Cobwebs and Cables by Hesba Stretton

Hesba Stretton was the pen name of Sarah Smith who was born on July 27th 1832 in Wellington, Shropshire, the younger daughter of bookseller, Benjamin Smith and his wife, Anne Bakewell Smith, a devout Methodist. Although she and her elder sister attended the Old Hall school in town, they were largely self-educated.

Smith became one of the most popular Evangelical writers of the 19th century. She used her "Christian principles as a protest against specific social evils in her children's books." Her moral tales and semi-religious stories, mainly directed towards the young, were printed in huge numbers.

After her sister submitted, without her knowledge, a story on her behalf ('The Lucky Leg', was a bizarre tale of a widower who proposes to women with wooden legs) Smith became a regular contributor to Household Words and All the Year Round, two popular periodicals begun by Charles Dickens. Dickens would collaborate with many writers to produce his part-work stories. Smith writing under the pseudonym Hesba Stretton (created from the initials of herself and four surviving siblings: **H**annah, **E**lizabeth, **S**arah, **B**enjamin, **A**nna and the name of a Shropshire village; All Stretton) contributed a well-regarded short story, 'The Ghost in the Cloak-Room', as part of 'The Haunted House'. She would go on to write over 40 novels.

Her break out book was 'Jessica's First Prayer', published in the Sunday at Home journal in 1866 and the following year as a book. By the end of the century it had sold over one and a half million copies. To put that into context; ten times the sales of 'Alice in Wonderland'. The book gave rise to a strand of books about homeless children in Victorian society combining elements of the sensational novel and the religious tract bringing the image of the poor, under-privileged, child into the Victorian social conscious.

A sequel, 'Jessica's Mother', was published in Sunday at Home in 1866 and eventually as a book, some decades later, in 1904. It was translated into fifteen European and Asiatic languages as well as Braille, depicted on coloured slides for magic lantern segments of Bands of Hope programmes, and placed in all Russian schools by order of Tsar Alexander II.

Smith became the chief writer for the Religious Tract Society. Her experience of working with slum children in Manchester in the 1860s gave her books great atmosphere and, of course, a sense of authenticity.

In 1884, Smith was one of the co-founders, together with Lord Shaftesbury and others, of the London Society for the Prevention of Cruelty to Children, which then combined, five years later, with societies in other cities to form the National Society for the Prevention of Cruelty to Children. Smith resigned a decade later in protest at financial mismanagement.

In retirement in Richmond, Surrey, the Smith sisters ran a branch of the Popular Book Club for working-class readers.

Sarah Smith died on October 8th, 1911 at home at Ivycroft on Ham Common. She had survived her sister by eight months.

Index of Contents

PART I

CHAPTER I

ABSCONDED

Late as it was, though the handsome office-clock on the chimney-piece had already struck eleven, Roland Sefton did not move. He had not stirred hand or foot for a long while now; no more than if he had been bound fast by many strong cords, which no effort could break or untie. His confidential clerk had left him two hours ago, and the undisturbed stillness of night had surrounded him ever since he had listened to his retreating footsteps. "Poor Acton!" he had said half aloud, and with a heavy sigh.

As he sat there, his clasped hands resting on his desk and his face hidden on them, all his life seemed to unfold itself before him; not in painful memories of the past only, but in terrified prevision of the black future.

How dear his native town was to him! He had always loved it from his very babyhood. The wide old streets, with ancient houses still standing here and there, rising or falling in gentle slopes, and called by quaint old names such as he never heard elsewhere; the fine old churches crowning the hills, and lifting up delicate tall spires, visible a score of miles away; the grammar school where he had spent the happiest days of his boyhood; the rapid river, brown and swirling, which swept past the town, and came back again as if it could not leave it; the ancient bridges spanning it, and the sharp-cornered recesses on them where he had spent many an idle hour, watching the boats row in and out under the arches; he saw every familiar nook and corner of his native town vividly and suddenly, as if he caught glimpses of them by the capricious play of lightning.

And this pleasant home of his; these walls which inclosed his birth-place, and the birth-place of his children! He could not imagine himself finding true rest and a peaceful shelter elsewhere. The spacious old rooms, with brown wainscoted walls and carved ceilings; the tall and narrow windows, with deep window-sills, where as a child he had so often knelt, gazing out on the wide green landscape and the far distant, almost level line of the horizon. His boy, Felix, had knelt in one of them a few hours ago, looking out with grave childish eyes on the sunset. The broad, shallow steps of the oaken staircase, trodden so many years by the feet of all who were dearest to him; the quiet chambers above where his mother, his wife, and his children were at this moment sleeping peacefully. How unutterably and painfully sweet all his home was to him!

Very prosperous his life had been; hardly overshadowed by a single cloud. His father, who had been the third partner in the oldest bank in Riversborough, had lived until he was old enough to step into his place. The bank had been established in the last century, and was looked upon as being as safe as the Bank of England. The second partner was dead; and the eldest, Mr. Clifford, had left everything in his hands for the last five years.

No man in Riversborough had led a more prosperous life than he had. His wife was from one of the county families; without fortune, indeed, but with all the advantages of high connections, which lifted him above the rank of mere business men, and admitted him into society hitherto closed even to the head partner in the old bank; in spite even of the fact that he still occupied the fine old house adjoining the bank premises. There was scarcely a townsman who was held to be his equal; not one who was considered his superior. Though he was little over thirty yet, he was at the head of all municipal affairs. He had already held the office of mayor for one year, and might have been re-elected, if his wife had not somewhat scorned the homely bourgeois dignity. There was no more popular man in the whole town than he was.

But he had been building on the sands, and the storm was rising. He could hear the moan of the winds growing louder, and the rush of the on-coming floods drawing nearer. He must make good his escape now, or never. If he put off flight till to-morrow, he would be crushed with the falling of his house.

He lifted himself up heavily, and looked round the room. It was his private office, at the back of the bank, handsomely furnished as a bank parlor should be. Over the fire-place hung the portrait of old Clifford, the senior partner, faithfully painted by a local artist, who had not attempted to soften the hard, stern face, and the fixed stare of the cold blue eyes, which seemed fastened pitilessly upon him. He had never seen the likeness before as he saw it now. Would such a man overlook a fault, or have any mercy for an offender? Never! He turned away from it, feeling cold and sick at heart; and with a heavy, and very bitter sigh he locked the door upon the room where he had spent so large a portion of his life. The place which had known him would know him no more.

As noiselessly and warily as if he was a thief breaking into the quiet house, he stole up the dimly-lighted staircase, and paused for a minute or two before a door, listening intently. Then he crept in. A low shaded lamp was burning, giving light enough to guide him to the cot where Felix was sleeping. It would be his birthday to-morrow, and the child must not lose his birthday gift, though the relentless floods were rushing on toward him also. Close by was the cot where his baby daughter, Hilda, was at rest. He stood between them, and could lay a hand on each. How soundly the children slept while his heart was breaking! Dear as they had been to him, he had never realized till now how priceless beyond all words such little tender creatures could be. He had called them into existence; and now the greatest good that could befall them was his death. It was unutterable agony to him.

His gift was a Bible, the boy's own choice; and he laid it on the pillow where Felix would find it as soon as his eyes opened. He bent over him, and kissed him with trembling lips. Hilda stirred a little when his lips touched her soft, rosy face, and she half opened her eyes, whispering "Father," and then fell asleep again smiling. He dared not linger another moment, but passing stealthily away, he paused listening at another door, his face white with anguish. "I dare not see Felicita," he murmured to himself, "but I must look on my mother's face once again."

The door made no sound as he opened it, and his feet fell noiselessly on the thick carpet; but as he drew near his mother's bed, her eyes opened with a clear steady gaze as if she had been awaiting his coming. There was a light burning here as well as in the night-nursery adjoining, for it was his mother who had charge of the children, and who would be the first the nurse would call if anything was the matter. She awoke as one who expects to be called upon at any hour; but the light was too dim to betray the misery on her son's face.

"Roland!" she said, in a slightly foreign accent.

"Were you calling, mother?" he asked. "I was passing by, and I came in here to see if you wanted anything."

"I did not call, my son," she answered, "but what have you the matter? Is Felicita ill? or the babies? Your voice is sad, Roland."

"No, no," he said, forcing himself to speak in a cheerful voice, "Felicita is asleep, I hope, and the babies are all right. But I have been late at bank-work; and I turned in just to have a look at you, mother, before I go to bed."

"That's my good son," she said, smiling, and taking his hand between her own in a fond clasp.

"Am I a good son?" he asked.

His mother's face was a fair, sweet face still, the soft brown hair scarcely touched with white, and with clear, dark gray eyes gazing up frankly into his own. They were eyes like these, with their truthful light shining through them, inherited from her, which in himself had won the unquestioning trust and confidence of those who were brought into contact with him. There was no warning signal of disloyalty in his face to set others on their guard. His mother looked up at him tenderly.

"Always a good son, the best of sons, Roland," she replied, "and a good husband, and a good father. Only one little fault in my good son: too spendthrift, too lavish. You are not a fine, rich lord, with large lands, and much, very much money, my boy. I do my best in the house; but women can only save pennies, while men fling about pounds."

"But you love me with all my faults, mother?" he said.

"As my own soul," she answered.

There was a profound solemnity in her voice and look, which penetrated to his very heart. She was not speaking lightly. It was in the same spirit with which. Paul wrote, after saying, "For I am persuaded that neither death, nor life, nor angels, nor principalities, nor powers, nor things present, nor things to come, nor height, nor depth, nor any other creature shall be able to separate us from the love of God, which is in Christ Jesus our Lord;" "I could wish that myself were separate from Christ for my brethren, my kinsmen according to the flesh." His mother had reached that sublime height of love for him.

He stood silent, looking down on her with dull, aching eyes, as he said to himself it was perhaps for the last time. It was the last time she would ever see him as her good son. With her, in her heart and memory, all his life dwelt; she knew the whole of it, with no break or interruption. Only this one hidden thread, which had been woven into the web in secret, and which was about to stand out with such clear and open disclosure; of this she had no faint suspicion. For a minute or two he felt as if he must tell her of it; that he must roll off this horrible weight from himself, and crush her faithful heart with it. But what could his mother do? Her love could not stay the storm; she had no power to bid the winds and waves be still. It would be best for all of them if he could make his escape secretly, and be altogether lost in impenetrable darkness.

At that moment a clock in the hall below struck one.

"Well," he said wearily, "if I'm to get any sleep to-night I must be off to bed. Good-by, mother."

"Good-by?" she repeated with a smile.

"Good-night, of course," he replied, bending over her and kissing her tenderly.

"God bless you, my son," she said, putting both her hands upon his head, and pressing his face close to her own. He could not break away from her fond embrace; but in a few moments she let him go, bidding him get some rest before the night was passed.

Once more he stood in the dimly-lighted passage, listening at his wife's door, with his fingers involuntarily clasping the handle. But he dared not go in. If he looked upon Felicita again he could not leave her, even to escape from ruin and disgrace. An agony of love and of terror took possession of him. Never to see her again was horrible; but to see her shrink from him as a base and dishonest man, his name an infamy to her, would be worse than death. Did she love him enough to forgive a sin committed chiefly for her sake? In the depths of his own soul the answer was no.

He stole down stairs again, and passed out by a side door into the streets. It was raining heavily, and the wind was moaning through the deserted thoroughfares, where no sound of footsteps could be heard. Behind him lay his pleasant home, never so precious as at this moment. He looked up at the windows, the two faintly lit up, and that other darkened window of the chamber he had not dared to enter. In a few hours those women, so unutterably dear to him, would be overwhelmed by the great sorrow he had prepared for them; those children would become the inheritors of his sin. He looked back longingly and despairingly, as if there only was life for him; and then hurrying on swiftly he lost sight of the old home, and felt as a drowning wretch at sea feels when the heaving billows hide from him the glimmering light of the beacon, which, however, can offer no harbor of refuge to him.

CHAPTER II

PHEBE MARLOWE

Though the night had been stormy, the sun rose brightly on the rain-washed streets, and the roofs and walls stood out with a peculiar clearness, and with a more vivid color than usual, against the deep blue of the sky. It was May-day, and most hearts were stirred with a pleasant feeling as of a holiday; not altogether a common day, though the shops were all open, and business was going on as usual. The old be-thought themselves of the days when they had gone a-Maying; and the young felt less disposed to work, and were inclined to wander out in search of May-flowers in the green meadows, or along the sunny banks of the river, which surrounded the town. Early, very early considering the ten miles she had ridden on her rough hill-pony, came a young country girl across one of the ancient bridges, with a large market-basket on her arm, brimful of golden May-flowers, set off well by their own glossy leaves, and by the dark blue of her dress. She checked her pony and lingered for a few minutes, looking over the parapet at the swift rushing of the current through the narrow arches. A thin line of alders grew along the margin of the river, with their pale green leaves half unfolded; and in the midst of the swirling waters, parting them into two streams, lay a narrow islet on which tall willow wands were springing, with soft, white buds on every rod, and glistening in the sunshine. Not far away a lofty avenue of lime-trees stretched along the banks, casting wavering shadows on the brown river; while beyond it, on the summit of one of the hills on which the town was built, there rose the spires of two churches built close together, with the gilded crosses on their tapering points glittering more brightly than anything else in the joyous light. For a little while the girl gazed dreamily at the landscape, her color coming and going quickly, and then with a deep-drawn sigh of delight she roused herself and her pony, and passed on into the town.

The church clocks struck nine as she turned into Whitefriars Road, the street where the old bank of Riversborough stood. The houses on each side of the broad and quiet street were handsome, old-fashioned dwelling-places, not one of which had as yet been turned into a shop. The most eminent lawyers and doctors lived in it; and there was more than one frontage which displayed a hatchment, left to grow faded and discolored long after the year of mourning was ended. Here too was the judge's residence, set apart for his occupation during the assizes. But the old bank was the most handsome and most ancient of all those urban mansions. It had originally stood alone on the brow of the hill overlooking the river and the Whitefriars Abbey. Toward the street, when Ronald Sefton's forefathers had realized a fortune by banking, now a hundred years ago, there had been a new frontage built to it, with the massive red brick workmanship and tall narrow windows of the eighteenth century. But on the river side it was still an old Elizabethan mansion, with gabled roofs standing boldly up against the sky; and low broad casements, latticed and filled with lozenge-shaped panes; and half-timber walls, with black beams fashioned into many forms: and with one story jutting out beyond that below, until the attic window under the gable seemed to hang in mid-air, without visible support, over the garden sloping down a steep bank to the river-side.

Phebe Marlowe, in her coarse dark blue merino dress, and with her market-basket of golden blossoms on her arm, walked with a quick step along the quiet street, having left her pony at a stable near the entrance to the town. There were few persons about; but those whom she met she looked at with a pleasant, shy, slight smile on her face, as if she almost claimed acquaintance with them, and was ready, even wishful, to bid them good-morning on a day so fine and bright. Two or three responded to this inarticulate greeting, and then her lips parted gladly, and her voice, clear though low, answered them with a sweet good-humor that had something at once peculiar and pathetic in it. She passed under a broad archway at one side of the bank offices, leading to the house entrance, and to the sloping garden beyond. A private door into the bank was ajar, and a dark, sombre face was peering out of it into the semi-darkness. Phebe's feet paused for an instant.

"Good-morning, Mr. Acton," she said, with a little rustic courtesy. But he drew back quickly, and she heard him draw the bolt inside the door, as if he had neither seen nor heard her. Yet the face, with its eager and scared expression, had been too quickly seen by her, and too vividly impressed upon her keen perception; and she went on, chilled a little, as if some cloud had come over the clear brightness of the morning.

Phebe was so much at home in the house, that when she found the housemaid on her knees cleaning the hall floor, she passed on unceremoniously to the dining-room, where she felt sure of finding some of the family. It was a spacious room, with a low ceiling where black beams crossed and recrossed each other; with wainscoted walls, and a carved chimney-piece of almost black oak. A sombre place in gloomy weather, yet so decorated with old china vases, and great brass salvers, and silver cups and tankards catching every ray of light, that the whole room glistened in this bright May-day. In the broad cushioned seat formed by the sill of the oriel window, which was almost as large as a room itself, there sat the elder Mrs. Sefton, Roland Sefton's foreign mother, with his two children standing before her. They had their hands clasped behind them, and their faces were turned toward her with the grave earnestness children's faces often wear. She was giving them their daily Bible lesson, and she held up her small brown hand as a signal to Phebe to keep silence, and to wait a moment until the lesson was ended.

"And so," she said, "those who know the will of God, and do not keep it, will be beaten with many stripes. Remember that, my little Felix."

"I shall always try to do it," answered the boy solemnly. "I'm nine years old to-day; and when I'm a man I'm going to be a pastor, like your father, grandmamma; my great-grandfather, you know, in the Jura. Tell us how he used to go about the snow mountains seeing his poor people, and how he met with wolves sometimes, and was never frightened."

"Ah! my little children," she answered, "you have had a good father, and a good grandfather, and a good great-grandfather. How very good you ought to be."

"We will," cried both the children, clinging round her as she rose from her chair, until they caught sight of Phebe standing in the doorway. Then with cries of delight they flew to her, and threw themselves upon her with almost rough caresses, as if they knew she could well bear it. She received them with merry laughter, and knelt down that their arms might be thrown more easily round her neck.

"See," she said, "I was up so early, while you were all in bed, finding May-roses for you, with the May-dew on them. And if your father and mother will let us go, I'll take you up the river to the osier island; or you shall ride my Ruby, and we'll go off a long, long way into the country, us three, and have dinner in a new place, where you have never been. Because it's Felix's birthday."

She was still kneeling on the floor, with the children about her, when the door opened, and the same troubled and haggard face, which had peered out upon her under the archway, looked into the room with restless and bloodshot eyes. Phebe felt a sudden chill again, and rising to her feet put the children behind her, as if she feared some danger for them.

"Where is Mr. Sefton?" he asked in a deep, hoarse voice; "is he at home, Madame?"

Ever since the elder Mr. Sefton had brought his young foreign wife home, now more than thirty years ago, the people of Riversborough had called her Madame, giving to her no other title or surname. It had always seemed to set her apart, and at a distance, as a foreigner, and so quiet had she been, so homely and domesticated, that she had remained a stranger, keeping her old habits of life and thought, and often yearning for the old pastor's home among the Jura Mountains.

"But yes," she answered, "my son is late this morning; but all the world is early, I think. It is not much beyond nine o'clock, Mr. Acton. The bank is not open yet."

"No, no," he answered hurriedly, while his eyes wandered restlessly about the room; "he is not ill, Madame?"

"I hope so not," she replied, with some vague uneasiness stirring in her heart.

"Nor dead?" he muttered.

"Dead!" exclaimed both Madame and Phebe in one breath; "dead!"

"All men die," he went on, "and it is a pleasant thing to lie down quietly in one's own grave, where the wicked cease from troubling, and the weary are at rest. He could rest soundly in the grave."

"I will go and see," cried Madame, catching Phebe by the arm.

"Pray God you may find him dead," he answered, with a low, miserable laugh, ending in a sob. He was mad; neither Madame nor Phebe had a doubt of it. They put the children before them, and bade them run away to the nursery, while they followed up the broad old staircase. Madame went into her son's bedroom; but in a few seconds she returned to Phebe with an anxious face.

"He is not there," she said, "nor Felicita. She is in her own sitting-room, where she likes not to be followed. It is her sacred place, and I go there never, Phebe."

"But she knows where Mr. Sefton is," answered Phebe, "and we must ask her. We cannot leave poor Mr. Acton alone. If nobody else dare disturb her, I will."

"She will not be vexed with you," said Madame Sefton. "Knock at this door, Phebe; knock till she answers. I am miserable about my son."

Several times Phebe knocked, more loudly each time, until at last a low voice, sounding far away, bade them go in. Very quietly, as if indeed they were stepping into some holy place barefooted, they crossed the threshold.

CHAPTER III

FELICITA

The room was a small one, with a dim, many-colored light pervading it; for the upper part of the mullioned casement was filled with painted glass, and even the panes of the lower part were of faintly tinted green. Like all the rest of the old house, the walls were wainscoted, but here there was no piece of china or silver to sparkle; the only glitter was that of the gilding on the handsomely bound books arranged in two bookcases. In this green gloom sat Felicita Sefton, leaning back in her chair, with her head resting languidly on the cushions, and her dark eyes turned dimly and dreamily toward the quietly opening door.

"Phebe Marlowe!" she said, her eyes brightening a little, as the fresh, sweet face of the young country girl met her gaze. Phebe stepped softly forward into the dim room, and laid the finest of the golden flowers she had gathered that morning upon Felicita's lap. It brought a gleam of spring sunshine into the gloom which caught Felicita's eye, and she uttered a low cry of delight as she took it up in her small, delicate hand. Phebe stooped down shyly and kissed the small hand, her face all aglow with smiles and blushes.

"Felicita," said Madame, her voice altering a little, "where is my son this morning?"

"Roland!" she repeated absently; "Roland? Didn't he say last night he was going to London?"

"To London!" exclaimed his mother.

"Yes," she answered, "he bade me good-by last night; I remember now. He said he would not disturb me again; he was going by the mail-train. He was sorry to be away on poor little Felix's birthday. I recollect quite distinctly now."

"He said not one word to me," said Madame. "It is strange."

"Very strange," asserted Felicita languidly, as if she were wandering away again into the reverie they had broken in upon.

"Did he say when he would be back?" asked his mother.

"In a few days, of course," she answered.

"But he has not told Acton," resumed Madame.

"Who did you say?" inquired Felicita.

"The head clerk, the manager when Roland is away," she said. "He has not said anything to him."

"Very strange," said Felicita again. It was plainly irksome to her to be disturbed by questions like these, and she was withdrawing herself into the remote and unapproachable distance where no one could follow her. Her finely-chiselled features and colorless skin gave her a singular resemblance to marble; and they might almost as well have addressed themselves to a marble image.

"Come," said Madame, "we must see Acton again."

They found him in the bank parlor, where Roland was usually to be met with at this hour. There was an unspoken hope in their hearts that he would be there, and so deliver them from the undefined trouble and terror they were suffering. But only Acton was there, seated at Roland's desk, and turning over the papers in it with a rapid and reckless hand. His face was hidden behind the great flap of the desk, and though he glanced over it for an instant as the door opened he concealed himself again, as if feigning unconsciousness of any one's presence.

"My son is gone to London," said Madame, keeping at a safe distance from him, with the door open behind her and Phebe to secure a speedy retreat. The flap of the desk fell with a loud crash, and Acton flung his arms above his head with a gesture of despair.

"I knew it," he exclaimed. "Oh, my dear young master! God grant he may get away safe. All is lost!"

"What do you mean?" cried Madame, forgetting one terror in another, and catching him by the arm; "what is lost?"

"He is gone!" he answered, "and it was more my fault than his—mine and Mrs. Sefton's. Whatever wrong he has done it was for her. Remember that, Madame, and you, Phebe Marlowe. If anything happens, remember it's my fault more than his, and Mrs. Sefton's fault more than mine."

"Tell me what you mean," urged Madame breathlessly.

"You'll know when Mr. Sefton returns, Madame," he answered, with a sudden return to his usually calm tone and manner, which was as startling as his former vehemence had been; "he'll explain all when he comes home. We must open the bank now; it is striking ten."

He locked the desk and passed out of the comfortably-furnished parlor into the office beyond, leaving them nothing to do but to return into the house with their curiosity unsatisfied, and the mother's vague trouble unsoothed.

"Phebe, Phebe!" cried Felix, as they slowly re-entered the pleasant home, "my mother says we may go up the river to the osier island; and, oh, Phebe, she will go with us her own self!"

He had run down the broad staircase to meet them, almost breathless with delight, and with eyes shining with almost serious rapture. He clasped Phebe's arm, and, leaning toward her, whispered into her ear,

"She took me in her arms, and said, 'I love you, Felix,' and then she kissed me as if she meant it, Phebe. It was better than all my birthday presents put together. My father said to me one day he adored her; and I adore her. She is my mother, you know—the mother of me, Felix; and I lie down on the floor and kiss her feet every day, only she does not know it. When she looks at me her eyes seem to go through me; but, oh, she does not look at me often."

"She is so different; not like most people," answered Phebe, with her arms round the boy.

Madame had gone on sadly enough up-stairs to see if she could find out anything about her son; and Phebe and Felix had turned into the terraced garden where the boat-house was built close under the bank of the river.

"I should be sorry for my mother to be like other people," said Felix proudly. "She is like the evening star, my father says, and I always look out at night to see if it is shining. You know, Phebe, when we row her up the river, my father and me, we keep quite quiet, only nodding at one another which way to pull, and she sits silent with eyes that shine like stars. We would not speak for anything, not one little word, lest we should disturb her. My father says she is a great genius; not at all like other people, and worth thousands and thousands of common women. But I don't think you are a common woman, Phebe," he added, lifting up his eager face to hers, as if afraid of hurting her feelings, "and my father does not think so, I know."

"Your father has known me all my life, and has always been my best friend," said Phebe, with a pleasant smile. "But I am a working-woman, Felix, and your mother is a lady and a great genius. It is God who has ordered it so."

She would have laughed if she had been less simple-hearted than she was, at the anxious care with which the boy arranged the boat for his mother. No cushions were soft enough and no shawls warm enough for the precious guest. When at length all was ready, and he fetched her himself from the house, it was not until she was comfortably seated in the low seat, with a well-padded sloping back, against which she could recline at ease, and with a soft, warm shawl wrapped round her—not till then did the slight cloud of care pass away from his face, and the little pucker of anxiety which knitted his brows grow smooth. The little girl of five, Hilda, nestled down by her mother, and Felix took his post at the helm. In unbroken silence they pushed off into the middle of the stream, the boat rowed easily by Phebe's strong young arms. So silent were they all that they could hear the rustling of the young leaves on the trees, under whose shadows they passed, and the joyous singing of the larks in the meadows on each side of the sunny reaches of water, down which they floated. It was not until they landed the children on the osier island, and bade them run about to play, and not then until they were some distance away, that their merry young voices were heard.

"Phebe," said Felicita, in her low-toned, softly-modulated voice, always languid and deliberate, "talk to me. Tell me how you spend your life."

Phebe was sitting face to face with her, balancing the boat with the oars against the swift flowing of the river, with smiles coming and going on her face as rapidly as the shadows and the sunshine chasing each other over the fields this May morning.

"You know," she answered simply, "we live a mile away from the nearest house, and that is only a cottage where an old farm laborer lives with his wife. It's very lonesome up there on the hills. Days and days go by, and I never hear a voice speaking, and I feel as if I could not bear the sound of my own voice when I call the cattle home, or the fowls to come for their corn. If it wasn't for the living things around me, that know me as well as they know one another, and love me more, I should feel sometimes as if I was dead. And I long so to hear somebody speak—to be near more of my fellow-creatures. Why, when I touch the hand of any one I love—yours, or Mr. Sefton's, or Madame's—it's almost a pain to me; it seems to bring me so close to you. I always feel as if I became a part of father when I touch him. Oh, you do not know what it is to be alone!"

"No," said Felicita, sighing; "never have I been alone, and I would give worlds to be as free as you are. You cannot imagine what it is," she went on, speaking rapidly and with intense eagerness, "never to belong to yourself, or to be alone; for it is not being alone to have only four thin walls separating you from a husband and children and a large busy household. 'What are you thinking, my darling?' Roland is always asking me; and the children break in upon me. Body, soul, and spirit, I am held down a captive; I have been in bondage all my life. I have never even thought as I should think if I could be free."

"But I cannot understand that," cried Phebe. "I could never be too near those I love. I should like to live in a large house, with many people all smiling and talking around me. And everybody worships you."

She uttered the last words shyly, partly afraid of bringing a frown on the lovely face opposite to her, which was quickly losing its vivid expression and sinking back into statuesque coldness.

"It is simply weariness to me and vexation of spirit," she answered. "If I could be quite alone, as you are, with only a father like yours, I think I could get free; but I have never been left alone from my babyhood; just as Felix and Hilda are never left alone. Oh, Phebe, you do not know how happy you are."

"No," she said cheerfully, "sometimes when I stand at our garden-gate, and look round me for miles and miles away, and the sweet air blows past me, and the bees are humming, and the birds calling to one another, and everything is so peaceful, with father happy over his work not far off, I think I don't know how happy I am. I try to catch hold of the feeling and keep it, but it slips away somehow. Only I thank God I am happy."

"I was never happy enough to thank God," Felicita murmured, lying back in her seat and shutting her eyes. Presently the children returned, and, after another silent row, slower and more toilsome, as it was up the river, they drew near home again, and saw Madame's anxious face watching for them over the low garden wall. Her heart had been too heavy for her to join them in their pleasure-taking, and it was no lighter now.

CHAPTER IV

UPFOLD FARM

Phebe rode slowly homeward in the dusk of the evening, her brain too busy with the varied events of the day for her to be in any haste to reach the end. For the last four miles her road lay in long by-lanes, shady with high hedgerows and trees which grew less frequent and more stunted as she rose gradually higher up the long spurs of the hills, whose rounded outlines showed dark against the clear orange tint of the western sky. She could hear the brown cattle chewing the cud, and the bleating of some solitary sheep on the open moor, calling to the flock from which it had strayed during the daytime, with the angry yelping of a dog in answer to its cry from some distant farm-yard. The air was fresh and chilly with dew, and the low wind, which only lifted the branches of the trees a little in the lower land she had left, was growing keener, and would blow sharply enough across the unsheltered table-land she was reaching. But still she loitered, letting her rough pony snatch tufts of fresh grass from the banks, and shamble leisurely along as he strayed from one side of the road to another.

Phebe was not so much thinking as pondering in a confused and unconnected manner over all the circumstances of the day, when suddenly the tall figure of a man rose from under the black hedgerow, and laid his arm across the pony's neck, with his face turned up to her. Her heart throbbed quickly, but not altogether with terror.

"Mr. Roland!" she cried.

"You know me in the dark then," he answered. "I have been watching for you all day, Phebe. You come from home?"

She knew he meant his home, not hers.

"Yes, it was Felix's birthday, and we have been down the river," she said.

"Is anything known yet?" he asked.

Though it was so solitary a spot that Phebe had passed no one for the last three miles, and he had been haunting the hills all day without seeing a soul, yet he spoke in a whisper, as if fearful of betraying himself.

"Only that you are away," she replied; "and they think you are in London."

"Is not Mr. Clifford come?" he asked.

"No, sir, he comes to-morrow," she answered.

"Thank God!" he exclaimed, in a louder tone. When he spoke again he did so without looking into her face, which indeed was scarcely visible in the deepening dusk.

"Phebe," he said, "we have known each other for many years."

"All my life, sir," she responded eagerly; "father and me, we are proud of knowing you."

Before speaking again he led her pony up the steep lane to a gate which opened on the moorland. It was not so dark here, from under the hedgerows and trees, and a little pool beside the gate caught the last lingering light in the west, and reflected it like a dim and dusty mirror. They could see one another's faces; his was working with strong excitement, and hers, earnest and friendly, looked frankly down upon him. He clasped her hand with the strong, desperate grip of a sinking man, and her fingers responded with a warm clasp.

"Can I trust you, Phebe?" he cried. "I have no other chance."

"I will help you, even to dying for you and yours," she answered. The girlish fervor of her manner struck him mournfully. Why should he burden her with his crime? What right had he to demand any sacrifice from her? Yet he felt she spoke the truth. Phebe Marlowe would rejoice in helping, even unto death, not only him, but any other fellow-creature who was sinking under sorrow or sin.

"Come on home," she said, "it is bitterly cold here; and you can tell me what to do."

He placed himself at the pony's head again, and trudged on speechlessly along the rough road, which was now nothing more than the tracks made by cart-wheels across the moor, with deep ruts over which he stumbled like a man who is worn out with fatigue. In a quarter of an hour the low cottage was reached, surrounded by a little belt of fields and a few storm-beaten fir-trees. There was a dull glow of red to be seen through the lattice window, telling Phebe of a smouldering fire, made up for her by her father before going back to his workshop at the end of the field behind the house. She stirred up the wood-ashes and threw upon them some dry, light fagots of gorse, and in a few seconds a dazzling light filled the little room from end to end. It was a familiar place to Roland Sefton, and he took no notice of it. But it was a curious interior. Every niche of the walls was covered with carved oak; no wainscoted hall in the country could be more richly or more fancifully decorated. The chimney-piece over the open hearth-stone, a wide chimney-piece, was deeply carved with curious devices. The doors and window-frames, the cupboards and the shelves for the crockery, were all of dark oak, fashioned into leaves and ferns, with birds on their nests, and timid rabbits, and still more timid wood-mice peeping out of their coverts, cocks crowing with uplifted crest, and chickens nestling under the hen-mother's wings, sheaves of corn, and tall, club-headed bulrushes—all the objects familiar to a country life. The dancing light played upon them, and shone also upon Roland Sefton's sad and weary face. Phebe drew her father's carved arm-chair close to the fire.

"Sit down," she said, "and let me get you something to eat."

"Yes," he answered, sinking down wearily in the chair, "I am nearly dying of hunger. Good Heavens! is it possible I can be hungry?"

He spoke with an indescribable expression of mingled astonishment and dread. Suddenly there broke upon him the possibility of suffering want in many forms in the future, and yet he felt ashamed of foreseeing them in this, the first day of his great calamity. Until this moment he had been too absorbed in dwelling upon the moral and social consequences of his crime, to realize how utterly worn out he was; but all his physical strength appeared to collapse in an instant.

And now for the first time Phebe beheld the change in him, and stood gazing at him in mute surprise and sorrow. He had always been careful of his personal appearance, with a refinement and daintiness which had grown especially fastidious since his marriage. But now his coat, wet through during the night, and dried only by the keen air of the hills, was creased and soiled, and his boots were thickly covered with mud and clay. His face and hands were unwashed, and his hair hung unbrushed over his forehead. Phebe's whole heart was stirred at this pitiful change, and she laid her hand on his shoulder with a timid but affectionate touch.

"Mr. Roland," she said, "go up-stairs and put yourself to rights a little; and give me your clothes and your boots to brush. You'll feel better when you are more like yourself."

He smiled faintly as he looked up at her quivering lips and eyes full of unshed tears. But her homely advice was good, and he was glad to follow it. Her little room above was lined with richly carved oak panels like the kitchen below, and a bookcase contained her books, many of which he had himself given to her. There was an easel standing under the highest part of the shelving roof, where a sky-light was let into the thatch, and a half-finished painting rested on it. But he did not give a glance toward it. There was very little interest to him just now in Phebe's pursuits, though she owed most of them to him.

By the time he was ready to go down, supper was waiting for him on the warm and bright hearth, and he fell upon it almost ravenously. It was twenty-four hours since he had last eaten. Phebe sat almost out of sight in the shadow of a large settle, with her knitting in her hand, and her eyes only seeking his face when any movement seemed to indicate that she could serve him in some way. But in these brief glances she noticed the color coming back to his face, and new vigor and resolution changing his whole aspect.

"And now," he said, when his hunger was satisfied, "I can talk to you, Phebe."

CHAPTER V

A CONFESSION

But Roland Sefton sat silent, with his shapely hands resting on his knees, and his handsome face turned toward the hearth, where the logs had burned down and emitted only a low and fitful flame. The little room was scarcely lighted by it, and looked all the darker for the blackness of the small uncurtained window, through which the ebony face of night was peering in. This bare, uncovered casement troubled him, and from time to time he turned his eyes uneasily toward it. But what need could there be of a curtain, when they were a mile away from any habitation, and where no road crossed the moor, except the rugged green pathway, worn into deep ruts by old Marlowe's own wagon? Yet as if touched by some vague sympathy with him, Phebe rose, and pinned one of her large rough working-aprons across it.

"Phebe," he said, as she stepped softly back to her seat, "you and I have been friends a long time; and your father and I have been friends all my life. Do you recollect me staying here a whole week when I was a school-boy?"

"Yes," she answered, her eyes glistening in the dusky light; "but for you I should have known nothing, only what work had to be done for father. You taught me my alphabet that week, and the hymns I have said every night since then before I go to sleep. You helped me to teach myself painting; and if I ever paint a picture worth looking at it will be your doing."

"No, no; you are a born artist, Phebe Marlowe," he said, "though perhaps the world may never know it. But being such friends as you say, I will trust you. Do you think me worthy of trust, true and honest as a man should be, Phebe?"

"As true and honest as the day," she cried, with eager emphasis.

"And a Christian?" he added, in a lower voice.

"Yes," she answered, "I do not know a Christian if you are not one."

"That is the sting of it," he groaned; "true, and honest, and a Christian! And yet, Phebe, if I were taken by the police to-night, or if I be taken by them to-morrow, I shall be lodged in Riversborough jail, and tried before a jury of my towns-people at the assizes next month."

"No, it is impossible!" she cried, stretching out her brown, hard-working hand, and laying it on his white and shapely one, which had never known toil.

"You would not send me to jail," he said, "I know that well enough. But I deserve it, my poor girl. They would find me guilty and sentence me to a convict prison. I saw Dartmoor prison on my wedding journey with Felicita, Heaven help me! She liked the wild, solitary moor, with its great tors and its desolate stillness, and one day we went near to the prison. Those grim walls seemed to take possession of me; I felt oppressed and crushed by them. I could not forget them for days after, even with Felicita by my side."

His voice trembled as he spoke, and a quiver ran through his whole frame, which seemed to thrill through Phebe's; but she only pressed her pitiful hand more closely on his.

"I might have escaped last night," he went on, "but I stumbled over a poor girl in the street, dying. A young girl, no older than you, without a penny or a friend; a sinner too like myself; and I could not leave her there alone. Only in finding help for her I lost my chance. The train to London was gone, and there was no other till ten this morning. I expected Mr. Clifford to be at the bank to-day; if I had only known he would not be there I could have got away then. But I came here, why I hardly know. You could not hide me for long if you would; but there was no one else to help me."

"But what have you done, sir?" she asked, with a tremulous, long-drawn sigh.

"Done?" he repeated; "ay! there's the question. I wonder if I can be honest and true now with only Phebe Marlowe listening. I could have told my mother, perhaps, if it had been of any use; but I would die rather than tell Felicita. Done, Phebe! I've appropriated securities trusted to my keeping, pledging some and selling others for my own use. I've stolen £10,000."

"And you could be sent to prison for it?" she said, in a low voice, glancing uneasily round as if she fancied she would be overheard.

"For I don't know how many years," he answered.

"It would kill Mrs. Sefton," she said. "Oh! how could you do it?"

"It was for Felicita I did it," he replied absently; "for my Felicita only."

For a few minutes Phebe's brain was busy, but not yet with the most sorrowful thoughts. There could be no shadow of doubt in her mind that this dearest friend of hers, sitting beside her in the twilight, was guilty of the crime he had confessed. But she could not as yet dwell upon the crime. He was in imminent peril; and his peril threatened the welfare of nearly all whom she loved. Ruin and infamy for him meant ruin and infamy for them all. She must save him if possible.

"Phebe," he said, breaking the dreary silence, "I ought to tell you one thing more. The money your father left with me—the savings of his life—six hundred pounds—it is all gone. He intrusted it to me, and made his will, appointing me your guardian; such confidence he had in me. I have made both him and you penniless."

"I think nothing of that," she answered. "What should I ever have been but for you? A dull, ignorant country girl, living a life little higher than my sheep and cattle. We are rich enough, my father and me. This cottage, and the fields about it, are our own. But I must go and tell father."

"Must he be told?" asked Roland Sefton anxiously.

"We've no secrets," she replied; "and there's no fear of him, you know. He would see if I was in trouble; and I shall be in trouble," she added, in a sorrowful voice.

She opened the cottage door, and going out left him alone. It was a familiar place to him; but hitherto it had been only the haunt of happy holidays, from the time when he had been a school-boy until his last autumn's shooting of grouse and woodcock on the wide moors. Old Marlowe had been one of his earliest friends, and Phebe had been something like a humble younger sister to him. If any one in the world could be depended upon to help him, outside his own family, it must be old Marlowe and his daughter.

And yet, when she left him, his first impulse was to rise and flee while yet there was time—before old Marlowe knew his secret. Phebe was a girl, living as girls do, in a region of sentiment and feeling, hardly understanding a crime against property. A girl like her had no idea of what his responsibility and his guilt were, money ranking so low in her estimate of life. But old Marlowe would look at it quite differently. His own careful earnings, scraped together by untiring industry and ceaseless self-denial, were lost—stolen by the man he had trusted implicitly. For Roland Sefton did not spare himself any reproaches; he did not attempt to hide or palliate his sin. There were other securities for small sums, like old Marlowe's, gone like his, and ruin would overtake half a dozen poor families, though the bulk of the loss would fall upon his senior partner, who was a hard man, of unbending sternness and integrity. If old Marlowe proved a man of the same inflexible stamp, he was lost.

But he sat still, waiting and listening. Round that lonely cottage, as he well knew, the wind swept from whatever quarter it was blowing; sighing softly, or wailing, moaning, or roaring past it, as ceaselessly as the sound of waves against a fisherman's hut on the sea-coast. It was crying and sobbing now, rising at intervals into a shriek, as if to warn him of coming peril. He went to the window and met the black face of the night, hiding everything from his eye. Neither moon nor star gleamed in the sky. But even if old Marlowe was merciful he could not stay there, but must go out, as he had done last night from his own home, lashed like a dog from every familiar hearth by an unseen hand and a heavy scourge.

Phebe had not lingered, though she seemed long away. As she drew near the little workshop she saw the wagon half-laden with some church furniture her father had been carving, and with which he and she were to start at daybreak for a village about twenty miles off. She heard the light tap of his carving tools as she opened the door, and found him finishing the wings of a spread-eagle. He had pushed back the paper cap he wore from his forehead, which was deeply furrowed, and shaded by a few straggling tufts of gray hair. He took no notice of her entrance until she touched his arm with her hand; and then he looked at her with eyes, blue like her own, but growing dim with age, and full of the pitiful, uncomplaining gaze of one who is deaf and dumb. But his face brightened and his smile was cheerful, as he began to talk eagerly with his fingers, throwing in many gestures to aid his slow speech. Phebe, too, smiled and gesticulated in silent answer, before she told him her errand.

"The carving is finished, father," she said. "Could we not start at once, and be at Upchurch before five to-morrow morning?"

"Twenty miles; eight hours; easily," he answered; "but why?"

"To help Mr. Sefton," she said. "He wants to get down to Southampton, and Upchurch is in the way. Father, it must be done; you would never see a smile upon my face again if we did not do it."

The keen, wistful eyes of her father were fastened alternately upon her troubled face and her moving hands, as slowly and silently she spelt out on her fingers the sad story she had just listened to. His own face changed rapidly from astonishment to dismay, and from dismay to a passionate rage. If Roland Sefton could have seen it he would have made good his escape. But still Phebe's fingers went on pleading for him; and the smile, which she said her father would never see again—a pale, wan smile—met his eyes as he watched her.

"He has been so good to you and me," she went on, with a sob in her throat; and unconsciously she spoke out the words aloud and slowly as she told them off on her fingers; "he learned to talk with you as I do, and he is the only person almost in the world who can talk to you without your slate and pencil, father. It was good of him to take that trouble. And his father was your best friend, wasn't he? How good Madame used to be when I was a little girl, and you were carving all that woodwork at the old bank, and she let me stay there with you! All our happiest days have come through them. And now we can deliver them from great misery."

"But my money?" he interposed.

"Money is nothing between friends," she said eagerly. "Will you make my life miserable, father? I shall be thinking of them always, night and day; and they will never see me again if he is sent to jail through our fault. There never was a kinder man than he is; and I always thought him a good man till now."

"A thief; worse than a common thief," said her father. "What will become of my little daughter when I am dead?"

Phebe made no answer except by tears. For a few minutes old Marlowe watched her bowed head and face hidden in her hands, till a gray hue came upon his withered face, and the angry gleam died away from his eyes. Hitherto her slightest wish had been a law to him, and to see her weeping was anguish to him. To have a child who could hear and speak had been a joy that had redeemed his life from wretchedness, and crowned it with an inexhaustible delight. If he never saw her smile again, what would become of him? She was hiding her face from him even now, and there was no medium of communication between them save by touch. He must call her attention to what he had to say by making her look at him. Almost timidly he stretched out his withered and cramped hand to lay it upon her head.

"I must do whatever you please," he said, when she lifted up her face and looked at him with tearful eyes; "if it killed me I must do it. But it is a hard thing you bid me do, Phebe."

He turned away to brush the last speck of dust from the eagle's wings, and lifting it up carefully carried it away to pack in his wagon, Phebe holding the lantern for him till all was done. Then hand in hand they walked down the foot-worn path across the field to the house, as they had done ever since she had been a tottering little child, hardly able to clasp his one finger with her baby hand.

Roland Sefton was crouching over the dying embers on the hearth, more in the utter misery of soul than in bodily chilliness, though he felt cold and shivering, as if stripped of all that made life desirable to him. There is no icy chill like that. He did not look round when the door opened, though Phebe spoke to him; for he could not face old Marlowe, or force himself to read the silent yet eloquent fingers, which only could utter words of reproach. The dumb old man stood on the threshold, gazing at his averted face and downcast head, and an inarticulate cry of mingled rage and grief broke from his silent lips, such as Phebe herself had never heard before, and which, years afterward, sounded at times in Roland Sefton's ears.

It was nearly ten o'clock before they were on the road, old Marlowe marching at the head of his horse, and Phebe mounted on her wiry little pony, while Roland Sefton rode in front of the wagon at times. Their progress was slow, for the oak furniture was heavy and the roads were rough, leading across the moor and down steep hills into valleys, with equally steep hills on the other side. The sky was covered with a thin mist drifting slowly before the wind, and when the moon shone through it, about two o'clock in the morning, it was the waning-moon looking sad and forlorn amid the floating vapor. The houses they passed were few and far between, showing no light or sign of life. All the land lay around them dark and desolate under the midnight sky; and the slow creaking of the wheels and sluggish hoof-beats of the horse dragging the wagon were the only sounds that broke the stillness.

In this gloom old Marlowe could hold no conversation either with Phebe or Roland Sefton, but from time to time they could hear him sob aloud as he trudged on in his speechless isolation. It was a sad sound, which pierced them to the heart. From time to time Roland Sefton walked up the long hills beside Phebe's pony, pouring out his whole heart to her. They could hardly see each other's faces in the dimness, and words came the more readily to him. All the burden of his confession was that he had fallen through seeking Felicita's happiness. For her sake he had longed for more wealth, and speculated in the hope of gaining it, and tampered with the securities intrusted to him in the hope of retrieving losses. It was for her, and her only, he maintained; and now he had brought infamy and wretchedness and poverty upon her and his innocent children.

"Would to God I could die to-night!" he exclaimed; "my death would save them from some portion of their trouble."

Phebe listened to him almost as heart-broken as himself. In her singularly solitary life, so far apart from ordinary human society, she had never been brought into contact with sin, and its profound, fathomless misery; and now it was the one friend, whom she had loved the longest and the best, who was walking beside her a guilty man, fleeing through the night from all he himself cared for, to seek a refuge from the consequences of his crime in an uncertain exile. In years afterward it seemed to her as if that night had been rather a terrible dream than a reality.

At length the pale dawn broke, and the utter separation caused by the darkness between them and old Marlowe passed away with it. He stopped his horse and came to them, turning a gray, despairing face upon Roland Sefton.

"It is time to leave you," he said; "over these fields lies the nearest station, where you can escape from a just punishment. You have made us beggars to keep up your own grandeur. God will see that you do not go unpunished."

"Hush, hush!" cried Phebe aloud, stretching out her hand to Roland Sefton; "he will forgive you by and by. Tell me: have you no message to send by me, sir? When shall we hear from you?"

"If I get away safe," he answered, in a broken voice, "and if nothing is heard of me before, tell Felicita I will be in the place where I saw her first, this day six months. Do not tell her till the time is near. It will be best for her to know nothing of me at present."

They were standing at the stile over which his road lay. The sun was not yet risen, but the gray clouds overhead were taking rosy and golden tints. Here and there in the quiet farmsteads around them the cocks were beginning to crow lazily; and there were low, drowsy twitterings in the hedges, where the nests were still new little homes. It was a more peaceful hour than sunset can ever be with its memories of the day's toils and troubles. All the world seemed bathed in rest and quietness except themselves. Their dark journey through the silent night had been almost a crime.

"Your father turns his back upon me, as all honest men will do," said Roland Sefton.

Old Marlowe had gone back to his horse, and stood there without looking round. The tears ran down Phebe's face; but she did not touch her father, and ask him to bid his old friend's son good-by.

"Some day no man will turn his back upon you, sir," she answered; "I would die now rather than do it. You will regain your good name some day."

"Never!" he exclaimed; "it is past recall. There is no place of repentance for me, Phebe. I have staked all, and lost all."

CHAPTER VI

THE OLD BANK

About the same hour that Roland Sefton set off under shelter of old Marlowe's wagon to attempt his escape, Mr. Clifford, the senior partner in the firm, reached Riversborough by the last train from London. It was too late for him to intrude on the household of his young partner, and he spent the night at a hotel.

The old bank at Riversborough had been flourishing for the last hundred years. It had the power of issuing its own notes; and until lately these notes, bearing the familiar names of Clifford and Sefton, had been preferred by the country people round to those of the Bank of England itself. For nobody knew who were the managers of the Bank of England; while one of the Seftons, either father or son, could be seen at any time for the last fifty years. On ordinary days there were but few customers to be seen in its handsome office, and a single clerk might easily have transacted all the business. But on market-days and fair-days the place was crowded by loud-voiced, red-faced country gentlemen, and by awkward and burly farmers, from the moment its doors were opened until they were closed at the last stroke of four sounding from the church clock near at hand. The strong room of the Old Bank was filled full with chests containing valuable securities and heirlooms, belonging to most of the county families in the neighborhood.

For the last twenty years Mr. Clifford had left the management of the bank entirely to the elder Sefton, and upon his death to his son, who was already a partner. He had lived abroad, and had not visited England for more than ten years. There was a report, somewhat more circumstantial than a rumor, but the truth of which none but the elder Sefton had ever known, that Mr. Clifford, offended by his only son, had let him die of absolute starvation in Paris. Added to this rumor was a vague story of some crime committed by the younger Clifford, which his father would not overlook or forgive. That he was a hard man, austere to utter pitilessness, everybody averred. No transgressor need look to him for pardon.

When Roland Sefton had laid his hands upon the private personal securities belonging to his senior partner, it was with no idea that he would escape the most rigorous prosecution, should his proceedings ever come to the light. But it was with the fixed conviction that Mr. Clifford would never return to England, or certainly not to Riversborough, where this hard report had been circulated and partly accepted concerning him. The very bonds he had dealt with, first borrowing money upon them, and at last selling them, had been bequeathed to him in Mr. Clifford's will, of which he was himself the executor. He had, as he persuaded himself, only forestalled the possession of them. But a letter he had received from Mr. Clifford, informing him that he was on his way home, with the purpose of thoroughly investigating the affairs of the bank, had fallen like a thunderbolt upon him, and upon Acton, through whose agency he had managed to dispose of the securities without arousing any suspicion.

Early the next morning Mr. Clifford arrived at the bank, and heard to his great surprise that his partner had started for London, and had been away the day before; possibly, Madame Sefton suggested with some anxiety, in the hope of meeting him there. No doubt he would be back early, for it was the day of the May fair, when there was always an unusual stir of business. Mr. Clifford took his place in the vacant bank parlor, and waited somewhat grimly for the arrival of the head clerk, Acton.

There was a not unpleasant excitement among the clerks, as they whispered to each other on arrival that old Clifford was come and Roland Sefton was still absent. But this excitement deepened into agitation and misgiving as the hour for opening the bank drew near and Acton did not arrive. Such a circumstance had never occurred before, for Acton had made himself unpopular with those beneath him by expecting devotion equal to his own to the interests of the firm. When ten o'clock was close at hand a clerk ran round to Acton's lodgings; but before he could return a breathless messenger rushed into the bank as the doors were thrown open, with the tidings that the head clerk had been found by his landlady lying dead in his bed.

More quickly than if the town-crier had been sent round the streets with his bell to announce the news, it was known that Roland Sefton was missing and the managing clerk had committed suicide. The populace from all the country round was flocking into the town for the fair, three fourths of whom did business with the Old Bank. No wonder that a panic took possession of them. In an hour's time the tranquil street was thronged with a dense mass of town's-people and country-people, numbers of whom were fighting their way to the bank as if for dear life. There was not room within for the crowds who struggled to get to the counters and present their checks and bank-notes, and demand instant settlement of their accounts. In vain Mr. Clifford assured them there was no fear of the firm being unable to meet its liabilities. In cases like these the panic cannot be allayed by words.

As long as the funds held out the checks and notes were paid over the counter; but this could not go on. Mr. Clifford himself was in the dark as to the state of affairs, and did not know how his credit stood. Soon after midday the funds were exhausted, and with the utmost difficulty the bank was cleared and the doors closed. But the crowd did not disperse; rather it grew denser as the news spread like wildfire that the Old Bank had stopped!

It was at the moment that the bank doors were closed that Phebe turned into Whitefriars Road. She had taken a train from Upchurch, leaving her father to return home alone with the empty wagon. It was a strange sight which met her. The usually quiet street was thronged from end to end, and the babble of many voices made all sounds indistinct. Even on the outskirts of the crowd there were men, some pale and some red with anxiety, struggling with elbows and shoulders to make their way through to the bank, in the vain hope that it would not be too late. A strongly-built, robust farmer fainted quietly away beside her, like a delicate woman, when he heard that the doors were shut; and his wife and son, who were following him, bore him out of the crush as well as they could. Phebe, pressing gently forward, and gliding in wherever a chance movement gave her an opportunity, at last reached the archway at the side of the house, and rapped urgently for admittance. A scared-looking man-servant, who opened the door with the chain upon it, let her in as soon as he recognized who she was.

"It's a fearsome day," he said; "master's away, gone nobody knows where; and old Acton's poisoned himself. Nobody dare tell Mrs. Sefton; but Madame knows. She is in the dining-room, Miss Marlowe."

Phebe found her, as she had done the day before, sitting in the oriel window; but the usually placid-looking little woman was in a state of nervous agitation. As soon as she caught sight of Phebe's pitiful face she ran to her, and clasping her in her arms, burst into a passion of tears and sobs.

"My son!" she cried; "what can have become of him, Phebe? Where can he be gone? If he would only come home, all these people would be satisfied, and go away. They don't know Mr. Clifford, but they know Roland; he is so popular. The servants say the bank is broken; what does that mean, Phebe? And poor Acton! They say he is dead—he did kill himself by poison. Is it not true, Phebe? Tell me it is not true!"

But Phebe could say nothing to comfort her; she knew better than any one else the whole truth of the calamity. But she held the weeping little woman in her strong young arms, and there was something consoling in her loving clasp.

"And where are the children?" she asked, after a while.

"I sent them to play in the garden," answered Madame; "their own little plots are far away, out of sight of the dreadful street. What good is it that they should know all this trouble?"

"No good at all," replied Phebe. "And where is Mrs. Sefton?"

"Alas, my Phebe!" she exclaimed, "who dare tell her? Not me; no, no! She is shut up in her little chamber, and she forgets all the world—her children even, and Roland himself. It is as if she went away into another life, far away from ours; and when she comes home again she is like one in a dream. Will you dare to tell her?"

"Yes, I will go," she said.

Yet with very slow and reluctant steps Phebe climbed the staircase, pausing long at the window midway, which overlooked the wide and sunny landscape in the distance, and the garden just below. She watched the children busy at their little plots of ground, utterly unconscious of the utter ruin that had befallen them. How lovely and how happy they looked! She could have cried out aloud, a bitter and lamentable cry. But as yet she must not yield to the flood of her own grief; she must keep it back until she was at home again, in her solitary home, where nobody could hear her sobs and cries. Just now she must think for, and comfort, if comfort were possible, these others, who stood even nearer than she did to the sin and the sinner. Gathering up all her courage, she quickened her footsteps and ran hurriedly up the remaining steps.

But at the drawing-room door, which was partly open, her feet were arrested. Within, standing behind the rose-colored curtains, stood the tall, slender figure of Felicita, with her clear and colorless face catching a delicate flush from the tint of the hangings that concealed her from the street. She was looking down on the crowd below, with the perplexity of a foreigner gazing on some unfamiliar scene in a strange land. There was a half-smile playing about her lips; but her whole attention was so absorbed by the spectacle beneath her that she did not see or hear Phebe until she was standing beside her, looking down also on the excited crowd.

"Phebe!" she exclaimed, "you here again? Then you can tell me, are the good people of Riversborough gone mad? or is it possible there is an election going on, of which I have heard nothing? Nothing less than an election could rouse them to such a pitch of excitement."

"Have you heard nothing of what they say?" asked Phebe.

"There is such a Babel," she answered; "of course I hear my husband's name. It would be just like him if he got himself elected member for Riversborough without telling me anything about it till it was over. He loves surprises; and I—why I hate to be surprised."

"But he is gone!" said Phebe.

"Yes, he told me he was going to London," she went on; "but if it is no election scene, what is it, Phebe? Why are all the people gathered here in such excitement?"

"Shall I tell you plainly?" asked Phebe, looking steadily into Felicita's dark, inscrutable eyes.

"Tell me the simple truth," she replied, somewhat haughtily; "if any human being can tell it."

"Then the bank has stopped payment," answered Phebe. "Poor Mr. Acton has been found dead in bed this morning; and Mr. Sefton is gone away, nobody knows where. It is the May fair to-day, and all the people are coming in from the country. There's been a run on the bank till they are forced to stop payment. That is what brings the crowd here."

Felicita dropped the curtain which she had been holding back with her hand, and stepped back a pace or two from the window. But her face scarcely changed; she listened calmly and collectedly, as if Phebe was speaking of some persons she hardly knew.

"My husband will come back immediately," she said. "Is not Mr. Clifford there?"

"Yes," said Phebe.

"Are you telling me all?" asked Felicita.

"No," she answered; "Mr. Clifford says he has been robbed. Securities worth nearly ten thousand pounds are missing. He must have found it out already."

"Who does he suspect?" she asked again imperiously; "he does not dare suspect my husband?"

Phebe replied only by a mute gesture. She had never had any secret to conceal before, and she did not see that she had betrayed herself by the words she had uttered. The deep gloom on her bright young face struck Felicita for the first time.

"Do you think it was Roland?" she asked.

Again the same dumb, hopeless gesture answered the question. Phebe could not bring her lips to shape a word of accusation against him. It was agony to her to feel her idol disgraced and cast down from his high pedestal; yet she had not learned any way of concealing or misrepresenting the truth.

"You know he did it?" said Felicita.

"Yes, I know it," she whispered.

For a minute or two Felicita stood, with her white hands resting on Phebe's shoulders, gazing into her mournful face with keen, questioning eyes. Then, with a rapid flush of crimson, betraying a strong and painful heart-throb, which suffused her face for an instant and left it paler than before, she pressed her lips on the girl's sunburnt forehead.

"Tell nobody else," she murmured; "keep the secret for his sake and mine."

Before Phebe could reply she turned away, and, with a steady, unfaltering step, went back to her study and locked herself in.

CHAPTER VII

AN INTERRUPTED DAY-DREAM

Felicita's study was so quiet a room, quite remote from the street, that it was almost a wonder the noise of the crowd had reached her. But this morning there had been a pleasant tumult of excitement in her own brain, which had prevented her from falling into an absorbed reverie, such as she usually indulged in, and rendered her peculiarly susceptible to outward influences. All her senses had been awake to-day.

On her desk lay the two volumes of a new book, handsomely got up, with pages yet uncut as it had come from the publishers. A dozen times she had looked at the title-page, as if unable to convince herself of the reality, and read her own name—Felicita Riversdale Sefton. It was the first time her name as an author had been published, though for the last three years she had from time to time written anonymously for magazines. This was her own book; thought out, written, revised, and completed in her chosen solitude and secrecy. No one knew of it; possibly Roland suspected something, but he had not ventured to make any inquiries, and she had no reason to believe that he even suspected its existence. It was simply altogether her own; no other mind had any part or share in it.

There was something like rapture in her delight. The book was a good book, she was sure of it. She had not succeeded in making it as perfect as her ideal, but she had not signally failed. It did in a fair degree represent her inmost thoughts and fancies. Yet she could not feel quite sure that the two volumes were real, and the letter from the publisher, a friendly and pleasant letter enough, seemed necessary to vouch for them. She read and re-read it. The little room seemed too small and close for her. She opened the window to let in the white daylight, undisguised by the faint green tint of the glass, and she leaned out to breathe the fresh sweet air of the spring morning. Life was very pleasurable to her to-day.

There were golden gleams too upon the future. She would no longer be the unknown wife of a country banker, moving in a narrow sphere, which was altogether painful to her in its provincial philistinism. It was a sphere to which she had descended in girlish ignorance. Her uncle, Lord Riversdale, had been willing to let his portionless niece marry this prosperous young banker, who was madly in love with her, and a little gentle pressure had been brought to bear on the girl of eighteen, who had been placed by her father's death in a position of dependence. Since then a smouldering fire of ambition and of dissatisfaction with her lot had been lurking unsuspected under her cold and self-absorbed manner.

But her thoughts turned with more tenderness than usual toward her husband. She had aroused in him also a restless spirit of ambition, though in him it was for her sake, not his own. He wished to restore her if possible to the position she had sacrificed for him; and Felicita knew it. Her heart beating faster with her success was softened toward him; and tears suffused her dark eyes for an instant as she thought of his astonishment and exultation.

The children were at play in the garden below her, and their merry voices greeted her ear pleasantly. The one human being who really dwelt in her inmost heart was her boy Felix, her first-born child. Hilda was an unnecessary supplement to the page of her maternal love. But for Felix she dreamed day-dreams of extravagant aspiration; no lot on earth seemed too high or too good for him. He was a handsome boy, the very image of her father, the late Lord Riversdale, and now as she gazed down on him, her eyes slightly dewed with tears, he looked up to her window. She kissed her hand to him, and the boy waved his little cap toward her with almost passionate gesticulations of delight. Felix would be a great man some day; this book of hers was a stone in the foundation of his fame as well as of her own.

It was upon this mood of exultation, a rare mood for Felicita, that the cry and roar from the street had broken. With a half-smile at herself, the thought flashed across her mind that it was like a shout of applause and admiration, such as might greet Felix some day when he had proved himself a leader of men. But it aroused her dormant curiosity, and she had condescended to be drawn by it to the window of the drawing-room overlooking Whitefriars Road, in order to ascertain its cause. The crowd filling the street was deeply in earnest, and the aim of those who were fighting their way through it was plainly the bank offices in the floor below her. The sole idea that occurred to her, for she was utterly ignorant of her husband's business, was that some unexpected crisis in the borough had arisen, and its people were coming to Roland Sefton as their leading townsman. When Phebe found her she was quietly studying the crowd and its various features, that she might describe a throng from memory, whenever a need should arise for it.

Felicita regained her luxurious little study, and sat down before her desk, on which the new volumes lay, with more outward calm than her face and movements had manifested before she left it. The transient glow of triumph had died away from her face, and the happy tears from her eyes. She closed the casement to shut out the bright, clear sunlight, and the merry voices of her children, before she sat down to think.

For a little while she had been burning incense to herself; but the treacherous fire was gone out, and the sweet, bewildering, intoxicating vapors were scattered to the winds. The recollection of her short-lived folly made her shiver as if a cold breath had passed over her.

Not for a moment did she doubt Roland's guilt. There was such a certainty of it lying behind Phebe's sorrowful eyes as she whispered "I know it," that Felicita had not cared to ask how she knew it. She did not trouble herself with details. The one fact was there: her husband had absconded. A dreamy panorama of their past life flitted across her brain—his passionate love for her, which had never cooled, though it had failed to meet with a response from her; his insatiable desire to make her life more full of pomp and luxury and display than that of her cousins at Riversdale; his constant thraldom to her, which had ministered only to her pride and coldness. His queen he had called her. It was all over now. His extraordinary absence was against any hope that he could clear himself. Her husband had brought fatal and indelible disgrace upon his name, the name he had given to her and their children.

Her name! This morning, and for many days to come, it would be advertised as the author of the new book, which was to have been one of her stepping-stones to fame. She had grasped at fame, and her hand had closed upon infamy. There was no fear now that she would remain among the crowd of the unknown. As the wife of a fraudulent banker she would be only too well and too widely talked of.

Why had she let her own full name be published? She had yielded, though with some reluctance, to the business-like policy of her publisher, who had sought to catch the public eye by it; for her father, Lord Riversdale, was hardly yet forgotten as an author. A vague sentiment of loyalty to her husband had caused her to add her married name. She hated to see the two blazoned together on the title-page.

Sick at heart, she sat for hours brooding over what would happen if Roland was arrested. The assizes held twice a year at Riversborough had been to her, as to many people of her position, an occasion of pleasurable excitement. The judges' lodgings were in the next house to the Old Bank, and for the few days the judges were Roland Sefton's neighbors there had been a friendly interchange of civilities. An assize ball was still held, though it was falling into some neglect and disrepute. Whenever any cause of special local interest took place she had commanded the best seat in the court, and had obsequious attention paid to her. She had learned well the aspect of the place, and the mode of procedure. But hitherto her recollections of a court of justice were all agreeable, and her impressions those of a superior being looking down from above on the miseries and crimes of another race.

How different was the vision that branded itself on her brain this morning! She saw her husband standing at the dock, instead of some coarse, ignorant, brutish criminal; the stern gravity of the judge; the flippant curiosity of the barristers not connected with the case, and the cruel eagerness of his fellow-townsmen to get good places to hear and see him. It would make a holiday for all who could get within the walls.

She could have written almost word for word the report of the trial as it would appear in the two papers published in Riversborough. She could foretell how lavish would be the use of the words "felon" and "convict;" and she would be that felon and convict's wife.

Oh, this intolerable burden of disgrace! To be borne through the long, long years of life; and not by herself alone, but by her children. They had come into a miserable heritage. What became of the families of notorious criminals? She could believe that the poor did not suffer from so cruel a notoriety, being quickly lost in the oblivious waters of poverty and distress, amid refuges and workhouses. But what would become of her? She must go away into endless exile, with her two little children, and live where there was no chance of being recognized. This was what her husband's sin had done for her.

"God help me! God deliver me!" she moaned with white lips. But she did not pray for him. In the first moments of anguish the spirit flies to that which lies at the very core. While Roland's mother and Phebe were weeping together and praying for him, Felicita was crying for help and deliverance for herself.

CHAPTER VIII

THE SENIOR PARTNER

Long as the daylight lasts in May it was after nightfall when Felicita left her study and went down to the drawing-room, more elegantly and expensively furnished for her than the drawing-room at Riversdale had been. Its extravagant display seemed to strike upon her suddenly as she entered it. Phebe was gone home, and Madame had retired to her own room, having given up the expectation of seeing Felicita that day. Mr. Clifford, the servant told her, was still in the bank, with his lawyer, for whom he had telegraphed to London. Felicita sent him a message that if he was not too busy she wished to see him for a few minutes.

Mr. Clifford almost immediately appeared, and Felicita saw him for the first time. She had always heard him called old; but he was a strong, erect, stern-looking man of sixty, with keen, cold eyes that could not be avoided. Felicita did not seek to avoid them. She looked as steadily at him as he did at her. There were traces of tears on her face, but there was no tremor or weakness about her. They exchanged a few civil words as calmly as if they were ordinary acquaintances.

"Tell me briefly what has happened," she said to him, when he had taken a seat near to her.

"Briefly," he repeated. "Well! I find myself robbed of securities worth nearly £8000; private securities, bond and scrip, left in custody only, not belonging to the firm. No one but Acton or Roland could have access to them. Acton has eluded me; but if Roland is found he must take the consequences."

"And what are those?" asked Felicita.

"I shall prosecute him as I would prosecute a common thief or burglar," answered Mr. Clifford. "His crime is more dishonorable and cowardly."

"Is it not cruel to say this to me?" she asked, yet in a tranquil tone which startled him.

"Cruel!" he repeated again; "I have not been in the habit of choosing words. You asked me a question, and I gave you the answer that was in my mind. I never forgive. Those who pass over crimes make themselves partakers in those crimes. Roland has robbed not only me, but half a dozen poor persons, to whom such a loss is ruin. Would it be right to let such a man escape justice?"

"You think he has gone away on purpose?" she said.

"He has absconded," answered Mr. Clifford, "and the matter is already in the hands of the police. A description of him has been telegraphed to every police station in the kingdom. If he is not out of it he can barely escape now."

Felicita's pale face could not grow paler, but she shivered perceptibly.

"I am telling you bluntly," he said, "because I believe it is best to know the worst at once. It is terrible to have it falling drop by drop. You have courage and strength; I see it. Take an old man's word for it, it is better to know all in its naked ugliness, than have it brought to light bit by bit. There is not the shadow of a doubt of Roland's crime. You do not believe him innocent yourself?"

"No," she replied in a low, yet steady voice; "no. I must tell the truth. I cannot comfort myself with the belief that he is innocent."

Mr. Clifford's keen eyes were fastened upon Felicita with admiration. Here was a woman, young and pallid with grief and dread, who neither tried to move him by prayers and floods of tears, nor shrank from acknowledging a truth, however painful. He had never seen her before, though the costly set of jewels she was wearing had been his own gift to her on her wedding. He recognized them with pleasure, and looked more attentively at her beautiful but gloomy face. When he spoke again it was in a manner less harsh and abrupt than it had been before.

"I am not going to ask you any questions about Roland," he said; "you have a right, the best right in the world, to screen him, and aid him in escaping from the just consequences of his folly and crime."

"You might ask me," she interrupted, "and I should tell you the simple truth. I do so now, when I say I know nothing about him. He told me he was going to London. But is it not possible that poor Acton alone was guilty?"

Mr. Clifford shook his head in reply. For a few minutes he paced up and down the floor, and then placed himself at the back of Felicita, with his hand upon her chair, as if to support him. In a glass opposite she could see the reflection of his face, gray and agitated, with closed eyes and quivering lips—a face that looked ten years older than that which she had seen when he entered the room. She felt the chair shaken by his trembling hand.

"I will tell you," he said in a voice which he strove to render steady. "I did not spare my own son when he had defrauded Roland's father. Though Sefton would not prosecute him, I left him to reap the harvest of his deed to the full; and it was worse than the penalty the law would have exacted. He perished, disgraced and forsaken, of starvation in Paris, the city of pleasures and of crimes. They told me that my son was little more than a living skeleton when he was found, so slowly had the end come. If I did not spare him, can I relent toward Roland? The justice I demand is, in comparison, mercy for him."

As he finished speaking he opened his eyes, and saw those of Felicita fastened on the reflection of his face in the mirror. He turned away, and in a minute or two resumed his seat, and spoke again in his ordinary abrupt tone.

"What will you do?" he asked.

"I cannot tell yet," she answered; "I must wait till suspense is over. If Roland comes back, or is brought back," she faltered, "then I must decide what to do. I shall keep to myself till then. Is there anything I can do?"

"Could you go to your uncle, Lord Riversdale?" suggested Mr. Clifford.

"No, no," she cried; "I will not ask any help from him. He arranged my marriage for me, and he will feel this disgrace keenly. I will keep out of their way; they shall not be compelled to forbid me their society."

"But to-morrow you had better go away for the day," he answered; "there will be people coming and going, who will disturb you. There will be a rigorous search made. There is a detective now with my lawyer, who is looking through the papers in the bank. The police have taken possession of Acton's lodgings."

"I have nowhere to go," she replied, "and I cannot show my face out of doors. Madame and the children shall go to Phebe Marlowe, but I must bear it as well as I can."

"Well," he said after a brief pause, "I will make it as easy as I can for you. You are thinking me a hard man? Yes, I have grown hard. I was soft enough once. But if I forgave any sinner now I should do my boy, who is dead, an awful injustice. I would not pass over his sin, and I dare not pass over any other. I know I shall pursue Roland until his death or mine; my son's fate cries out for it. But I'm not a hard man toward innocent sufferers, like you and his poor mother. Try to think of me as your friend; nay, even Roland's friend, for what would a few years' penal servitude be compared with my boy's death? Shake hands with me before I go."

The small, delicate hand she offered him was icy cold, though her face was still calm and her eyes clear and dry. He was himself more moved and agitated than she appeared to be. The mention of his son always shook him to the very centre of his soul; yet he had not been able to resist uttering the words that had passed his lips during this painful interview with Roland's young wife. Unshed tears were burning under his eyelids. But if it had not been for that death-like hand he might have imagined her almost unmoved.

Felicita was down-stairs before Madame the next morning, and had ordered the carriage to be ready to take her and the children to Upfold Farm directly after breakfast. It was so rare an incident for their mother to be present at the breakfast-table that Felix and Hilda felt as if it were a holiday. Madame was pale and sad, and for the first time Felicita thought of her as being a sufferer by Roland's crime. Her husband's mother had been little more to her than a superior housekeeper, who had been faithfully attached to her and her children. The homely, gentle, domestic foreigner, from a humble Swiss home, had looked up to her young aristocratic daughter-in-law as a being from a higher sphere. But now the downcast, sorrowful face of the elder woman touched Felicita's sympathy.

"Mother!" she said, as soon as the children had run away to get ready for their drive. She had never before called Madame "mother," and a startled look, almost of delight, crossed Madame's sad face.

"My daughter!" she cried, running to Felicita's side, and throwing her arms timidly about her, "he is sure to come back soon—to-day, I think. Oh, yes, he will be here when we return! You do well to stay to meet him; and I should be glad to be here, but for the children. Yes, the little ones must be out of the way. They must not see their father's house searched; they must never know how he is suspect. Acton did say it was all his fault; his fault and—"

But here Madame paused for an instant, for had not Acton said it was Felicita's fault more than any one's?

"Phebe heard him," she went on hastily; "and if it is not his fault, why did he kill himself? Oh, it is an ill-fortune that my son went to London that day! It would all be right if he were here; but he is sure to come to-day and explain it all; and the bank will be opened again. So be of good comfort, my daughter; for God is present with us, and with my son also."

It was a sorrowful day at the Upfold Farm in spite of the children's unconscious mirthfulness. Old Marlowe locked himself into his workshop, and would see none of them, taking his meals there in sullen anger. Phebe's heart was almost broken with listening to Madame's earnest asseverations of her son's perfect innocence, and her eager hopes to find him when she reached home. It was nearly impossible to her to keep the oppressive secret, which seemed crushing her into deception and misery, and her own muteness appeared to herself more condemnatory than any words could be. But Madame did not notice her silence, and her grief was only natural. Phebe's tears fell like balm on Madame's aching heart. Felicita had not wept; but this young girl, and her abandonment to passionate bursts of tears, who needed consoling herself, was a consolation to the poor mother. They knelt together in Phebe's little bedroom, while the children were playing on the wide uplands around them, and they prayed silently, if heavy sobs and sighs could be called silence; but they prayed together, and for her son; and Madame returned home comforted and hopeful.

It had been a day of fierce trial to Felicita. She had not formed any idea of how searching would be the investigation of the places where any of her husband's papers might be found. Her own study was not exempt from the prying eyes of the detectives. This room, sacred to her, which Roland himself never entered without permission was ransacked, and forever desecrated in her eyes. This official meddling with her books and her papers could never be forgotten. The pleasant place was made an abomination to her.

The bank was reopened the next morning at the accustomed hour, for a very short investigation by Mr. Clifford and the experienced advisers summoned from London to assist him proved that the revenues of the firm were almost as good as ever. The panic had been caused by the vague rumor afloat of some mysterious complicity in crime between the absent partner and the clerk who had committed suicide. It was, therefore, considered necessary for the prosperous re-establishment of the bank to put forth a cautiously worded circular, in which Mr. Clifford's return was made the reason for the absence on a long journey of Roland Sefton, whose disappearance had to be accounted for. By the time he was arrested and brought to trial the confidence of the bank's customers in its stability would in some measure be regained.

There was thus a good deal of conjecture and of contradictory opinion abroad in Riversborough concerning Roland Sefton, which continued to be the town's-talk for some weeks. Even Madame began to believe in a half-bewildered manner that her son had gone on a journey of business connected with the bank, though she could not account for his total silence. Sometimes she wondered if he and Felicita could have had some fatal quarrel, which had driven him away from home in a paroxysm of passionate disappointment and bitterness. Felicita's coldness and indifference might have done it. With this thought, and the hope of his return some day, she turned for relief to the discharge of her household duties, and to the companionship of the children, who knew nothing except that their father was gone away on a journey, and might come back any day.

Neither Madame nor the children knew that whenever they left the house they were followed by a detective, and every movement was closely watched. But Felicita was conscious of it by some delicate sensitiveness of her imaginative temperament. She refused to quit the house except in the evening, when she rambled about the garden, and felt the fresh air from the river breathing against her often aching temples. Even then she fancied an eye upon her—an unsleeping, unblinking eye; the unwearying vigilance of justice on the watch for a criminal. Night and day she felt herself living under its stony gaze.

It was a positive pain to her when reviews of her book appeared in various papers, and were forwarded to her with congratulatory letters from her publishers. She was living far enough from London to be easily persuaded, without much vanity, that her name was upon everybody's lips there. She read the reviews, but with a sick heart, and the words were forgotten as soon as she put them away; but the Riversborough papers, which had been very guarded in their statements about the death of Acton and the events at the Old Bank, took up the book with what appeared to her fulsome and offensive enthusiasm. It had never occurred to her that local criticism was certain to follow the appearance of a local writer; and she shrank from it with morbid and exaggerated disgust. Even if all had been well, if Roland had been beside her, their notices would have been well-nigh intolerable to her. She could not have endured being stared at and pointed out in the streets of her own little town. But now Fame had come to her with broken wings and a cracked trumpet, and she shuddered at the sound of her own name harshly proclaimed through it.

It soon became evident that Roland Sefton had succeeded in getting away out of the country. The police were at fault; and as no one in his own home knew how to communicate with him, no clew had been discovered by close surveillance of their movements. Such vigilance could be kept up only for a few months at longest, and as the summer drew toward the end it ceased.

CHAPTER IX

FAST BOUND

Roland Sefton had met with but few difficulties in getting clear away out of England, and there was little chance of his being identified, from description merely, by any of the foreign police, or by any English detective on the Continent who was not as familiar with his personal appearance as the Riversborough force were. In his boyhood he had spent many months, years even, in his mother's native village with her father, M. Roland Merle, the pastor of a parish among the Jura Mountains. It was as easy for him to assume the character of a Swiss mountaineer as to sustain that of a prosperous English banker. The dress, the patois, the habits of the peasant were all familiar to him, and his disguise in them was as complete as disguise ever can be. The keen eye either of love or hate can pierce through all disguises.

Switzerland was all fatherland to him, as much so as his native country, and the county in which Riversborough was situated. There was no ignorance in him of any little town, or the least known of the Alps, which might betray the stranger. He would never need to attract notice by asking a question. He had become a member of an Alpine club as soon as his boyish thews and sinews were strong enough for stiff and perilous climbing. He had crossed the most difficult passes and scaled some of the worst peaks. And there had been within him that passionate love of the country common to the Swiss which an English Alpine climber can never feel. His mother's land had filled him with an ardent flame, smouldering at times amid the absorbing interests of his somewhat prominent place in English life, but every now and then breaking out into an irrepressible longing for the sight of its white mountains and swift, strong streams. It was at once the safest and the most dangerous of refuges. He would be certainly sought for there; but there he could most effectually conceal himself. He flew thither with his burden of sin and shame.

Roland adopted at once the dress of a decent artisan of the Jura—such a man as he had known in his boyhood as a watchmaker of Locle or the Doubs. For a few days he stayed in Geneva, lodging in such a street as a Locle artisan would have chosen; but he could not feel secure there, in spite of his own certainty that his transformation was complete. A restless dread haunted him. He knew well that there are in every one little personal traits, tricks of gesture, and certain tones of voice always ready to betray us. It was yet too early in the year for many travellers to be journeying to Switzerland; but already a few straggling pioneers of the summer flight were appearing in the larger towns, and what would be his fate if any one of them recognized him? He quitted Geneva, and wandered away into the mountain villages.

It was May-time, and the snow-line was still lingering low down on the steep slopes, though the flowers were springing into life up to its very margin, seeming to drive it higher and higher every day. The High Alps were still fast locked in midwinter, and with untrodden wastes and plains of snow lying all around them. The deserted mountain farms and great solitary hotels, so thronged last summer, were empty. But in the valleys and the little villages lying on the warm southern slopes, or sheltered by precipitous rocks from the biting winds, there was everywhere a joyous stir of awakening from the deep sleep of winter. The frozen streams were thawed and ran bubbling and gurgling along their channels, turning water-wheels and filling all the quiet places with their merry noise. The air itself was full of sweet exhilaration. In the forests there was the scent of stirring sap and of the up-springing wild-flowers, and the rosy blossoms of the tender young larch-trees shone like jewels in the bright sunshine. The mountain-peaks overhead, gleaming through the mists and clouds, were of dazzling whiteness, for none of the frozen snow had yet fallen from their sharp, lance-like summits.

Journeying on foot from one village to another, Roland roamed about aimlessly, yet as one hunted, seeking for a safe asylum. He bore his troubled conscience and aching heart from one busy spot to another, homesick and self-exiled. Oh, what a fool he had been! Life had been full to the brim for him with gladness and prosperity, and in trying to make its cup run over he had dashed it away from his lips forever.

His money was not yet spent, for a very little went a long way among these simple mountain villages, and in his manner of travelling. He had not yet been forced to try to earn a living, and he felt no anxiety for the future. In his boyhood he had learned wood-carving, both in Switzerland and from old Marlowe, and he had acquired considerable skill in the art. Some of the panels in his home at Riversborough were the workmanship of his own hands. It was a craft to turn to in extremity; but he did not think of it yet.

Labor of any kind would have made the interminable hours pass more quickly. The carving of a piece of wood might have kept him from torturing his own heart perpetually; but he did not turn to this slight solace. There were times when he sat for hours, for a whole age, as it seemed to him, in some lonely spot, hidden behind a great rock or half lost in a forest, thinking. And yet it was not thought, but a vague, mournful longing and remembrance, the past and the absent blended in dim, shadowy reverie, of which nothing was clear but the sharp anguish of having forfeited them. There was a Garden of Eden still upon earth, and he had been dwelling in it. But he had banished himself from it by his own folly and sin, and when he turned his eyes toward it he could see only the "flaming brand, and the gate with dreadful faces thronged and fiery arms." But even Adam had his Eve with him, "to drop some natural tears, and wipe them soon." He was utterly alone.

If his thoughts, so dazed and bewildered usually, became clear for a little while, it was always Felicita whose image stood out most distinctly before him. He had loved her passionately; surely never had any man loved a woman with the same intensity—so he said to himself. Even now the very crime he had committed seemed as nothing to him, because he had been guilty of it for her. His love for her covered its heinousness from his eyes. His conscience had become the blind and dumb slave of his passion. So blind and dumb had it been that it had scarcely stirred or murmured until his sin was found out, and it was scarcely aroused to life even yet.

In a certain sense he had been religious, having been most sedulously trained in religion from his earliest consciousness. He had accepted the ordinary teachings of our nineteenth-century Christianity. His place in church, beside his mother or his wife, had seldom been empty, and several times in the year he had knelt with them at the Lord's table, and taken the Lord's Supper, feeling himself distinctly a more religious man than usual on such occasions. No man had ever heard him utter a profane word, nor had he transgressed any of the outward rules of a religious life. It is true he had never made a vehement and extraordinary profession of piety, such as some men do; but there was not a person in Riversborough who would not have spoken of him as a good churchman and a Christian. While he had been gradually appropriating Mr. Clifford's money and the hard-earned savings of poorer men confided to him, he had felt no qualm of conscience in giving liberally to many a religious and philanthropic object, contributing such sums as figure well in a subscription list; though it was generally his wife's name that figured there. He had never taken up a subscription list without glancing first for that beloved name, Mrs. Roland Sefton.

In those days he had never doubted that he was a Christian. So far as he knew, so far as words could teach him, he was living a Christian life. Did he not believe in God, the Father Almighty? Yes, as fully as those who lived about him. Had he not followed Christ? As closely as the mass of people who call themselves Christians. Nay, more than most of them. Not as much as his mother perhaps, in her simple, devout faith. But then religion is always a different thing with women than with men, a fairer and more delicate thing, wearing a finer bloom and gloss, which does not wear well in a work-a-day world such as he did battle in. But if he had not lived a Christian life, what man in Riversborough had done so, except a few fanatics?

But his religion had been powerless to keep him from falling into subtle temptations, and into a crime so heinous in the sight of his fellow-men that it was only to be expiated by the loss of character, the loss of liberty, and the loss of every honorable man's esteem. The web had been closely and cunningly woven, and now he was fast bound in it, with no way of escape.

CHAPTER X ·

LEAVING RIVERSBOROUGH

The weeks passed by in Riversborough, and brought no satisfactory conclusion to the guarded investigations of the police. A close search made among Acton's private papers produced no discovery. His will was among them, leaving all he had to leave, which was not much, to Felix, the son of his friend and employer, Roland Sefton. There was no memorandum or letter which could throw any light upon the transactions, or give any clew to what had been done with Mr. Clifford's securities.

Nor was the watch kept over the movements of the family more successful. The police were certain that no letter was posted by any member of the household, which could be intended for the missing culprit. Even Phebe Marlowe's correspondence was subject to their vigilance. But not a trace could be discovered. He was gone; whether he had fled to America, or concealed himself nearer home on the Continent, no one could make a guess.

Mr. Clifford remained in Riversborough, and resumed his position as head of the firm. He had returned with the intention of doing so, having heard abroad of the extravagant manner in which his junior partner was living. The bank, though seriously crippled in its credit and resources, was in no danger of insolvency, and there seemed no reason why it should not regain its former prosperity, if only confidence could be restored. He had reserved to himself the power of taking in another partner, if he should deem it advisable; and an eligible one presenting himself, in the person of a Manchester man of known wealth, the deeds of partnership were drawn up, and the Old Bank was once more set up on a firm basis.

During the time that elapsed while these arrangements were being made, Felicita was visibly suffering, and failing in health. So sensitive had she grown to the dread of seeing any one not in the immediate circle of her household, that it became impossible to her to leave her home. The clear colorlessness of her face had taken on a transparency and delicacy which did not lessen its beauty, but added to it an unearthly grace. She no longer spent hours alone in her desecrated room; it had grown intolerable to her; but she sat speechless, and almost motionless, in the oriel window overlooking the garden and the river; and Felix, a child of dreamy and sensitive temperament, would sit hour after hour at her feet, pressing his cheek against her knee, or with his uplifted eyes gazing into her face.

"Mother," he said one day, when Roland had been gone more than a month, "how long will my father be away on his journey? Doesn't he ever write to you, and send messages to me? Grandmamma says she does not know how soon he will be back. Do you know, mother?"

Felicita looked down on him with her beautiful dark eyes, which seemed larger and sadder than of old, sending a strange thrill through the boy's heart, and for a minute or two she seemed uncertain what to say.

"I cannot tell you, Felix," she answered; "there are many things in life which children cannot understand. If I told you what was true about your father, your little brain would turn it into an untruth. You could not understand it if I told you."

"But I shall understand it some day," he said, lifting his head up proudly; "will you tell me when I am old enough, mother?"

How could she promise him to do that? This proud young head, tossed back with the expectant triumph of some day knowing all that his father and mother knew, must be bowed down with grief and shame then, as hers was now. It was a sad knowledge he must inherit. How would she ever be able to tell him that the father who had given him life, and whose name he bore, was a criminal; a convict if he was arrested and brought to judgment; an outlaw and an exile if he made good his escape? Roland had never been as dear to her as Felix was. She was one of those women who love more deeply and tenderly as mothers than as wives. To see that bright, fond face of his clouded with disgrace would be a ceaseless torment to her. There would be no suffering to compare with it.

"But you will tell me all about it some day, mother," urged the boy.

"If I ever tell you," she answered, "it will be when you are a man, and can understand the whole truth. You will never hear me tell a falsehood, Felix."

"I know that, mother," he replied, "but oh! I miss my father! He used to come to my bedside at nights, and kiss me, and say 'God bless you.' I tried always to keep awake till he came; but I was asleep the last time of all, and missed him. Sometimes I feel frightened, as if he would never come again. But grandmamma says he is gone on a long journey, and will come home some day, only she doesn't know when. Phebe cries when I ask her. Would it be too much trouble for you to come in at night sometimes, like my father did?" he asked timidly.

"But I am not like your father," she answered. "I could not say 'God bless you' in the same way. You must ask God yourself for His blessing."

For Felicita's soul had been thrust down into the depths of darkness. Her early training had been simply and solely for this world: how to make life here graceful and enjoyable. She could look back upon none but the vaguest aspirations after something higher in her girlhood. It had been almost like a new revelation to her to see her mother-in-law's simple and devout piety, and to witness her husband's cheerful and manly profession of religion. This was the point in his character which had attracted her most, and had been most likely to bind her to him. Not his passionate love to herself, but his unselfishness toward others, his apparently happy religion, his energetic interest in all good and charitable schemes—these had reconciled her more than anything else to the step she had taken, the downward step, in marrying him.

This unconscious influence of Roland's life and character had been working secretly and slowly upon her nature for several years. They were very young when they were married, and her first feeling of resentment toward her own family for pressing on the marriage had at the outset somewhat embittered her against her young husband. But this had gradually worn away, and Felicita had never been so near loving him heartily and deeply as during the last year or two, when it was evident that his attachment to her was as loyal and as tender as ever. He had almost won her, when he staked all and lost all.

For now, she asked herself, what was the worth of all this religion, which presented so fair a face to her? She had a delicate sense of honor and truthfulness, which never permitted her to swerve into any byways of expediency or convenience. What use was Roland's religion without truthfulness and honor? She said to herself that there was no excuse for him even feeling tempted to deal with another man's property. It ought to have been as impossible to him as it was impossible to her to steal goods from a tradesman's counter. Was it possible to serve God—and Roland professed to serve Him—yet cheat his fellow-men? The service of God itself must then be a vanity—a mere bubble, like all the other bubbles of life.

It had never been her habit to speak out her thoughts, even to her husband. Speech seemed an inefficient and blundering medium of communication, and she found it easier to write than to talk. There was a natural taciturnity about her which sealed her lips, even when her children were prattling to her. Only in writing could she give expression to the multitude of her thoughts within her; and her letters were charming, and of exceeding interest. But in this great crisis in her life she could not write. She would sit for hours vainly striving to arouse her languid brain. It seemed to her that she had lost this gift also in the utter ruin that had overtaken her.

Felicita's white, silent, benumbed grief, accepting the conviction of her husband's guilt with no feminine contradicting or loud lamenting, touched Mr. Clifford with more pity than he felt for Madame, who bore her son's mysterious absence with a more simple and natural sorrow. There was something irritating to him in the fact that Roland's mother ignored the accusation he made against him. But when Roland had been away three months, and the police authorities had given up all expectation of discovering anything by watching his home and family, Mr. Clifford felt that it was time something should be arranged which would deliver Felicita from her voluntary imprisonment.

"Why do you not go away?" he asked her; "you cannot continue to live mewed up here all your days. If Roland should be found, it would be better for you not to be in Riversborough. And I for one have given up the expectation that he will be found; the only chance is that he may return and give himself up. Go to some place where you are not known. There is Scarborough; take Madame and the children there for a few months, and then settle in London for the winter. Nobody will know you in London."

"But how can we leave this house?" she said, with a gleam of light in her sad eyes.

"Let me come in just as it is," he answered. "I will pay you a good rent for it, and you can take a part of the furniture to London, to make your new dwelling there more like home. It would be a great convenience to me, and it would be the best thing for you, depend upon it. If Roland returns he never will live here again."

"No, he could never do that," she said, sighing deeply. "Mr. Clifford, sometimes I think he must be dead."

"I have thought so too," he replied gravely; "and if it were so, it would be the salvation of you and your children. There would be no public trial and conviction, and though suspicion might always rest upon his memory, he would not be remembered for long. Justice would be defrauded, yet on the whole I should rejoice for your sake to hear that he was dead."

Felicita's lips almost echoed the words. Her heart did so, though it smote her as she recollected his passionate love for her. But Mr. Clifford's speech sank deeply into her mind, and she brooded over it incessantly. Roland's death meant honor and fair fame for herself and her children; his life was perpetual shame and contempt to them.

It was soon settled that they must quit Riversborough; but though Felicita welcomed the change, and was convinced it would be the best thing to do, Madame grieved sorely over leaving the only home which had been hers, except the little manse in the Jura, where her girlhood had passed swiftly and happily away. She had brought with her the homely, thrifty ways in which she had been trained, and every spot in her husband's dwelling had been taken under her own care and supervision. Her affections had rooted themselves to the place, and she had never dreamed of dying anywhere else than among the familiar scenes which had surrounded her for more than thirty years. The change too could not be made without her consent, for her marriage settlement was secured upon the house, and her husband had left to her the right of accepting or refusing a tenant. To leave the familiar, picturesque old mansion, and to carry away with her only a few of the household treasures, went far to break her heart.

"It is where my husband intended for me to live and die," she moaned to Phebe Marlowe; "and, oh, if I go away I can never fancy I see him sitting in his own chair as he used to do, at the head of the table, or by the fire. I have not altogether lost him, though he's gone, as long as I can think of how he used to come in and go out of this room, always with a smile for me. But if I go where he never was, how can I think I see him there? And my son will be angry if we go; he will come back, and clear up all this mystery, and he will think we went away because we thought he had done evil. Ought we not to come home again after we have been to Scarborough?"

"I think Mrs. Sefton will die if she stays here," said Phebe. "It is necessary for her to make this change; and you'd rather go with her and the children than live here alone without them."

"Oh, yes, yes!" answered Madame; "I cannot leave my little Felix and Hilda, or Felicita: she is my son's dear wife. But he will come home some day, and we can return then; you hope so, don't you, Phebe?"

"If God pleases!" said Phebe, sighing.

"In truth, if God pleases!" repeated Madame.

When the last hour came in which Phebe could see Roland's wife, she sought for her in her study, where she was choosing the books to be sent after her. In the very words in which Roland had sent his message he delivered it to Felicita. The cold, sad, marble-like face did not change, though her heart gave a throb of disappointment and anguish as the dread hope that he was no longer alive died out of it.

"I will meet him there," she said. But she asked Phebe no questions, and did not tell her where she was to meet her husband.

CHAPTER XI

OLD MARLOWE

Life had put on for Phebe a very changed aspect. The lonely farmstead on the uplands had been till now a very happy and tranquil home. She had had no sorrow since her mother died when she was eight years of age, too young to grieve very sorely. On the other hand, she was not so young as to require a woman's care, and old Marlowe had made her absolute mistress of the little home. His wife, a prudent, timid woman, had always repressed his artistic tendencies, preferring the certainty of daily bread to the vague chances of gaining renown and fortune. Old Marlowe, so marred and imperfect in his physical powers, had submitted to her shrewd, ignorant authority, and earned his living and hers by working on his little farm and going out occasionally as a carpenter. But when she was gone, and his little girl's eyes only were watching him at his work, and the child's soul delighted in all the beautiful forms his busy hands could fashion, he gave up his out-door toil, and, with all the pent-up ardor of the lost years, he threw himself absorbingly into the pleasant occupation of the present. Though he mourned faithfully for his wife, the woman who had given to him Phebe, he felt happier and freer without her.

Phebe's girlhood also had been both free and happy. All the seasons had been sweet to her: dear to her was "the summer, clothing the general earth with greenness," and the winter, when "the redbreast sits and sings be-twixt the tufts of snow on the bare branch of the mossy apple-tree." She had listened to "the eave-drops falling in the trances of the blast," and seen them "hang in silent icicles, quietly shining to the quiet moon." There had been no change in nature unnoticed or unbeloved by her. The unbroken silence reigning around her, heightened by the mute speech between herself and her father, which needed eyes only, not lips, had grown so familiar as to be almost dear to her, in spite of her strong delight in fellowship with others. The artistic temperament she had inherited from her father, which very early took vivid pleasure in expressing itself in color as well as in form, had furnished her with an occupation of which she could never tire. As long as there was light in the sky, long after the sun had gone down, in the lingering twilight, loath to forsake the uplands, she was at her canvas catching the soft gray tones, and dim-colored tints, and clearer masses of foliage, which only the evening could show.

To supply her need of general companionship there had been so full and satisfying a sense of friendship between herself and the household at the Old Bank at Riversborough that one day spent with them gave her thought for a month. Every word uttered by Roland and Felicita was treasured up in her memory and turned over in her mind for days after. Madame's simple and cheerful nature made her almost like a mother to the simple and cheerful country girl; and Felix and Hilda had been objects of the deepest interest to her from the days of their birth. But it was Roland, who had known her best and longest, to whom she owed the direction and cultivation of her tastes and intellect, who had been almost like a god to her in her childhood; it was he who dominated over her simple heart the most. He was to Phebe so perfect that she had never imagined that there could be a fault in him.

There is one token to us that we are meant for a higher and happier life than this, in the fact that sorrow and sin always come upon us as a surprise. Happy days do not astonish us, and the goodness of our beloved ones awakens no amazement. But if a sorrow comes we cry aloud to let our neighbors know something untoward has befallen us; and if one we love has sinned, we feel as if the heavens themselves were darkened.

It was so with Phebe Marlowe. All her earthly luminaries, the greater lights and the lesser lights, were under an eclipse, and a strange darkness had fallen upon her. For the first time in her life she found herself brooding over the sin of one who had been her guide, her dearest friend, her hero. From the time when as a child she had learned to look up to him as the paragon of all perfection, until now, as a girl on the verge of womanhood, she had offered up to him a very pure and maidenly worship. There was no one else whom she could love as much; for her dumb and deaf father she loved in quite a different manner—with more of pity and compassion than of admiration. Roland too had sometimes talked with her, especially while she was a child, about God and Christ; and she had regarded him as a spiritual director. Now her guide was lost in the dense darkness. There was no sure example for her to follow.

She had told her father he would never see her smile again if Roland Sefton was taken to jail. There had been, of course, an implied promise in this, but the promise was broken. Old Marlowe looked in vain for the sweet and merry smiles that had been used to play upon her face. She was too young and too unversed in human nature to know how jealously her father would watch her, with inward curses on him who had wrought the change. When he saw her stand for an hour or more, listlessly gazing with troubled, absent eyes across the wide-spreading moor, with its broad sweep of deep-purpled bloom, and golden gorse, and rich green fern, yet taking no notice, nor hastening to fix the gorgeous hues upon her canvas while the summer lasted; and when he watched her in the long dusk of the autumn evenings sit motionless in the chimney corner opposite to him, her fingers lying idly on her lap instead of busily prattling some merry nonsense to him, and with a sad preoccupation in her girlish face; then he felt that he had received his own death-blow, and had no more to live for.

The loss of his hard-earned money had taken a deeper hold upon him than a girl so young as Phebe could imagine. For what is money to a young nature but the merest dross, compared with the love and faith it has lavished upon some fellow-mortal? While she was mourning over the shipwreck of all her best affections, old Marlowe was brooding over his six hundred pounds. They represented so much to him, so many years of toil and austere self-denial. He had risen early, and late taken rest, and eaten the bread of carefulness. His grief was not all ignoble, for it was for his girl he grieved most; his wonderful child, so much more gifted than the children of other men, whom nature had treated more kindly than himself, men who could hear and speak, but whose daughters were only commonplace creatures. The money was hers, not his; and it was too late now for him to make up the heavy loss. The blow which had deprived him of the fruits of his labor seemed to have incapacitated him for further work.

Moreover, Phebe was away oftener than usual: gone to the house of the spoiler. Nor did she come home, as she had been wont to do, with radiant eyes, and a soft, sweet smile coming and going, and many a pleasant piece of news to tell off on her nimble fingers. She returned with tear-stained eyelids and a downcast air, and was often altogether silent as to the result of the day's absence.

He strove, notwithstanding a haunting dread of failure, to resume his old occupation. Doggedly every morning he put on his brown paper cap, and went off to his crowded little workshop, but with unequal footsteps, quite unlike his former firm tread. But it would not do. He stood for hours before his half-shaped blocks of oak, with birds and leaves and heads partly traced upon them; but he found himself powerless to complete his own designs. Between him and them stood the image of Phebe, a poverty-stricken, work-worn woman, toiling with her hands, in all weathers, upon their three or four barren fields, which were now the only property left to him. It had been pleasant to him to see her milk the cows, and help him to fetch in the sheep from the moors; but until now he had been able to pay for the rougher work on the farmstead. His neighbor, Samuel Nixey, had let his laborers do it for him, since he had kept his own hands and time for his artistic pursuit. But he could afford this no longer, and the thought of the next winter's work which lay before him and Phebe harassed him terribly.

"Father," she said to him one evening, after she had been at Riversborough, "they are all going away—Mrs. Sefton, and Madame, and the children. They are going Scarborough, and after that to London, never to come back. I shall not see them again."

"Thank God!" thought the dumb old man, and his eyes gleamed brightly from under their thick gray eyebrows. But he did not utter the words, so much less easy was it for his fingers to betray his thoughts than it would have been for his lips. And Phebe did not guess them.

"Is there any news of him?" he asked.

"Not a word," she answered. "Mr. Clifford has almost given it up. He is an unforgiving man, an awful man."

"No, no; he is a just man," said old Marlowe; "he wants nothing but his own again, like me, and that a scoundrel should not get off scot free. I want my money back; it's not money merely, but my years, and my brain, and my love for thee, and my power to work: that's what he has robbed me of. Let me have my money back, and I'll forgive him."

"Poor father!" said Phebe aloud, with a little sob. How easy it seemed to her to forgive a wrong that could be definitely stated at six hundred pounds! All her inward grief was that Roland had fallen—he himself. If by a whole sacrifice of herself she could have reinstated him in the place he had forfeited, she would not have hesitated for an instant. But no sacrifice she could make would restore him.

"Does Mrs. Sefton know what he has done?" inquired her father.

She nodded only in reply.

"Does she believe him innocent?" he asked.

"No," answered Phebe.

"And Madame, his mother?" he pursued.

"No, no, no! she cannot believe him guilty," she replied; "she thinks he could free himself, if he would only come home. She is far happier than Mrs. Sefton or me. I would lay down my life to have him true and honest and good again, as he used to be. I feel as if I was in a miserable dream."

They were sitting together outside their cottage-door, with the level rays of the setting sun shining across the uplands upon them, and the fresh air of the evening breathing upon their faces. It was an hour they both loved, but neither of them felt its beauty and tranquillity now.

"You love him next to me?" asked old Marlowe.

"Next to you, father," she repeated.

But the subtle jealousy in the father's heart whispered that his daughter loved these grand friends of hers more than himself. What could he be to her, deaf mute that he was? What could he do for her? All he had done had been swept away by the wrong-doing of this fine gentleman, for whom she was willing to lay down her life. He looked at her with wistful eyes, longing to hold closer, swifter communication with her than could be held by their slow finger-speech. How could he ever make her know all the love and pride pent up in his voiceless heart? Phebe, in her girlish, blind preoccupation, saw nothing of his eager, wistful gaze, did not even notice the nervous trembling of his stammering fingers; and the old man felt thrown back upon himself, in more utter loneliness of spirit than his life had ever experienced before. Yet he was not so old a man, for he was little over sixty, but his hard life of incessant toil and his isolation from his fellow-creatures had aged him. This bitter calamity added many years to his actual age, and he began to realize that his right hand was forgetting its cunning, his eye for beauty was growing dim, and his craft failing him. The long, light summer days kept him for a while from utter hopelessness. But as the autumn winds began to moan and mutter round the house he told himself that his work was done, and that soon Phebe would be a friendless and penniless orphan.

"I ought not to have let Roland Sefton go," he thought to himself; "if I'd done my duty he would have been paying for his sin now, and maybe there would have been some redress for us that lost by him. None of his people will come to poverty like my Phebe. I could have held up my head if I had not helped him to escape from punishment."

CHAPTER XII

RECKLESS OF LIFE

If old Marlowe, or Mr. Clifford himself, could have followed Roland Sefton during his homeless wanderings, their rigorous sense of justice would have been satisfied that he was not escaping punishment, though he might elude the arbitrary penalty of the law.

As the summer advanced, and the throng of yearly tourists poured into the playground of Europe from every country, but especially from England, he was driven away from all the towns and villages where he might by chance be recognized by some fellow-countryman. Up into the mountain pastures he retreated, where he rambled from one chalet to another, sleeping on beds of fodder, with its keen night air piercing through the apertures of the roof and walls, yet bringing with it those intolerable stenches which exhale from the manure and mire lying ankle-deep round each picturesque little hut. The yelping of the watch-dogs; the snoring of the tired herdsmen lying within arm's length of him; the shrill tinkling of cow-bells, musical enough by day and in the distance, but driving sleep away too harshly; the sickness and depression produced by unwholesome food, and the utter compulsory abandonment of all his fastidious and dainty personal habits, made his mere bodily life intolerable to him. He had borne something like these discomforts and privations for a day or two at a time, when engaged in Alpine climbing, but that he should be forced to live a life compared with which that of an Irish bog-trotter was decent and civilized, was a daily torment to him.

It is true that during the long hours of daylight he wandered among the most sublime scenery. Sometimes he scaled solitary peaks and looked down upon far-stretching landscapes below him, with broad dead rivers of glaciers winding between the high and terrible masses of snow-clad rocks, and creeping down into peaceful valleys, where little living streams of silvery gray wandered among chalets looking no larger than the rocks strewn around them, with a tiny church in their midst lifting up its spire of glittering metal with a kind of childish confidence and exultation. Here and there in deep sunken hollows lay small tarns, black as night, and guilty looking, with precipices overhanging them fringed with pointed pine-trees, which sought in vain to mirror themselves in those pitch-dark waters. And above them all, gazing down in silent greatness, rose the snow-mountains, very cold, whiter than any other whiteness on earth, pure and stainless, and apparently as unapproachable in their far-off loveliness as the deep blue of the pure sky behind them.

But there was something unutterably awful to Roland Sefton in this sublimity. A bad man, whose ear has never heard the voice of Nature, and whose eye is blind to her ineffable beauty, may dwell in such places and not be crushed by them. The dull herdsmen, thinking only of their cattle and of the milking to be done twice a day, might live their own stupid, commonplace lives there. The chance visitor who spent a few hours in scaling difficult cliffs would perhaps catch a brief and fleeting sense of their awfulness, only too quickly dissipated by the unwonted toil and peril of his situation. But Roland Sefton felt himself exiled to their ice-bound solitudes, cut off from all companionship, and attended only by an accusing conscience.

Morning after morning, when his short and feverish night was ended, he went out in the early dawn while all the valleys below were still slumbering in darkness, self-driven into the wilderness of rock and snow rising above the wretched chalets. With coarse food sufficient for the wants of the day he strayed wherever his aimless footsteps led him. It was seldom that he stayed more than a night or two in the same herdsman's hut. When he was well out of the track of tourists he ventured down into the lower villages now and then, seeking a few days of comparative comfort. But some rumor, or the arrival of some chance traveller more enterprising and investigating than the mass, always drove him away again. There was no peace for him, either in the high Alps or the most secluded valleys.

How could there be peace while memory and conscience were gnawing at his heart? In a dreary round his thoughts went back to the first beginnings of the road that had led him hither; with that vague feeling which all of us have when retracing the irrevocable past, as if by some mighty effort of our will we could place ourselves at the starting-point again and run our race—oh, how differently!

Roland could almost fix the date when he had first wished that Mr. Clifford's bonds, bequeathed to him, were already his own. He recollected the very day when old Marlowe had asked him to invest his money for him in some safe manner for Phebe's benefit, and how he had persuaded himself that nothing could be safer than to use it for his own purposes, and to pay a higher interest than the old man could get elsewhere. What he had done for him had been still easier to do for other clients—ignorant men and women who knew nothing of business, and left it all to him, gratefully pleased with the good interest he paid them. The web had been woven with almost invisible threads at the first, but the finest thread among them was a heavy cable now.

But the one thought that haunted him, never leaving him for an instant in these terrible solitudes, was the thought of Felicita. His mother he could forget sometimes, or remember her with a dewy tenderness at his heart, as if he could feel her pitiful love clinging to him still; and his children he dreamed of at times in a day-dream, as playing merrily without him, in the blissful ignorance of childhood. But Felicita, who did not love him as his mother did, and could not remain in ignorance of his crime! Was she not something like these pure, distant snowy pinnacles, inapproachable and repellent, with icy-cold breath which petrified all lips that drew too near to them? And he had set a stain upon that purity as white as the driven snow. The name he had given to her was tarnished, and would be publicly dishonored if he failed in evading the penalty he merited. His death alone could save her from notorious and intolerable disgrace.

But though he was reckless of his life, he could not bring himself to be guilty of suicide. Death was wooing him in many forms, day by day, to seek refuge with him. When his feet slipped among the yawning crevasses of the glaciers, the smallest wilful negligence would have buried him in their blue depths. The common impulse to cast himself down the precipices along whose margin he crept had only to be yielded to, and all his earthly woe would be over. Even to give way to the weary drowsiness that overtook him at times as the sun went down, and the night fell upon him far away from shelter, might have soothed him into the slumber from which there is no awaking. But he dared not. He was willing enough to die, if dying had been all. But he believed in the punishment of sin here, or hereafter; in the dealing out of a righteous judgment to every man, whether he be good or evil.

As the autumn passed by, and the mountain chalets were shut up, the cattle and the herdsmen descending to the lower pastures, Roland Sefton was compelled to descend too. There was little chance of encountering any one who knew him at this late season; yet there were still stragglers lingering among the Alps. But when he saw himself again in a looking-glass, his face burned and blistered with the sun, and now almost past recognition, and his ragged hair and beard serving him better than any disguise, he was no longer afraid of being detected. He began to wonder in mingled hope and dread whether Felicita would come out to seek him. The message he had sent to her by Phebe could be interpreted by her alone. Would she avail herself of it to find him out? Or would she shrink from the toil and pain and danger of quitting England? A few weeks more would answer the question.

Sometimes he was overwhelmed with terror lest she should be watched, and her movements tracked, and that behind her would come the pursuers he had so successfully evaded. At other times an unutterable heart-sickness possessed him to see her once more, to hear her voice, to press his lips, if he dared, to her pale cheeks; to discover whether she would suffer him to hold her in his arms for one moment only. He longed to hear from her lips what had happened at home since he fled from it six months ago; what she had done, and was going to do, supposing that he were not arrested and brought to justice. Would she forgive him? would she listen to his pleas and explanations? He feared that she would hate him for the shame he had brought upon her. Yet there was a possibility that she might pity him, with a pity so much akin to love as that with which the angels look down upon sinful human beings.

Every day brought the solution of his doubts nearer. The rains of autumn had begun, and fell in torrents, driving him to any shelter he could find, to brood there hour after hour upon these hopes and fears. The fog and thick clouds hid the mountains, and all the valleys lay forlorn and cold under clinging veils of mist, through which the few brown leaves left upon the trees hung limp and dying on the bare branches. The villagers were settling down to their winter life; and though along the frequented routes a few travellers were still passing to and fro, the less known were deserted. It was safe now to go down to Engelberg, where, if ever again except as a prisoner in the hands of justice, he would see Felicita.

Impatient to anticipate the day on which he might again see her, he reached Engelberg a week before the appointed time. The green meadows and the forests of the little valley were hidden in mist and rain, and the towering dome of the Titlis was folded from sight in dense clouds, with only a cold gleam now and then as its snowy summit glanced through them for a minute. The innumerable waterfalls were swollen, and fell with a restless roar through the black depths of the forests. The daylight was short, for the sun rose late behind the encircling mountains, and hastened to sink again below them. But the place where he had first met Felicita was dear to him, though dark and gloomy with the cloudy days. He hastened to the church where his eyes had fallen upon the young, silent, absorbed girl so many years ago; and here, where the sun was shining fitfully for a brief half hour, he paced up and down the aisles, wondering what the coming interview would bring. Day after day he lingered there, with the loud chanting of the monks ringing in his ears, until the evening came when he said to himself, "To-morrow I shall see her once more."

CHAPTER XIII

SUSPENSE

Roland Sefton did not sleep that night. As the time drew near for Felicita to act upon his message to her, he grew more desponding of her response to it; yet he could not give up the feeble hope still flickering in his heart. If she did not come he would be a hopeless outcast indeed; yet if she came, what succor could she bring to him? He had not once cherished the idea that Mr. Clifford would forbear to prosecute him; yet he knew well that if he could be propitiated, the other men and women who had claims upon him would be easily satisfied and appeased. But how many things might have happened during the long six months, which had seemed almost an eternity to him. It was not impossible that Mr. Clifford might be dead. If so, and if a path was thus open to him to re-enter life, how different should his career be in the future! How warily would he walk; with what earnest penitence and thorough uprightness would he order all his ways! He would be what he had only seemed to be hitherto: a man following Christ, as his forefathers had done.

He was staying at a quiet inn in the village, and as soon as daybreak came he started down the road along which Felicita must come, and waited at the entrance of the valley, four miles from the little village. The road was bad, for the heavy rains had washed much of it away, and it had been roughly repaired by fir-trees laid along the broken edges; but it was not impassable, and a one-horse carriage could run along it safely. The rain had passed away, and the sun was shining. The high mountains and the great rocks were clear from base to summit. If she came to-day there was a splendid scene prepared for her eyes. Hour after hour passed by, the short autumnal day faded into the dusk, and the dusk slowly deepened into the blackness of night. Still he waited, late on into the night, till the monastery bells chimed for the last time; but there was no sign of her coming.

The next day passed as that had done. Felicita, then, had deserted him! He felt so sure of Phebe that he never doubted that she had not received his message. He had left only one thread of communication between himself and home—a slender thread—and Felicita had broken it. There was now no hope for him, no chance of learning what had befallen all his dear ones, unless he ran the risk of discovery, and ventured back to England.

But for Felicita and his children, he said to himself, it would be better to go back, and pay the utmost penalty he owed to the broken laws of his country. No hardships could be greater than those he had already endured; no separation from companionship could be more complete. The hard labor he would be doomed to perform would be a relief. His conscience might smite him less sharply and less ceaselessly if he was suffering the due punishment for his sin, in the society of his fellow-criminals. Dartmoor Prison would be better for him than his miserable and degrading freedom.

Still, as long as he could elude publicity and preserve his name from notoriety, the burden would not fall upon Felicita and his children. His mother would not shrink from bearing her share of any burden of his. But he must keep out of the dock, lest their father and husband should be branded as a convict.

A dreary round his thoughts ran. But ever in the centre of the circling thoughts lay the conviction that he had lost his wife and children forever. Whether he dragged out a wretched life in concealment, or was discovered, or gave himself up to justice, Felicita was lost to him. There were some women—Phebe Marlowe was one—who could have lived through the shame of his conviction and the dreary term of his imprisonment, praying to God for her husband, and pitying him with a kind of heavenly grace, and at the end of the time met him at the prison door, and gone out with him, tenderly and faithfully, to begin a new life in another country. But Felicita was not one of these women. He could never think of her as pardoning a transgression like his, though committed for her sake. Even now she would not stoop so low as to seek a meeting with one who deserved a penal punishment.

Night had set in, and he was trudging along the road, still heavy with recent rains, though the sky above was hung with glittering stars, and the crystal snow on Titlis shone against the deep blue depths, casting a wan light over the valley. Suddenly upon the stillness there came the sound of several voices, and a shrill yodel, pitched in a key that rang through the village, to call attention to the approaching party. It was in advance of him, nearer to Engelberg; yet though he had been watching the route from Stans all day, and was satisfied that Felicita could not have entered the valley unseen by himself, the hope flashed through him that she was before him, belated by the state of the roads. He hurried on, seeing before him a small group of men carrying lanterns. But in their midst they bore a rude litter, made of a gate taken hastily off the hinges. They passed out of sight behind a house as he caught sight of the litter, and for a minute or two he could not follow them, from the mere shock of dread lest the litter held her. Then he hurried on, and reached the hotel door as the procession marched into the hall and laid their burden cautiously down.

"An accident?" said the landlord.

"Yes," answered one of the peasants; "we found him under Pfaffenwand. He must have been coming from Engstlensee Alp; how much farther the good God alone knows. The paths are slippery this wet weather, and he had no guide, or there was no guide to be seen."

"That must be searched into," said the landlord; "is he dead?"

"No, no," replied two or three together.

"He has spoken twice," continued the peasant who had answered before, "and groaned much. But none of us knew what he said. He is dying, poor fellow!"

"English?" asked the landlord, looking down on the scarred face and eager eyes of the stranger, who lay silent on the litter, glancing round uneasily at the faces about him.

"Some of us would have known French, or German, or Italian," was the reply, "but not one of us knows English."

"Nor I," said the landlord; "and our English speaker went away last week, over the St. Gothard to Italy for the winter. Send round, Marie," he went on, speaking to his wife, "and find out any one in Engelberg who knows English. See! The poor fellow is trying to say something now."

"I can speak English," said Roland, pushing his way in amid the crowd and kneeling down beside the litter, on which a rough bed of fir pine-branches had been made. The unknown face beneath his eyes was drawn with pain, and the gaze that met his was one of earnest entreaty.

"I am dying," he murmured; "don't let them torture me. Only let me be laid on a bed to die in peace."

"I will take care of you," said Roland in his pleasant and soothing voice, speaking as tenderly as if he had been saying "God bless you!" to Felix in his little cot; "trust yourself to me. They shall do for you only what I think best."

The stranger closed his eyes with an expression of relief, and Roland, taking up one corner of the litter, helped to carry it gently into the nearest bedroom. He was gifted with something of a woman's softness of touch, and with a woman's delicate sympathy with pain; and presently, though not without some moans and cries, the injured man was resting peacefully on a bed: not unconscious, but looking keenly from face to face on the people surrounding him.

"Are you English?" he asked, looking at Roland's blistered face and his worn peasant's dress.

"Yes," he answered.

"Is there any surgeon here?" he inquired.

"No English surgeon," replied Roland. "I do not know if there is one even at Lucerne, and none could come to you for many hours. But there must be some one at the monastery close by, if not in the village—"

"No, no!" he interrupted, "I shall not live many hours; but promise me—I am quite helpless as you see—promise me that you will not let any village doctor pull me about."

"They are sometimes very skilful," urged Roland, "and you do not know that you must really die."

"I knew it as I was slipping," he answered; "at the first moment I knew it, though I clutched at the very stones to keep me from falling. Why! I was dead when they found me; only the pain of being pulled about brought me back to life. I'm not afraid to die if they will let me die in peace."

"I will promise not to leave you," replied Roland; "and if you must die, it shall be in peace."

That he must die, and was actually dying, was affirmed by all about him. One of the brothers from the monastery, skilled in surgery, came in unrecognized as a doctor by the stranger, and shook his head hopelessly when he saw him, telling Roland to let him do whatever he pleased so long as he lived, and to learn all he could from him during the hours of the coming night. There was no hope, he said; and if he had not been found by the peasants he would have been dead now. Roland must ask if he was a good Catholic or a heretic. When the monk heard that he was a heretic and needed none of the consolations of the Church, he bade him farewell kindly, and went his way.

Roland Sefton sat beside the dying man all the night, while he lingered from hour to hour: free from pain at times, at others restless and racked with agony. He wandered a little in delirium, and when his brain was clear he had not much to say.

"Have you no message to send to your friends?" inquired Roland, in one of these lucid intervals.

"I have no friends," he answered, "and no money. It makes death easier."

"There must be some one who would care to hear of you," said Roland.

"They'll see it in the papers," he replied. "No, I come from India, and was going to England. I have no near relations, and there is no one to care much. 'Poor Austin,' they'll say; 'he wasn't a bad fellow.' That's all. You've been kinder to me than anybody I know. There's about fifty pounds in my pocket-book. Bury me decently and take the rest."

He dozed a little, or was unconscious for a few minutes. His sunburnt face, lying on the white pillow, still looked full of health and the promise of life, except when it was contracted with pain. There was no weakness in his voice or dimness in his eye. It seemed impossible to believe that this strong young man was dying.

"I lost my valise when I fell," he said, opening his eyes again and speaking in a tranquil tone; "but there was nothing of value in it. My money and my papers are in my pocket-book. Let me see you take possession of it."

He watched Roland search for the book in the torn coat on the chair beside him, and his eyes followed its transfer to his breast-pocket under his blue blouse.

"You are an English gentleman, though you look a Swiss peasant," he said; "you are poor, perhaps, and my money will be of use to you. It is the only return I can make to you. I should like you to write down that I give it to you, and let me sign the paper."

"Presently," said Roland; "you must not exert yourself. I shall find your name and address here?"

"I have no address; of course I have a name," he answered; "but never mind that now. Tell me, what do you think of Christ? Does He indeed save sinners?"

"Yes," said Roland reluctantly; "He says, 'I came to seek and to save that which was lost.' Those are His own words."

"Kneel down quickly," murmured the dying man. "Say 'Our Father!' so that I can hear every word. My mother used to teach it to me."

"And she is dead?" said Roland.

"Years ago," he gasped.

Roland knelt down. How familiar, with what a touch of bygone days, the attitude came to him; how homely the words sounded! He had uttered them innumerable times; never quite without a feeling of their sacredness and sweetness. But he had not dared to take them into his lips of late. His voice faltered, though he strove to keep it steady and distinct, to reach the dying ears that listened to him. The prayer brought to him the picture of his children kneeling, morning and evening, with the self-same petitions. They had said them only a few hours ago, and would say them again a few hours hence. Even the dying man felt there was something more than mere emotion for him expressed in the tremulous tones of Roland Sefton's voice. He held out his hand to him when he had finished, and grasped his warmly.

"God bless you!" he said. But he was weary, and his strength was failing him. He slumbered again fitfully, and his mind wandered. Now and then during the rest of the night he looked up with a faint smile, and his lips moved inarticulately. He thought he had spoken, but no sound disturbed the unbroken silence.

CHAPTER XIV

ON THE ALTAR STEPS

It was as the bells of the Abbey rang for matins that the stranger died. For a few minutes Roland remained beside him, and then he called in the women to attend to the dead, and went out into the fresh morning air. It was the third day that the mountains had been clear from fog and cloud, and they stood out against the sky in perfect whiteness. The snow-line had come lower down upon the slopes, and the beautiful crystals of frost hung on the tapering boughs of the pine-trees in the forests about Engelberg. Here and there a few villagers were going toward the church, and almost unconsciously Roland followed slowly in their track.

The short service was over and the congregation was dispersing when he crossed the well-worn door-sill. But a few women, especially the late comers, were still scattered about praying mechanically, with their eyes wandering around them. The High Altar was deserted, but candles burning on it made a light in the dim place, and he listlessly sauntered up the centre aisle. A woman was kneeling on the steps leading up to it, and as the echo of his footsteps resounded in the quiet church she rose and looked round. It was Felicita! At that moment he was not thinking of her; yet there was no doubt or surprise in the first moment of recognition. The uncontrollable rapture of seeing her again arrested his steps, and he stood looking at her, with a few paces between them. It was plain that she did not know him.

How could she know him, he thought bitterly, in the rough blue blouse and coarse clothing and heavy hobnail boots of a Swiss peasant? His hair was shaggy and uncut, and the skin of his face was so peeled and blistered and scorched that his disguise was sufficient to conceal him even from his wife. Yet as he stood there with downcast head, as a devout peasant might have done before the altar, he saw Felicita make a slight but imperious sign to him to advance. She did not take a step toward him, but leaning against the altar rails she waited till he was near to her, within hearing. There Roland paused.

"Felicita," he said, not daring to draw closer to her.

"I am here," she answered, not looking toward him; her large, dark, mournful eyes lifted up to the cross above the altar, before which a lamp was burning, whose light was reflected in her unshed tears.

Neither of them spoke again for a while. It seemed as if there could be nothing said, so great was the anguish of them both. The man who had just died had passed away tranquilly, but they were drinking of a cup more bitter than death. Yet the few persons lingering over their morning devotions before the shrines in the side aisles saw nothing but a stranger looking at the painting over the altar, and a peasant kneeling on the lowest step deep in prayer.

"I come from watching a fellow-man die," he said at last; "would to God it had been myself!"

"Yes!" sighed Felicita, "that would have been best for us all."

"You wish me dead!" he exclaimed, in a tone of anguish.

"For the children's sake," she murmured, still looking away from him; "yes! and for the sake of our name, your father's name, and mine. I thought to bring honor to it, and you have brought flagrant dishonor to it."

"That can never be wiped away," he added.

"Never!" she repeated.

As if exhausted by these passionate words, they fell again into silence. The murmur of whispered prayers was about them, and the faint scent of incense floated under the arched roof. A gleam of morning light, growing stronger, though the sun was still far below the eastern mountains, glittered through a painted window, and threw a glow of color upon them. Roland saw her standing in its many-tinted brightness, but her wan and sorrowful face was not turned to look at him. He had not caught a glance from her yet. How vividly he remembered the first moment his eyes had ever beheld her, standing as she did now on these very altar steps, with uplifted eyes and a sweet seriousness on her young face! It was only a poor village church, but it was the most sacred spot in the whole world to him; for there he had met Felicita and received her image into his inmost heart. His ambition as well as his love had centred in her, the penniless daughter of the late Lord Riversford, an orphan, and dependent upon her father's brother and successor. But to Roland his wife Felicita was immeasurably dearer than the girl Felicita Riversford had been. All the happy days since he had won her, all the satisfied desires, all his successes were centred in her and represented by her. All his crime too.

"I have loved you," he cried, "better than the whole world."

There was no answer by word or look to his passionate words.

"I have loved you," he said, more sadly, "better than God."

"But you have brought me to shame!" she answered; "if I am tracked here—and who can tell that I am not?—and if you are taken and tried and convicted, I shall be the wife of the fraudulent banker and condemned felon, Roland Sefton. And Felix and Hilda will be his children."

"It is true," he groaned; "I could not escape conviction."

He buried his face in his hands, and rested them on the altar-rails. Now his bowed-down head was immediately beneath her eyes, and she looked down upon it with a mournful gaze; it could not have been more mournful if she had been contemplating his dead face lying at rest in his coffin. How was all this shame and misery for him and her to end?

"Felicita," he said, lifting up his head, and meeting the sorrowful farewell expression in her face, "if I could die it would be best for the children and you."

"Yes," she answered, in the sweet, too dearly loved voice he had listened to in happy days.

"I dare not open that door of escape for myself," he went on, "and God does not send death to me. But I see a way, a possible way. I only see it this moment; but whether it be for good or evil I cannot tell."

"Will it save us?" she asked eagerly.

"All of us," he replied. "This stranger, whose corpse I have just left—nobody knows him, and he has no friends to trouble about him—shall I give to him my name, and bury him as myself? Then I shall be dead to all the world, Felicita; dead even to you; but you will be saved. I too shall be safe in the grave, for death covers all sins. Even old Clifford will be satisfied by my death."

"Could it be done?" she asked breathlessly.

"Yes," he said; "if you consent it shall be done. For my own sake I would rather go back to England and deliver myself up to the law I have broken. But you shall decide, my darling. If I return you will be known as the wife of the convict Sefton. Say: shall I be henceforth dead forever to you and my mother and the children? Shall it be a living death for me, and deliverance and safety and honor for you all? You must choose between my infamy or my death."

"It must be," she answered, slowly yet without hesitation, looking away from him to the cross above the altar, "your death."

A shudder ran through her slight frame as she spoke, and thrilled through him as he listened. It seemed to them both as if they stood beside an open grave, on either side one, and parted thus. He stretched out his hand to her, and laid it on her dress, as if appealing for mercy; but she did not turn to him, or look upon him, or open her white lips to utter another word. Then there came more stir and noise in the church, footsteps sounded upon the pavement, and an inquisitive face peeped out of the vestry near the altar where they stood. It was no longer prudent to remain as they were, subject to curiosity and scrutiny. Roland rose from his knees, and without glancing again toward her, he spoke in a low voice of unutterable grief and supplication.

"Let me see you and speak to you once more," he said.

"Once more," she repeated.

"This evening," he continued, "at your hotel."

"Yes," she answered. "I am travelling under Phebe Marlowe's name. Ask for Mrs. Marlowe."

She turned away and walked slowly and feebly down the aisle; and he watched her, as he had watched the light tread of the young girl eleven years ago, passing through alternate sunshine and shadow. There was no sunshine now. Was it possible that so long a time had passed since then? Could it be true that for ten years she had been his wife, and that the tie between them was forever dissolved? From this day he was to be dead to her and to all the world. He was about to pass voluntarily into a condition of death amid life, as utterly bereft of all that had once been his as if the grave had closed over him. Roland Sefton was to exist no more.

CHAPTER XV

A SECOND FRAUD

Roland Sefton went back to the room in which the corpse of the stranger was now lying. The women were gone, and he turned down the sheet to look at the face of the man who was about to bear his name and the disgrace of his crime into the safe asylum of the grave. It was perfectly calm, with no trace of the night's suffering upon it; there was even a faint vestige of a smile about the mouth, as of one who sleeps well, and has pleasant dreams. He was apparently about Roland's own age, and a description given by strangers would not be such as would lead to any suspicion that there could have been a mistake as to identity. Roland looked long upon it before covering it up again, and then he sat down beside the bed and opened the pocket-book.

There were notes in it worth fifty pounds, but not many papers. There was a memorandum made here and there of the places he had visited, and the last entry was dated the day before at Engstlenalp. Roland knew every step of the road, and for a while he seemed to himself to be this traveller, starting from the little inn, not yet vacated by its peasant landlord, but soon to be left to icy solitude, and taking the narrow path along the Engstlensee, toiling up the Joch pass under the mighty Wendenstöcke and the snowy Titlis, clear of clouds from base to summit yesterday. The traveller must have had a guide with him, some peasant or herdsman probably, as far as the Trübsee Alp; for even in summer the route was difficult to find. The guide had put him on to the path for Engelberg, and left him to make his way along the precipitous slopes of the Pfaffenwand. All this would be discovered when an official inquiry was made into the accident. In the mean time it was necessary to invest this stranger with his own identity.

There were two or three well-worn letters in the pocket-book, but they contained nothing of importance. It seemed true, what the dying man had said, that there was no link of kinship or friendship binding him specially to his fellow-men. Roland opened his own pocket-book, and looked over a letter or two which he had carried about with him, one of them a childish note from Felix, preferring some simple request. His passport was there also, and his mother's portrait and those of the children, over which his eyes brooded with a hungry sorrow in his heart. He looked at them for the last time. But Felicita's portrait he could not bring himself to give up. She would be dead to him, and he to her. In England she would live among her friends as his widow, pitied, and comforted, and beloved. But what would the coming years bring to him? All that would remain to him of the past would be a fading photograph only.

So long he lingered over this mournful conflict that he was at last aroused from it by the entrance of the landlord, and the mayor and other officials, who had come to look at the body of the dead. Roland's pocket-book lay open on the bed, and he was still gazing at the portraits of his children. He raised his sunburnt face as they came in, and rose to meet them.

"This traveller," he said, "gave to me his pocket-book as I watched beside him last night. It is here, containing his passport, a few letters, and fifty pounds in notes, which he told me to keep, but which I wish to give to the commune."

"They must be taken charge of," said the mayor; "but we will look over them first. Did he tell you who he was?"

"The passport discloses that," answered Roland; "he desired only a decent funeral."

"Ah!" said the mayor, taking out the passport, "an English traveller; name Roland Sefton; and these letters, and these portraits—they will be enough for identification."

"He said he had no friends or family in England," pursued Roland, "and there is no address among his letters. He told me he came from India."

"Then there need be no delay about the interment," remarked the mayor, "if he had no family in England, and was just come from India. Bah! we could not keep him till any friends came from India. It is enough. We must make an inquiry; but the corpse cannot be kept above ground. The interment may take place as soon as you please, Monsieur."

"I suppose you will wish for some trifle as payment?" said the landlord, addressing Roland.

"No," he answered, "I only watched by him through the night; and I am but a passing traveller like himself."

"You will assist at the funeral?" he asked.

"If it can be to-morrow," replied Roland; "if not I must go on to Lucerne. But I shall come back to Engelberg. If it be necessary for me to stay, and the commune will pay my expenses, I will stay."

"Not necessary at all," said the mayor; "the accident is too simple, and he has no friends. Why should the commune lose by him?"

"There are the fifty pounds," suggested Roland.

"And there are the expenses!" said the mayor. "No, no. It is not necessary for you to stay; not at all. If you are coming back again to Engelberg it will be all right. You say you are coming back?"

"I am sure to come back to Engelberg," he answered, with gloomy emphasis.

For already Roland began to feel that he, himself, was dead, and a new life, utterly different from the old, was beginning for him. And this new life, beginning here, would often draw him back to its birth-place. There would be an attraction for him here, even in the humble grave where men thought they had buried Roland Sefton. It would be the only link with his former life, and it would draw him to it irresistibly.

"And what is your name and employment, my good fellow?" asked the mayor.

"Jean Merle," he answered promptly. "I am a wood-carver."

The deed he had only thought of an hour ago was accomplished, and there could be no undoing it. This passport and these papers would be forwarded to the embassy at Berne, where doubtless his name was already known as a fugitive criminal. He could not reclaim them, for with them he took up again the burden of his sin. He had condemned himself to a penalty and sacrifice the most complete that man could think of, or put into execution. Roland Sefton was dead, and his wife and children were set free from the degradation he had brought upon them.

He spent the remaining hours of the day in wandering about the forests in the Alpine valley. The autumn fogs and the dense rain-clouds were gathering again. But it was nothing to him that the snowy crests of the surrounding mountains were once more shrouded from view, or that the torrents and waterfalls which he could not see were thundering and roaring along their rocky channels with a vast effluence of waters. He saw and heard no more than the dead man who bore his name. He was insensible to hunger or fatigue. Except for Felicita's presence in the village behind him he would have felt himself in another world; in a beamless and lifeless abyss, where there was no creature like unto himself; only eternal gloom and solitude.

It was quite dark before he passed again through the village on his way to Felicita's hotel. The common light of lamps, and the every-day life of ordinary men and women busy over their evening meal, astonished him, as if he had come from another state of existence. He lingered awhile, looking on as at some extraordinary spectacle. Then he went on to the hotel standing a little out of and above the village.

The place, so crowded in the summer, was quiet enough now. A bright light, however, streamed through the window of the salon, which was uncurtained. He stopped and looked in at Felicita, who was sitting alone by the log fire, with her white forehead resting on her small hand, which partly hid her face. How often had he seen her sitting thus by the fireside at home! But though he stood without in the dark and cold for many minutes, she did not stir; neither hand nor foot moved. At last he grew terrified at this utter immobility, and stepping through the hall he told the landlady that the English lady had business with him. He opened the door, and then Felicita looked up.

CHAPTER XVI

PARTING WORDS

Roland advanced a few paces into the gaudy salon, with its mirrors reflecting his and Felicita's figures over and over again, and stood still, at a little distance from her, with his rough cap in his hand. He looked like one of the herdsmen with whom he had been living during the summer. There was no one else in the large room, but the night was peering in through half a dozen great uncurtained windows, which might hold many spectators watching them, as he had watched her a minute ago. She scarcely moved, but the deadly pallor of her face and the dark shining of her tearless eyes fixed upon him made him tremble as if he had been a woman weaker than herself.

"It is done," he said.

"Yes," she answered, "I have been to see him."

There was an accent in her voice, of terror and repugnance, as of one who had witnessed some horrifying sight and was compelled to bear a reluctant testimony to it. Roland himself felt a shock of antipathy at the thought of his wife seeing this unknown corpse bearing his name. He seemed to see her standing beside the dead, and looking down with those beloved eyes upon the strange face, which would dwell for evermore in her memory as well as his. Why had she subjected herself to this needless pang?

"You wished it?" he said. "You consented to my plan?"

"Yes," she answered in the same monotonous tone of reluctant testimony.

"And it was best so, Felicita," he said tenderly; "we have done the dead man no wrong. Remember he was alone, and had no friends to grieve over his strange absence. If it had been otherwise there would have been a terrible sin in our act. But it has set you free; it saves you and my mother and the children. As long as I lived you would have been in peril; but now there is a clear, safe course laid open for you. You will go home to England, where in a few months it will be forgotten that your husband was suspected of crime. Only old Clifford, and Marlowe, and two or three others will remember it. When you have the means, repay those poor people the money I owe them. And take comfort, Felicita. It would have done them no good if I had been taken and convicted; that would not have restored their money. My name then will be clear of all but suspicion, and you will make it a name for our children to inherit."

"And you?" she breathed with lips that scarcely moved.

"I?" he said. "Why, I shall be dead! A man's life is not simply the breath he draws: it is his country, his honor, his home. You are my life, Felicita: you and my mother and Felix and Hilda; the old home where my forefathers dwelt; my townsmen's esteem and good-will; the work I could do, and hoped to do. Losing those I lost my life. I began to die when I first went wrong. The way seemed right in my own eyes, but the end of it was death. I told old Marlowe his money was as safe as in the Bank of England, when I was keeping it in my own hands; but I believed it then. That was the first step; this is the last. Henceforth I am dead."

"But how will you live?" she asked.

"Never fear; Jean Merle will earn his living," he answered. "Let us think of your future, my darling. Nay, let me call you darling once more. My death provides for you, for your marriage-settlement will come into force. You will have to live differently, my Felicita; all the splendor and the luxury I would have surrounded you with must be lost. But there will be enough, and my mother will manage your household well for you. Be kind to my poor mother, and comfort her. And do not let my children grow up with hard thoughts of their father. It will be a painful task to you."

"Yes," she said. "Oh, Roland, we ought not to have done this thing!"

"Yet you chose," he replied.

"Yes; and I should choose it again, though I hate the falsehood," she exclaimed vehemently. "I cannot endure shame. But all our future life will be founded on a lie."

"Let the blame be mine, not yours," he said; "it was my plan, and there is no going back from it now. But tell me about home. How are my children and my mother? They are still at home?"

"No," she answered; "the police watched it day and night, till it grew hateful to me. I shall never enter it again. We went away to the sea-side three months ago, and there our mother and the children are still. But when I get back we shall remove to London."

"To London!" he repeated. "Will you never go home to Riversborough?"

"Never again!" she replied. "I could not live there now; it is a hateful spot to me. Your mother grieves bitterly over leaving it; but even she sees that we can never live there again."

"I shall not even know how to think of you all!" he cried. "You will be living in some strange house, which I can never picture to myself. And the old home will be empty."

"Mr. Clifford is living in it," she said.

He threw up his hands with a gesture of grief and vexation. Whenever his thoughts flew to the old home, the only home he had ever known, it would be only to remember that the man he most dreaded, he who was his most implacable enemy, was dwelling in it. And when would he cease to think of his own birth-place and the birth-place of his children, the home where Felicita had lived? It would be impossible to blot the vivid memory of it from his brain.

"I shall never see it again," he said; "but I should have felt less banished from you if I could have thought of you as still at home. We are about to part forever, Felicita—as fully as if I lay dead down yonder, as men will think I do."

"Yes," she answered, with a mournful stillness.

"Even if we wished to hold any intercourse with each other," he continued, gazing wistfully at her, "it would be dangerous to us both. It is best for us both to be dead to one another."

"It is best," she assented; "only if you were ever in great straits, if you could not earn your living, you might contrive to let me know."

"There is no fear of that," he answered bitterly. "Felicita, you never loved me as I love you."

"No," she said, with the same inexpressible sadness, yet calmness, in her voice and face; "how could I? I was a child when you married me; we were both children. There is such a difference between us. I suppose I should never love any one very much—not as you mean. It is not in my nature. I can live alone, Roland. All of you, even the children, seem very far away from me. But I grieve for you in my inmost soul. If I could undo what you have done I would gladly lay down my life. If I could only undo what we did this morning! The shadow of it is growing darker and darker upon me. And yet it seemed so wise; it seems so still. We shall be safe again, all of us, and we have done that dead man no wrong."

"None," he said.

"But when I think of you," she went on, "how you, still living, will long to know what is befalling us, how the children are growing up, and how your mother is, and how I live, yet never be able to satisfy this longing; how you will have to give us up, and never dare to make a sign; how you will drag on your life from year to year, a poor man among poor, ignorant, stupid men; how I may die, and you not know it, or you may die, and I not know it; I wonder how we could have done what we did this morning."

"Oh, hush, hush, Felicita!" he exclaimed; "I have said all this to myself all this day, until I feel that my punishment is harder than I can bear. Tell me, shall we undo it? Shall I go to the mayor and deliver myself up as the man whose name I have given to the dead? It can be done still; it is not too late. You shall decide again."

"No; I cannot accept disgrace," she answered passionately; "it is an evil thing to do, but it must be done. We must take the consequences. You and I are dead to one another for evermore; but your death is more terrible than mine. I shall grieve over you more than if you were really dead. Why does not God send death to those that desire it? Good-by now forever, Roland. I return to England to act this lie, and you must never, never seek me out as your wife. Promise me that. I would repudiate you if I lay on my death-bed."

"I will never seek you out and bring you to shame," he said; "I promise it faithfully, by my love for you. As I hope ever to obtain pardon, I promise it."

"Then leave me," she cried; "I can bear this no longer. Good-by, Roland."

They were still some paces apart, he with his shaggy mountain cap in his hand standing respectfully at a distance, and she, sitting by the low, open hearth with her white, quiet face turned toward him. All the village might have witnessed their interview through the uncurtained windows. Slowly, almost mechanically, Felicita left her seat and advanced toward him with an outstretched hand. It was cold as ice as he seized it eagerly in his own; the hand of the dead man could not have been colder or more lifeless. He held it fast in a hard, unconscious grip.

"Good-by, my wife," he said; "God bless and keep you!"

"Is there any God?" she sobbed.

But there was a sound at the door, the handle was being turned, and they fell apart guiltily. A maid entered to tell Madame her chamber was prepared, and without another word Felicita walked quickly from the salon, leaving him alone.

He caught a glimpse of her again the next morning as she came down-stairs and entered the little carriage which was to take her down to Stansstad in time to catch the boat to Lucerne. She was starting early, before it was fairly dawn, and he saw her only by the dim light of lamps, which burned but feebly in the chilly damp of the autumn atmosphere. For a little distance he followed the sound of the carriage wheels, but he arrested his own footsteps. For what good was it to pursue one whom he must never find again? She was gone from him forever. He was a young man yet, and she still younger. But for his folly and crime a long and prosperous life might have stretched before them, each year knitting their hearts and souls more closely together; and he had forfeited all. He turned back up the valley broken-hearted.

Later in the day he stood beside the grave of the man who was bearing away his name from disgrace. The funeral had been hurried on, and the stranger was buried in a neglected part of the churchyard, being friendless and a heretic. It was quickly done, and when the few persons who had taken part in it were dispersed, Roland Sefton lingered alone beside the desolate grave.

CHAPTER XVII

WAITING FOR THE NEWS

Felicita hurried homeward night and day without stopping, as if she had been pursued by a deadly enemy. Madame and the children were not at Scarborough, but at a quiet little fishing village on the eastern coast; for Felicita had found Scarborough too gay in the month of August, and her cousins, the Riversfords, having appeared there, she retreated to the quietest spot that could be found. To this village she returned, after being absent little more than a week.

Madame knew nothing of her journey; but the mere fact that Felicita was going away alone had aroused in her the hope that it was connected in some way with Roland. In some vague manner this idea had been communicated to Felix, and both were expecting to see the long-lost father and son come back with her. Roland's prolonged and mysterious absence had been a sore trial to his mother, though her placid and trustful nature had borne it patiently. Surely, she thought, the trial was coming to an end.

Felicita reached their lodgings utterly exhausted and worn out. She was a delicate woman, in no way inured to fatigue, and though she had been insensible to the overstrain of the unbroken journey as she was whirled along railways and passed from station to station, a sense of complete prostration seized upon her as soon as she found herself at home. Day after day she lay in bed, in a darkened room, unwilling to lift her voice above a whisper, waiting in a kind of torpid dread for the intelligence that she knew must soon come.

She had been at home several days, and still there was no news. Was it possible, she asked herself, that this unknown traveller, and his calamitous fate, should pass on into perfect oblivion and leave matters as they were before? For a cloud would hang over her and her children as long as Roland was the object of pursuit. While he was a fugitive criminal, of interest to the police officers of all countries, there was no security for their future. The lie to which she had given a guilty consent was horrible to her, but her morbid dread of shame was more horrible. She had done evil that good might come; but if the good failed, the evil would still remain as a dark stain upon her soul, visible to herself, if to none else.

"I will get up to-day," she said at last, to Madame's great delight. She never ventured to exert any authority over her beautiful and clever daughter-in-law—not even the authority of a mildly expressed wish. She was willing to be to Felicita anything that Felicita pleased—her servant and drudge, her fond mother, or her quiet, attentive companion. Since her return from her mysterious journey she had been very tender to her, as tenderly and gently demonstrative as Felicita would ever permit her to be.

"Have you seen any newspapers lately?" asked Felicita.

"I never read the papers, my love," answered Madame.

"I should like to see to-day's Times," said Felicita.

But it was impossible to get it in this village without ordering it beforehand, and Felicita gave up her wish with the listless indifference of an invalid. When the late sun of the November day had risen from behind a heavy bank of clouds she ventured down to the quiet shore. There were no visitors left beside themselves, so there were no curious eyes to scan her white, sad face. For a short time Felix and Hilda played about her; but by and by Madame, thinking she was weary and worried, allured them away to a point where they were still in sight, though out of hearing. The low, cold sun shed its languid and watery rays upon the rocks and creeping tide, and, unnoticed, almost unseen, Felicita could sit there in stillness, gazing out over the chilly and mournful sea. There was something so unutterably sad about Felicita's condition that it awed the simple, cheerful nature of Madame. It was more than illness and exhaustion. The white, unsmiling face, the drooping head, the languor of the thin, long hands, the fathomless sorrow lurking behind her dark eyes—all spoke of a heart-sickness such as Madame had never seen or dreamed of. The children did not cheer their mother. When she saw that, Madame felt that there was nothing to be done but to leave her in the cold solitude she loved.

But as Felicita sat alone on the shore, looking listlessly at the fleeting sails which were passing to and fro upon the sea, she saw afar off the figure of a girl coming swiftly toward her from the village, and before many moments had passed she recognized Phebe Marlowe's face. A great throb of mingled relief and dread made her heart beat violently. Nothing could have brought Phebe away, so far from home, except the news of Roland's death.

The rosy color on Phebe's face was gone, and the brightness of her blue eyes was faded; but there was the same out-looking of a strong, simple, unselfish soul shining through them. As she drew near to Felicita she stretched out her arms with the instinctive gesture of one who was come to comfort and support, and Felicita, with a strange, impulsive feeling that she brought consolation and help, threw herself into them.

"I know it all," said Phebe in a low voice. "Oh, what you must have suffered! He was going to Engelberg to meet you, and you never saw him alive! Oh, why did not God let you meet each other once again? But God loved him. I can never think that God had not forgiven him, for he was grieved because of his sin when I saw him the night he got away. And in all things else he was so good! Oh, how good he was!"

Phebe's tears were falling fast, and her words were choked with sobs. But Felicita's face was hidden against her neck, and she could not see if she was weeping.

"Everybody is talking of him in Riversborough," she went on, "and now they all say how good he always was, and how unlikely it is that he was guilty. They will forget it soon. Those who remember him will think kindly of him, and be grieved for him. But oh, I would give worlds for him to have lived and made amends! If he could only have proved that he had repented! If he could only have outlived it all, and made everybody know that he was really a good man, one whom God had delivered out of sin!"

"It was impossible!" murmured Felicita.

"No, not impossible!" she cried earnestly; "it was not an unpardonable sin. Even if he had gone to prison, as he would, he might have faced the world when he came out again; and if he'd done all the good he could in it, it might have been hard to convince them he was good, but it would never be impossible. If God forgives us, sooner or later our fellow-creatures will forgive us, if we live a true life. I would have stood by him in the face of the world, and you would, and Madame and the children. He would not have been left alone, and it would have ended in every one else coming round to us. Oh, why should he die when you were just going to see each other again!"

Felicita had sunk down again into the chair which had been carried for her to the shore, and Phebe sat down on the sands at her feet. She looked up tearfully into Felicita's wan and shrunken face.

"Did any one ever win back their good name?" asked Felicita with quivering lips.

"Among us they do sometimes," she answered. "I knew a working-man who had been in jail five years, and he became a Christian while he was there, and he came back home to his own village. He was one of the best men I ever knew, and when he died there was such a funeral as had never been seen in the parish church. Why should it not be so? If God is faithful and just to forgive us our sins, why shouldn't we forgive? If we are faithful and just, we shall."

"It could never be," said Felicita; "it cannot be the same as if Roland had not been guilty. No one can blot out the past; it is eternal."

"Yes," she replied, covering Felicita's hand with kisses and tears; "but oh, we love him more now than ever. He is gone into the land of thick darkness, and I cannot follow him in my thoughts. It is like a gulf between us and him. Even if he had been farthest away from us in the world—anywhere—we could imagine what he was doing; but we cannot see him or call across the gulf to him. It is all unknown. Only God knows!"

"God!" echoed Felicita; "if there is a God, let Him help me, for I am the most wretched woman on His earth to-day."

"God cannot keep from helping us all," answered Phebe. "He cannot rest while we are wretched. I understand it better than I used to do. I cannot rest myself while the poorest creature about me is in pain that I can help. It is impossible that He should not care. That would be an awful thing to think; that would make His love and pity less than ours. This I know, that God loves every creature He has made. And oh, He must have loved him, though he was suffered to fall over that dreadful precipice, and die before you saw him. It happened before you reached Engelberg?"

"Yes," said Felicita, shivering.

"The papers were sent on to Mr. Clifford," continued Phebe, "and he sent for me to come with him, and see you before the news got into the papers. It will be in to-morrow. But I knew more than he did, and I came on here to speak to you. Shall you tell him you went there to meet him?"

"Oh, no, no!" cried Felicita; "it must never be known, dear Phebe."

"And his mother and the children—they, know nothing?" she said.

"Not a word, and it is you who must tell them, Phebe," she answered. "How could I bear to tell them that he is dead? Never let them speak about it to me; never let his name be mentioned."

"How can I comfort you?" cried Phebe.

"I can never be comforted," she replied despairingly; "but it is like death to hear his name."

The voices of the children coming nearer reached their ears. They had seen from their distant playground another figure sitting close beside Felicita, and their curiosity had led them to approach. Now they recognized Phebe, and a glad shout rang through the air. She bent down hurriedly to kiss Felicita's cold hand once again, and then she rose to meet them, and prevent them from seeing their mother's deep grief.

"I will go and tell them, poor little things!" she said, "and Madame. Oh, what can I do to help you all? Mr. Clifford is at your lodgings, waiting to see you as soon as you can meet him."

She did not stay for an answer, but ran to meet Felix and Hilda; while slowly, and with much guilty shrinking from the coming interview, Felicita went back to the village, where Mr. Clifford was awaiting her.

CHAPTER XVIII

THE DEAD ARE FORGIVEN

Roland Sefton's pocket-book, containing his passport and the papers and photographs, had reached Mr. Clifford the day before, with an official intimation of his death from the consulate at Berne. The identification was complete, and the inquiry into the fatal accident had resulted in blame to no one, as the traveller had declined the services of a trustworthy guide from Meirengen to Engelberg. This was precisely what Roland would have done, the whole country being as familiar to him as to any native. No doubt crossed Mr. Clifford's mind that his old friend's son had met his untimely end while a fugitive from his country, from dread chiefly of his own implacable sense of justice.

Roland was dead, but justice was not satisfied. Mr. Clifford knew perfectly well that the news of his tragic fate would create an immediate and complete reaction in his favor among his fellow-townsmen. Hitherto he had been only vaguely accused of crime, which his absence chiefly had tended to fasten upon him; but as there had been no opportunity of bringing him to public trial, it would soon be believed that there was no evidence against him. Many persons thought already that the junior partner was away either on pleasure or business, because the senior had taken his place. Only a few, himself and the three or four obscure people who actually suffered from his defalcations, would recollect them. By and by Roland Sefton would be remembered as the kind, benevolent, even Christian man, whose life, so soon cut short, had been full of promise for his native town.

Mr. Clifford himself felt a pang of regret and sorrow when he heard the news. Years ago he had loved the frank, warm-hearted boy, his friend's only child, with a very true affection. He had an only boy, too, older than Roland by a few years, and these two were to succeed their fathers in the long-established firm. Then came the bitter disappointment in his own son. But since he had suffered his son to die in his sins, reaping the full harvest of his transgressions, he had felt that any forgiveness shown to other offenders would be a cruel injustice to him. Yet as Roland's passport and the children's photographs lay before him on his office desk—the same desk at which Roland was sitting but a few months ago, a man in the full vigor of life, with an apparently prosperous and happy future lying before him—Mr. Clifford for a moment or two yielded to the vain wish that Roland had thrown himself on his mercy. Yet his conscience told him that he would have refused to show him mercy, and his regret was mingled with a tinge of remorse.

His first care was to prevent the intelligence reaching Felicita by means of the newspapers, and he sent immediately for Phebe Marlowe to accompany him to the sea-side, in order to break the news to her. Phebe's excessive grief astonished him, though she had so much natural control over herself, in her sympathy for others, as to relieve him of all anxiety on her account, and to keep Felicita's secret journey from being suspected. But to Phebe, Roland's death was fraught with more tragic circumstances than any one else could conceive. He was hastening to meet his wife, possibly with some scheme for their future, which might have hope and deliverance in it, when this calamity hurried him away into the awful, unknown world, on whose threshold we are ever standing. But for her ardent sympathy for Felicita, Phebe would have been herself overwhelmed. It was the thought of her, with this terrible and secret addition to her sorrow, which bore her through the long journey and helped her to meet Felicita with something like calmness.

From the bay-window of the lodging-house Mr. Clifford watched Felicita coming slowly and feebly toward the house. So fragile she looked, so unutterably sorrow-stricken, that a rush of compassion and pity opened the floodgates of his heart, and suffused his stern eyes with tears. Doubtless Phebe had told her all. Yet she was coming alone to meet him, her husband's enemy and persecutor, as if he was a friend. He would be a friend such as she had never known before. There would be no vain weeping, no womanish wailing in her; her grief was too deep for that. And he would respect it; he would spare her all the pain he could. At this moment, if Roland could have risen from the dead, he would have clasped him in his arms, and wept upon his neck, as the father welcomed his prodigal son.

Felicita did not speak when she entered the room, but looked at him with a steadfastness in her dark sad eyes which again dimmed his with tears. Almost fondly he pressed her hands in his, and led her to a chair, and placed another near enough for him to speak to her in a low and quiet voice, altogether unlike the awful tones he used in the bank, which made the clerks quail before him. His hand trembled as he took the little photographs out of their envelope, so worn and stained, and laid them before her. She looked at them with tearless eyes, and let them fall upon her lap as things of little interest.

"Phebe has told you?" he said pitifully.

"Yes," she whispered.

"You did not know before?" he said.

She shook her head mutely. A long, intricate path of falsehood stretched before her, from which she could not turn aside, a maze in which she was already entangled and lost; but her lips were reluctant to utter the first words of untruth.

"These were found on him," he continued, pointing to the children's portraits. "I am afraid we cannot doubt the facts. The description is like him, and his papers and passport place the identity beyond a question. But I have dispatched a trusty messenger to Switzerland to make further inquiries, and ascertain every particular."

"Will he see him?" asked Felicita with a start of terror.

"No, my poor girl," said the old banker; "it happened ten days ago, and he was buried, so they say, almost immediately. But I wish to have a memorial stone put over his grave, that if any of us, I or you, or the children, should wish to visit it at some future time, it should not be past finding."

He spoke tenderly and sorrowfully, as if he imagined himself standing beside the grave of his old friend's son, recalling the past and grieving over it. His own boy was buried in some unknown common fosse in Paris. Felicita looked up at him with her strange, steady, searching gaze.

"You have forgiven him?" she said.

"Yes," he answered; "men always forgive the dead."

"Oh, Roland! Roland!" she cried, wringing her hands for an instant. Then, resuming her composure, she gazed quietly into his pitiful face again.

"It is kind of you to think of his grave," she said; "but I shall never go there, nor shall the children go, if I can help it."

"Hush!" he answered imperatively. "You, then, have not forgiven him? Yet I forgive him, who have lost most."

"You!" she exclaimed, with a sudden outburst of passion. "You have lost a few thousand pounds; but what have I lost? My faith and trust in goodness; my husband's love and care. I have lost him, the father of my children, my home—nay, even myself. I am no longer what I thought I was. That is what Roland robs me of; and you say it is more for you to forgive than for me!"

He had never seen her thus moved and vehement, and he shrank a little from it, as most men shrink from any unusual exhibition of emotion. Though she had not wept, he was afraid now of a scene, and hastened to speak of another subject.

"Well, well," he said soothingly, "that is all true, no doubt. Poor Roland! But I am your husband's executor and the children's guardian, conjointly with yourself. It will be proved immediately, and I shall take charge of your affairs."

"I thought," she answered, in a hesitating manner, "that there was nothing left, that we were ruined and had nothing. Why did Roland take your bonds if he had money? Why did he defraud other people? There cannot be any money coming to me and the children, and why should the will be proved?"

"My dear girl," he said, "you know nothing about affairs. Your uncle, Lord Riversford, would never have allowed Roland to marry you without a settlement, and a good one too. His death was the best thing for you. It saves you from poverty and dependence, as well as from disgrace. I hardly know yet how matters stand, but you will have little less than a thousand a year. You need not trouble yourself about these matters; leave them to me and Lord Riversford. He called upon me yesterday, as soon as he heard the sad news, and we arranged everything."

Felicita did not hear his words distinctly, though her brain caught their meaning vaguely. She was picturing herself free from poverty, surrounded with most of her accustomed luxuries, and shielded from every hardship, while Roland was homeless and penniless, cast upon his own resources to earn his daily bread and a shelter for every night, with nothing but a poor handicraft to support him. She had not expected this contrast in their lot. Poverty had seemed to lie before her also. But now how often would his image start up before her as she had seen him last, gaunt and haggard, with rough hair and blistered skin serving him as a mask, clad in coarse clothing, already worn and ragged, not at rest in the grave, as every one but herself believed him, but dragging out a miserable and sordid existence year by year, with no hopes for the future, and no happy memories of the past!

"Mr. Clifford," she said, when the sound of his voice humming in her ears had ceased, "I shall not take one farthing of any money settled upon me by my husband. I have no right to it. Let it go to pay the sums he appropriated. I will maintain myself and my children."

"You cannot do it," he replied; "you do not know what you are talking about. The money is settled upon your children; all that belongs to you is the yearly income from it."

"That, at least, I will never touch," she said earnestly; "it shall be set aside to repay those just claims. When all those are paid I will take it, but not before. Yours is the largest, and I will take means to find out the others. With my mother's two hundred a year and what I earn myself, we shall keep the children. Lord Riversford has no control over me. I am a woman, and I will act for myself."

"You cannot do it," he repeated; "you have no notion of what you are undertaking to do. Mrs. Sefton, my dear young lady, I am come, with Lord Riversford's sanction, to ask you to return to your home again, to Madame's old home—your children's birth-place. I think, and Lord Riversford thinks, you should come back, and bring up Felix to take his grandfather's and father's place."

"His father's place!" interrupted Felicita. "No, my son shall never enter into business. I would rather see him a common soldier or sailor, or day-laborer, earning his bread by any honest toil. He shall have no traffic in money, such as his father had; he shall have no such temptations. Whatever my son is, he shall never be a banker."

"Good heavens, madam!" exclaimed Mr. Clifford. Felicita's stony quietude was gone, and in its place was such a passionate energy as he had never witnessed before in any woman.

"It was money that tempted Roland to defraud you and dishonor himself," she said; "it drove poor Acton to commit suicide, and it hardened your heart against your friend's son. Felix shall be free from it. He shall earn his bread and his place in the world in some other way, and till he can do that I will earn it for him. Every shilling I spend from henceforth shall be clean, the fruit of my own hands, not Roland's—not his, whether he be alive or dead."

Before Mr. Clifford could answer, the door was flung open, and Felix, breathless with rapid running, rushed into the room and flung himself into his mother's arms. No words could come at first; but he drew long and terrible sobs. The boy's upturned face was pale, and his eyes, tearless as her own had been, were fastened in an agony upon hers. She could not soothe or comfort him, for she knew his grief was wasted on a falsehood; but she looked down on her son's face with a feeling of terror.

"Oh, my father! my beloved father!" he sobbed at last. "Is he dead, mother? You never told me anything that wasn't true. He can't be dead, though Phebe says so. Is it true, mother?"

Felicita bent her head till it rested on the boy's uplifted face. His sobs shook her, and the close clasp of his arms was painful; but she neither spoke nor moved. She heard Phebe coming in, and knew that Roland's mother was there, and Hilda came to clasp her little arms about her as Felix was doing. But her heart had gone back to the moment when Roland had knelt beside her in the quiet little church, and she had said to him deliberately, "I choose your death." He was dead to her.

"Is it true, mother?" wailed Felix. "Oh, tell me it isn't true!"

"It is true," she answered. But the long, tense strain had been too much for her strength, and she sank fainting on the ground.

CHAPTER XIX

AUTHOR AND PUBLISHER

It was all in vain that Mr. Clifford tried to turn Felicita from her resolution. Phebe cordially upheld her, and gave her courage to persist against all arguments. Both of them cared little for poverty—Phebe because she knew it, Felicita because she did not know it. Felicita had never known a time when money had to be considered; it had come to her pretty much in the same way as the air she breathed and the food she ate, without any care or prevision of her own. Phebe, on the other hand, knew that she could earn her own living at any time by the work of her strong young arms, and her wants were so few that they could easily be supplied.

It was decided before Phebe went home again, and decided in the face of Mr. Clifford's opposition, that a small house should be taken in London, and partly furnished from the old house at Riversborough, where Felicita would be in closer and easier communication with the publishers. Mr. Clifford laughed to himself at the idea that she could gain a maintenance by literature, as all the literary people he had ever met or heard of bewailed their poverty. But there was Madame's little income of two hundred a year: that formed a basis, not altogether an insecure or despicable one. It would pay more than the rent, with the rates and taxes.

The yearly income from Felicita's marriage settlement, which no representations could persuade her to touch, was to go to the gradual repayment of Roland's debts, the poorest men being paid first, and Mr. Clifford, who reluctantly consented to the scheme, to receive his the last. Though Madame had never believed in her son's guilt, her just and simple soul was satisfied and set at rest by this arrangement. She had not been able to blame him, but it had been a heavy burden to her to think of others suffering loss through him. It was then almost with cheerfulness that she set herself to keep house for her daughter-in-law and her grand-children under such widely different circumstances.

Before Christmas a house was found for them in Cheyne Walk. The Chelsea Embankment was not then thought of, and the streets leading to it, like those now lying behind it, were mean and crowded. It was a narrow house, with rooms so small that when the massive furniture from their old house was set up in it there was no space for moving about freely. Madame had known only two houses—the old straggling, picturesque country manse in the Jura, with its walnut-trees shading the windows, and tossing up their branches now and then to give glimpses of snow-mountains on the horizon, and her husband's pleasant and luxurious house at Riversborough, with every comfort that could be devised gathered into it. There was the river certainly flowing past this new habitation, and bearing on its full and rapid tide a constantly shifting panorama of boats, of which the children never tired, and from Felicita's window there was a fair reach of the river in view, while from the dormer windows of the attic above, where Felix slept, there was a still wider prospect. But in the close back room, which Madame allotted to herself and Hilda, there was only a view of back streets and slums, with sights and sounds which filled her with dismay and disgust.

But Madame made the best of the woeful change. The deep, quiet love she had given to her son she transferred to Felicita, who, she well knew, had been his idol. She believed that the sorrows of these last few months had not sprung out of the ground, but had for some reason come down from God, the God of her fathers, in whom she put her trust. Her son had been called away by Him; but three were left, her daughter and her grand-children, and she could do nothing better in life than devote herself to them.

But to Felicita her new life was like walking barefoot on a path of thorns. Until now she had been so sheltered and guarded, kept from the wind blowing too roughly upon her, that every hour brought a sharp pin-prick to her. To have no carriage at her command, no maid to wait upon, her—not even a skilful servant to discharge ordinary household duties well and quickly—to live in a little room where she felt as if she could hardly breathe, to hear every sound through the walls, to have the smell of cooking pervade the house—these and numberless similar discomforts made her initiation into her new sphere a series of surprises and disappointments.

But she must bestir herself if even this small amount of comfort and well-being were to be kept up. Madame's income would not maintain their household even on its present humble footing. Felicita's first book had done well; it had been fairly reviewed by some papers, and flatteringly reviewed by other critics who had known the late Lord Riversford. On the whole it had been a good success, and her name was no longer quite unknown. Her publishers were willing to take another book as soon as it could be ready: they did more, they condescended to ask for it. But the £50 they had paid for the first, though it had seemed a sufficient sum to her when regarded from the stand-point of a woman surrounded by every luxury, and able to spend the whole of it on some trinket, looked small enough—too small—as the result of many weeks of labor, by which she and her children were to be fed. If her work was worth no more than that, she must write at least six such books in the year, and every year! Felicita's heart sank at the thought!

There seemed to be only one resource, since one of her publishers had offered an advance of £10 only, saying they were doing very well for her, and running a risk themselves. She must take her manuscript and offer it as so much merchandise from house to house, selling it to the best bidder. This was against all her instincts as an author, and if she had remained a wealthy woman she would not have borne it. She was too true and original an artist not to feel how sacred a thing earnest and truthful work like hers was. She loved it, and did it conscientiously. She would not let it go out of her hands disgraced with blunders. Her thoughts were like children to her, not to be sent out into the world ragged and uncouth, exposed to just ridicule and to shame.

Felicita and Madame set out on their search after a liberal publisher on a gloomy day in January. For the first time in her life Felicita found herself in an omnibus, with her feet buried in damp straw, and strange fellow-passengers crushing against her. In no part of London do the omnibuses bear comparison with the well-appointed carriages rich people are accustomed to; and this one, besides other discomforts, was crowded till there was barely room to move hand or foot.

"It is very cheap," said Madame cheerfully after she had paid the fare when they were set down in Trafalgar Square "and not so very inconvenient."

A fog filled the air and shrouded all the surrounding buildings in dull obscurity; while the fountains, rising and falling with an odd and ghostly movement as of gigantic living creatures, were seen dimly white in the midst of the gray gloom. The ceaseless stream of hurrying passers-by lost itself in darkness only a few paces from them. The chimes of unseen belfries and the roll of carriages visible only for a few seconds fell upon their ears. Felicita, in the secret excitement of her mood, felt herself in some impossible world, some phantasmagoria of a dream, which must presently disperse, and she would find herself at home again, in her quiet, dainty study at Riversborough, where most of the manuscript, which she held so closely in her hand, had been written. But the dream was dispelled when she found herself entering the publishing-house she had fixed upon as her first scene of venture. It was a quiet place, with two or three clerks busily engaged in some private conversation, too interesting to be abruptly terminated by the entrance of two ladies dressed in mourning, one of whom carried a roll of manuscript. If Felicita had been wise the manuscript would not have been there to betray her. It made it exceedingly difficult for her to obtain admission to the publisher, in his private room beyond; and it was only when she turned away to go, with a sudden outflashing of aristocratic haughtiness, that the clerk reluctantly offered to take her card and a message to his employer.

In a few moments Felicita was entering the dark den where the fate of her book was in the balance. Unfortunately for her she presented too close a resemblance to the well-known type of a distressed author. Her deep mourning, the thick veil almost concealing her face; a straw clinging to the hem of her dress and telling too plainly of omnibus-riding; her somewhat sad and agitated voice; Madame's widow's cap, and unpretending demeanor—all were against her chances of attention. The publisher, who had risen from his desk, did not invite them to be seated. He glanced at Felicita's card, which bore the simple inscription, "Mrs. Sefton."

"You know my name?" she asked, faltering a little before his keen-eyed, shrewd, business-like observation. He shook his head slightly.

"I am the writer of a book called 'Haughmond Towers,'" she added, "published by Messrs. Price and Gould. It came out last May."

"I never heard of it," he answered solemnly. Felicita felt as if he had struck her. This was an unaccountable thing; he was a publisher, and she an author; yet he had never heard of her book. It was impossible that she had understood him, and she spoke again eagerly.

"It was noticed in all the reviews," she said, "and my publishers assured me it was quite a success. I could send you the reviews of it."

"Pray do not trouble yourself," he answered; "I do not doubt it in the least. But there are hundreds of books published every season, and it is impossible for one head, even a publisher's, to retain all the titles and the names of the authors."

"But I hope mine was not like hundreds of others," remarked Felicita.

"Every author hopes so," he said; "and besides the mass that is printed, somehow, at some one's expense, there are hundreds of manuscripts submitted to us. Pardon me, but may I ask if you write for amusement or for remuneration."

"For my living," she replied, with a sorrowful inflection of her voice which alarmed the publisher. How often had he faced a widowed mother and her daughter, in mourning so deep as to suggest the recentness of their loss. There was a slight movement of his hand, unperceived by either of them, and a brisk rap was heard on the door behind them.

"In a moment," he said, looking over their heads. "I am afraid," he went on, "if I asked you to leave your manuscript on approbation, it might be months before our readers could look at it. We have scores, if not hundreds, waiting."

"Could you recommend any publisher to me?" asked Felicita.

"Why not go again to Price and Gould?" he inquired.

"I must get more money than they pay me," she answered ingenuously.

The publisher shrugged his shoulders. If her manuscript had contained Milton's "Paradise Lost" or Goldsmith's "Vicar of Wakefield," such an admission would have swamped it. There is no fate swift enough for an unknown author who asks for more money than that which a publisher's sense of justice awards to him.

"I am sorry I can do nothing for you," he said, "but my time is very precious. Good-morning—No thanks, I beg. It would be a pleasure, I am sure, if I could do anything."

Felicita's heart sank very low as she turned into the dismal street and trod the muddy pavement. A few illusions shrivelled up that wintry morning under that murky sky. The name she was so fearful of staining; the name she had fondly imagined as noised from mouth to mouth; the name for which she had demanded so great a sacrifice, and had sacrificed so much herself, was not known in those circles where she might most have expected to find it a passport to attention and esteem. It had travelled very little indeed beyond the narrow sphere of Riversborough.

CHAPTER XX

A DUMB MAN'S GRIEF

The winter fogs which made London so gloomy did not leave the country sky clear and bright. All the land lay under a shroud of mist and vapor; and even on the uplands round old Marlowe's little farmstead the heavens were gray and cold, and the wide prospect shut out by a curtain of dim clouds.

The rude natural tracks leading over the moor to the farm became almost impassable. The thatched roof was sodden with damp, and the deep eaves shed off the water with the sound of a perpetual dropping. Behind the house the dark, storm-beaten, distorted firs, and the solitary yew-tree blown all to one side, grew black with the damp. The isolation of the little dwelling-place was as complete as if a flood had covered the face of the earth, leaving its two inmates the sole survivors of the human race.

Several months had passed since old Marlowe had executed his last piece of finished work. The blow that Rowland Sefton's dishonesty had inflicted upon him had paralyzed his heart—that most miserable of all kinds of paralysis. He could still go about, handle his tools, set his thin old fingers to work; but as soon as he had put a few marks upon his block of oak his heart died with him, and he threw down his useless tools with a sob as bitter as ever broke from an old man's lips.

There was no relief for him, as for other men, in speech easily, perhaps hastily uttered, in companionship with his fellows. Any solace of this kind was too difficult and too deliberate for him to seek it in writing his lamentations on a slate or spelling them off on his fingers, but his grief and anger struck inward more deeply.

Phebe saw his sorrow, and would have cheered him if she could; but she, too, was sorely stricken, and she was young. She tried to set him an example of diligent work, and placed her easel beside his carving, painting as long as the gray and fleeting daylight permitted. Now and then she attempted to sing some of her old merry songs, knowing that his watchful eyes would see the movement of her lips; but though her lips moved, her face was sad and her heart heavy. Sometimes, too, she forgot all about her, and fell into an absorbed reverie, brooding over the past, until a sob or half-articulate cry from her father aroused her. These outcries of his troubled her more than any other change in him. He had been altogether mute in the former tranquil and placid days, satisfied to talk with her in silent signs; but there was something in his mind to express now which quiet and dumb signs could not convey. At intervals, both by day and night, her affection for him was tortured by these hoarse and stifled cries of grief mingled with rage.

There was a certain sense of the duties of citizenship in old Marlowe's mind which very few women, certainly not a girl as young as Phebe, could have shared. Many years ago the elder Sefton had perceived that the companionless man was groping vaguely after many a dim thought, political and social, which few men of his class would have been troubled with. He had given to him several books, which old Marlowe had pondered over. Now he felt that, quite apart from his own personal ground of resentment, he had done wrong to the laws of his country by aiding an offender of them to escape and elude the just penalty. He felt almost a contempt for Roland Sefton that he had not remained to bear the consequences of his crime.

The news of Roland's death brought something like satisfaction to his mind; there was a chill, dejected sense of justice having been done. He had not prospered in his crime. Though he had eluded man's judgment, yet vengeance had not suffered him to live. There was no relenting toward him, as there was in Mr. Clifford's mind. Something like the old heathen conception of a divine righteousness in this arbitrary punishment of the evil-doer gave him a transient content. He did not object therefore to Phebe's hasty visit to Mrs. Sefton at the sea-side, in order to break the news to her. The inward satisfaction he felt sustained him, and he even set about a piece of work long since begun, a hawk swooping down upon his prey.

The evening on which Phebe reached home again he was more like his former self. He asked her many questions about the sea, which he had never seen, and told her what he had been doing while she was away. An old, well-thumbed translation of Plato's Dialogues was lying on the carved dresser behind him, in which he had been reading every night. Instead of the Bible, he said.

"It was him, Mr. Roland, that gave it to me," he continued; "and listen to what I read last night: 'Those who have committed crimes, great yet not unpardonable, they are plunged into Tartarus, where they go who betray their friends for money, the pains of which they undergo for a year. But at the end of the year they come forth again to a lake, over which the souls of the dead are taken to be judged. And then they lift up their voices, and call upon the souls of them they have wronged to have pity upon them, and to forgive them, and let them come out of their prison. And if they prevail they come forth, and cease from their troubles; but if not they are carried back again into Tartarus, until they obtain mercy of them whom they have wronged.' But it seems as if they have to wait until them they have wronged are dead themselves."

The brown, crooked fingers ceased spelling out the solemn words, and Phebe lifted up her eyes from them to her father's face. She noticed for the first time how sunken and sallow it was, and how dimly and wearily his eyes looked out from under their shaggy eyebrows. She buried her face in her hands, and broke down into a passion of tears. The vivid picture her father's quotation brought before her mind filled it with horror and grief that passed all words.

The wind was wailing round the house with a ceaseless moan of pain, in which she could almost distinguish the tones of a human voice lamenting its lost and wretched fate. The cry rose and fell, and passed on, and came back again, muttering and calling, but never dying away altogether. It sounded to her like the cry of a belated wanderer calling for help. She rose hastily and opened the cottage door, as if she could hear Roland Sefton's voice through the darkness and the distance. But he was dead, and had been in his grave for many days already. Was she to hear that lost, forlorn cry ringing in her ears forever? Oh, if she could but have known something of him between that night, when he walked beside her through the dark deserted roads, pouring out his whole sorrowful soul to her, and the hour when in the darkness again he had strayed from his path, and been swallowed up of death! Was it true that he had gone down into that great gulf of secrecy and silence, without a word of comfort spoken, or a ray of light shed upon its profound mystery?

The cold wind blew in through the open door, and she shut it again, going back to her low chair on the hearth. Through her blinding tears she saw her father's brown hands stretched out to her, and the withered fingers speaking eagerly.

"I shall be there before long," he said; "he will not have to wait very long for me. And if you bid me I will forgive him at once. I cannot bear to see your tears. Tell me: must I forgive him? I will do anything, if you will look up at me again and smile."

It was a strange smile that gleamed through Phebe's tears, but she had never heard an appeal like this from her dumb father without responding to it.

"Must I forgive him?" he asked.

"'If ye forgive men their trespasses,'" she answered, "'your heavenly Father will also forgive yours; but if ye forgive not men their trespasses, neither will your heavenly Father forgive yours.' It was our Lord Jesus Christ who said that, not your old Socrates, father."

"It is a hard saying," he replied.

"I don't think so," she said; "it was what Jesus Christ was doing every day he lived."

From that time old Marlowe did not mention Roland Sefton again, or his sin against him.

As the dark stormy days passed on he sometimes put a touch or two to the outstretched wings of his swooping hawk, but it did not get on fast. With a pathetic clinging to Phebe he seldom let her stay long out of his sight, but followed her about like a child, or sat on the hearth watching her as she went about her house-work. Only by those unconscious sobs and outcries, inaudible to himself, did he betray the grief that was gnawing at his heart. Very often did Phebe put aside her work, and standing before him ask such questions as the following on her swiftly moving fingers.

"Don't you believe in God, our Father in heaven, the Father Almighty, who made us?"

"Yes," he would reply by a nod.

"And in Jesus Christ, His Son, our Lord, who lived, and died for us, and rose again?"

"Yes, yes," was the silent, emphatic answer.

"And yet you grieve and fret over the loss of money!" she would say, with a wistful smile on her young face.

"You are a child; you know nothing," he replied.

For without a sigh the old man was going forward consciously to meet death. Every morning when the dawn awoke him he felt weaker as he rose from his bed; every day his sight was dimmer and his hand less steady; every night the steep flight of stairs seemed steeper, and he ascended them feebly by his hands as well as feet. He could not bring himself to write upon his slate or to spell out upon his fingers the dread words, "I am dying;" and Phebe was not old or experienced enough to read the signs of an approaching death. That her father should be taken away from her never crossed her thoughts.

It was the vague, mournful prospect of soon leaving her alone in the wide world that made his loss loom more largely and persistently before the dumb old man's mind. Certainly he believed all that Phebe said to him. God loved her, cared for her, ordered her life; yet he, her father, could not reconcile himself to the idea of her being left penniless and friendless in the cold and cruel world. He could have left her more peacefully in God's hands if she had those six hundred pounds of his earnings to inherit.

The sad winter wore slowly away. Now and then the table-land around them put on its white familiar livery of snow, and old Marlowe's dim eyes gazed at it through his lattice window, recollecting the winters of long years ago, when neither snow nor storm came amiss to him. But the slight sprinkling soon melted away, and the dun-colored fog and cloudy curtain shut them in again, cutting them off from the rest of the world as if their little dwelling was the ark stranded on the hill's summit amid a waste of water.

CHAPTER XXI

PLATO AND PAUL

Phebe's nearest neighbor, except the farm-laborer who did an occasional day's labor for her father, was Mrs. Nixey, the tenant of a farmhouse, which lay at the head of a valley running up into the range of hills. Mrs. Nixey had given as much supervision to Phebe's motherless childhood as her father had permitted, in his jealous determination to be everything to his little daughter. Of late years, ever since old Marlowe in the triumph of making an investment had communicated that important fact to her on his slate, she had indulged in a day-dream of her own, which had filled her head for hours while sitting beside her kitchen fire busily knitting long worsted stockings for her son Simon.

Simon was thirty years of age, and it was high time she found a wife for him. Who could be better than Phebe, who had grown up under her own eyes, a good, strong, industrious girl, with six hundred pounds and Upfold Farm for her fortune? As she brooded over this idea, a second thought grew out of it. How convenient it would be if she herself married the dumb old father, and retired to the little farmstead, changing places with Phebe, her daughter-in-law. She would still be near enough to come down to her son's house at harvest-time and pig-killing, and when the milk was abundant and cheese and butter to make. And the little house on the hills was built with walls a yard thick, and well lined with good oak wainscoting; she could keep it warm for herself and the old man. The scheme had as much interest and charm for her as if she had been a peeress looking out for an eligible alliance for her son.

But it had always proved difficult to take the first steps toward so delicate a negotiation. She was not a ready writer; and even if she had been, Mrs. Nixey felt that it would be almost impossible to write her day-dream in bold and plain words upon old Marlowe's slate. If Marlowe was deaf, Phebe was singularly blind and dull. Simon Nixey had played with her when she was a child, but it had been always as a big, grown-up boy, doing man's work; and it was only of late that she had realized that he was not almost an old man. For the last year or two he had lingered at the church door to walk home with her and her father, but she had thought little of it. He was their nearest neighbor, and made himself useful in giving her father hints about his little farm, besides sparing his laborer to do them an occasional day's work. It seemed perfectly natural that he should walk home with them across the moors from their distant parish church.

But as soon as the roads were passable Mrs. Nixey made her way up to the solitary farmstead. The last time she had seen old Marlowe he had been ailing, yet she was quite unprepared for the rapid change that had passed over him. He was cowering in the chimney-corner, his face yellow and shrivelled, and his eyes, once blue as Phebe's own, sunken in their sockets, and glowering dimly at her, with the strange intensity of gaze in the deaf and dumb. There was a little oak table before him, with his copy of Plato's Dialogues and a black leather Bible that had belonged to his forefathers, lying upon it; but both of them were closed, and he looked drowsy and listless.

"Good sakes! Phebe," cried Mrs. Nixey, "whatever ails thy father? He looks more like dust and ashes than a livin' man. Hast thou sent for no physic for him?"

"I didn't know he was ill," answered Phebe. "Father always feels the winter long and trying. He'll be all right when the spring comes."

"I'll ask him what's the matter with him," said Mrs. Nixey, drawing his slate to her, and writing in the boldest letters she could form, as if his deafness made it needful to write large.

"What's the matter?" she asked.

"Nothing, save old age," he answered in his small, neat hand-writing. There was a gentle smile on his face as he pushed the slate under the eyes of Mrs. Nixey and Phebe. He had sometimes thought he must tell Phebe he would not be long with her, but his hands refused to convey such sad warnings to his young daughter. He had put it off from day to day, though he was not sorry now to give some slight hint of his fears.

"Old! he's no older nor me," said Mrs. Nixey. "A pretty thing it'ud be if folks gave up at sixty or so. There's another ten years' work in you," she wrote on the slate.

"Ten years' work." How earnestly he wished it was true! He might still earn a little fortune for Phebe; for he was known all through the county, and beyond, and could get a good price for his carving. He stretched out his hand and took down his unfinished work, looking longingly at it.

Phebe's fingers were moving fast, so fast that he could not follow them. Of late he had been unable to seize the meaning of those swift, glancing finger-tips. He had reached the stage of a man who can no longer catch the lower tones of a familiar voice, and has to guess at the words thus spoken. If he lived long enough to lose his sight he would be cut off from all communion with the outer world, even with his daughter.

"Come close to me, and speak more slowly," he said to her. "I am growing old and dark. Yet I am only sixty, and my father lived to be over seventy. I was over forty when you were born. It was a sunny day, and I kept away from the house, in the shed, till I saw Mrs. Nixey there beckoning to me. And when I came in the house here she laid you in my arms. God was very good to me that day."

"He is always good," answered Phebe.

"So the parson teaches us," he continued; "but it was very hard for me to lose that money. It struck me a dreadful blow, Phebe. If I'd been twenty years younger I could have borne it; but when a man's turned sixty there's no chance. And he robbed me of more than money: he robbed me of love. I loved him next to you."

She knew that so well that she did not answer him. Her love for Roland Sefton lived still; but it was altogether changed from the bright, girlish admiration and trustful confidence it had once been. His conduct had altered life itself to her; it was colder and darker, with deeper and longer shadows in it. And now there was coming the darkest shadow of all.

"Read this," he said, opening the "Phædo," and pointing to some words with his crooked and trembling finger. She stooped her head till her soft cheek rested against his with a caressing and soothing touch.

"I go to die, you to live; but which is best God alone can know," she read. Her arm stole round his neck, and her cheek was pressed more closely against his. Mrs. Nixey's hard face softened a little as she looked at them; but she could not help thinking of the new turn affairs were taking. If old Marlowe died, it might be more convenient, on the whole, than for her to marry him. How snugly she could live up here, with a cow or two, and a little maid from the workhouse to be her companion and drudge!

Quite unconscious of Mrs. Nixey's plans, Phebe had drawn the old black leather Bible toward her, turning over the stained and yellow leaves with one hand, for she would not withdraw her arm from her father's neck. She did not know exactly where to find the words she wanted; but at last she came upon them. The gray shaggy locks of the old man and the rippling glossy waves of Phebe's brown hair mingled as they bent their heads again over the same page.

"For whether we live, we live unto the Lord; and whether we die, we die unto the Lord: whether we live therefore or die, we are the Lord's. For to this end Christ both died, and rose, and revived, that he might be Lord both of the dead and the living."

"That is better than your old Socrates," said Phebe, with tears in her eyes and a faint smile playing about her lips. "Our Lord has gone on before us, through life and death. There is nothing we can have to bear that He has not borne."

"He never had to leave a young girl like you alone in the world," answered her father.

For a moment Phebe's fingers were still, and old Marlowe looked up at her like one who has gained a miserable victory over a messenger of glad tidings.

"But He had to leave His mother, who was growing old, when the sword had pierced through her very soul," answered Phebe. "That was a hard thing to do."

The old man nodded, and his withered hands folded over each other on the open page before him. Mrs. Nixey, who could understand nothing of their silent speech, was staring at them inquisitively, as if trying to discover what they said by the expression of their faces.

"Ask thy father if he's made his will," she said. "I've heard say as land canno' go to a woman if there's no will; and it'ud niver do for Upfold to go to a far-away stranger. May be he reckons on all he has goin' to you quite natural. But there's law agen' it; the agent told me so years ago. I niver heard of any relations thy father had, but they'll find what's called an heir-at-law, take my word for it, if he doesn't leave iver a will."

But, instead of answering, Phebe rushed past her up the steep, dark staircase, and Mrs. Nixey heard her sobbing and crying in the little room above. It was quite natural, thought the hard old woman, with a momentary feeling of pity for the lonely girl; but it was necessary to make sure of Upfold Farm, and she drew old Marlowe's slate to her, and wrote on it, very distinctly, "Has thee made thy will?"

The dejected, miserable expression came back to his face, as his thoughts were recalled to the loss he had sustained, and he nodded his answer to Mrs. Nixey.

"And left all to Phebe?" she wrote again.

Again he nodded. It was all right so far, and Mrs. Nixey felt glad she had made sure of the ground. The little farm was worth £15 a year, and old Marlowe himself had once told her that his money brought him in £36 yearly, without a stroke of work on his part. How money could be gained in this way, with simply leaving it alone, she could not understand. But here was Phebe Marlowe with £50 a year for her fortune: a chance not to be lost by her son Simon. She hesitated for a few minutes, listening to the soft low sobs overhead, but her sense of judicious forestalling of the future prevailed over her sympathy with the troubled girl.

"Phebe'll be very lonesome," she wrote, and old Marlowe looked sadly into her face with his sunken eyes. There was no need to nod assent to her words.

"I've been like a mother to her," wrote Mrs. Nixey, and she rubbed both the sentences off the slate with her pocket-handkerchief, and sat pondering over the wording of her next communication. It was difficult and embarrassing, this mode of intercourse on a subject which even she felt to be delicate. How much easier it would have been if old Marlowe could hear and speak like other men! He watched her closely as she wrote word after word and rubbed them out again, unable to satisfy herself. At last he stretched out his hand and seized the slate, just as she was again about to rub out the sentence.

"Our Simon'd marry her to-morrow," was written upon it.

Old Marlowe sat looking at the words without raising his eyes or making any sign. He had never seen the man yet worthy of being the husband of his daughter, and Simon Nixey was not much to his mind. Still, he was a kind-hearted man, and well-to-do for his station; he kept a servant to wait on his mother, and he would do no less for his wife. Phebe would not be left desolate if she could make up her mind to marry him. But with a deep instinctive jealousy, born of his absolute separation from his kind, he could not bear the thought of sharing her love with any one. She must continue to be all his own for the little time he had to live.

"If Phebe likes to marry him when I'm gone, I've no objection," he wrote, and then, with a feeling of irritation and bitterness, he rubbed out the words with the palm of his hand and turned his back upon Mrs. Nixey.

CHAPTER XXII

A REJECTED SUITOR

All the next day Phebe remained very near to her father, leaving her house-work and painting to sit beside him on the low chair he had carved for her when she was a child. For the first time she noticed how slowly he caught her meaning when she spoke to him, and how he himself was forgetting how to express his thoughts on his fingers. The time might come when he could no longer hold any intercourse with her or she with him. There was unutterable sadness in this new dread.

"You used to laugh and sing," he said, "but you never do it now: never since he robbed me. He robbed me of that too. I'm a poor, helpless, deaf old man; and God never let me hear my child's voice. He used to tell me it was sweet and pleasant to hear; and your laugh made every one merry who heard it. But I could see you laugh, and now I never see it."

She could not laugh now, and her smile was sadder than tears; so she bent down her head and laid it against his knee where he could not see her face. By and by he touched her, and she lifted up her tear-dimmed eyes to his fingers.

"Promise me," he said, "not to sell this old place. It has belonged to the Marlowes from generation to generation. Who can tell but the dead come back to the place where they've lived so long? If you can, keep it for my sake."

"I promise it," she answered. "I will never sell it."

"Perhaps I shall lose my power to speak to you," he went on, "but don't you fret as if I did not forgive him as robbed me. He learnt to talk on his fingers for my sake, and I'll say 'God bless him' for your sake. If we meet one another in the next world I'll forgive him freely, and if need be I'll ask pardon for him. Phebe, I do forgive him."

As he spoke there was a brighter light in his sunken eyes, and a smile on his face such as she had not seen since the day he had helped Roland Sefton to escape. She took both of his hands into hers and kissed them fondly. But by and by, though it was yet clear day, he crept feebly up-stairs to his dark little loft under the thatched roof, and lay down on the bed where his father and grandfather had died before him.

At first he was able to talk a little in short, brief sentences; but very soon that which he had dreaded came upon him. His fingers grew too stiff to form the signs, and his eyes too dim to discern even the slowest movement of her dear hands. There was now no communication between them but that of touch, and he could not bear to miss the gentle clasp of Phebe's hand. When she moved away from him he tossed wearily from side to side, groping restlessly with his thin fingers. In utter silence and darkness, but hand to hand with her, he at last passed away.

The next few days was a strange and bewildering time to Phebe. Neighbors were coming and going, and taking the arrangements for the funeral into their own hands, with little reference to her. The clergyman of the parish, who lived three miles off, rode over the hills to hold a solemn interview with her. Mrs. Nixey would not leave her alone, and if she could have had her way would have carried her off to her own house. But this Phebe would not submit to; except the two nights she had been away when she went to the sea-side to break the news of Roland's death to Felicita and her mother, she had never been absent for a night from home. Why should she be afraid of that quiet, still form, which even in death was dearer to her than any other upon earth?

But Mrs. Nixey walked beside her, next the coffin, when the small funeral procession wound its way slowly over the uplands to the country churchyard, where the deaf and dumb old wood-carver was laid in a grave beside his wife. It was almost impossible to shake her off on their return, but Phebe could bear companionship no longer. She must walk back alone along the familiar fields, where the green corn was springing among the furrows, and under the brown hedgerows where all the buds were swelling, to the open moor lying clear and barren in an unbroken plain before her. How often had she walked along these narrow sheep-tracks with her father pacing on in front, speechless, but so full of silent sympathy with her that words were not missed between them. Their little homestead lay like an island in a sea of heather and fern, with no other dwelling in sight; but, oh, how empty and desolate it seemed!

The old house-dog crept up quietly to her, and whined softly; and the cow, as she went into the shed to milk her, turned and licked her hand gently, as if these dumb creatures knew her sorrow. There were some evening tasks to be performed, for the laborer, who had been to the funeral, was staying in the village with the other men who had helped to carry her father's coffin, to rest themselves and have some refreshment in the little inn there. She lingered over each duty with a dreary sense of the emptiness of the house haunting her, and of the silence of the hearth where all the long evening must be spent alone.

It was late in February, and though the fern and heather and gorse were not yet in bud, there was a purple tinge upon the moor fore-telling the quickly coming spring. The birds that had been silent all winter were chirping under the eaves, or fluttered up from the causeway where she had been scattering corn, at the sound of her footsteps across the little farm-yard. The sun, near its setting, was shining across the uplands, and throwing long shadows from every low bush and brake. Phebe mounted the old horse-block by the garden wicket, and looked around her, shading her eyes with her hands. The soft west wind, blowing over many miles of moor and meadows and kissing her cheek, seemed like the touch of a dear old friend, and the thin gray cloud overhead appeared only as a slight veil scarcely hiding a beloved face. It would not have startled her if she had seen her father come to the door, beckoning to her with his quiet smile, or if she had caught sight of Roland Sefton crossing the moor, with his swift, strong stride, and his face all aglow with the delight of his mountain ramble.

"But they are both dead," she said to herself. "If only Mr. Roland had been living in Riversborough he would have told me what to do."

She was too young to connect her father's death in any way with Roland Sefton's crime. They two were the dearest persons in the world to her; and both were now gone into the mysterious darkness of the next world, meeting there perhaps with all earthly discords forgiven and forgotten more perfectly than they could have been here. She remembered how her father's dull, joyless face used to brighten when Roland was talking to him—talking with slow, unaccustomed fingers, which the dumb man would watch intently, and catch the meaning of the phrase before it was half finished, flashing back an eager answer by signs and changeful expression of his features. There would be no need of signs and gestures where they had gone. Her father, perhaps, was speaking to him now.

Phebe had passed into a reverie, as full of pleasure as of pain, and she fancied she heard her father's voice—that voice which she had never heard. She started, and awoke herself. It was growing dusk, and she was faint with hunger and fatigue. The wintry sun had sunk some time since behind the brow of the hill, leaving only a few faint lines of clouds running across a clear amber light. She stepped down from the horse-block reluctantly, and with slow steps loitered up the garden-path to the deserted cottage.

It might have been better, she thought, if she had let Mrs. Nixey come home with her; but, oh, how tired she was of her aimless chatter, which seemed to din the ear and drive away all quiet thought from the heart. She had been very weary of all the fuss that had made a Babel of the little homestead since her father's death. But now she was absolutely alone, the loneliness seemed awful.

It was quite dark before the fire burned up and threw its flickering light over her old home. She sat down on the hearth opposite her father's empty chair, in her own place—the place which had been hers ever since she could remember. How long would it be hers? She knew that one volume of her life was ended and closed; the new volume was all hidden from her. She was not afraid of opening it, for there was a fund of courage and hope in her nature of which she did not know all the wealth. There was also the simple trust of a child in the goodness of God.

She had finished her tea and was sitting apparently idle, with her hands lying on her lap, when a sudden knock at the door startled and almost frightened her. Until this moment she had never thought of the loneliness of the house as possessing any element of danger; but now she turned her eyes to the uncurtained window, through which she had been so plainly visible, and wished that she had taken the precaution of putting the bar on the door. It was too late, for the latch was already lifted, and she had scarcely time to say with a tremulous voice, "Come in."

"It's me—Simon Nixey," said a loud, familiar voice, as the door opened and the tall ungainly figure of the farmer filled up the doorway. He had been at her father's funeral, and was still in his Sunday suit, standing sheepishly within the door and stroking the mourning-band round his hat, as he gazed at her with a shamefaced expression, altogether unlike the bluntness of his usual manner.

"Is there anything the matter, Mr. Nixey?" asked Phebe. "Have you time to take a seat?"

"Oh, ay! I'll sit down," he answered, stepping forward readily and settling himself down in her father's chair, in spite of her hasty movement to prevent it. "Mother thought as you'd be lonesome," he continued; "her and me've been talking of nothing else but you all evening. And mother said your heart'ud be sore and tender to-night, and more likely to take to comfort. And I'd my best clothes on, and couldn't go to fodder up, so I said I'd step up here and see if you was as lonesome as we thought. You looked pretty lonesome through the window. You wouldn't mind me staying a half hour or so?"

"Oh, no," said Phebe simply; "you're kindly welcome."

"That's what I'd like to be always," he went on, "and there's a deal about me to make me welcome, come to think on it. Our house is a good one, and the buildings they're all good; and I got the first prize for my pigs at the last show, and the second prize for my bull the show before that. Nobody can call me a poor farmer. You recollect painting my prize-bull for me, don't you, Phebe?"

"To be sure I do," she answered.

"Ay! and mother shook like a leaf when I told her you'd gone into his shed, and him not tied up. 'Never you mind, mother,' I says, 'there's neither man nor beast'ud hurt little Phebe.' You'd enjoy painting my prize-pigs, I know; and there'd be plenty o' time. Wouldn't you now?"

"Very much," she said, "if I have time."

"That's something to look forward to," he continued. "I'm always thinking what you'd like to paint, and make a picture of. I should like to be painted myself, and mother; and there'll be plenty o' time. For I'm not a man to see you overdone with work, Phebe. I've been thinking about it for the last five year, ever since you were a pretty young lass of fifteen. 'She'll be a good girl,' mother said, 'and if old Marlowe dies before you're wed, Simon, you'd best marry Phebe.' I've put it off, Phebe, over and over again, when there's been girls only waiting the asking; and now I'm glad I can bring you comfort. There's a home all ready for you, with cows and poultry for you to manage and get the good of, for mother always has the butter money and the egg money, and you'll have it now. And there's stores of linen, mother says, and everything that any farmer's wife could desire."

Phebe laughed, a low, gentle, musical laugh, which had surprise in it, but no derision. The sight of the gaunt embarrassed man opposite to her, his face burning red, and his clumsy hands twisting and untwisting as he uttered his persuasive sentences, drove her sadness away for the moment. Her pleasant, surprised laugh made him laugh too.

"Ay! mother was right; she always is," said Nixey, rubbing his great hands gleefully. "'There'll be scores of lads after her,' says mother, 'for old Marlowe has piles o' money in Sefton's Old Bank, everybody knows that.' But, Phebe, there aren't a many houses like mine for you to step right into. I'm glad I came to bring you comfort to-night."

"But father lost all his money in the Old Bank nine months ago," answered Phebe.

"Lost all his money!" repeated Nixey slowly and emphatically. There was a deep silence in the little house, while he gazed at her with open mouth and astonished eyes. Phebe had covered her face with her hands, forgetting him and everything else in the recollection of that bitter sorrow of hers nine months ago; worse than her sorrow now. Nixey spoke again after a few minutes, in a husky and melancholy voice.

"It shan't make no difference, Phebe," he said; "I came to bring you comfort, and I'll not take it away again. There they all are for you, linen and pigs, and cows and poultry. I don't mind a straw what mother'ill say. Only you wipe away those tears and laugh again, my pretty dear. Look up at Simon and laugh again."

"It's very good of you," she answered, looking up into his face with her blue eyes simply and frankly, "and I shall never forget it. But I could not marry you. I could not marry anybody."

"But you must," he said imperiously; "a pretty young girl like you can't live alone here in this lonesome place. Mother says it wouldn't be decent or safe. You'll want a home, and it had best be mine. Come, now. You'll never have a better offer if you've lost all your money. But your land lies nighest to my farm, and it's worth more to me than anybody else. It wouldn't be a bad bargain for me, Phebe; and I've waited five years for you besides. If you'll only say yes, I'll go down and face mother, and have it out with her at once."

But Phebe could not be brought to say yes, though Nixey used every argument and persuasion he could think. He went away at last, in dudgeon, leaving her alone, but not so sad as before. The new volume of her life had already been opened.

CHAPTER XXIII

ANOTHER OFFER

The next day Phebe locked up her house and rode down to Riversborough. As she descended into the valley and the open plain beyond her sorrowfulness fell away from her. Her social instincts were strong, and she delighted in companionship and in the help she could render to any fellow-creature. If she overtook a boy trudging reluctantly to school she would dismount from her rough pony and give him a ride; or if she met with a woman carrying a heavy load, she took the burden from her, and let her pony saunter slowly along, while she listened to the homely gossip of the neighborhood. Phebe was a great favorite along these roads, which she had traversed every week during summer to attend Riversborough market for the last eight years. Her spirits rose as she rode along, receiving many a kindly word, and more invitations to spend a little while in different houses than she could have accepted if she had been willing to give twelve months to visiting. It was market-day at Riversborough, and the greetings there were still more numerous, and, if possible, more kindly. Everybody had a word for Phebe Marlowe; especially to-day, when her pretty black dress told of the loss she had suffered.

She made her way to Whitefriars Road. The Old Bank was not so full as it had formerly been, for immediately after the panic last May a new bank had been opened more in the centre of the town, and a good many of the tradesmen and farmers had transferred their accounts to it. The outer office was fairly busy, but Phebe had not long to wait before being summoned to see Mr. Clifford. The muscles of his stern and careworn features relaxed into something approaching a smile as she entered, and he caught sight of her sweet and frank young face.

"Sit down, Phebe," he said. "I did not hear of your loss before yesterday; and I was just about to send for you to see your father's will. It is in our strong room. You are not one-and-twenty yet?"

"Not till next December, sir," she replied.

"Roland Sefton is the only executor appointed," he continued, his face contracting for an instant, as if some painful memory flashed across him; "and, since he is dead, I succeed to the charge as his executor. You will be my ward, Phebe, till you are of age."

"Will it be much trouble, sir?" she asked anxiously.

"None at all," he answered; "I hope it will be a pleasure; for, Phebe, it will not be fit for you to live alone at Upfold Farm; and I wish you to come here—to make your home with me till you are of age. It would be a great pleasure to me, and I would take care you should have every opportunity for self-improvement. I know you are not a fine young lady, my dear, but you are sensible, modest, and sweet-tempered, and we should get on well together. If you were happy with me I should regard you as my adopted daughter, and provide accordingly for you. Think of it for a few minutes while I look over these letters. Perhaps I seem a grim and surly old man to you; but I am not naturally so. You would never disappoint me."

He turned away to his desk, and appeared to occupy himself with his letters, but he did not take in a single line of them. He had set his heart once more on the hope of winning love and gratitude from some young wayfarer on life's rough road, whose path he could make smooth and bright. He had been bitterly disappointed in his own son and his friend's son. But if this simple, unspoiled, little country maiden would leave her future life in his keeping, how easy and how happy it should be!

"It's very good of you," said Phebe, in a trembling voice; "and I'm not afraid of you, Mr. Clifford, not in the least; but I could not keep from fretting in this house. Oh, I loved them so, every one of them; but Mr. Roland most of all. No one was ever so good to me as he was. If it hadn't been for him I should have learned nothing, and father himself would have been a dull, ignorant man. Mr. Roland learnt to talk to father, and nobody else could talk with him but me. I used to think it was as much like our Lord Jesus Christ as anything any one could do. Mr. Roland could not open father's ears, but he learned how to talk to him, to make him less lonely. That was the kindest thing any one on earth could do."

"Do you believe Mr. Roland was innocent?" asked Mr. Clifford.

"I know he was guilty," answered Phebe sadly. "He told me all about it himself, and I saw his sorrow. Before that he always seemed to me more like what I think Jesus Christ was than any one else. He could never think of himself while there were other people to care for. And I know," she went on, with simple sagacity, "that it was not Mr. Roland's sin that fretted father, but the loss of the money. If he had made six hundred pounds by using it without his consent, and said, 'Here, Marlowe, are twelve hundred pounds for you instead of six; I did not put your money up as you wanted, but used it instead;' why, father would have praised him up to the skies, and could never have been grateful enough."

Mr. Clifford's conscience smote him as he listened to Phebe's unworldly comment on Roland Sefton's conduct. If Roland had met him with the announcement of a gain of ten thousand pounds by a lucky though unauthorized speculation, he knew very well his own feeling would have been utterly different from that with which he had heard of the loss of ten thousand pounds. The world itself would have cried out against him if he had prosecuted a man by whose disregard of the laws he had gained so large a profit. Was it, then, a simple love of justice that had actuated him? Yet the breach of trust would have been the same.

"But if you will not come to live with me, my dear," he said, "what do you propose to do? You cannot live alone in your old home."

"May I tell you what I should like to do?" she asked.

"Certainly," he answered. "I am bound to know it."

"Those two who are dead," she said, "thought so much of my painting. Mr. Roland was always wishing I could go to a school of art, and father said when he was gone he should wish it too. But now we have lost our money, the next best thing will be for me to go to live as servant to some great artist, where I could see something of painting till I've saved enough money to go to school. I can let Upfold Farm for fifteen pounds a year to Simon Nixey, so I shall soon have money enough. I promised father I would never sell our farm, that has belonged to Marlowes ever since it was inclosed from the common. And if I go to London, I shall be near Madame and the children, and Mrs. Roland Sefton."

The color had come back to Phebe's face, and her voice was steady and musical again. There was a clear, frank shining in her blue eyes, looking so pleasantly into his, that Mr. Clifford sighed regretfully as he thought of his solitary and friendless life—self-chosen partly, but growing more dreary as old age, with its infirmities, crept on.

"No, no; you need not go into service," he said; "there is money enough of your own to do what you wish with. Mrs. Roland refuses to receive the income from her marriage settlement till every claim against her husband is paid off. I shall pay your claim off at the rate of one hundred a year, or more, if you like. You may have a sum sufficient to keep you at an art school as long as you need be there."

"Why, I shall be very rich!" exclaimed Phebe; "and father dreaded I should be poor."

"I will run up to London and see what arrangements I can make for you," he continued. "Perhaps Mrs. Roland Sefton could find a corner for you in her own house, small as it is, and Madame would make you as welcome as a daughter. You are more of a daughter to her than Felicita. Only I must make a bargain, that you and the children come down often to see me here in the old house. I should have grown very fond of you, Phebe; and then you would have married some man whom I detested, and disappointed me bitterly again. It is best as it is, I suppose. But if you will change your mind now, and stay with me as my adopted daughter, I'll run the risk."

"If it was anywhere else!" she answered with a wistful look into his face, "but not here. If Mrs. Roland Sefton could find room for me I'd rather live with them than anywhere else in the world. Only don't think I'm ungrateful because I can't stay here."

"No, no, Phebe," he replied; "it was for my own sake I asked it. As you grow older, child, you'll find out that the secret root of nine tenths of the benevolence you see is selfishness."

Six weeks later all the arrangements for Phebe leaving her old home and entering upon an utterly new life were completed. Simon Nixey, after vainly urging her to accept himself, and to give herself and her little farm and her restored fortune to him, offered to become her tenant at £10 a year for the land, leaving the cottage uninhabited; for Phebe could not bear the idea of any farm laborer and his family dwelling in it, and destroying or injuring the curious carvings with which her father had lined its walls. The spot was far out of the way of tramps and wandering vagabonds, and there was no danger of damage being done to it by the neighbors. Mrs. Nixey undertook to see that it was kept from damp and dirt, promising to have a fire lighted there occasionally, and Simon would see to the thatch being kept in repair, on condition that Phebe would come herself once a year to receive her rent, and see how the place was cared for. There was but a forlorn hope in Mrs. Nixey's heart that Phebe would ever have Simon now she was going to London; but it might possibly come about in the long run if he met with no girl to accept him with as much fortune.

Before leaving Upfold Farm Phebe received the following letter from Felicita:

"DEAR PHEBE: I shall be very glad to have you under my roof. I believe I see in you a freshness and truthfulness of nature on which I can rely for sympathy. I have always felt a sincere regard for you, but of late I have learned to love you, and to think of you as my friend. I love you next to my children. Let me be a friend to you. Your pursuits will interest me, and you must let me share them as your friend.

"But one favor I must ask. Never mention my husband's name to me. Madame will feel solace in talking of him, but the very sound of his name is intolerable to me. It is my fault; but spare me. You are the dearer to me because you love him, and because he prized your affections so highly; but he must never be mentioned, if possible not thought of, in my presence. If you think of him I shall feel it, and be wounded. I say this before you come that you may spare me as much pain as you can.

"This is the only thing I dread. Otherwise your coming to us would be the happiest thing that has befallen me for the last year.

"Yours faithfully,

"Felicita."

If Felicita was glad to have her, Phebe knew that Madame and the children would be enraptured. Nor had she judged wrongly. Madame received her as if she had been a favorite child, whose presence was the very comfort and help she stood most in need of. Though she devoted herself to Felicita, there was a distance between them, an impenetrable reserve, that chilled her spirits and threw her love back upon herself. But to Phebe she could pour out her heart unrestrainedly, dwelling upon the memory of her lost son, and mourning openly for him. And Phebe never spoke a word that could lead Roland's mother to think she believed him to be guilty. With a loving tact she avoided all discussion on that point; and, though again and again the pang of her own loss made itself poignantly felt, she knew how to pour consolation into the heart of Roland's mother.

But to Felix and Hilda Phebe's companionship was an endless delight. She came from her lonely homestead on the hills into the full stream of London life, and it had a ceaseless interest for her. She could not grow weary of the streets with their crowd of passers-by; and the shop windows filled with wealth and curiosities fascinated her. All the stir and tumult were joyous to her, and the faces she met as she walked along the pavement possessed an unceasing influence over her. The love of humanity, scarcely called into existence before, developed rapidly in her. Felix and Hilda shared in her childish pleasure without understanding the deep springs from which it came.

It was an education in itself for the children. A drive in an omnibus, with its frequent stoppages and its constant change of passengers, was delightful to Phebe, and never lost its charm for her. She and the children explored London, seeing all its sights, which Phebe, in her rustic curiosity, wished to see. From west to east, from north to south, they became acquainted with the great capital as few children, rich or poor, have a chance of doing. They sought out all its public buildings, every museum and picture gallery, the birthplaces of its famous men, the places where they died, and their tombs if they were within London. Westminster Abbey was as familiar to them as their own home. It seemed as if Phebe was compensating herself for her lonely girlhood on the barren and solitary uplands. Yet it was not simply sight-seeing, but the outcome of an intelligent and genuine curiosity, which was only satisfied by understanding all she could about the things and places she saw.

To the children, as well as to Madame, she often talked of Roland Sefton. Felix loved nothing more than to listen to her recollections of his lost father, who had so strangely disappeared out of his life. On a Sunday evening when, of course, their wanderings were over, she would sit with them in summer by the attic window, which overlooked the river, and in winter by the fireside, recounting again and again all she knew of him, especially of how good he always was to her. There were a vividness and vivacity in all she said of him which charmed their imagination and kept the memory of him alive in their hearts. Phebe gave dramatic effect to her stories of him. Hilda could scarcely remember him, though she believed she did; but to Felix he remained the tall, handsome, kindly father, who was his ideal of all a man should be; while Phebe, perhaps unconsciously, portrayed him as all that was great and good.

For neither Madame nor Phebe could find it in their hearts to tell the boy, so proud and fond of his father's memory, that any suspicion had ever been attached to his name. Madame, who had mourned so bitterly over his premature death in her native land, but so far from his own, had never believed in his guilt; and Phebe, who knew him to be guilty, had forgiven him with that forgiveness which possesses an almost sacred forgetfulness. If she had been urged to look back and down into that dark abyss in which he had been lost to her, she must have owned reluctantly that he had once done wrong. But it was hard to remember anything against the dead.

CHAPTER XXIV

AT HOME IN LONDON

Every summer Phebe went down to her own home on the uplands, according to her promise to the Nixeys. Felix and Hilda always accompanied her, for a change was necessary for the children, and Felicita seldom cared to go far from London, and then only to some sea-side resort near at hand, when Madame always went with her. Every summer Simon Nixey repeated his offer the first evening of Phebe's residence under her own roof; for, as Mrs. Nixey said, as long as she was wed to nobody else there was a chance for him. Though they could see with sharp and envious eyes the change that was coming over her, transforming her from the simple, untaught country girl into an educated and self-possessed woman, marking out her own path in life, yet the sweetness and the frankness of Phebe's nature remained unchanged.

"She's growing a notch or two higher every time she comes down," said Mrs. Nixey regretfully; "she'll be far above thee, lad, next summer."

"She's only old Dummy's daughter after all," answered Simon; "I'll never give her up."

To Phebe they were always old friends, whom she must care for as long as she lived, however far she might travel from them or rise above them. The free, homely life on the hills was as dear to her and the children as their life in London. The little house, with its beautiful and curious decorations; the small fields and twisted trees surrounding it; the wide, purple moors, and all the associations Phebe conjured up for them connected with their father, made the dumb old wood-carver's place a second home to them.

The happiest season of the year to Mr. Clifford was that when Phebe and Roland Sefton's children were in his neighborhood. Felicita remained firm to her resolution that Felix should have nothing to do with his father's business, and the boy himself had decided in his very childhood that he would follow in the footsteps of his ancestor, Felix Merle, the brave pastor of the Jura. There was no hope of having him to train up for the Old Bank. But every summer they spent a few days with him, in the very house where their father had lived, and where Felix could still associate him with the wainscoted rooms and the terraced garden. When Felix talked of his father and asked questions about him, Mr. Clifford always spoke of him in a regretful and affectionate tone. No hint reached the boy that his father's memory was not revered in his native town.

"There is no stone to my father in the church," he said, one Sunday, after he had been looking again and again at a tablet to his grandfather on the church walls.

"No; but I had a granite cross put over his grave in Engelberg," answered Mr. Clifford; "when you can go to Switzerland you'll have no trouble in finding it. Perhaps you and I may go there together some day. I have some thoughts of it."

"But my mother will not hear a word of any of us ever going to Switzerland," said Felix. "I've asked her how soon she would think us old enough to go, and she said never! Of course we don't expect she would ever bear to go to the place where he was killed; but Phebe would love to go, and so would I. We've saved enough money, Phebe and I; and my mother will not let me say one word about it. She says I am never, never to think of such a thing."

"She is afraid of losing you as well as him," replied Mr. Clifford; "but when you are more of a man she will let you go. You are all she has."

"Except Hilda," said the boy fondly, "and I know she loves me most of all. I do not wonder she cannot bear to hear about my father. My mother is not like other women."

"Your mother is a famous woman," rejoined Mr. Clifford; "you ought to be proud of her."

For as years passed on Felicita had attained some portion of her ambition. In Riversborough it seemed as if she was the first writer of the age; and though in London she had not won one of those extraordinary successes which place an author suddenly at the top of the ladder, she was steadily climbing upward, and was well known for her good and conscientious work. The books she wrote were clever, though cynical and captious; yet here and there they contained passages of pathos and beauty which insured a fair amount of favor. Her work was always welcome and well paid, so well that she could live comfortably on the income she made for herself, without falling back on her marriage settlement. Without an undue strain upon her mental powers she could earn a thousand a year, which was amply sufficient for her small household.

Though Roland Sefton had lavished upon his high-born wife all the pomp and luxury he considered fitting to the position she had left for him, Felicita's own tastes and habits were simple. Her father, Lord Riversford, had been but a poor baron with an encumbered estate, and his only child had been brought up in no extravagant ways. Now that she had to earn most of the income of the household, for herself she had very few personal expenses to curtail. Thanks to Madame and Phebe, the house was kept in exquisite order, saving Felicita the shock of seeing the rooms she dwelt in dingy and shabby. Excepting the use of a carriage, there was no luxury that she greatly missed.

As she became more widely known, Felicita was almost compelled to enter into society, though she did it reluctantly. Old friends of her father's, himself a literary man, sought her out; and her cousins from Riversford insisted upon visiting her and being visited as her relations. She could not altogether resist their overtures, partly on account of her children, who, as they grew up, ought not to find themselves without friends. But she went from home with unwillingness, and returned to the refuge of her quiet study with alacrity.

There was only one house where she visited voluntarily. A distant cousin of hers had married a country clergyman, whose parish was about thirty miles from London, in the flat, green meadows of Essex. The Pascals had children the same age as Felix and Hilda; and when they engaged a tutor for their own boys and girls they proposed to Felicita that her children should join them. In Mr. Pascal's quiet country parsonage were to be met some of the clearest and deepest thinkers of the day, who escaped from the conventionalities of London society to the simple and pleasant freedom they found there. Mr. Pascal himself was a leading spirit among them, with an intellect and a heart large and broad enough to find companionship in every human being who crossed his path. There was no pleasure in life to Felicita equal to going down for a few days' rest to this country parsonage.

That she was still mourning bitterly for the husband, whose name could never be mentioned to her, all the world believed. It made those who loved her most feel very tenderly toward her. Though she never put on a widow's garb she always wore black dresses. The jewels Roland had bought for her in profusion lay in their cases, and never saw the light. She could not bring herself to look at them; for she understood better now the temptation that had assailed and conquered him. She knew that it was for her chiefly, to gratify an ambition cherished on her account, that he had fallen into crime.

"I worship my mother still," said Felix one day to Phebe, "but I feel more and more awe of her every day. What is it that separates her from us? It would be different if my father had not died."

"Yes, it would have been different," answered Phebe, thinking of how terrible a change it must have made in their young lives if Roland Sefton had not died. She, too, understood better what his crime had been, and how the world regarded it; and she thanked God in her secret soul that Roland was dead, and his wife and children saved from sharing his punishment. It had all been for the best, sad as it was at the time. Madame also was comforted, though she had not forgotten her son. It was the will of God: it was God who had called him, as He would call her some day. There was no bitterness in her grief, and she did not perplex her soul with brooding over the impenetrable mystery of death.

CHAPTER XXV

DEAD TO THE WORLD

In an hospital at Lucerne a peasant had been lying ill for many weeks of a brain fever, which left him so absolutely helpless that it was impossible to turn him out into the streets on his recovery from the fever, as he had no home or friends to go to. When his mind seemed clear enough to give some account of himself, he was incoherent and bewildered in the few statements he made. He did not answer to his own name, Jean Merle; and he appeared incapable of understanding even a simple question. That his brain had been, perhaps, permanently affected by the fever was highly probable.

When at length the authorities of the hospital were obliged to discharge him, a purse was made up for him, containing enough money to keep him in his own station for the next three months.

By this time Jean Merle was no longer confused and unintelligible when he opened his lips, but he very rarely uttered a word beyond what was absolutely necessary. He appeared to the physicians attending him to be bent on recollecting something that had occurred in the past before his brain gave way. His face was always preoccupied and moody, and scarcely any sound would catch his ear and make him lift up his head. There must be mania somewhere, but it could not be discovered.

"Have you any plans for the future, Merle?" he was asked the day he was discharged as cured.

"Yes, Monsieur," he replied; "I am a wood-carver by trade."

"And where are you going to now?" was the next question.

"I must go to Engelberg," answered Merle, with a shudder.

"Ah! to Monsieur Nicodemus; then," said the doctor, "you must be a good hand at your work to please him, my good fellow."

"I am a good hand," replied Merle.

The valley of Engelberg lies high, and is little more than a cleft in the huge mass of mountains; a narrow gap where storms gather, and bring themselves into a focus. In the summer thunder-clouds draw together, and fill up the whole valley, while rain falls in torrents, and the streams war and rage along their stony channels. But when Jean Merle returned to it in March, after four months' absence, the valley was covered with snow stretching up to the summits of the mountains around it, save only where the rocks were too precipitous for it to lodge.

He had come back to Engelberg because there was the grave of the friendless man who bore his former name. It had a fascination for him, this grave, where he was supposed to be at rest. The handsome granite cross, bearing only the name of Roland Sefton and the date of his death, attracted him, and held him by an irresistible spell. At first, in the strange weakness of his mind, he could hardly believe but that he was dead, and this inexplicable second life as Jean Merle was an illusion. It would not have amazed him if he had been invisible and inaudible to those about him. That which filled him with astonishment and terror was the fact that the people took him to be what he said he was, a Swiss peasant, and a wood-carver.

He had no difficulty in getting work as soon as he had done a piece as a specimen of his skill. Monsieur Nicodemus recognized a delicate and cultivated hand, and a faithful delineator of nature. As he acquired more skill with steady practice he surpassed the master's most dexterous helper, and bid fair to rival Monsieur Nicodemus himself. But Jean Merle had no ambition; there was no desire to make himself known, or put his productions forward. He was content with receiving liberal wages, such as the master, with the generosity of a true artist, paid to him. But for the unflagging care he expended upon his work, his fellow-craftsmen would have thought him indifferent to it.

For nine months in the year Jean Merle remained in Engelberg, giving himself no holiday, no leisure, no breathing time. He lived on the poorest fare, and in the meanest lodging. His clothing was often little better than rags. His wages brought him no relaxation from toil, or delivered him from self-chosen wretchedness. Silent and morose, he lived apart from all his fellows, who regarded him as a half-witted miser.

When the summer season brought flights of foreign tourists, Merle disappeared, and was seen no more till autumn. Nobody knew whither he went, but it was believed he acted as a guide to some of the highest and most perilous of the Alps. When he came back to his work at the end of the season, his blackened and swarthy face, from which the skin had peeled, and his hands wounded and torn as if from scaling jagged cliffs, bore testimony to these conjectures.

He never entered the church when mass was performed, or any congregation assembled; but at rare intervals he might be seen kneeling on the steps before the high altar, his shaggy head bent down, and his frame shaken with repressed sobs which no one could hear. The curé had tried to win his confidence, but had failed. Jean Merle was a heretic.

When he was spoken to he would speak, but he never addressed himself to any one. He was not a native-born Swiss, and he did not seek naturalization, or claim any right in the canton. He did not seek permission to marry or to build a house, but as he was skilful and industrious and thrifty, a man in the prime of life, the commune left him alone.

He seemed to have taken it as a self-imposed task that he should have the charge of the granite cross, erected over the man whose death he had witnessed. He was recognized in Engelberg as the man who had spent the last hours with the buried Englishman, but no suspicion attached to him. So careful was he of the monument that it was generally rumored he received a sum of money yearly for keeping it in order. No doubt the friends of the rich Englishman, who had erected so handsome a stone to his memory, made it worth the man's while to attend to it. Besides this grave, which he could not keep himself from haunting, Engelberg attracted him by its double association with Felicita. Here he had seen her for the first and for the last time. There was no other spot in the world, except the home he had lost forever, so full of memories of her. He could live over again every instant of each interview with her, with all the happy interval that lay between them. The rest of his life was steeped in shadow; the earlier years before he knew Felicita were pale and dim; the time since he lost her was unreal and empty, like a confused dream.

After a while a dull despondency succeeded to the acute misery of his first winter and summer. His second fraud had been terribly successful; in a certain measure he was duped by it himself. All the world believed him to be dead, and he lived as a shadow among shadows. The wild and solitary ice-peaks he sometimes scaled seemed to him the unsubstantial phantasmagoria of a troubled sleep. He wondered with a dull amazement if the crevasses which yawned before him would swallow him up, or the shuddering violence of an avalanche bury him beneath it. His life had been as a tale that is told, even to its last word, death.

PART II

CHAPTER I

The busy, monotonous years ran through their course tranquilly, marked only by a change of residence from the narrow little house suited to Felicita's slender means to a larger, more commodious, and more fashionable dwelling-place in a West End square. Both Felicita and Phebe had won their share of public favor and a fair measure of fame; and the new home was chosen partly on account of an artist's studio with a separate entrance, through which Phebe could go in and out, and admit her visitors and sitters, in independence of the rest of the household.

Never once had Felix wavered in his desire to take orders and become a clergyman, from the time his boyish imagination had been fired by the stories of his great-grandfather's perils and labors in the Jura. Felicita had looked coldly on his resolution, having a quiet contempt for English clergymen, in spite of her friendship for Mr. Pascal, if friendship it could be called. For each year as it passed over Felicita left her in a separation from her fellow-creatures, always growing more chilly and dreary. It seemed to herself as if her lips were even losing the use of language, and that only with her pen could she find vent in expression. And these written thoughts of hers, printed and published for any eye to read, how unutterably empty of all but bitterness she found them. She almost marvelled at the popularity of her own books. How could it be that the cynical, scornful pictures she drew of human nature and human fellowship could be read so eagerly? She felt ashamed of her children seeing them, lest they should learn to distrust all men's truth and honor, and she would not suffer a word to be said about them in her own family.

But Madame Sefton, in her failing old age, was always ready to sympathize with Felix, and to help to keep him steady to her own simple faith; and Phebe was on the same side. These two women, with their quiet, unquestioning trust in God, and sweet charity toward their fellow-men, did more for Felix than all the opposing influences of college life could undo; and when his grandmother's peaceful and happy death set the last seal on her truthful life, Felix devoted himself with renewed earnestness to the career he had chosen. To enter the lists in the battle against darkness, and ignorance, and sin, wherever these foes were to be met in close quarters, was his ambition; and the enthusiasm with which he followed it made Felicita smile, yet sigh with unutterable bitterness as she looked into the midnight gloom of her own soul.

It became quite plain to Felicita as the years passed by that her son was no genius. At present there was a freshness and singleness of purpose about him, which, with the charm of his handsome young face and the genial simplicity of his manners, made him everywhere a favorite, and carried him into circles where a graver man and a deeper thinker could not find entrance; but let twenty years pass by, and Felix, she said to herself, would be nothing but a commonplace country clergyman, looking after his glebe lands and riding lazily about his parish, talking with old women and consulting farmers about his crops and cattle. She felt disappointed in him; and this disappointment removed him far away from her. The enchanted circle of her own isolation was complete.

The subtle influence of Felicita's dissatisfaction was vaguely felt by Felix. He had done well at Oxford, and had satisfied his friend and tutor, Mr. Pascal; but he knew that his mother wished him to make a great name there, and he had failed to do it. Every day, when he spent a few minutes in Felicita's library, lined with books which were her only companions, their conversation grew more and more vapid, unless his mother gave utterance to some of her sarcastic sayings, which he only half understood and altogether disliked.

But in Phebe's studio all was different; he was at home there. Though it was separate from the house, it had from the first been the favorite haunt of all the other members of the family. Madame had been wont to bring her knitting and sit beside Phebe's easel, talking of old times, and of the dear son she had lost so sorrowfully. Felix had read his school-boy stories aloud to her whilst she was painting; and Hilda flitted in and out restlessly, carrying every bit of news she picked up from her girl friends to Phebe. Even Felicita was used to steal in silently in the dusk, when no one else was there, and talk in her low sad voice as she talked to no one else.

As soon as Felix was old enough, within a few months of Madame's death, he took orders, and accepted a curacy in a poor and densely populated London district. It was not much more than two miles from home, but it was considered advisable that he should take lodgings near his vicar's church, and dwell in the midst of the people with whom he had to do. The separation was not so complete as if he had gone into a country parish, but it brought another blank into the home, which had not yet ceased to miss the tranquil and quiet presence of the old grandmother.

"I shall not have to fight with wolves like Felix Merle, my great-grandfather," said Felix, the evening before he left home, as he and Phebe were sitting over her studio fire. "I think sometimes I ought to go out as a missionary to some wild country. Yet there are dangers to meet here in London, and risks to run; ay! and battles to fight. I shall have a good fist for drunken men beating helpless women in my parish. I couldn't stand by and see a woman ill-used without striking a blow, could I, Phebe?"

"I hope you'll strike as few blows as you can," she answered, smiling.

"How could I help standing up for a woman when I think of my mother, and you, and little Hilda, and her who is gone?" asked Felix.

"Is there nobody else?" inquired Phebe, with a mischievous tone in her pleasant voice.

"When I think of the good women I have known," he answered evasively, "the sweet true, noble women, I feel my blood boil at the thought of any man ill-using any woman. Phebe, I can just remember my father speaking of it with the utmost contempt and anger, with a fire in his eyes and a sternness in his voice which made me tremble with fear. He was in a righteous passion; it was the other side of his worship of my mother."

"He was always kind and tender toward all women," answered Phebe. "All the Seftons have been like that; they could never be harsh to any woman. But your father almost worshipped the ground your mother trod upon; nothing on earth was good enough for her. Look here, my dear boy, I've been trying to paint a picture for you."

She lifted up a stretcher which had been turned with the canvas to the wall, and placed it on her easel in the full light of a shaded lamp. For a moment she stood between him and it, gazing at it with tears in her blue eyes. Then she fell back to his side to look at it with him, clasping his hand in hers, and holding it in a warm, fond grasp.

It was a portrait of Roland Sefton, painted from her faithful memory, which had been aided by a photograph taken when he was the same age Felix was now. Phebe could only see it dimly through her tears, and for a moment or two both of them were silent.

"My father?" said Felix, his face flushing and his voice faltering; "is it like him, Phebe? Yes, yes! I recollect him now; only he looked happier or merrier than he does there. There is something sad about his face that I do not remember. What a king he was among men! I'm not worthy to be the son of such a man and such a woman."

"No, no; don't say that," she answered eagerly; "you're not as handsome, or as strong, or as clever as he was; but you may be as good a man—yes, a better man."

She spoke with a deep, low sigh that was almost a sob, as the memory of how she had seen him last—crushed under a weight of sin and flying from the penalty of crime—flashed across her brain. She knew now why there had lurked a subtle sadness in the face she had been painting, which she had not been able to banish.

"I think," she said, as if speaking to herself, "that the sense of sin links us to God almost as closely as love does. I never understood Jesus Christ until I knew something of the wickedness of the world, and the frailty of our nature at its best. It is when a good man has to cry, 'Against Thee, Thee only, have I sinned, and done this evil in Thy sight,' that we feel something of the awful sinfulness of sin."

"And have you this sense of sin, Phebe?" asked Felix in a low voice. "I have thought sometimes that you, and my mother, and men like my father and Mr. Pascal, felt but little of the inward strength of sin. Your lives stand out so clear and true. If there is a stain upon them it is so slight, so plainly a defect of the physical nature, that it often seems to me you do not know what evil is."

"We all know it," she answered, "and that shadow of sorrow you see in your father's face must bear witness for him to you that he has passed through the same conflict you may be fighting. The sins of good men are greater than the sins of bad men. One lie from a truthful man is more hurtful than all the lies of a liar. The sins of a man after God's own heart have done more harm than all the crimes of all the Pagan emperors."

"It is true," he said thoughtfully.

"If I told you a falsehood, what would you think of me?"

"I believe it would almost break my heart if you or my mother told me a falsehood," he answered.

"I could not paint this portrait while your grandmother was living," said Phebe, after a short silence; "I tried it once or twice, but I could never succeed. See; here is the photograph your father gave me when I was quite a little girl, because I cried so bitterly at his going away for a few months on his wedding trip. There were only two taken, and your mother has the other. They were both very young; he was only your age, and your mother was not twenty. But Lord Riversford was dead, and she was not happy with her cousins; and your grandfather, who was living then, was eager for the match. Everybody said it was a great match for your father."

"They were very happy; they were not too young to be married," answered Felix, with a deep flush on his handsome face. "Why should not people marry young, if they love one another?"

"I would ask Canon Pascal that question if I were you," she said, smiling significantly.

"I have a good mind to ask him to-night," he replied, stooping down to kiss Phebe's cheek; "he is at Westminster, and Alice is there too. Bid me good speed, Phebe."

"God bless you, my Felix," she whispered.

He turned abruptly away, though he lingered for a minute or two longer, gazing at his father's portrait. How like him, and yet how unlike him, he was in Phebe's eyes! Then, with a gentle pressure of her hand, he went away in silence; while she took down the painting, and set it again with its face to the wall, lest Felicita coming in should catch a sight of it.

CHAPTER II

CANON PASCAL

The massive pile of the old Abbey stood darkly against the sky, with not a glimmer of light shining through its many windows; whilst behind it the Houses of Parliament, now in full session, glittered from roof to basement with innumerable lamps. All about them there was the rush and rattle of busy life, but the Abbey seemed inclosed in a magic circle of solitude and stillness. Overhead a countless host of little silvery clouds covered the sky, with fine threads and interspaces of dark blue lying between them. The moon, pale and bright, seemed to be drifting slowly among them, sometimes behind them, and faintly veiled by their light vapor; but more often the little clouds made way for her, and clustered round, in a circle of vaguely outlined cherub-heads, golden brown in the halo she shed about her. These child-like angel-heads, floating over the greater part of the sky, seemed pressing forward, one behind the other, and hastening into the narrow ring of light, with a gentle eagerness; and fading softly away as the moon passed by.

Felix stood still for a minute or two looking up from the dark and silent front of the Abbey to the silent and silvery clouds above it. Almost every stone of the venerable old walls was familiar and dear to him. For Phebe, when she came from the broad, grand solitude of her native moors, had fixed at once upon the Abbey as the one spot in London where she could find something of the repose she had been accustomed to meet with in the sight of the far-stretching horizon, and the unbroken vault of heaven overarching it. Felicita, too, had attended the cathedral service every Sunday morning, since she had been wealthy enough to set up a carriage, which was the first luxury she had allowed herself. The music, the chants, the dim light of the colored windows, the long aisle of lofty arches, and the many persistent and dominant associations taking possession of her memory and imagination, made the Abbey almost as dear to Felicita as it was through its mysterious and sacred repose to Phebe.

Felix had paced along the streets with rapid and headlong haste, but now he hesitated before turning into Dean's Yard. When he did so, he sauntered round the inclosure two or three times, wondering in what words he could best move the Canon, and framing half a dozen speeches in his mind, which seemed ridiculous to himself when he whispered them half aloud. At last, with a sudden determination to trust to the inspiration of the moment, he turned his steps hurriedly into the dark, low arches of the cloisters.

But he had not many steps to take. The tall, somewhat stooping figure of Canon Pascal, so familiar to him, was leaving through one of the archways, with head upturned to the little field of sky above the quadrangle, where the moon was to be seen with her attendant clouds. Felix could read every line in his strongly marked features, and the deep furrows which lay between his thick brows. The tinge of gray in his dark hair was visible in the moonlight, or rather the pale gleam caused all his hair to seem silvery. His eyes were glistening with delight, and as he heard steps pausing at his side, he turned, and at the sight of Felix his harsh face melted into almost a womanly smile of greeting.

"Welcome, my son," he said, in a pleasant and deep voice; "you are just in time to share this glorious sight with me. Pity 'tis it vanishes so soon!"

He clasped Felix's hand with a warm, hearty pressure, such as few hands know how to give; though it is one of the most tender and most refined expressions of friendship. Felix grasped his with an unconscious grip which made Canon Pascal wince, though he said nothing. For a few minutes the two men stood gazing upward in reverent silence, each brain busy with its own thoughts.

"You were coming to see me?" said Canon Pascal at last.

"Yes," answered Felix, in a voice faltering with eager emotion.

"On some special errand?" pursued Canon Pascal. "Don't let us lose time in beating about the bush, then. You cannot say anything that will not be interesting to me, Felix; for I always find a lad like you, and at your age, has something in his mind worth listening to. What is it, my son?"

"I don't want to beat about the bush," stammered Felix, "but oh! if you only knew how I love Alice! More than words can tell. You've known me all my life, and Alice has known me. Will you let her be my wife?"

The smile was gone from Canon Pascal's face. A moment ago, and he, gazing up at the moon, had been recalling, with a boyish freshness of heart, the days of his own happy though protracted courtship of the dear wife, who might be gazing at the same scene from her window in his country rectory. His face grew almost harsh with its grave thoughtfulness as his eyes fastened upon the agitated features of the young man beside him. A fine-looking young fellow, he said to himself; with a frank, open nature, and a constitution and disposition unspoiled by the world. He needed nobody to tell him what his old pupil was, for he knew him as well as he knew his own boys, but he had never thought of him as any other than a boy. Alice, too, was a child still. This sudden demand struck him into a mood of silent and serious thought; and he paced to and fro for a while along the corridor, with Felix equally silent and serious at his side.

"You've no idea how much I love her!" Felix at last ventured to say.

"Hush, my boy!" he answered, with a sharp, imperative tone in his voice. "I loved Alice's mother before you were born; and I love her more every day of my life. You children don't know what love means."

Felix answered by a gesture of protest. Not know what love meant, when neither day nor night was the thought of Alice absent from his inmost heart! He had been almost afraid of the vehemence of his own passion, lest it should prove a hindrance to him in God's service. Canon Pascal drew his arm affectionately through his and turned back to pace the cloister once more.

"I'm trying to think," he said, in a gentler voice, "that Alice is out of the nursery, and you out of the schoolroom. It is difficult, Felix."

"You were present at my ordination last week," exclaimed Felix, in an aggrieved tone; "the Church, and the Bishop, and you did not think me too young to take charge of souls. Surely you cannot urge that I am not old enough to take care of one whom I love better than my own life!"

Canon Pascal pressed Felix's arm closer to his side.

"Oh, my boy!" he said, "you will discover that it is easier to commit unknown souls to anybody's charge, than to give away one's child, body, soul, and spirit. It is a solemn thing we are talking of; more solemn, in some respects, than my girl's death. I would rather follow Alice to the grave than see her enter into a marriage not made for her in heaven."

"So would I," answered Felix tremulously.

"And to make sure that any marriage is made in heaven!" mused the Canon, speaking as if to himself, with his head sunk in thought. "There's the grand difficulty! For oh! Felix, my son, it is not love only that is needed, but wisdom; yes! the highest wisdom, that which cometh down from above, and is first pure, and then peaceable. For how could Christ Himself be the husband of the Church, if He was not both the wisdom of God and the love of God? How could God be the heavenly Father of us all, if He was not infinite in wisdom? Know you not what Bacon saith; 'To love and to be wise is not granted unto man?'"

"I dare not say I am wise," answered Felix, "but surely such love as I bear to Alice will bring wisdom."

"And does Alice love you?" asked Canon Pascal.

"I did not think it right to ask her?" he replied.

"Then there's some hope still," said the Canon, more joyously; "the child is scarcely twenty yet. Do not you be in a hurry, my boy. You do not know what woman is yet; how delicately and tenderly organized; how full of seeming contradictions and uncertainties, often with a blessed meaning in them, ah, a heavenly meaning, but hard to be understood and apprehended by the rougher portion of humanity. Study them a little longer, Felix; take another year or two before you fix on your life mistress."

"You forget how many years I have lived under the same roof as Alice," replied Felix eagerly, "and how many women I have lived with; my mother, my grandmother, Phebe, and Hilda. Surely I know more about them than most men."

"All good women," he answered, "happy lad! blessed lad, I should rather say. They have been better to thee than angels. Phebe has been more than a guardian angel to thee, though thou knowest not all thou owest to her yet. But a wife, Felix, is different, God knows, from mother, or sister, or friend. God chooses our kinsfolk for us; but man chooses his own wife; having free will in that choice on which hangs his own life, and the lives of others. Yet the wisest of men said, 'Whoso findeth a wife findeth a good thing, and obtaineth favor of the Lord.' Ay, a good wife is the token of such loving favor as we know not yet in this world."

The Canon's voice had fallen into a low and gentle tone, little louder than a whisper. The dim, obscure light in the cloisters scarcely gave Felix a chance of seeing the expression of his face; but the young man's heart beat high with hope.

"You don't say No to me?" he faltered.

"How can I say No or Yes?" asked Canon Pascal, almost with an accent of surprise. "I will talk it over with your mother and Alice's mother; but the Yes or No must come from Alice herself. What am I that I should stand between you two and God, if it is His will to bestow His sweet boon upon you both? Only do not disturb the child, Felix. Leave her fancy-free a little longer."

"And you are willing to take me as your son? You do not count me unworthy?" he exclaimed.

"I've boys of my own," he answered, "whose up-growing I've watched from the day of their birth, and who are precious to me as my own soul; and you, Felix, come next to them. You've been like another son to me. But I must see your mother. Who knows what thoughts she may not have for her only son?"

"None, none that can come between Alice and me," cried Felix rapturously. "Father! yes, I shall know again what it is to have a father."

A sob rose to his throat as he uttered the word. He seemed to see his own father again, as he remembered him in his childhood, and as Phebe's portrait had recalled him vividly to his mind. If he had only lived till now to witness, and to share in this new happiness! It seemed as if his early death gathered an additional sadness about it, since he had left the world while so much joy and gladness had been enfolded in the future. Even in this first moment of ineffable happiness he promised himself that he would go and visit his father's foreign grave.

CHAPTER III

FELICITA'S REFUSAL

Now there was no longer a doubt weighing upon his spirit, Felix longed to tell his mother all. The slight cloud that had arisen of late years between them was so gossamer-like yet, that the faintest breath could drive it away. Though her boy was not the brilliant genius she had secretly and fondly hoped he would prove, he was still dearer to Felicita than ought else on earth or, indeed, in heaven; and her love for him was deeper than she supposed. On his part he had never lost that chivalrous tenderness, blended with deferential awe, with which he had regarded her from his early boyhood. His love for Alice was so utterly different from his devotion to her, that he had never compared them, and they had not come into any kind of collision yet.

Felix sought his mother in her library. Felicita was alone, reading in the light of a lamp which shed a strong illumination over her. In his eyes she was incomparably the loveliest woman he had ever seen, not even excepting Alice; and the stately magnificence of her velvet dress, and rich lace, and costly jewels, was utterly different from that of any other woman he knew. For Mrs. Pascal dressed simply, as became the wife of a country rector; and Phebe, in her studio, always wore a blouse or apron of brown holland, which suited her well, making her homely and domestic in appearance as she was in nature. Felicita looked like a queen in his eyes.

When she heard his voice speaking to her, having not caught the sound of his step on the soft carpet, Felicita looked up with a smile in her dark eyes. In a day or two her son was about to leave her roof, and her heart felt very soft toward him. She had scarcely realized that he was a man, until she knew that he had decided to have a place and a dwelling of his own.

She stretched out both hands to him, with a gesture of tenderness peculiar to herself, and shown only to him. It was as if one hand could not link them closely enough; could not bring them so nearly heart to heart. Felix took them both into his own, and knelt down before her; his young face flushed with eagerness, and his eyes, so like her own, fastened upon hers.

"Your face speaks for you," she said, pressing one of her rare kisses upon it. "What is it my boy has to tell me?"

"Oh, mother," he cried, "you will never think I love you less than I have always done? See, I kiss your feet still as I used to do when I was a boy."

He bent his head to caress the little feet, and then laid it on his mother's lap, while she let her white fingers play with his hair.

"Why should you love me less than you have always done?" she asked, in a sweet languid voice. "Have I ever changed toward you, Felix?"

"No, mother, no," he answered, "but to-night I feel how different I am from what I was but a year or two ago. I am a man now; I was a boy then."

"You will always be a boy to me," she said, with a tender smile.

"Yet I am as old as my father was when you were married," he replied.

Felicita's face grew white, and she leaned back in her chair with a sudden feeling of faintness. It was years since the boy had spoken of his father; why should he utter his name now? He had raised his head when he felt her move, and her dim and failing eyes saw his face in a mist, looking so like his father when she had known him first, that she shrank from him, with a terror and aversion too deep to be concealed.

"Roland!" she cried.

He did not speak or move, being too bewildered and wonderstruck at his mother's agitation. Felicita hid her face in her white hands, and sat still recovering herself. The pang had been sudden, and poignant; it had smitten her so unawares that she had betrayed its anguish. But, she felt in an instant, her boy had no thought of wounding her; and for her own sake, as well as his, she must conquer this painful excitement. There must be no scene to awaken observation or suspicion.

"Mother, forgive me," he exclaimed, "I did not mean to distress you."

"No," she breathed with difficulty, "I am sure of it. Go on Felix."

"I came to tell you," he said gravely, "that as long as I can remember—at least as long as we have been in London and known the Pascals—I have loved Alice. Oh, mother, I've thought sometimes you seemed as fond of her as you are of Hilda. You will be glad to have her as your daughter?"

Felicita closed her eyes with a feeling of helpless misery. She could hardly give a thought to Felix and the words he uttered; yet it was those words which brought a flood of hidden memories and fears sweeping over her shrinking soul. It was so long since she had thought much of Roland! She had persuaded herself that as so many years had passed by bringing to her no hint or token of his existence, he must be dead; and as one dead passes presently out of the active thoughts, busy only with the present, so had her husband passed away from her mind into some dim, hidden cell of memory, with which she had long ceased to trouble herself.

Her husband seemed to stand before her as she had seen him last, a haggard, way-worn, ruined man, beggared and stripped of all that makes life desirable. And this was only six months after he had lost all. What would he be after thirteen years if he was living still?

But if it had appeared to her out of the question to face and bear the ignominy and disgrace he had brought upon her thirteen years ago, how utterly impossible it was now. She could never retrace her steps. To confess the deception she had herself consented to, and taken part in, would be to pull down with her own hands the fair edifice of her life. The very name she had made for herself, and the broader light in which her fame had placed her, made any repentance impossible. "A city that is set on a hill cannot be hid." Her hill was not as lofty as she had once fancied it would be; but still she was not on the low and safer level of the plain. She was honorably famous. She could not stain her honor by the acknowledgment of dishonor. The chief question, after all, was whether Roland was alive or dead.

Her colorless face and closed eyes, the expression of unutterable perplexity and anguish in her knitted brows and quivering lips, filled Felix with wonder and grief. He had risen from his kneeling posture at her feet, and now his reverential awe of her yielded to the tender compassion of a man for a weak and suffering woman. He drew her beloved head on to his breast, and held her in a firm and loving grasp.

"I would not grieve or pain you for worlds," he said falteringly, "nor would Alice. I love you better than myself; as much as I love her. We will talk of it another day, mother."

She pressed close to him, and he felt her arms strained about him, as if she could not hold him near enough to her. It seemed to him as if she was striving to draw him into the very heart of her motherhood; but she knew how deep the gulf was between her and him, and shuddered at her own loneliness.

"It is losing you, my son," she whispered with her quivering lips.

"No, no," he said eagerly; "it is not losing me, but finding another child. Don't take a gloomy view of it, mother. I shall be as happy as my father was with you."

He could not keep himself from thinking of his father, or of speaking of him. He understood more perfectly now what his father's worship of his mother had been; the tenderness of a stronger being toward a weaker one, blended with the chivalrous homage of a generous nature to the one woman chosen to represent all womanhood. There was a keener trouble to him to-night, than ever before, in the thought that his mother was a widow.

"Leave me now, Felix," she said, loosing him from her close embrace, and shutting her eyes from the sight of him. "Do not let any one come to me again to-night. I must be alone."

But when she was alone it was only to let her thoughts whirl round and round in one monotonous circle. If Roland was dead, her secret was safe, and Felix might be happy. If he was not dead, Felix must not marry Alice Pascal. She had not looked forward to this difficulty. There had been an unconscious and vague feeling in her heart that her son loved her too passionately to be easily pleased by any girl; and, almost unawares to herself, she had been in the habit of comparing her own attractions and loveliness with those of the younger women who crossed his path. Yet there was no personal vanity in the calm conviction she possessed that Felix had never seen a woman more beautiful and fascinating than the mother he had always admired with so much enthusiasm.

She was not jealous of Alice Pascal, she said to herself, and yet her heart was sore when she said it. Why could not Felix remain simply constant to her? He was the only being she had ever really loved; and her love for him was deeper than she had known it to be. Yet to crush his hopes, to wound him, would be like the bitterness of death to her. If she could but let him marry his Alice, how much easier it would be than throwing obstacles in the way of his happiness; obstacles that would seem but the weak and wilful caprices of a foolish mother.

When the morning came, and Canon Pascal made his appearance, Felicita received him in her library, apparently composed, but grave and almost stern in her manner. They were old friends; but the friendship on his side was warm and genial, while on hers it was cold and reserved. He lost no time in beginning on the subject which had brought him to her.

"My dear Felicita," he said, "Felix tells me he had some talk with you last night. What do you think of our young people?"

"What does Alice say?" she asked.

"Oh, Alice!" he answered in an amused yet tender tone; "she would be of one mind with Felix. There is something beautiful in the innocent, unworldly love of children like these, who are ready to build a nest under any eaves. Felicita, you do not disapprove of it?"

"I cannot disapprove of Alice," she replied gloomily; "but I do disapprove of Felix marrying so young. A man should not marry under thirty."

"Thirty!" echoed Canon Pascal; "that would be in seven years. It is a long time; but if they do not object I should not. I'm in no hurry to lose my daughter. But they will not wait so long."

"Do not let them be engaged yet," she said in hurried and sad tones. "They may see others whom they would love more. Early marriages and long engagements are both bad. Tell them from me that it is better for them to be free a while longer, till they know themselves and the world better. I would rather Felix and Hilda never married. When I see Phebe so free from all the gnawing cares and anxieties of this life, and so joyous in her freedom, I wish to heaven I could have had a single life like hers."

"Why! Felicita!" he exclaimed; "this is morbid. You have never forgiven God for taking away your husband. You have been keeping a grudge against Him all these years of your widowhood."

"No, no!" she interrupted; "it is not that. They married me too soon, my uncle and Mr. Sefton. I never loved Roland as I ought. Oh! if I had loved him, how different my life would have been, and his!"

Her voice faltered and broke into deep sobs, which cut off all further speech. For a few minutes Canon Pascal endeavored to reason with her and comfort her, but in vain. At length he quietly went away and sent Phebe to her. There could be no more discussion of the subject for the present.

CHAPTER IV

TAKING ORDERS

The darkness that had dwelt so long in the heart of Felicita began now to cast its gloom over the whole household. A sharp attack of illness, which followed immediately upon her great and inexplicable agitation, caused great consternation to her friends, and above all to Felix. The eminent physician who was called in said her brain had been over-worked, and she must be kept absolutely free of all worry and anxiety. How easily is this direction given, and how difficult, how impossible, in many cases, is it to follow! That any soul, except that of a child, can be freed from all anxiety, is possible only to the soul that knows and trusts God.

All further mention of his love for Alice was out of the question now for Felix. Bitter as silence was, it was imperative; for while his mother's objections and prejudices were not overcome, Canon Pascal would not hear of any closer tie than that which already existed being formed between the young people. He had, however, the comfort of believing that Alice had heard so much of what had passed from her mother, as that she knew he loved her, and had owned his love to her father. There was a subtle change in her manner toward him; she was more silent in his presence, and there was a tremulous tone in her voice at times when she spoke to him, yet she lingered beside him, and listened more closely to all he had to say; and when they left Westminster to return to their country rectory the tears glistened in her eyes as they had never done before when he bade her good-by.

"Come and see us as soon as it will not vex your mother, my boy," said Canon Pascal; "you may always think of our home as your own."

The only person who was not perplexed by Felicita's inexplicable conduct and her illness, was Phebe Marlowe, who believed that she knew the cause, and was drawn closer to her in the deepest sympathy and pity. It seemed to Phebe that Felicita was creating the obstacle, which existed chiefly in her fancy; and with her usual frankness and directness she went to Canon Pascal's abode in the Cloisters at Westminster, to tell him simply what she thought.

"I want to ask you," she said, with her clear, honest gaze fastened on his face, "if you know why Mrs. Sefton left Riversborough thirteen years ago?"

"Partly," he answered; "my wife is a Riversdale, you know, Felicita's second or third cousin. There was some painful suspicion attaching to Roland Sefton."

"Yes," answered Phebe sadly.

"Was it not quite cleared up?" asked Canon Pascal.

Phebe shook her head.

"We heard," he went on, "that it was believed Roland Sefton's confidential clerk was the actual culprit; and Sefton himself was only guilty of negligence. Mr. Clifford himself told Lord Riversdale that Sefton was gone away on a long holiday, and might not be back for months; and something of the same kind was put forth in a circular issued from the Old Bank. I had one sent to me; for some little business of my wife's was in the hands of the firm. I recollect thinking it was an odd affair, but it passed out of my mind; and the poor fellow's death quite obliterated all accusing thoughts against him."

"That is the scruple in Felicita's mind," said Phebe in a sorrowful tone; "she feels that you ought to know everything before you consent to Alice marrying Felix, and she cannot bring herself to speak of it."

"But how morbid that is!" he answered; "as if I did not know Felix, every thought of him, and every motion of his soul! His father was a careless, negligent man. He was nothing worse, was he, Phebe?"

"He was the best friend I ever had," she answered earnestly, though her face grew pale, and her eyelids drooped, "I owe all I am to him. But it was not Acton who was guilty. It was Felix and Hilda's father."

"And Felicita knew it?" he exclaimed.

"She knew nothing about it until I told her," answered Phebe. "Roland Sefton came to me when he was trying to escape out of the country, and my father and I helped him to get away. He told me all; and oh! he was not so much to blame as you might think. But he was guilty of the crime; and if he had been taken he would have been sent to jail. I would have died then sooner than let him be taken to jail."

"If I had only known this from the beginning!" said Canon Pascal.

"What would you have done?" asked Phebe eagerly. "Would you have refused to take Felix into your home? He has done no wrong. Hilda has done no wrong. There would have been disgrace and shame for them if their father had been sent to jail; but his death saved them from all danger of that. Nobody would ever speak a word against Roland Sefton now. Yet this is what is preying on Felicita's mind. If she was sure you knew all, and still consented to Felix marrying Alice, she would be at peace again. And I too think you ought to know all. But you—will not visit the sins of the father upon the son—"

"Divine providence does so," he interrupted; "if the fathers eat sour grapes the teeth of the sons are set on edge. Phebe, Phebe, that is only too true."

"But Roland's death set the children free from the curse," answered Phebe, weeping. "If he had been taken, they would have gone away to some foreign land where they were not known; or even if he had not died, we must have done differently from what we have done. But there is no one now to bring this condemnation against them. Even old Mr. Clifford has more than forgiven Roland; and if possible would have the time back again, that he might act so as to reinstate him in his position. No one in the world bears a grudge against Roland."

"I'm not hard-hearted, God knows," he answered, "but no man likes to give his child to the son of a felon, convicted or unconvicted."

"Then I have done harm by telling you."

"No, no; you have done rightly," he replied, "it was good for me to know the truth. We will let things be for awhile. And yet," he added, his grave, stern face softening a little, "if it would be good for Felicita, tell her that I know all, and that after a battle or two with myself, I am sure to yield. I could not see Alice unhappy; and that lad holds her heart in his hands. After all, she too must bear her part in the sins of the world."

But though Phebe watched for an opportunity for telling Felicita what she had done, no chance came. If Felicita had been reserved before, she inclosed herself in almost unbroken silence now. During her illness she had been on the verge of delirium; and then she had shut her lips with a stern determination, which even her weak and fevered brain could not break. She had once begged Phebe, if she grew really delirious, to dismiss all other attendants, so that no ear but hers might hear her wanderings; but this emergency had not arisen. And since then she had sunk more and more into a stern silence.

Felix had left home, and entered into his lodgings, taking his father's portrait with him. He was not so far from home but that he either visited it, or received visitors from it almost every day. His mother's illness troubled him; or otherwise the change in his life, his first step in independent manhood, would have been one of great happiness to him. He did not feel any deep misgivings as to Alice, and the blessedness of the future with her; and in the mean-time, while he was waiting, there was his work to do.

He had taken orders, not from ambition or any hope of worldly gain, those lay quite apart from the path he had chosen, but from the simple desire of fighting as best he might against the growing vices and miseries of civilization. Step for step with the ever-increasing luxury of the rich he saw marching beside it the gaunt degradation of the poor. The life of refined self-indulgence in the one class was caricatured by loathsome self-indulgence in the other. On the one hand he saw, young as he was, something of the languor and weariness of life of those who have nothing to do, and from satiety have little to hope or to fear; and on the other the ignorance and want which deprived both mind and body of all healthful activity, and in the pressure of utter need left but little scope for hope or fear. He fancied that such civilization sank its victims into deeper depths of misery than those of barbarism.

Before him seemed to lie a huge, weltering mass of slime, a very quagmire of foulness and miasma, in the depths and darkness of which he could dimly discern the innumerable coils of a deadly dragon, breathing forth poison and death into the air, which those beloved of God and himself must breathe, and crushing in its pestilential folds the bodies and souls of immortal men. He was one of the young St. Michaels called by God to give combat to that old serpent, called the Devil and Satan, which was deceiving the old world.

CHAPTER V

A LONDON CURACY

The district on which his vicar directed Felix to concentrate his efforts was by no means a neglected one. It was rather suffering from the multitude of laborers, who had chosen it as their part of the great vineyard. Lying close to a wealthy and fashionable neighborhood, it had long been a kind of pleasure-ground, or park for hunting sinners in, to the charitable and religious inhabitants of the comfortable dwellings standing within a stone's throw of the wretched streets. There was interest and excitement to be found there for their own unoccupied time, and a pleasant glow of approbation for their consciences. Every denomination had a mission there; and the mission-halls stood thickly on the ground. There were Bible-women, nurses, city missionaries, tract distributors at work; mothers' meetings were held; classes of all sorts were open; infirmaries and medical mission-rooms were established; and coffee-rooms were to be found in nearly every street. Each body of Christians acted as if there were no other workers in the field; each was striving to hunt souls into its own special fold; and each distributed its funds as if no money but theirs was being laid out for the welfare of the poor district. Hence there were greater pauperism and more complete poverty than in many a neglected quarter of the East End, with all its untold misery. Spirit-vaults flourished; the low lodging-houses were crowded to excess; rents rose rapidly; and the narrow ill lighted streets swarmed with riff-raff after nightfall, when the greater part of the wealthy district-visitors were spending their evening hours in their comfortable homes, satisfied with their day's work for the Lord.

But Felix began his work in the evenings, when the few decent working men, who still continued to live in the Brickfields, had come home from their day's toil, and the throng of professional beggars and thieves, who found themselves in good quarters there, poured in from their day's prowling. It was well for him that he had an athletic and muscular frame, well-knitted together, and strengthened by exercise, for many a time he had to force his way out of houses, where he found himself surrounded by a crew of half-drunken and dangerous men. Presently they got to know and respect him both for his strength and forbearance, which he exercised with good temper and generosity. He could give a blow, as well as take one, when it was necessary. At one time his absence from church was compulsory, because he had received a black eye when defending a querulous old crone from her drunken son; he was seen about the wretched streets of the Brickfields with this too familiar decoration, but he took care not to go home until it was lost.

With the more decent inhabitants of the district he was soon a great favorite; but he was feared and abhorred by the others. Felix belonged to the new school of philanthropic economy, which discerns, and protests against thoughtless almsgiving; and above all, against doles to street beggars. He would have made giving equally illegal with begging. But he soon began to despair of effecting a reformation in this direction; for even Phebe could not always refrain from finding a penny for some poor little shivering urchin, dogging her steps on a winter's day.

"You do not stop to think how cruel you are," Felix would say indignantly; "if it was not for women giving to them, these poor little wretches would never be sent out, with their naked feet on the frozen pavement, and scarcely rags enough to hide their bodies, blue with cold. If you could only step inside the gin-shops as I do, you would see a drunken sinner of a father or a mother drinking down the pence you drop into the children's hands. Your thoughtless kindness is as cruel as their vice."

But still, with all that fresh ardor and energy which is sneered at in the familiar proverb, "A new broom sweeps clean," Felix swept away at the misery, and the ignorance, and the vice of his degraded district. He was not going to spare himself; it should be no sham fight with him. The place was his first battlefield; and it had a strong attraction for him.

So through the pleasant months of spring, which for the last four years had been spent at Oxford, and into the hot weeks of summer, Felix was indefatigably at work, giving himself no rest and no recreation, besides writing long and frequent letters to Mrs. Pascal, or rather to Alice. For would not Alice always read those letters, every word of them? would she not even often be the first to open them? it being the pleasant custom of the Pascal household for most letters to be in common, excepting such as were actually marked "private." And Mrs. Pascal's answer might have been dictated by Alice herself, so exactly did they express her mind. They did not as yet stand on the footing of betrothed lovers; but neither of them doubted but that they soon would do so.

It was not without a sharp pang, however, that Felix learned that the Pascals were going to Switzerland for the summer. He had an intense longing to visit the land, of which his grandmother had so often spoken to him, and where his father's grave lay. But quite apart from his duty to the district placed under his charge, there was an obstacle in the absolute interdiction Felicita laid upon the country where her husband had met with his terrible death. It was impossible even to hint at going to Switzerland whilst she was in her present state of health. She had only partially recovered from the low, nervous fever which had attacked her during the winter; and still those about her strove their utmost to save her from all worry and anxiety.

The sultry, fervid days of August came; and if possible the narrow thoroughfares of the Brickfields seemed more wretched than in the winter. The pavements burned like an oven, and the thin walls of the houses did not screen their inmates from the reeking heat. Not a breath of fresh air seemed to wander through the low-lying streets, and a sickly glare and heaviness brooded over them. No wonder there was fever about. The fields were too far away to be reached in this tiring weather; and when the men and women returned home from their day's work, they sunk down in silent and languid groups on their door-steps, or on the dirty flag-stones of the causeway. Even the professional beggars suffered more than in the winter, for the tide of almsgiving is at its lowest ebb during the summer, when the rich have many other and pleasanter occupations.

Felix walked through his "parish," as he called it, with slow and weary steps. Yet his holiday was come, and this was the last evening he would work thus for the present. The Pascals were in Switzerland; he had had a letter from Mrs. Pascal, with a few lines from Alice herself in a postscript, telling him she and her father were about to start for Engelberg to visit his father's grave for him. It was a loving and gracious thing to do, just suited to Canon Pascal's kindly nature; and Felix felt his whole being lifted up by it to a happier level. Phebe and Hilda were gone to their usual summer haunt, Phebe's quaint little cottage on the solitary mountain-moor; where he was going to join them for a day or two, before they went to Mr. Clifford, in the old house at Riversborough. His mother alone, of all the friends he had, was remaining in London; and she had refused to leave until Phebe and Hilda had first paid their yearly visits to the old places.

He reached his mission-room at last, through the close, unwholesome atmosphere, and found it fairly filled, chiefly with working men, some of whom had turned into it as being a trifle less hot and noisy than the baking pavements without, crowded with quarrelsome children. It was, moreover, the pay-night for a Providence club which Felix had established for any, either men or women, who chose to contribute to it. There was a short and simple lecture given first; and afterwards the club-books were brought out, and a committee of working men received the weekly subscriptions, and attended to the affairs of the little club.

The lecture was near its close, when a drunken man, in the quarrelsome stage of intoxication, stumbled in through the open door. Felix knew him by sight well; a confirmed drunkard, a mere miserable sot, who hung about the spirit-vaults, and lived only for the drink he could pour down his throat. There had been a vague instinctive dread and disgust for the man, mingled with a deep interest he could not understand, in Felix's mind. He paused for an instant, looking at the dirty rags, and bleared eyes, and degraded face of the drunkard standing just in the doorway, with the summer's light behind him.

"What's the parson's name?" he called in a thick, unsteady voice. "Is it Sefton?"

"Hush! hush!" cried two or three voices in answer.

"I'll not hush! If it's Sefton, it were his father as made me what I am. It were his father as stole every blessed penny of my earnings. It were his father as drove me to drink, and ruined me, soul and body. Sefton! I've a right to know the name of Sefton if any man on earth does. Curse it!"

Felix had ceased speaking, and stood facing his little congregation, listening as in a dream. The men caught the drunken accuser by the arms, and were violently expelling him, but his rough voice rose above the noise of the scuffle.

"Ay!" he shouted, "the parson won't hear the truth told. But take care of your money, mates, or it'll go where mine went."

"Don't turn him out," called Felix; "it's a mistake, my men. Let him alone. He never knew my father."

The drunkard turned round and confronted him, and the little assembly was quiet again, with an intense quietness, waiting to hear what would follow.

"Your father's name was Roland Sefton?" said the drunkard.

"Yes," answered Felix.

"And he was banker of the Old Bank at Riversborough?" he asked.

"Yes," said Felix.

"Then what I've got to say is this," went on the rough, thick voice of the half-drunken man; "and the tale's true, mates. Roland Sefton, o' Riversborough, cheated me out o' all my hard earnings—one hundred and nineteen pounds—as I'd trusted him with, and drove me to drink. I were a steady man till then, as steady as the best of ye; and he were a fine, handsome, fair-spoken gentleman as ever walked; and we poor folks trusted him as if he'd been God Almighty. There was a old deaf and dumb man, called Marlowe, lost six hundred pound by him, and it broke his heart; he never held his head up after, and he died. Me, it drove to drink. That's the father o' the parson who stands here telling you about Jesus Christ, and maybe trusted with your money, as I trusted mine with him as cheated me. It's a true tale, mates, if God Almighty struck me dead for it this moment."

There was such a tone of truth in the hoarse and passionate tones, which grew steadier as the speaker gained assurance by the silence of the audience, that there was not one there who did not believe the story. Even Felix, listening with white face and flaming eyes, dared not cry out that the accusation was a lie. Horrible as it was, he could not say to himself that it was all untrue. There came flashing across his mind confused reminiscences of the time when his father had disappeared from out of his life. He remembered asking his mother how long he would be away, and did he never write to her? and she had answered him that he was too young to understand the truth about his father. Was it possible that this was the truth?

In after years he never forgot that sultry evening, with the close, noisome atmosphere of the hot mission-hall, and the confused buzzing of many voices, which after a short silence began to hum in his ears. The drunkard was still standing in the doorway, the very wreck and ruin of a man; and every detail of his loathsome, degraded appearance was burnt in on Felix's brain. He felt stupefied and bewildered—as if he had received almost a death-blow. But in his inmost soul a cry went up to heaven, "Lord, Thou also hast been a man!"

Then he saw that the cross lay before him in his path. "Whosoever will come after me, let him deny himself, and take up his cross, and follow me." It had seemed to Felix at times as if he had never been called upon to bear any cross. But now it lay there close before him. He could not take another step forward unless he lifted it up and laid it on his shoulders, whatever its weight might be. The cross of shame—the bearing of another's sin—his father's sin. His whole soul recoiled from it. Any other cross but this he could have borne after Christ with willing feet and rejoicing heart. But to know that his father was a criminal; and to bear the shame of it openly!

Yet he could not stand there longer, fighting his battle, in the presence of these curious eyes so keenly fastened upon him. The clock over the door showed upon its dial only a minute or two gone; but to Felix the time consumed in his brief foretaste of the cross seemed years. He gathered together so much of his self-possession as could be summoned at a moment's notice, and looked straight into the faces of his audience.

"Friends," he said, "if this is true, it is as new to me as it is to you. My father died when I was a boy of ten; and no one had a heart hard enough to tell me then my father was a rogue. But if I find it is true, I'll not rest day nor night till this man has his money again. What is his name?"

"Nixey," called out three or four voices; "John Nixey."

Again Felix's heart sank, for he knew Simon Nixey, whose farm lay nearest to Phebe's little homestead; and there was a familiar ring in the name.

"Ay, ay!" stammered Nixey; "but old Clifford o' the Bank paid me the money back all right; only I'd sworn a dreadful oath I'd never lay by another farthin', and it soon came to an end. It were me as were lost as well as the money."

"Then what do you come bothering here for," asked one of the men, "if you've had your money back all right? Get out with you."

For a minute or two there was a scuffle, and then the drunkard was hustled outside and the door shut behind him. For another half hour Felix mechanically conducted the business of the club, as if he had been in a dream; and then, bidding the members of the little committee good night, he paced swiftly away from his district in the direction of his home.

CHAPTER VI

OTHER PEOPLE'S SINS

"But why go home?" Felix stopped as he asked himself this question. He could not face his mother with any inquiry about the mystery that surrounded his father's memory, that mystery which was slowly dissipating like the mists which vanish imperceptibly from a landscape. He was beginning to read his mother's life in a more intelligible light, and all along the clearer line new meanings were springing into sight. The solitude and sadness, the bitterness of spirit, which had separated her from the genial influences of a society that had courted her, was plain to him now at their fountain-head. She had known—if this terrible thing was true—that shame, not glory, was hers; confusion of face, not the bearing of the palm. His heart ached for her more than for himself.

In his heart of hearts, Felix had triumphed greatly in his mother's fame. From his very babyhood the first thought impressed upon his mind had been that his mother was different from other women; far above them. It had been his father who had given him that first impression, but it had grown with strong and vigorous growth from its deep root, through all the years which had passed since his father died. Even his love for Alice had not touched his passionate loyalty and devotion to his mother. He had rejoiced in thinking that she was known, not in England alone, but in other countries into whose language her books had been translated. Her celebrity shone in his eyes with a very strong and brilliant splendor. How could he tell her that he had been thrust into the secret of his father's infamy!

There was only Phebe to whom he could just yet lay open the doubt and terror of his soul. If it was true that her father, old Marlowe, had died broken-hearted from the loss of his money, she would be sure to know of it. His preparations for his journey to-morrow morning were complete; and if he chose there was time enough for him to catch the night train, and start at once for Riversborough. There would be no sleep for him until some of these tormenting questions were answered.

It was a little after sunrise when he reached Riversborough, where with some difficulty he roused up a hostler and obtained a horse at one of the inns. Before six he was riding up the long, steep lanes, fresh and cool with dew, and overhung with tall hedgerows, which led up to the moor. He had not met a living soul since he left the sleeping town behind him, and it seemed to him as if he was in quite a different world from the close, crowded, and noisome streets he had traversed only a few hours ago. In the natural exhilaration of the sweet mountain air, and the silence broken only by the singing of the birds, his fears fell from him. There must be some mistake which Phebe would clear up. It was nothing but the accusation of a besotted brain which had frightened him.

He shouted boyishly when the quaint little cottage came in sight, with a thin column of blue smoke floating upward from its ivy-clad chimney. Phebe herself came to the door, and Hilda, with ruffled hair and a sleepy face, looked out of the little window in the thatched roof. There was nothing in his appearance a few hours earlier than he was expected to alarm them, and their surprise and pleasure were complete. Even to himself it seemed singular that he should sit down at the little breakfast-table with them, the almost level rays of the morning sun shining through the lattice window, instead of in the dingy parlor of his London lodgings.

"Come with me on to the moors, Phebe," he said as soon as breakfast was over.

She went out with him bareheaded, as she had been used to do when a girl at home, and led him to a little knoll covered with short heath and ferns, from which a broad landscape of many miles stretched under their eyes to a far-off horizon. The hollow of the earth curved upwards in perfect lines to meet the perfect curve of the blue dome of the sky bending over it. They were resting as some small bird might rest in the rounded shelter of two hands which held it safely. For a few minutes they sat silent, gazing over the wide sweep of sky and land, till Felix caught sight of a faint haze, through which two or three spires were dimly visible. It was where Riversborough was lying.

"Phebe," he said, "I want you to tell me the naked truth. Did my father defraud yours of some money?"

"Felix!" she cried, in startled tones.

"Say only yes or no to me first," he continued; "explain it afterward. Only say yes or no."

Through Phebe's brain came trooping the vivid memories of the past. She saw Roland again hurrying over the moors from his day's shooting to mount his horse, which she had saddled for him, and to ride off down the steep lanes, with a cheery shout of "Good-night" to her when he reached the last point where she could catch sight of him; and she saw him as his dark form walked beside her pony that night when he was already crushed down beneath his weight of sin and shame, pouring out his burdened heart into her ears. If Felix had asked her this question in London it might have hurt her less poignantly; but here, where Roland and her father filled all the place with the memory of their presence, it wounded her like the thrust of a sword. She burst into a passion of tears.

"Yes or no?" urged Felix, setting his face like a flint, and striking out blindly and pitilessly.

"Yes!" she sobbed; "but, oh, your father was the dearest friend I ever had!"

The sharp, cruel sound of the yes smote him with a deadly force. He could not tell himself what he had expected to hear; but now for a certainty, his father, whom he had been taught to regard as a hero and a saint, proved no other than a rogue.

It was a long time before he spoke again, or lifted up his head; so long that Phebe ceased weeping, and laid her hand tenderly on his to comfort him by her mute sympathy. But he took no notice of her silent fellowship in his suffering; it was too bitter for him to feel as yet that any one could share it.

"I must give up Alice!" he groaned at last.

"No, no!" said Phebe. "I told Canon Pascal all, and he does not say so. It is your mother who cannot give her consent, and she will do it some day."

"Does he know all?" cried Felix. "Is it possible he knows all, and will let me love Alice still? I think I could bear anything if that is true. But, oh! how could I offer to her a name stained like mine?"

"Nay, the name was saved by his death," answered Phebe sadly. "There are only three who knew he was guilty—Mr. Clifford, and your mother, and I. If he had lived he might have been brought to trial and sent to a convict prison; I suppose he would; but his death saved him and you. Down in Riversborough yonder some few uncharitable people might tell you there was some suspicion about him, but most of them speak of him still as the kindest and the best man they ever knew. It Was covered up skilfully, Felix, and nobody knew the truth but we three."

"Alice is visiting my father's grave this very day," he said falteringly.

"Ah! how like that is to Canon Pascal!" answered Phebe; "he will not tell Alice; no, she will never know, nor Hilda. Why should they be told? But he will stand there by the grave, sorrowing over the sin which drove your father into exile, and brought him to his sorrowful death. And his heart will feel more tenderly than ever for you and your mother. He will be devising some means for overcoming your mother's scruples and making you and Alice happy."

"I never ran be happy again," he exclaimed. "I never thought of such a sorrow as this."

"It was the sorrow that fell to Christ's lot," she answered; "the burden of other people's sins."

"Phebe," he said, "if I felt the misery of my fellow-man before, and I did feel it, how can I bear now to remember the horrible degradation of the man who told me of my father's sin? It was a drunkard——"

"John Nixey," she interrupted; "ay, but he caught at your father's sin as an excuse for his own. He was always a drinking man. No man is forced into sin. Nothing can harm them who are the followers of God. Don't lay on your father's shoulders more than his own wrong-doing. Sin spreads misery around it only when there is ground ready for the bad seed. Your father's sin opened my soul to deeper influences from God; I did not love him less because he had fallen, but I learned to trust God more, and walk more closely with Him. You, too, will be drawn nearer to God by this sorrow."

"Phebe," he said, "can I speak to Mr. Clifford about it? It would be impossible to speak to my mother."

"Quite impossible," she answered emphatically. "Yes, go down to Riversborough, and hear what Mr. Clifford can tell you. Your father repented of his sin bitterly, and paid a heavy price for it; but he was forgiven. If my poor old father could not withhold his forgiveness, would our heavenly Father fall short of it? You, too, must forgive him, my Felix."

CHAPTER VII

AN OLD MAN'S PARDON

To forgive his father—that was a strange inversion of the attitude of Felix's mind in regard to his father's memory. He had been taught to think of him with reverence, and admiration, and deep filial love. As Felicita looked back on the long line of her distinguished ancestry with an exaltation of feeling which, if it was pride, was a legitimate pride, so had Felix looked back upon the line of good men from whom his own being had sprung. He had felt himself pledged to a Christian life by the eminently Christian lives of his forefathers.

Now, suddenly, with no warning, he was called upon to forgive his father for a crime which had made him amenable to the penal laws of his country; a mean, treacherous, cowardly crime. Like Judas, he had borne the bag, and his fellow-pilgrims had trusted him with their money; and, like Judas, he had been a thief. Felix could not understand how a Christian man could be tempted by money. To attempt to serve Mammon as well as God seemed utterly comtemptible and incredible to him.

His heart was very heavy as he rode slowly down the lanes and along the highway to Riversborough, which his father had so often traversed before him. When he had come this way in the freshness and stillness of the early morning there had been more hope in his soul than he had been aware of, that Phebe would be able to remove this load from him; but now he knew for a certainty that his father had left to him a heritage of dishonor. She had told him all the circumstances known to her, and he was going to learn more from Mr. Clifford.

He entered his old home with more bitterness of spirit than he had ever felt before in his young life. Here, of all places in the world, clustered memories of his father; memories which he had fondly cherished and graved as deeply as he could upon his mind. He could almost hear the joyous tones of his father's voice, and see the summer gladness of his face, as he remembered them. How was it possible that with such a hidden load of shame he could have been so happy.

Mr. Clifford, though a very old man, was still in full and clear possession of his faculties, and had not yet given up an occasional attention to the business of the bank. He was nearly eighty years of age, and his hair was white, and the cold, stern blue eyes were watery and sunken in their sockets. Some years ago, when Samuel Nixey had given up his last hope of winning Phebe, and had married a farmer's daughter, his mother, Mrs. Nixey, had come to the Old Bank as housekeeper to Mr. Clifford, and looked well after his welfare. Felix found him sitting in the wainscoted parlor, a withered, bent, old man, seldom leaving the warm hearth, but keen in sight and memory, living over again in his solitude the many years that had passed over him from his childhood until now. He welcomed Felix with delight, holding his hands, and looking earnestly into his face, with the half-childlike affection of old age.

"I've not seen you since you became a parson," he said, with a sigh; "ah, my lad, you ought to have come to me. You don't get half as much as my cashier, and not a tenth part of what I give my manager. But there! that's your mother's fault, who would never let you touch business. She would never hear of you taking your father's place."

"How could she?" said Felix, indignantly. "Do you think my mother would let me come into the house my father had disgraced and almost ruined?"

"So you've plucked that bitter apple at last!" he answered, in a tone of regret. "I thought it was possible you might never have to taste it. Felix, my boy, your mother paid every farthing of the money your father had, with interest and compound interest; even to me, who begged and entreated to bear the loss. Your mother is a noble woman."

A blessed ray of comfort shot across the gloom in Felix's heart, and lit up his dejected face with a momentary smile; and Mr. Clifford stretched out his thin old hand again, and clasped his feebly.

"Ah, my boy!" he said, "and your father was not a bad man. I know how you are sitting in judgment upon him, as young people do, who do not know what it is to be sorely tempted. I judged him, and my son before him, as harshly as man could do. Remember we judge hardest where we love the most; there's selfishness in it. Our children, our fathers, must be better than other folk's children and fathers. Don't begin to reckon up your father's sins before you are thirty, and don't pass sentence till you're fifty. Judges ought to be old men."

Felix sat down near to the old man, whose chair was in the oriel window, on which the sun was shining warmly. There below him lay the garden where he had played as a child, with the river flowing swiftly past it, and the boat-house in the corner, from which his father and he had so often started for a pleasant hour or two on the rapid current. But he could never think of his father again without sorrow and shame.

"Sin hurts us most as it comes nearest to us," said old Mr. Clifford; "the crime of a Frenchman does not make our blood boil as the crime of an Englishman; our neighbor's sin is not half as black as our kinsman's sin. But when we have to look it in the face in a son, in a father, then we see the exceeding sinfulness of it. Why, Felix, you knew that men defrauded one another; that even men professing godliness were sometimes dishonest."

"I knew it," he answered, "but I never felt it before."

"And I never felt it till I saw it in my son," continued the old man, sadly; "but there are other sins besides dishonesty, of a deeper dye, perhaps, in the sight of our Creator. If Roland Sefton had met with a more merciful man than I am he might have been saved."

For a minute or two his white head was bowed down, and his wrinkled eyelids were closed, whilst Felix sat beside him as sorrowful as himself.

"I could not be merciful," he burst out with a sudden fierceness in his face and tone, "I could not spare him, because I had not spared my own son. I had let one life go down into darkness, refusing to stretch out so much as a little finger in help, though he was as dear to me as my own life; and God required me yet again to see a life perish because of my hardness of heart. I think sometimes if Roland had come and cast himself on my mercy, I should have pardoned him; but again I think my heart was too hard then to know what mercy was. But those two, Felix, my son Robert, who died of starvation in the streets of Paris, and your father, who perished on a winter's night in Switzerland, they are my daily companions. They sit down beside me here, and by the fireside, and at my solitary meals; and they watch beside me in the night. They will never leave me till I see them again, and confess my sin to them."

"It was not you alone whom my father wronged," said Felix, "there were others besides you who might have prosecuted him."

"Yes, but they were ignorant, simple men," replied Mr. Clifford, "they need never have known of his crime. All their money could have been replaced without their knowledge; it was of me Roland was afraid. If the time could come over again—and I go over and over it in my own mind all in vain—I would act altogether differently. I would make him feel to the utmost the sin and peril of his course; but I would keep his secret. Even Felicita should know nothing. It was partly my fault too. If I had fulfilled my duty, and looked after my affairs instead of dreaming my time away in Italy, your father, as the junior partner, could not have fallen into this snare. When a crime is committed the criminal is not the only one to be blamed. Consciously or unconsciously those about him have been helping by their own carelessness and indolence, by cowardice, by indifference to right and wrong. By a thousand subtle influences we help our brother to disobey God; and when he is found out we stand aloof and raise an outcry against him. God has made every one of us his brother's keeper."

"Then you too have forgiven him," said Felix, with a glowing sense of comfort in his heart.

"Forgiven him? ay!" he answered, "as he sits by me at the fireside, invisible to all but me, I say to him again and again in words inaudible to all but him:

'Even as I hope for pardon in that day,
When the great Judge of heaven in scarlet sits,
So be thou pardoned.'"

The tremulous, weak old voice paused, and the withered hands lay feebly on his knees as he looked out on the summer sky, seeing nothing of its brightness, for the thoughts and memories that were flocking to his brain. Felix's younger eyes caught every familiar object on which the sun was shining, and knitted them up for ever with the memory of that hour.

"God help me!" he cried, "I forgive my father too; but I have lost him. I never knew the real man."

CHAPTER VIII

THE GRAVE AT ENGELBERG

On the same August morning when Felix was riding up the long lovely lanes to Phebe Marlowe's little farmstead, Canon Pascal and Alice were starting by the earliest boat which left Lucerne for Stansstad, in the dewy coolness of the dawn. The short transit was quickly over, and an omnibus carried them into Stans, where they left their knapsacks to be sent on after them during the day. The long pleasant walk of fourteen miles to Engelberg lay before them, to be taken leisurely, with many a rest in the deep cool shades of the woods, or under the shadow of some great rock. The only impediment with which Alice burdened herself was a little green slip of ivy, which Felix had gathered from the walls of her country home, and which she had carried in a little flower-pot filled with English soil, to plant on his father's grave. It had been a sacred, though somewhat troublesome charge to her, as they had travelled from place to place, and she had not permitted any one to take the care of it off her hands. This evening, with her own hands, she was going to plant it upon the foreign grave of Roland Sefton; which had been so long neglected, and unvisited by those whom he had left behind him. That Felicita should never have made a pilgrimage to this sacred spot was a wonder to her; but that she should so steadily resist the wish of Felix to visit his father's resting-place, filled Alice's heart with grave misgivings for her own future happiness.

But she was not troubling herself with any misgivings to-day, as they journeyed onward and upward through the rich meadows and thick forests leading to the Alpine valley which lay under the snowy dome of the Titlis. Her father's enjoyment of the sweet solitude and changeful beauty of their pathway was too perfect for her to mar it by any mournful forebodings. He walked beside her under the arched aisles of the pine-woods bareheaded, singing snatches of song as joyously as a school-boy, or waded off through marshy and miry places in quest of some rare plant which ought to be growing there, splashing back to her farther on in the winding road, scarcely less happy if he had not found it than if he had. How could she be troubled whilst her father was treading on enchanted ground?

But the last time they allowed themselves to sit down to rest before entering the village, Canon Pascal's face grew grave, and his manner toward his daughter became more tender and caressing than usual.

The secret which Phebe had told him of Roland Sefton had been pondered over these many weeks in his heart. If it had concerned Felix only he would have felt himself grieved at this story of his father's sin, but he knew too well it concerned Alice as closely. This little ivy-slip, so carefully though silently guarded through all the journey, had been a daily reminder to him of his girl's love for her old playfellow and companion. Though she had not told him of its destiny he had guessed it, and now as she screened it from the too direct rays of the hot sun it spoke to her of Felix, and to him of his father's crime.

He had no resolve to make his daughter miserable by raising obstacles to her marriage with Felix, who was truly as dear to him as his own sons. But yet, if he had only known this dishonest strain in the blood, would he, years ago, have taken Felix into his home, and exposed Alice to the danger of loving him? Felix was out of the way of temptation; there was no stream of money passing through his hands, and it would be hard and vile indeed for him to fall into any dishonest trickery. But it might be that his children, Alice's children, might tread in the steps of their forefather, Roland Sefton, and pursue the same devious course. Thieves breed thieves, it was said, in the lowest dregs of social life. Would there be some fatal weakness, some insidious improbity, in the nature of those descending from Roland Sefton?

It was a wrong against God, a faithless distrust of Him, he said to himself, to let these dark thoughts distress his mind, at the close of a day such as that which had been granted to him, almost as a direct and perfect gift from heaven itself. He looked into the sweet, tranquil face of his girl, and the trustful loving eyes which met his anxious gaze with so open and frank an expression; yet he could not altogether shake off the feeling of solicitude and foreboding which had fallen upon his spirit.

"Let us go on, and have a quiet dinner by ourselves," said Alice, at last, "and then we shall have all the cool of the evening to wander about as we please."

They left their resting-place, and walked on in silence, as if they were overawed by the snow-clad mountains and towering peaks hanging over the valley. A little way off the road they saw a poor and miserable hut, built on piles of stones, with deep, sheltering eaves, but with a broken roof, and no light except such as entered it by the door. In the dimness of the interior they just caught sight of a gray-headed man, sitting on the floor, with his face hidden on his knees. It was an attitude telling of deep wretchedness, and heaviness of heart; and though neither of them spoke of the glimpse they had had, they drew nearer to one another, and walked closely together until they reached the hotel.

It was still broad daylight, though the sun had sunk behind the lofty mountains when they strolled out again into the picturesque, irregular street of the village. The clear blue sky above them was of the color of the wild hyacinth, the simplest, purest blue, against which the pure and simple white of the snowy domes and pinnacles of the mountain ranges inclosing the valley stood out in sharp, bold outlines; whilst the dark green of the solemn pine-forests climbing up the steep slopes looked almost black against the pale grey peaks jutting up from among them, with silver lines of snow marking out every line and crevice in their furrowed and fretted architecture. Canon Pascal bared his head, as if he had been entering his beloved Abbey in Westminster.

"God is very glorious!" he said, in a low and reverent tone. "God is very good!"

In silence they sauntered on, with loitering steps, to the little cemetery, where lay the grave they had come to seek. They found it in a forlorn and deserted corner, but there was no trace of neglect about the grey unpolished granite of the cross that marked it. No weeds were growing around it, and no moss was gathering upon it; the lettering, telling the name, and age, and date of death, of the man who lay beneath it, was as clear as if it had just come from the chisel of the graver. The tears sprang to Alice's eyes as she stood before it with reverently bowed head, looking down on Roland Sefton's grave.

"Did you ever see him, father?" she asked, almost in a whisper.

"I saw him once," he answered, "at Riversdale Towers, when Felix was still only a baby. He was a finer and handsomer man than Felix will ever be; and there was more foreign blood in his veins, which gave him greater gaiety and simpler vivacity than Englishmen usually have. I remember how he watched over Felicita, and waited on her in an almost womanly fashion; and fetched his baby himself for us to see, carrying him in his own arms with the deft skill of a nurse. Felix is as tender-hearted, but he would not make a show of it so openly."

"Cousin Felicita must have loved him with her whole heart," sighed Alice, "yet if I were in her place, I should come here often; it would be the one place I loved to come to. She is a hard woman, father; hard, and bitter, and obstinate. Do you think Felix's father would have set himself against me as she has done?"

She turned to him, her sad and pensive face, almost the dearest face in the world to him; and he gazed into it with penetrating and loving eyes. Would it not be best to tell the child the secret this grave covered, here, by the grave itself? Better for her to know the truth concerning the dead, than cherish hard and unjust thoughts of the living. Even if Felicita consented, he could not let her marry Felix ignorant of the facts which Phebe had disclosed to him. Felix himself must know them some day; and was not this the hour and the place for revealing them to Alice?

"My darling," he said, "I know why Felicita never comes here, nor lets her children come; and also why she is at present opposed to the thought of Felix marrying. Roland Sefton, her husband, the unhappy man whose body lies here, was guilty of a crime; and died miserably while a fugitive from our country. His death consigned the crime to oblivion; no one remembered it against her and her children. But if he had lived he would have been a convict; and she, and Felix, and Hilda would have shared his ignominy. She feels that she must not suffer Felix to enter our family until she has told me this; and it is the mere thought and dread of such a disclosure that has made her ill. We must wait till her mind recovers its strength."

"What was it he had done?" asked Alice, with quivering lips.

"He had misappropriated a number of securities left in his charge," answered Canon Pascal, "Phebe says to the amount of over £10,000; most of it belonging to Mr. Clifford."

"Is that all?" cried Alice, the color rushing back again to her face, and the light to her eyes, "was it only money? Oh! I thought it was more dreadful than that. Why! we should never blame cousin Felicita because her husband misappropriated some securities belonging to old Mr. Clifford. And Felix is not to blame at all; how could he be? Poor Felix!"

"But, Alice," he said, with a half smile, "if, instead of being buried here, Roland Sefton had lived, and been arrested, and sent to a convict prison for a term of imprisonment, Felicita's life, and the life of her children, would have been altogether overshadowed by the disgrace and infamy of it. There could have been no love between you and Felix."

"It was a good thing that he died," she answered, looking down on the grave again almost gladly. "Does Felix know this? But I am sure he does not," she added quickly, and looking up with a heightened color into her father's face, "he is all honor, and truth, and unselfishness. He could not be guilty of a crime against any one."

"I believe in Felix; I love him dearly," her father said, "but if I had known of this I do not think I could have brought him up in my own home, with my own boys and girls. God knows it would have been a difficult point to settle; but it was not given to my poor wisdom to decide."

"I shall not love Felix one jot less," she said, "or reverence him less. If all his forefathers had been bad men I should be sure still that he was good. I never knew him do or say anything that was mean or selfish. My poor Felix! Oh, father! I shall love him more than ever now I know there is something in his life that needs pity. When he knows it he will come to me for comfort; and I will comfort him. His father shall hear me promise it by this grave here. I will never, never visit Roland Sefton's sin on his son; I will never in my heart think of it as a thing against him. And if all the world came to know it, I would never once feel a moment's shame of him."

Her voice faltered a little, and she knelt down on the parched grass at the foot of the cross, hiding her face in her hands. Canon Pascal laid his hand fondly on her bowed head; and then he left her that she might be alone with the grave, and God.

CHAPTER IX

THE LOWEST DEEPS

The miserable, delapidated hut at the entrance of Engelberg, with no light save that which entered by the doorway, had been Jean Merle's home since he had fixed his abode in the valley, drawn thither irresistibly by the grave which bore Roland Sefton's name. There was less provision for comfort in this dark hovel than in a monk's cell. A log of rough, unbarked timber from the forest was the only seat, and a rude framework of wood filled with straw or dry ferns was his bed. The floor was bare, except near the door, the upper half of which usually stood open, and here it was covered with fine chips of box and oak-wood, and the dust which fell from his busy graver, the tool which was never out of his fingers while the light served him. There was no more decoration then there was comfort; except that on the smoke-stained walls the mildew had pencilled out some strange and grotesque lines, as if some mural painting had mouldered into ruin there. Two or three English books alone, of the cheap continental editions, lay at one end of a clumsy shelf; with the few cooking utensils which were absolutely necessary, piled together on the other. There was a small stove in one corner of the hovel, where a handful of embers could be seen at times, like the eye of some wild creature lurking in the deep gloom.

Jean Merle, though still two or three years under fifty, was looked upon by his neighbors as being a man of great, though unknown age. Yet, though he stooped in the shoulders a little, and walked with his head bent down, he was not infirm, nor had he the appearance of infirmity. His long mountain expeditions kept his muscles in full force and activity. But his grey face was marked with many lines, so fine as to be seen only at close quarters; yet on the whole forming a wrinkled and aged mask as of one far advanced in life. In addition to this singularity of aspect there was the extraordinary seclusion and sordid miserliness of his mode of existence, more in harmony with the passiveness of extreme old age, than with the energy of a man still in the prime of his days. The village mothers frightened their children with tales about Jean Merle's gigantic strength, which made him an object of terror to them. He sought acquaintanceship with none of his neighbors; and they avoided him as a heretic and a stranger.

The rugged, simple, narrow life of his Swiss forefathers gathered around him, and hedged him in. They had been peasant-farmers, with the exception of the mountain-pastor his grandfather, and he still well-remembered Felix Merle, after whom his boy had been called. All of them had been men toiling with their own hands, with a never-ceasing bodily activity, which had left them but little time or faculty for any mental pursuit. This half of his nature fitted him well for the life that now lay before him. As his Swiss ancestors had been for many generations toil-worn and weather-beaten men, whose faces were sunburnt and sun-blistered, whose backs were bent with labor, and whose weary feet dragged heavily along the rough paths, so he became. The social refinement of the prosperous Englishman, skin deep as it is, vanished in the coarse and narrow life to which he had partly doomed himself, had partly been doomed, by the dull, despondent apathy which had possessed his soul, when he first left the hospital in Lucerne.

His mode of living was as monotonous as it was solitary. His work only gave him some passing interest, for in the bitterness of his spirit he kept himself quite apart from all relation with his fellow-men. As far as in him lay he shut out the memory of the irrevocable past, and forbade his heart to wander back to the years that were gone. He strove to concentrate himself upon his daily toil, and the few daily wants of his body; and after a while a small degree of calm and composure had been won by him. Roland Sefton was dead; let him lie motionless, as a corpse should do, in the silence of his grave. But Jean Merle was living, and might continue to live another twenty years or more, thus solitarily and monotonously.

But there was one project which he formed early in his new state of existence, which linked him by a living link to the old. As soon as he found he could earn handsome wages for his skilled and delicate work, wages which he could in no way spend, and yet continue the penance which he pronounced upon himself, the thought came to him of restoring the money which had been intrusted to him by old Marlowe, and the other poor men who had placed their savings in his care. To repay the larger amount to which he was indebted to Mr. Clifford would be impossible; but to earn the other sums, though it might be the work of years, was still practicable, especially if from time to time he could make safe and prudent speculations, such as his knowledge of the money-market might enable him to do, so as to insure more rapid returns. At the village inn he could see the newspapers, with their lists of the various continental funds, and the share and stock markets; and without entering at all into the world he could direct the buying in and selling out of his stock through some bankers in Lucerne.

Even this restitution must be made in secret, and be so wrapped up in darkness and stealth that no one could suspect the hand from which it came. For he knew that the net he had woven about himself was too strong and intricate to be broken through without deadly injury to others, and above all to Felicita. The grave yonder, and the stone cross above it, barred the way to any return by the path he had come. But would it be utterly impossible for him to venture back, changed as he was by these many years, to England? It would be only Jean Merle who would travel thither, there could be no resurrection for Roland Sefton. But could not Jean Merle see from afar off the old home; or Phebe Marlowe's cottage on the hill-side; or possibly his mother, or his children; nay, Felicita herself? Only afar off; as some banished, repentant soul, drawing a little nearer to the walls of the eternal city, might be favored with a glimpse of the golden streets, and the white-robed citizens therein, the memory of which would dwell within him for evermore.

As he drew nearer the end he grew more eager to reach it. The dull apathy of the past thirteen years was transformed into a feverish anticipation of his secret journey to England with the accumulated proceeds of his work and his speculations; which in some way or other must find their way into the hands of the men who had trusted him in time past. But at this juncture the bankers at Lucerne failed him, as he had failed others. It was not simply that his speculations turned out badly; but the men to whom he had intrusted the conduct of them, from his solitary mountain-home, had defrauded him; and the bank broke. The measure he had meted out to others had been measured to him again. Whatsoever he had done unto men they had done unto him.

For three days Jean Merle wandered about the eternal frosts of the ice-bound peaks and snow-fields of the mountains around him, living he did not himself know how. It was not money he had lost. Like old Marlowe he realized how poor a symbol money was of the long years of ceaseless toil, the days of self-denial, the hours of anxious thoughts it represented. And besides this darker side, it stood also for the hopes he had cherished, vaguely, almost unconsciously, but still with strong earnestness. He had fled from the penalty the just laws of his country demanded from him, taking refuge in a second and more terrible fraud, and now God suffered him not to make this small reparation for his sin, or to taste the single drop of satisfaction that he hoped for in realizing the object he had set before him. There was no place of repentance for him; not a foot-hold in all the wide wilderness of his banishment on which he could stand, and repair one jot a little of the injury he had inflicted upon his fellow-men.

What passed through his soul those three days, amidst the ice-solitudes where no life was, and where the only sounds that spoke to him were the wild awful tones of nature in her dreariest haunts, he could never tell; he could hardly recall it to his own memory. He felt as utterly alone as if no other human being existed on the face of the earth; yet as if he alone had to bear the burden of all the falsehood, and dishonesty and dishonor of the countless generations of false and dishonorable men which this earth has seen.

All hope was dead now. There was nothing more to work for, or to look forward to. Nothing lay before him but his solitary blank life in the miserable hut below. There was no interest in the world for him but Roland Sefton's grave.

He descended the mountain-side at last. For the first time since he had left the valley he noticed that the sun was shining, and that the whole landscape below him was bathed in light. The village was all astir, and travellers were coming and going. It was not in the sight of all the world that he could drag his weary feet to the cemetery, where Roland Sefton's grave was; and he turned aside into his own hut to wait till the evening was come.

At last the sun went down upon his misery, and the cool shades of the long twilight crept on. He made a circuit round the village to reach the spot he longed to visit. His downcast eyes saw nothing but the rough ground he trod, and the narrow path his footsteps had made to the solitary grave, until he was close to it; and then, looking up to read the name upon the cross, he discerned the figure of a girl kneeling before it, and carefully planting a little slip of ivy into the soil beneath it.

CHAPTER X

ALICE PASCAL

Alice Pascal looked up into Jean Merle's face with the frank and easy self-possession of a well-bred English woman; coloring a little with girlish shyness, yet at the same time smiling with a pleasant light in her dark eyes. The oval of her face, and the color of her hair and eyes, resembled, though slightly, the more beautiful face of Felicita in her girlhood; it was simply the curious likeness which runs through some families to the remotest branches. But her smile, the shape of her eyes, the kneeling attitude, riveted him to the spot where he stood, and struck him dumb. A fancy flashed across his brain, which shone like a light from heaven. Could this girl be Hilda, his little daughter, whom he had seen last sleeping in her cot? Was she then come, after many years, to visit her father's grave?

There had always been a corroding grief to him in the thought that it was Felicita herself who had erected that cross over the tomb of the stranger, with whom his name was buried. He did not know that it was Mr. Clifford alone who had thus set a mark upon the place where he believed that the son of his old friend was lying. It had pained Jean Merle to think that Felicita had commemorated their mutual sin by the erection of an imperishable monument; and it had never surprised him that no one had visited the grave. His astonishment came now. Was it possible that Felicita had revisited Switzerland? Could she be near at hand, in the village down yonder? His mother, also, and his boy, Felix, could they be treading the same soil, and breathing the same air as himself? An agony of mingled terror and rapture shot through his inmost soul. His lips were dry, and his throat parched: he could not articulate a syllable.

He did not know what a gaunt and haggard madman he appeared. His grey hair was ragged and tangled, and his sunken eyes gleamed with a strange brightness. The villagers, who were wont at times to call him an imbecile, would have been sure they were right at this moment, as he stood motionless and dumb, staring at Alice; but to her he looked more like one whose reason was just trembling in the balance. She was alone, her father was no longer in sight; but she was not easily frightened. Rather a sense of sacred pity for the forlorn wretch before her filled her heart.

"See!" she said, in clear and penetrating accents, full, however, of gentle kindness, and she spoke unconsciously in English, "see! I have carried this little slip of ivy all the way from England to plant it here. This is the grave of a man I should have loved very dearly."

A rapid flush of color passed over her face as she spoke, leaving it paler than before, while a slight sadness clouded the smile in her eyes.

"Was he your father?" he articulated, with an immense effort.

"No," she answered; "not my father, but the father of my dearest friends. They cannot come here; but it was his son who gathered this slip of ivy from our porch at home, and asked me to plant it here for him. Will it grow, do you think?"

"It shall grow," he muttered.

It was not his daughter, then; none of his own blood was at hand. But this English girl fascinated him; he could not turn away his eyes, but watched every slight movement as she carefully gathered the soil about the root of the little plant, which he vowed within himself should grow. She was rather long about her task, for she wished this madman to go away, and leave her alone beside Roland Sefton's grave. What her father had told her about him was still strange to her, and she wanted to familiarize it to herself. But still the haggard-looking peasant lingered at her side, gazing at her with his glowering and sunken eyes; yet neither moving nor speaking.

"You know English?" she said, as all at once it occurred to her that she had spoken to him as she would have spoken to one of the villagers in their own country churchyard at home, and that he had answered her. He replied only by a gesture.

"Can you find me some one who will take charge of this little plant?" she asked.

Jean Merle raised his head and lifted up his dim eyes to the eastern mountain-peaks, which were still shining in the rays of the sinking sun, though the twilight was darkening everywhere in the valley. Only last night he had slept among some juniper-bushes just below the boundary of that everlasting snow, feeling himself cast out forever from any glimpse of his old Paradise. But now, if he could only find words and utterance, there was come to him, even to him, a messenger, an angel direct from the very heart of his home, who could tell him all that last night he believed that he should never know. The tears sprang to his eyes, blessed tears; and a rush of uncontrollable longing overwhelmed him. He must hear all he could of those whom he loved; and then, whether he lived long or died soon, he would thank God as long as his miserable life continued.

"It is I who take care of this grave," he said; "I was with him when he died. He spoke to me of Felix and Hilda and his mother; and I saw their portraits. You hear? I know them all."

"Was it you who watched beside him?" asked Alice eagerly. "Oh! sit down here and tell me all about it; all you can remember. I will tell it all again to Felix, and Hilda, and Phebe Marlowe; and oh! how glad, and how sorry they will be to listen!"

There was no mention of Felicita's name, and Jean Merle felt a terrible dread come over him at this omission. He sank down on the ground beside the grave, and looked up into Alice's bright young face, with eyes that to her were no longer lit up with the fire of insanity, however intense and eager they might seem. It was an undreamed-of chance which had brought to her side the man who had watched by the death-bed of Felix's father.

"Tell me all you remember," she urged.

"I remember nothing," he answered, pressing his dark hard hand against his forehead, "it is more than thirteen years ago. But he showed to me their portraits. Is his wife still living?"

"Oh, yes!" she answered, "but she will not let either of them come to Switzerland; neither Felix nor Hilda. Nobody speaks of this country in her hearing; and his name is never uttered. But his mother used to talk to us about him; and Phebe Marlowe does so still. She has painted a portrait of him for Felix."

"Is Roland Sefton's mother yet alive?" he asked, with a dull, aching foreboding of her reply.

"No," she said. "Oh! how we all loved dear old Madame Sefton! She was always more like Felix and Hilda's mother than Cousin Felicita was. We loved her more a hundred times than Cousin Felicita, for we are afraid of her. It was her husband's death that spoiled her whole life and set her quite apart from everybody else. But Madame—she was not made so utterly miserable by it; she knew she would meet her son again in heaven. When she was dying she said to Cousin Felicita, 'He did not return to me, but I go to him; I go gladly to see again my dear son.' The very last words they heard her say were, 'I come, Roland!'"

Alice's voice trembled, and she laid her hand caressingly on the name of Roland Sefton graved on the cross above her. Jean Merle listened, as if he heard the words whispered a long way off, or as by some one speaking in a dream. The meaning had not reached his brain, but was travelling slowly to it, and would surely pierce his heart with a new sorrow and a fresh pang of remorse. The loud chanting of the monks in the abbey close by broke in upon their solemn silence, and awoke Alice from the reverie into which she had fallen.

"Can you tell me nothing about him?" she asked. "Talk to me as if I was his child."

"I have nothing to tell you," answered Jean Merle. "I remember nothing he said."

She looked down on the poor ragged peasant at her feet, with his gaunt and scarred features, and his slowly articulated speech. There seemed nothing strange in such a man not being able to recall Roland Sefton's dying words. It was probable that he barely understood them; and most likely he could not gather up the meaning of what she herself was saying. The few words he uttered were English, but they were very few and forced.

"I am sorry," she said gently, "but I will tell them you promised to take care of the ivy I have planted here."

She wished the dull, gray-headed villager would go home, and leave her alone for awhile in this solemn and sacred place; but he crouched still on the ground, stirring neither hand nor foot. When at last she moved as if to go away, he stretched out a toil-worn hand, and laid it on her dress.

"Stay," he said, "tell me more about Roland Sefton's children; I will think of it when I am tending this grave."

"What am I to tell you?" she asked gently, "Hilda is three years younger than me, and people say we are like sisters. She and Felix were brought up with me and my brothers in my father's house; we were like brothers and sisters. And Felix is like another son to my father, who says he will be both good and great some day. Good he is now; as good as man can be."

"And you love him!" said Jean Merle, in a low and humble voice, with his head turned away from her, and resting on the lowest step of the cross.

Alice started and trembled as she looked down on the grave and the prostrate man. It seemed to her as if the words had almost come out of this sad, and solitary, and forsaken grave, where Roland Sefton had lain unvisited so many years. The last gleam of daylight had vanished from the snowy peaks, leaving them wan and pallid as the dead. A sudden chill came into the evening air which made her shiver; but she was not terrified, though she felt a certain bewilderment and agitation creeping through her. She could not resist the impulse to answer the strange question.

"Yes, I love Felix," she said simply. "We love each other dearly."

"God bless you!" cried Jean Merle, in a tremulous voice. "God in heaven bless you both, and preserve you to each other."

He had lifted himself up, and was kneeling before her, eagerly scanning her face, as if to impress it on his memory. He bent down his gray head and kissed her hand humbly and reverently, touching it only with his lips. Then starting to his feet he hastened away from the cemetery, and was soon lost to her sight in the gathering gloom of the dusk.

For a little while longer Alice lingered at the grave, thinking over what had passed. It was not much as she recalled it, but it left her agitated and disturbed. Yet after all she had only uttered aloud what her heart would have said at the grave of Felix's father. But this strange peasant, so miserable and poverty-stricken, so haggard and hopeless-looking, haunted her thoughts both waking and sleeping. Early the next morning she and Canon Pascal went to the hovel inhabited by Jean Merle, but found it deserted and locked up. Some laborers had seen him start off at daybreak up the Trübsee Alps, from which he might be either ascending the Titlis or taking the route to the Joch-Pass. There was no chance of his return that day, and Jean Merle's absence might last for several days, as he was eccentric, and bestowed his confidence on nobody. There was little more to be learned of him, except that he was a heretic, a stranger, and a miser. Canon Pascal and Alice visited once more Roland Sefton's grave, and then they went on their way over the Joch-Pass, with some faint hopes of meeting with Jean Merle on their route, hopes that were not fulfilled.

CHAPTER XI

COMING TO HIMSELF

When he left the cemetery Jean Merle went home to his wretched chalet, flung himself down on his rough bed, and slept for some hours the profound and dreamless sleep of utter exhaustion. The last three nights he had passed under the stars, and stretched upon the low juniper-bushes. He awoke suddenly, from the bright, clear moonlight of a cloudless sky and dry atmosphere streaming in through his door, which he had left open. There was light enough for him to withdraw some money from a safe hiding-place he had constructed in his crazy old hut, and to make up a packet of most of the clothing he possessed. There were between twenty and thirty pounds in gold pieces of twenty francs each—the only money he was master of now his Lucerne bankers had failed him. A vague purpose, dimly shaping itself, was in his brain, but he was in no hurry to see it take definite form. With his small bundle of clothes and his leathern purse he started off in the earliest rays of the dawn to escape being visited by the young English girl, whom he had seen at the grave, and who would probably seek him out in the morning with her father. Who they were he could find out if he himself returned to Engelberg.

If he returned; for, as he ascended the steep path leading up to the Trübsee Alp, he turned back to look at the high mountain-valley where he had dwelt so long, as though he was looking upon it for the last time. It seemed to him as if he was awaking out of a long lethargy and paralysis. Three days ago the dull round of incessant toil and parsimonious hoarding had been abruptly broken up by the loss of all he had toiled for and hoarded up, and the shock had driven him out like a maniac, to wander about the desolate heights of Engelberg in a mood bordering on despair, which had made him utterly reckless of his life. Since then news had come to him from home—stray gleams from the Paradise he had forfeited. Strongest of them all was the thought that these fourteen years had transformed his little son Felix into a man, loving as he himself had loved, and already called to take his part in the battle of life. He had never realized this before, and it stirred his heart to the very depths. His children had been but soft, vague memories to him; it was Felicita who had engrossed all his thought. All at once he comprehended that he was a father, the father of a son and daughter, who had their own separate life and career. A deep and poignant interest in these beings took possession of him. He had called them into existence; they belonged to him by a tie which nothing on earth, in heaven, or in hell itself could destroy. As long as they lived there must be an indestructible interest for him in this world. Felicita was no longer the first in his thoughts.

The dim veil which time had drawn around them was rent asunder, and they stood before him bathed in light, but placed on the other side of a gulf as fathomless, as impassable, and as death-like as the ice-crevasses yawning at his feet. He gazed down into the cold, gleaming abyss, and across it to the sharp and slippery margin where there could be no foot-hold, and he pictured to himself the springing across that horrible gulf to reach them on the other side, and the falling, with outstretched hands and clutching fingers, into the unseen icy depths below him. For the first time in his life he shrank back shivering and terror-stricken from the edge of the crevasse, with palsied limbs and treacherous nerves. He felt that he must get back into safer standing-ground than this solitary and perilous glacier.

He reached at last a point of safety, where he could lie down and let his trembling limbs rest awhile. The whole slope of the valley lay below him, with its rich meadows of emerald green, and its silvery streams wandering through them. Little farms and chalets were dotted about, some of them clinging to the sides of the rocks opposite to him, or resting on the very edge of precipices thousands of feet deep, and looking as if they were about to slip over them. He felt his head grow giddy as he looked at them, and thought of the children at play in such dangerous playgrounds. There were a few gray clouds hanging about the Titlis, and caught upon the sharp horns of the rugged peaks around the valley. Every peak and precipice he knew; they had been his refuge in the hours of his greatest anguish. But these palsied limbs and this giddy head could not be trusted to carry him there again. He had lost his last hope of making any atonement. Hope was gone; was he to lose his indomitable courage also? It was the last faculty which made his present life endurable.

He lay motionless for hours, neither listening nor looking. Yet he heard, for the memory of it often came back to him in after years, the tinkling of innumerable bells from the pastures below him, and around him; and the voices of many waterfalls rushing down through the pine-forests into the valley; and the tossing to and fro of the interwoven branches of the trees. And he saw the sunlight stealing from one point to another, chased by the shadows of the clouds, that gathered and dispersed, dimming the blue sky for a little time, and then leaving it brighter and deeper than before. He was unconscious of it all; he was even unaware that his brain was at work at all, until suddenly, like a flash, there rose upon him the clear, resolute, unchangeable determination, "I will go to England."

He started up at once, and seized his bundle and his alpenstock. The afternoon was far advanced, but there was time enough to reach the Engstlenalp, where he could stay the night, and go on in the morning to Meiringen. He could be in England in three days.

Three days: so short a time separated him from the country and the home from which he had been exiled so many years. Any day during those fourteen years he might have started homeward as he was doing now; but there had not been the irresistible hunger in his heart that at this moment drove him thither. He had been vainly seeking to satisfy himself with husks; but even these, dry and empty, and bitter as they were, had failed him. He had lost all; and having lost all, he was coming to himself.

There was not the slightest fear of detection in his mind. A gray-haired man with bowed shoulders, and seamed and marred face, who had lost every trace of the fastidiousness, which had verged upon foppery in the handsome and prosperous Roland Sefton, ran no risk of recognition, more especially as Roland Sefton had been reckoned among the dead and buried for many a long year. The lineaments of the dead die with them, however cunningly the artist may have used his skill to preserve them. The face is gone, and the memory of it. Some hearts may long to keep it engraven sharp and clear in their remembrance; but oh, when the "inward eye" comes to look for it how dull and blurred it lies there, like a forgotten photograph which has grown faded and stained in some seldom-visited cabinet!

Jean Merle travelled, as a man of his class would travel, in a third-class wagon and a slow train; but he kept on, stopping nowhere for rest, and advancing as rapidly as he could, until on the third day, in the gray of the evening, he saw the chalk-line of the English coast rising against the faint yellow light of the sunset; and as night fell his feet once more trod upon his native soil.

So far he had been simply yielding to his blind and irresistible longing to get back to England, and nearer to his unknown children. He had heard so little of them from Alice Pascal, that he could no longer rest without knowing more. How to carry out his intention he did not know, and he had hardly given it a thought. But now, as he strolled slowly along the flat and sandy shore for an hour or two, with the darkness hiding both sea and land from him, except the spot on which he stood, he began to consider what steps he must take to learn what he wanted to know, and to see their happiness afar off without in any way endangering it. He had purchased it at too heavy a price to be willing to place it in any peril now.

That Felicita had left Riversborough he had heard from her own lips, but there was no other place where he was sure of discovering her present abode, for London was too wide a city, even if she had carried out her intention of living there, for him to ascertain where she dwelt. Phebe Marlowe would certainly know where he could find them, for the English girl at Roland Sefton's grave had spoken of Phebe as familiarly as of Felix and Hilda—spoken of her, in fact, as if she was quite one of the family. There would be no danger in seeking out Phebe Marlowe. If his own mother could not have recognized her son in the rugged peasant he had become, there was no chance of a young girl such as Phebe had been ever thinking of Roland Sefton in connection with him; and he could learn all he wished to know from her.

He was careful to take the precaution of exchanging his foreign garb of a Swiss peasant for the dress of an English mechanic. The change did not make him look any more like his old self, for there was no longer any incongruity in his appearance. No soul on earth knew that he had not died many years ago, except Felicita. He might saunter down the streets of his native town in broad daylight on a market-day, and not a suspicion would cross any brain that here was their old townsman, Roland Sefton, the fraudulent banker.

Yet he timed his journey so as not to reach Riversborough before the evening of the next day; and it was growing dusk when he paced once more the familiar streets, slowly, and at every step gathering up some sharp reminiscence of the past. How little were they changed! The old grammar-school, with its gray walls and mullioned windows, looked exactly as it had done when he was yet a boy wearing his college-cap and carrying his satchel of school-books. His name, he knew, was painted in gold on a black tablet on the walls inside as a scholar who had gained a scholarship. Most of the shops on each side of the streets bore the same names and looked but little altered. In the churchyard the same grave-stones were standing as they stood when he, as a child, spelt out their inscriptions through the open railings which separated them from the causeway. There was a zigzag crack in one of the flag-stones, which was one of his earliest recollections; he stood and put his clumsy boot upon it as he had often placed his little foot in those childish years, and leaning his head against the railings of the churchyard, where all his English forefathers for many a generation were buried, he waited as if for some voice to speak to him.

Suddenly the bells in the dark tower above him rang out a peal, clanging and clashing noisily together as if to give him a welcome. They had rung so the day he brought Felicita home after their long wedding journey. It was Friday night, the night when the ringers had always been used to practise, in the days when he was churchwarden. The pain of hearing them was intolerable; he could bear no more that night. Not daring to go on and look at the house where he was born, and where his children had been born, but which he could never more enter, he sought out a quiet inn, and shut himself up in a garret there to think, and at last to sleep.

CHAPTER XII

A GLIMPSE INTO PARADISE

I cannot tell whether it was fancy merely, but the morning light which streamed into his room seemed more familiar and home-like to him than it had ever done in Switzerland. He was awakened by one of those sounds which dwell longest in the memory—the chiming of the church bells nearest home, which in childhood had so often called to him to shake off his slumbers, and which spoke to him now in sweet and friendly tones, as if he was still an innocent child. The tempest-tossed, sinful man lay listening to them for a minute or two, half asleep yet. He had been dreaming that he was in truth dead, but that the task assigned to him was that of an invisible guardian and defender to those who had lost him. He had been present all these years with his wife, and mother, and children, going out and coming in with them, hearing all their conversation, and sharing their family life, but himself unseen and unheard, felt only by the spiritual influence he could exercise over them. It had been a blissful dream, such as had never visited him in his exile; and as the familiar chiming of the bells, high up in the belfry not far from his attic, fell upon his ear, the dream for a brief moment gathered a stronger sense of reality.

It was with a strange feeling, as if he was himself a phantom mingling with creatures of flesh and blood, that he went out into the streets. His whole former life lay unrolled before him, but there was no point at which he could touch it. Every object and every spot was commonplace, yet invested with a singular and intense significance. Many a man among the townsfolk he knew by name and history, whose eyes glanced at him as a stranger, with no surprise at his appearance, and no show of suspicion or of welcome. Certainly he was nothing but a ghost revisiting the scenes of a life to which there was no possible return. Yet how he longed to stretch out his hand and grasp those of these old towns-people of his! Even the least interesting of the shopkeepers in the streets, bestirring themselves to meet the business of a new day, seemed to him one of the most desirable of companions.

His heart was drawing him to Whitefriars Road, to that spot on earth of all others most his own, but his resolution failed him whenever he turned his face that way. He rambled into the ancient market square, where stood a statue of his Felicita's great uncle, the first Baron Riversdale. The long shadow of it fell across him as he lingered to look in at a bookseller's window. He and the bookseller had been school-fellows together at the grammar-school, and their friendship had lasted after each was started in his own career. Hundreds of times he had crossed this door-sill to have a chat with the studious and quiet bookworm within whose modest life was so great a contrast with his own. Jean Merle stopped at the well-remembered shop-window.

His eyes glanced aimlessly along the crowded shelves, but suddenly his attention was arrested, and his pulses, which had been beating somewhat fast, throbbed with eager rapidity. A dozen volumes or more, ranged together, were labelled, "Works by Mrs. Roland Sefton." Surprise, and pride, and pleasure were in the rapid beatings of his heart. By Felicita! He read over the titles with a new sense of delight and admiration; and in the first glow of his astonishment he stepped quickly into the shop, with erect head and firm tread, and found himself face to face with his old school-fellow. The sight of his blank, unrecognizing gaze brought him back to the consciousness of the utter change in himself. He looked down at his coarse hands and mechanic's dress, and remembered that he was no longer Roland Sefton. His tongue was parched; it was difficult to stammer out a word.

"Do you want anything, my good man?" asked the bookseller quietly.

There was something in the words "my good man" that brought home to him at once the complete separation between his former life and the present, and the perfect security that existed for him in the conviction that Roland Sefton was dead. With a great effort he commanded himself, and answered the bookseller's question collectedly.

"There are some books in the window by Mrs. Roland Sefton," he said, "how much are they?"

"That is the six shilling edition," replied the bookseller.

Jean Merle was on the point of saying he would take them all, but he checked himself. He must possess them all, and read every line that Felicita had ever written, but not now, and not here.

"Which do you think is the best?" he asked.

"They are all good," was the answer; "we are very proud of Mrs. Roland Sefton, who belongs to Riversborough. That is her great uncle yonder, the first Lord Riversdale; and she married a prominent townsman, Roland Sefton, of the Old Bank. I have a soiled copy or two, which I could sell to you for half the price of the new ones."

"She is famous then?" said Jean Merle.

"She has won her rank as an author," replied the bookseller. "I knew her husband well, and he always foretold that she would make her mark; and she has. He died fourteen years ago; and, strange to say, there was something about your step as you came in which reminded me of him. Do you belong to Riversborough?"

"No," he answered; "but my name is Jean Merle, and I am related to Madame Sefton, his mother. I suppose there is some of the same blood in Roland Sefton and me."

"That is it," said the bookseller cordially. "I thought you were a foreigner, though you speak English so well."

"There was some mystery about Roland Sefton's death?" remarked Jean Merle.

"No, no; at least not much," was the answer. "He went away on a long holiday, unluckily without announcing it, on account of bank business; but Mr. Clifford, the senior partner, was on his way to take charge of affairs. There was but one day between Roland Sefton's departure and Mr. Clifford's arrival, but during that very day, for some reason or other unknown, the head clerk committed suicide, and there was a panic and a run upon the bank. Unfortunately there was no means of communicating with Sefton, who had started at once for the continent. Mr. Clifford did not see any necessity for his return, as the mischief was done; but just as his six months' absence was over—not all holiday, as folks said, for there was foreign business to see after—he died by accident in Switzerland. I knew the truth better than most people; for Mr. Clifford came here often, and dropped many a hint. Some persons still say the police were seeking for Roland; but that is not true. It was an unfortunate concatenation of circumstances."

"You knew him well?" said Jean Merle.

"Yes; we were school-fellows and friends," answered the bookseller, "and a finer fellow never breathed. He was always eager to get on, and to help other people on. We have not had such a public-spirited man amongst us since he died. It cuts me to the heart when anybody pretends that he absconded. Absconded! Why! there were dozens of us who would have made him welcome to every penny we could command. But I own appearances were against him, and he never came back to clear them up, and prove his innocence."

"And this is his wife's best book," said Jean Merle, holding it with shaking, nerveless hands. Felicita's book! The tears burned under his eyelids as he looked down on it.

"I won't say it is the best; it is my favorite," replied the bookseller. "Her son, Felix Sefton, a clergyman now, was in here yesterday, asking the same question. If you are related to Madame Sefton, you'll be very welcome at the Old Bank; and you'll find both of Madame's grand-children visiting old Mr. Clifford. I'll send one of my boys to show you the house."

"Not now," said Jean Merle. If Mr. Clifford was living yet he must be careful what risks he ran. Hatred has eyes as keen as love; and if any one could break through his secret it would be the implacable old man, who had still the power of sending him to a convict prison.

A shudder ran through him at the dread idea of detection. What would it be to Felicita now, when her name was famous, to have it dragged down to ignominy and utter disgrace? The dishonor would be a hundred-fold the greater for the fair reputation she had won, and the popularity she had secured. And her children too! Worse for them past all words would it be than if they were still little creatures, ignorant of the value of the world's opinion. He bade the bookseller good-morning, and threaded his way through many alleys and by-lanes of the old town until he reached a ferry and a boat-house, where many a boat lay ready for him, as they had always done when he was a boy. He seated himself in one of them, and taking the oars fell down with the current to the willows under the garden-wall of his old home.

He steered his boat aside into a small creek, where the willow-wands grew tall and thick, from which he could see the whole river frontage of the old house. Was there any change in it? His keen, despairing gaze could not detect one. The high tilted gables in the roof stood out clear against the sky, with their spiral wooden rods projecting above them. The oriel window cast its slowly moving shadow on the half-timber walls; and the many lattice casements, with their small diamond-shaped panes, glistened in the sun as in the days gone by. The garden-plots were unchanged, and the smooth turf on the terraces was as green and soft as when he ran along them at his mother's side. The old house brought to his mind his mother rather than his wife. It was full of associations and memories of her, with her sweet, humble, self-sacrificing nature. There was repose and healing in the very thought of her, which seemed to touch his anguish with a strong and soothing hand. Was there an echo of her voice still lingering for him about the old spot where he had listened to it so often? Could he hear her calling to him by his name, the name he had buried irrecoverably in a foreign grave? For the first time for many years he bent down his face upon his hands, and wept many tears; not bitter ones, full of grief as they were. His mother was dead; he had not wept for her till now.

Presently there came upon the summer silence the sound of a young, clear, laughing voice, calling "Phebe;" and he lifted up his head to look once more at the house. An old man, with silvery white hair was pacing slowly to and fro on the upper terrace, and a slight girlish figure was beside him. That was old Clifford, his enemy; but could that girl be Hilda? A face looked out of one of the windows, smiling down upon this young girl, which he knew again as Phebe Marlowe's. By and by she came down to the terrace, with a tall, fine-looking young man walking beside her; and all three, bidding farewell to the old man, descended from terrace to terrace, becoming every minute more distinct to his eyes. Yes, there was Phebe; and these others must be his girl Hilda and his son Felix. They were near to him, every word they spoke reached his ears, and penetrated to his heart. They seemed more beautiful, more perfect than any young creatures he had ever beheld. He listened to them unfastening the chain which secured the boat, and to the creaking of the row-locks as they fitted the oars into them. It was as if one of his own long-lost days was come back again to earth, when he had sat where Felix was now sitting, with Felicita instead of Hilda dipping her little white hand into the water. He had scarcely eyes for Phebe; but he was conscious that she was there, for Hilda was speaking to her in a low voice which just reached him. "See," she said, "that man has one of my mother's books! And he is quite a common man!"

"As much a common man, perhaps, as I am a common woman," answered Phebe, in a gentle though half-reproving tone.

As long as his eyes could see them they were fastened upon the receding boat; and long after, he gazed in the direction in which they had gone. He had had the passing glimpse he longed for into the Paradise he had forfeited. This had been his place, appointed to him by God, where he could have served God best, and served Him in as perfect gladness and freedom as the earth gives to any of her children. What lot could have been more blessed? The lines had fallen unto him in pleasant places; he had had a goodly heritage, and he had lost it through grasping dishonestly at a larger share of what this world called success. The madness and the folly of his sin smote him with unutterable bitterness.

He could bear to look at it no longer. The yearning he had felt to see his old home was satisfied; but the satisfaction seemed an increase of sorrow. He would not wait to witness the return of his children. The old man was gone into the house, and the garden was quiet and deserted. With weary strokes he rowed back again up the river; and with a heavier weight of sorrow and a keener consciousness of sin he made his way through the streets so familiar to his tread. It was as if no eye saw him, and no heart warmed to him in his native town. He was a stranger in a strange place; there was none to say to him, here or elsewhere on earth, "You are one of us."

CHAPTER XIII

A LONDON GARRET

There was one other place he must see before he went out again from this region of many memories, to which all that he could call life was linked—the little farmstead on the hills, which, of all places, had been his favorite haunt when a boy, and which had been the last spot he had visited before fleeing from England. Phebe Marlowe he had seen; if he went away at once he could see her home before her return to it. Next to his mother and his wife, he knew that Phebe was most likely to recognize him, if recognition by any one was possible. Most likely old Marlowe was dead; but if not, his senses would surely be too dull to detect him.

The long, hot, white highway, dusty with a week's drought, carried back his thoughts so fully to old times that he walked on unconscious of the noontide heat and the sultriness of the road. Yet when he came to the lanes, green overhead and underfoot, and as silent as the mountain-heights round Engelberg, he felt the solace of the change. All the recollections treasured up in the secret cells of memory were springing into light at every step; and these were remembrances less bitter than those the sight of his lost home had called to mind. He felt himself less of a phantom here, where no one met him or crossed his path, than in the streets where many faces looking blankly at him wore the well-known features of old comrades. By the time he gained the moorlands, and looked across its purple heather and yellow gorse, his mind was in a healthier mood than it had been for years. The low thatched roof of the small homestead, and the stunted and twisted trees surrounding it, seemed like a possible refuge to him, where for a little while he might find shelter from the storm of life. He pressed on with eagerness, and found himself quickly at the door, which he had never met with fastened.

But it was locked now. After knocking twice he tried the latch, but it did not open. He went to the little window, uncurtained as usual and peered in, but all was still and dark; there was not a glimmer of light on the hearth, where he had always seen some glimmering embers. There was no sign of life about the place; no dog barking, no sheep bleating, or fowls fluttering about the little farm-yard. All the innocent, joyous gayety of the place had vanished; yet he could see that it was not falling into decay; the thatch was in repair, the dark interior, dimly visible through the window, was as it used to be. It was not a ruin, but it was not a home. A home might have received him with its hospitable walls, or a ruin might have given him an hour's shelter. But Phebe's door was shut against him, though it would have done him good to stand within it once more, a penitent man.

He was turning away sadly, when a loud rustic voice called to him; and Simon Nixey, almost hidden under a huge load of dried ferns, came into sight. Jean Merle stepped down the stone causeway of the farm-yard to open the gate for him.

"What are you doing here?" he inquired suspiciously.

"A wood-carver, called old Marlowe, used to live here," he answered, "what has become of him?"

"Dead!" said Simon; "dead this many a year. Why, if you know anything you ought to know that."

"What did he die of?" asked Jean Merle.

"A broken heart, if ever man did," answered Simon; "he'd saved a mint o' money by scraping and moiling; and he lost it all when there was a run on the Old Bank over thirteen years ago. He couldn't talk about it like other folks, poor old Dummy! and it struck inwards, as you may say. It killed him as certain as if they'd shot a bullet into him."

Jean Merle staggered as if Simon had struck him a heavy blow. He had not thought of anything like this, old Marlowe dying broken-hearted, and Phebe left alone in the world. Simon Nixey seemed pleased at the impression his words had produced.

"Ay!" he said, "it was hard on old Marlowe; and drove my cousin, John Nixey, into desperate ways o' drinking. Not but all the money was paid up; only it was too late for them two. Every penny was paid, so as folks had nothing to say against the Old Bank. Only money won't bring a dead man back to life again. I offered Phebe to make her my wife before I knew it'ud be paid back; but she always said no, till I grew tired of it, and married somebody else."

"And where is she now?" inquired Jean Merle.

"Oh! she's quite the fine lady," answered Simon. "Mrs. Roland Sefton, Lord Riversdale's daughter that was, took quite a fancy to her, and had her to live with her in London; not as a servant, you know, but as a friend; and she paints pictures wonderful. My mother, who lives housekeeper with Mr. Clifford, hears say she can get sixty pounds or more for one likeness. Think of that now! If she'd been my wife what a fortune she'd have been to me!"

"Has she sold this place?" asked Jean Merle.

"There it is," he replied; "she gave her father a faithful promise never to part with it, or I'd have bought it myself. She comes here once a year with Miss Hilda and Mr. Felix, and they stay a week or two; and it's shut up all the rest of the time. I've got the key here if you'd like to look inside at old Dummy's carving."

How familiar, yet how different, the interior of the cottage seemed! He knew all these carvings, curious and beautiful, which lined the walls and decorated every article of the old oak furniture. But the hearth was cold, and there was no pleasant disorder about the small house telling its story of daily work. In the deep recess of the window-frame, where the western sun was already shining, stood old Marlowe's copy of a carved crucifix, which he had himself once brought from the Tyrol, and lent to him before finding a place for it in his own home. The sacred head was bowed down so low as to be almost hidden under the shadow of the crown of thorns. At the foot of the cross, in delicately small old English letters, the old man had carved the words, "Come unto me all ye that be weary and heavy laden, and I will give you rest." He remembered pointing out the mistake that he had made to old Marlowe.

"I like it best," said the dumb man; "I have often been weary, but not with labor; weary of myself, weary of the world, weary of life, weary of everything but my Phebe. That is what Christ says to me."

Jean Merle could see the old man's speaking face again, and the fingers moving less swiftly when spelling out the words to him, than when he was talking to Phebe. Weary! weary! was it not so with him? Could any man on earth be more weary than he was?

He loitered back to Riversborough through the cool of the evening, with the pale stars shining dimly in the twilight of the summer sky; pondering, brooding over what he had seen and heard that day. He had already done much of what he had come to England to do; but what next? What was the path he ought to take now? He was in a labyrinth, where there were many false openings leading no-whither; and he had no clue to guide him. All these years he had lain as one dead in the coil he had wound about himself, but now he was living again. There was agony in the life that he had entered into, but it was better than the apathy of his death in life.

He returned to London, and hired a garret for a small weekly rent, where he would lodge until he could resolve what to do. But week after week passed without bringing to his mind the solution of the problem. Remorse had given place to repentance; but despair had not been succeeded by hope. There was nothing to hope for. The irrevocable past stood between him and any reparation for his sin which his soul earnestly desired to make. An easy thing, and light, it would have been to put himself into the power of his enemy, Mr. Clifford, and bear the penalty of the law. He had suffered a hundred fold more than justice would have exacted. The broken law demanded satisfaction, and it would have been a blessed relief to him to give it. But that could never be. He could never bear the penalty of his crime without dragging Felicita into depths of shame and suffering deeper than they would have been if he had borne it at first. The fame she had won for herself would lift up his infamy and hers to the intolerable gaze of a keen and bitter publicity. He must blacken her fair reputation if he sought to appease his own conscience.

He made no effort to find out where she and his children were living. But one after another, in the solitude of his garret, he read every book Felicita had written. They gave him no pleasure, and awoke in him no admiration, for he read them through different eyes from her other readers. There was great bitterness of soul for him in many of the sentences she had penned; now and then he came upon some to which he alone held the true key. He felt that he, her husband, was dwelling in her mind as a type of subtle selfishness and weak ambition. When she depicted a good or noble character it was almost invariably a woman, not a man; it was never a man past his early manhood. However varied their circumstances and temperaments, they were in the main worldly and mean; sometimes they were successful hypocrites, deceiving those nearest and dearest to them.

It was a wholesome penance to him, perhaps, but it shook and troubled his soul to its very depths. His sin had ruined the poor weak-minded drunkard, John Nixey, and hastened the end of dumb old Marlowe; these consequences of it must, at any time, have clouded his own after-life. But it had also wrought a baneful change in the spirit of the woman whom he loved. It was he who had slain within her the hope, and the love, and the faith in her fellow-men which had been needed for the full perfecting of her genius.

CHAPTER XIV

HIS FATHER'S SIN

When Felix returned from his brief and clouded holiday to his work in that corner of the great vineyard, so overcrowded with busy husbandmen that they were always plucking up each others' plants, and pruning and repruning each others' vines, till they made a wilderness where there should have been a harvest, he found that his special plot there had suffered much damage. John Nixey, following up the impression he had so successfully made, had spread his story abroad, and found ears willing to listen to it, and hearts willing to believe it. The small Provident Club, instituted by Felix to check the waste and thriftlessness of the people, had already, in his short absence, elected another treasurer of its scanty funds; and the members who formed it, working men and women who had been gathered together by his personal influence, treated him with but scant civility. His evening lectures in the church mission-house were sometimes scarcely attended, whilst on other days there was an influx of hearers, among whom John Nixey was prominent, with half-a-dozen rough and turbulent fellows like himself, hangers-on at the nearest spirit-vaults, who were ready for any turn that might lead to a row. The women and children who had been accustomed to come stayed away, or went to some other of the numerous preaching-places, as though afraid of this boisterous element in his little congregation.

Now and then, too, he heard his name called out aloud in the streets by some of Nixey's friends, as he passed the prospering gin-palaces with their groups of loungers about the doors; but though he could catch the sound of the laugh and the sneer that followed him, he could take no notice. He could not turn round in righteous indignation and tell the fellows, and the listening bystanders, that what they said of his father was a lie. The poor young curate, with his high hopes and his enthusiastic love of the work he had chosen for the sake of his fellow-men, was compelled to pass on with bowed head, and silent lips, and a heart burdened with the conviction that his influence was altogether blighted and uprooted.

"It isn't true, sir, is it, what folks are tellin' about your father?" was a question put to him more than once, when he entered some squalid home, in the hope of giving counsel, or help, or comfort. There was something highly welcome and agreeable to these people, themselves thieves or bordering on thievedom, in the idea that this fine, handsome, gentlemanly young clergyman, who had set to work among them with so much energy and zeal, was the son of a dishonest rogue, who ought to have been sent to jail as many of them had been. Felix had not failed to make enemies in the Brickfields by his youthful intolerance of idleness, beggary, and drunkenness. The owners of the gin-palaces hated him, and not a few of the rival religious sects were, to say the least, uncharitably disposed towards one who had drawn so many of their followers to himself. There was very little common social interest in the population of the district, for the tramping classes of the lowest London poor, such as were drawn to the Brickfields by its overflowing charities, have as little cohesion as a rope of sand; but Felix was so conspicuous a figure in its narrow and dirty streets, that even strangers would nudge one another's elbows, and almost before he was gone by narrate Nixey's story, with curious additions and alterations.

It was gall and wormwood to Felix that he was unable to contradict the story in full. He could say that his father had never been a convict; but no inducement on earth could have wrung from him the declaration that his father had never been guilty of fraud. Sometimes he wondered whether it would not be well to own the simple truth, and endure the shame: if he had been the sole survivor of his father's sin this he would have done, and gone on toilsomely regaining the influence he had lost. But the secret touched his mother even more closely than himself, and Hilda was equally concerned in it. It had been sacredly kept by those older than he was, and it was not for him to betray it. "My poor mother!" he called her. Never, before he learned the secret burden she had borne, had he called her by that tender and pitiful epithet; but as often as he thought of her now his heart said, "My poor mother!"

As soon as Canon Pascal returned to England Felix took a day's holiday, and ran down by train to the quiet rectory in Essex, where he had spent the greater portion of his boyhood. Only a few years separated him from that careless and happiest period of his life; yet the last three months had driven it into the far background. He almost smiled at the recollection of how young he was half-a-year ago, when he had declared his love for Alice. How far dearer to him she was now than then! The one letter he had received from her, written in Switzerland, and telling him in loving detail of her visit to his father's grave, would be forever one of his most precious treasures. But he was not going to share his blemished name with her. He had had nothing worthy of her, or of his father, to lay at her feet, whilst he was yet in utter ignorance of the shame he had inherited; and now? He must never more think of her as his wife.

She was at home, he knew; but he sternly forbade himself to seek for her. It was Canon Pascal he had come down to see, and he went straight on to his well-known study. He was busy in the preparation of next Sunday's sermons, but at the sight of Felix's dejected, unsmiling face, he swept away his books and papers with one hand, whilst he stretched out his hand to give him such a warm, strong, hearty grip as he might have given to a drowning man.

"What is it, my son?" he asked.

There was such a full sympathetic tone in the friendly voice speaking to him, that Felix felt his burden already shared, and pressing less heavily on his bruised spirit. He stood a little behind Canon Pascal, with his hand upon his shoulder, as he had often placed himself before when he was pleading for some boyish indulgence, or begging pardon for some boyish fault.

"You have been like a true father to me, and I come to tell you a great trouble," he began in a tremulous voice.

"I know it, my boy," replied Canon Pascal; "you have found out how true it is, 'The fathers have eaten sour grapes, and the children's teeth are set on edge.' Ah! Felix, life teaches us so, as well as this wise old Book."

"You know it?" stammered Felix.

"Phebe told me," he interrupted, "six months since. And now you and I can understand Felicita. There was no prejudice against our Alice in her mind; no unkindness to either of you. But she could not bring herself to say the truth against the husband whom she has wept and mourned over so long. And your mother is the soul of truth and honor; she could not let you marry whilst we were ignorant of this matter. It has been a terrible cross to bear, and she has borne it in silence. I love and revere your mother more than ever."

"Yes!" said Felix with a sob. He had not yet seen her since coming to this fateful knowledge; for Phebe and Hilda had joined her at the sea-side where they were still staying. But if his father had gone down into depths of darkness, his mother had risen so much the higher in his reverence and love. She had become a saint and a martyr in his eyes; and to save her from a moment's grief seemed to be a cause worth dying for.

"I came to tell you all," he went on, "and to say I cannot any more hope that you will give Alice to me. God alone knows what it costs me to give her up: and she will suffer too for a while, a long while, I fear; for we have grown together so. But it must be. Alice cannot marry a man who has not even an unblemished name to offer to her."

"You should ask Alice herself about that," said Canon Pascal quietly.

A thrill of rapture ran through Felix, and he grasped the shoulder, on which his hand still rested, more firmly. What! was it possible that this second father of his knew all his disgrace and dishonor, how his teeth were set on edge by the sour grapes which he had not eaten, and yet was willing that Alice should share his name and his lot? There was no fear as to what Alice would say. He recollected how Phebe spoke, as if her thoughts dwelt more on his father's sorrow and sad death, than on his sin; and Alice would be the same. She would cover it with a woman's sweet charity. He could not command his voice to speak; and after a minute's pause Canon Pascal continued—

"Yes! Alice, too, knows all about it. I told her beside your father's grave. And do you suppose she said, 'Here is cause enough for me to break with Felix'? Nay, I believe if the sin had been your own, Alice would have said it was her duty to share it, and your repentance. Shall our Lord come to save sinners, and we turn away from their blameless children? Yet I thought it must be so at first, I own it, Felix; at first, while my eyes were blinded and my heart hardened; and I looked at it in the light of the world. But then I be-thought me of your mother. Shall not she make good to you the evil your father has wrought? If he dishonored your name in the eyes of a few, she has brought honor to it, and made it known far beyond the limits it could have been known through him. The world will regard you as her son, not as his."

"But I came also to tell you that I wish to leave the country," said Felix. "There is a difficulty in getting young men for our colonial work; and I am young and strong, stronger than most young men in the Church. I could endure hardships, and go in for work that feebler men must leave untried; you have taken care of that for me. Such a life would be more like old Felix Merle's than a London curacy. You let your own sons emigrate, believing that the old country is getting over-populated; and I thought I would go too."

"Why?" asked Canon Pascal, turning round in his chair, and looking up searchingly into his face.

In a few words, and in short broken sentences, Felix told him of Nixey's charge, and the change it had wrought in the London curacy, upon which he had entered with so much enthusiasm and delight.

"It will be the same wherever I go in England," he said in conclusion; "and I cannot face them boldly and say it is all a falsehood."

"You must live it down," answered Canon Pascal; "go on, and take no notice of it."

"But it hinders my work sadly," said Felix, "and I cannot go on in the Brickfields. There might be a row any evening, and then the story would come out in the police-courts; and what could I say? At least, I must give up that."

For a few minutes Canon Pascal was lost in thought. If Felix was right in his apprehension, and the whole story came out in the police-court, there were journals pandering to public curiosity that would gladly lay hold of any gossip or scandal connected with Mrs. Roland Sefton. Her name would ensure its publicity. And how could Felicita endure that, especially now that her health was affected? If the dread of disclosing her secret to him had wrought so powerfully upon her physical and mental constitution, what would she suffer if it became a nine days' talk for the world?

"I will get your rector to exchange curates with me till we can see our way clear," he said. "He is Alice's godfather, you know, and will do it willingly. I am going up to Westminster in November, and you will be here in my place, where everybody knows your face and you know theirs. There will be no question here about your father, for you are looked upon as my son. Now go away, and find Alice."

When Felix turned out of Liverpool Street station that evening, a tall, gaunt-looking workman man offered to carry his bag for him. It was filled with choice fruit from the rectory garden, grown on trees grafted and pruned by Canon Pascal's own hands; and Felix had helped Alice to gather it for some of his sick parishioners in the unwholesome dwelling-places he visited.

"I am going no farther than the Mansion House," he answered, "and I can carry it myself."

"You'd do me a kindness if you'd let me carry it," said the man.

It was not the tone of a common loafer, hanging about the station for any chance job, and Felix turned to look at him in the light of the street-lamp. It was the old story, he thought to himself, a decent mechanic from the country, out of work, and lost in this great labyrinth of a city. He handed his bag to him and walked on along the crowded thoroughfare, soon forgetting that he was treading the flagged streets of a city; he was back again, strolling through dewy fields in the cool twilight, with Alice beside him, accompanying him to the quiet little station. He thought no more of the stranger behind him, or of the bag he carried, until he hailed an omnibus travelling westward.

"Here is your bag, sir," said the man.

"Ah! I'd forgotten it," exclaimed Felix. "Good night, and thank you."

He had just time to drop a shilling into his hand before the omnibus was off. But the man stood there in front of the Mansion House, motionless, with all the busy sea of life roaring around him, hearing nothing and seeing nothing. This coin that lay in his hand had been given to him by his son; his son's voice was still sounding in his ears. He had walked behind him taking note of his firm strong step, his upright carriage and manly bearing. It had been too swift a march for him, full of exquisite pain and pleasure, which chance might never offer to him again.

"Move on, will you?" said a policeman authoritatively; and Jean Merle, rousing himself from his reverie, went back to his lonely garret.

CHAPTER XV

HAUNTING MEMORIES

Felicita was slowly recovering her strength at the sea-side. She had never before felt so seriously shaken in health, as since she had known of the attachment of Felix to Alice Pascal; an attachment which would have been quite to her mind, if there was no loss of honor in allowing it whilst she held a secret which, in all probability, would seem an insuperable barrier in the eyes of Canon Pascal.

This secret she had kept resolutely in the background of her own memory, conscious of its existence, but never turning her eyes towards it. The fact that it was absolutely a secret, suspected by no one, made this more possible; for there was no gleam of cognizance in any eye meeting hers which could awaken even a momentary recollection of it. It seemed so certain that her husband was dead to every one but herself, that she came at last almost to believe that it was true.

And was it not most likely to be true? Through all these long years there had come no hint to her in any way that he was living. She had never seen or heard of any man lingering about her home where she and her children lived, all whom Roland loved, and loved so passionately. Certainly she had made no effort to discover whether he was yet alive; but though it would be well for her if he was dead—a cause of rest almost amounting to satisfaction—it was not likely that he would remain content with unbroken and complete ignorance of how she and her children were faring. If he had been living, surely he would have given her some sign.

There was a terrible duty now lying in her path. Before she could give her consent to Felix marrying Alice, she must ascertain positively if her husband was dead. Should it be so, her secret was safe, and would die with her. Nobody need ever know of this fraud, so successfully carried out. But if not? Then she knew in herself that her lips could never confess the sin in which she had shared; and nothing would remain for her to do but to oppose with all the energy and persistence possible the marriage either of her son or daughter. And she fully believed that neither of them would marry against her will.

Her health had not permitted her hitherto to make the exertion necessary for ascertaining this fact, on which her whole future depended—hers and her children's. The physician whom she had consulted in London had urged upon her the imperative necessity of avoiding all excitement and fatigue, and had ordered her down to this dull little village of Freshwater, where not even a brass band on the unfinished pier or the arrival of an excursion steamer could disturb or agitate her. She had nothing to do but to sit on the quiet downs, where no sound could startle her, and no spectacle flutter her, until the sea-breezes had brought back her usual tone of health.

How long this promised restoration was in coming! Phebe, who watched for it anxiously, saw but little sign of it. Felicita was more silent than ever, more withdrawn into herself, gazing for hours upon the changeful surface of the sea with absent eyes, through which the brain was not looking out. Neither sound nor sight reached the absorbed soul, that was wandering through some intricate mazes to which Phebe had no clue. But no color came to Felicita's pale face, and no light into her dim eyes. There was a painful and weird feeling often in Phebe's heart that Felicita herself was not there; only the fair, frail form, which was as insensible as a corpse, until this spirit came back to it. At such times Phebe was impelled to touch her, and speak to her, and call her back again, though it might be to irritability and displeasure.

"Phebe," said Felicita, one day when they sat on the cliff, so near the edge that nothing but the sea lay within the range of their sight, "how should you feel if, instead of helping a fellow-creature to save himself from drowning, you had thrust him back into the water, and left him, sure that he would perish?"

"But I cannot tell you how I should feel," answered Phebe, "because I could never do it. It makes me shudder to think of such a thing. No human being could do it."

"But if you had thrust the one fellow-creature nearest to you, the one who loved you the most," pursued Felicita, "into sin, down into a deeper gulf than he could have fallen into but for you—"

"My dear, my dear!" cried Phebe, interrupting her in a tone of the tenderest pity. "Oh! I know now what is preying upon you. Because Felix loves Alice it has brought back all the sorrowful past to you, and you are letting it kill you. Listen! Let me speak this once, and then I will never speak again, if you wish it. Canon Pascal knows it all; I told him. And Felix knows it, and he loves you more than ever; you are dearer to him a hundred times than you were before. And he forgives his father—fully. God has cast his sin as a stone into the depths of the sea, to be remembered against him no more forever!"

A slight flush crept over Felicita's pale face. It was a relief to her to learn that Canon Pascal and Felix knew so much of the truth. The darker secret must be hidden still in the depths of her heart until she found out whether she was altogether free from the chance of discovery.

"It was right they should know," she said in a low and dreamy tone; "and Canon Pascal makes no difficulty of it?"

"Canon Pascal said to me," answered Phebe, "that your noble life and the fame you had won atoned for the error of which Felix and Hilda's father had been guilty. He said they were your children, brought up under your training and example, not their father's. Why do you dwell so bitterly upon the past? It is all forgotten now."

"Not by me," murmured Felicita, "nor by you, Phebe."

"No; I have never forgotten him," cried Phebe, with a passionate sorrow in her voice. "How good he was to me, and to all about him! Yes, he was guilty of a sin before God and against man; I know it. But oh! if he had only suffered the penalty, and come back to us again, for us to comfort him, and to help him to live down the shame! Possibly we could not have done it in Riversborough; I do not know; but I would have gone with you, as your servant, to the ends of the earth, and you would have lived happy days again—happier than the former days. And he would have proved himself a good man, in spite of his sin; a Christian man, whom Christ would not have been ashamed to own."

"No, no," said Felicita; "that is impossible. I never loved Roland; can you believe that, Phebe?"

"Yes," she answered in a whisper, and with downcast eyes.

"Not as I think of love," continued Felicita in a dreary voice. "I have tried to love you all; but you seem so far away from me, as if I could never touch you. Even Felix and Hilda, they are like phantom children, who do not warm my heart, or gladden it, as other mothers are made happy by their children. Sometimes I have dreamed of what life would have been if I had given myself to some man for whom I would have forfeited the world, and counted the loss as nothing. But that is past now, and I feel old. There is nothing more before me; all is gray and flat and cold, a desolate monotony of years, till death comes."

"You make me unhappy," said Phebe. "Ought we not to love God first, and man for God's sake? There is no passion in that; but there is inexhaustible faithfulness and tenderness."

"How far away from me you are!" answered Felicita with a faint smile.

She turned her sad face again towards the sea, and sat silent, watching the flitting sails pass by, but holding Phebe's hand fast in her own, as if she craved her companionship. Phebe, too, was silent, the tears dimming her blue eyes and blotting out the scene before her. Her heart was very heavy and troubled for Felicita.

"Will you go to Engelberg with me by-and-by?" asked Felicita suddenly, but in a calm and tranquil tone.

"To Engelberg!" echoed Phebe.

"I must go there before Felix thinks of marrying," she answered in short and broken sentences; "but it cannot be till spring. Yet I cannot write again until I have been there; the thought of it haunts me intolerably. Sometimes, nay, often, the word Engelberg has slipped from my pen unawares when I have tried to write; so I shall do no more work till I have fulfilled this duty; but I will rest another few months. When I have been to Engelberg again, for the last time, I shall be not happy, but less miserable."

"I will go with you wherever you wish," said Phebe.

It was so great a relief to have said this much to Phebe, to have broken through so much of the icy reserve which froze her heart, that Felicita's spirits at once grew more cheerful. The dreaded words had been uttered, and the plan was settled; though its fulfilment was postponed till spring; a reprieve to Felicita. She regained health and strength rapidly, and returned to London so far recovered that her physician gave her permission to return to work.

But she did not wish to take up her work again. It had long ago lost the charm of novelty to her, and though circumstances had compelled her to write, or to live upon her marriage settlement, which in her eyes was to live upon the proceeds of a sin successfully carried out, her writing itself had become tedious to her. "Vanity of vanities; all is vanity!" and there is much vexation of spirit, as well as weariness of the flesh, in the making of many books. She had made enemies who were spiteful, and friends who were exacting; she, who felt equally the irksomeness of petty enmities and of small friendships, which, like gnats buzzing monotonously about her, were now and then ready to sting. The sting itself might be trivial, but it was irritating.

Felicita had soon found out how limited is the circle of fame for even a successful writer. For one person who would read a book, there were fifty who would go to hear a famous singer or actor, and a hundred who would crowd to see a clever acrobat. As she read more she discovered that what she had fondly imagined were ideas originated by her own intellect, was, in reality, the echo only of thought long since given to mankind by other minds, in other words, often better than her own. Her own silent claim to genius was greatly modified; she was humbler than she had been. But she knew painfully that her name was now a hundred-fold better known than it had been while she was yet only the wife of a Riversborough banker. All her work for the last fourteen years had placed it more and more prominently before the public. Any scandal attaching to it now would be blazoned farther and wider, in deeper and more enduring characters, than if her life as an author had been a failure.

The subtle hope, very real, vague as it was, that her husband was in truth dead, gathered strength. The silence that had engulfed him had been so profound that it seemed impossible he should still be treading the same earth as herself, and wearing through its slow and commonplace days, sleeping and waking, eating and drinking like other men. Felicita was not superstitious, but there was in her that deep-rooted, instinctive sense of mystery in this double life of ours, dividing our time into sleeping and waking hours, which is often apt to make our dreams themselves omens of importance. She had never dreamed of Roland as she did of those belonging to her who had already passed into the invisible world about us. His spirit was not free, perhaps, from its earthly fetters so as to be able to visit her, and haunt her sleeping fancies. But now she began to dream of him frequently, and often in the daytime flashes of memory darted vividly across her brain, lighting up the dark forgotten past, and recalling to her some word of his, or a glance merely. It was an inward persecution from which she could not escape, but it seemed to her to indicate that her persecutor was no more a denizen of this world.

To get rid of these haunting memories as much as possible, she made such a change in her mode of life as astonished all about her. She no longer shut herself up in her library; as she had told Phebe, she resolved to write no more, nor attempt to write, until she had been to Engelberg. She seemed wishful to attract friends to her, and she renewed old acquaintanceships with members of her own family which she had allowed to drop during these many years. No sooner was it evident that Felicita Sefton was willing to come out of the extremely quiet and solitary life she had led hitherto, and take her place in society both as Lord Riversdale's daughter and as the author of many popular books, than the current of fashion set towards her. She was still a remarkably lovely woman, possessing irresistible attractions in her refined face and soft yet distant manners, as of one walking in a trance, and seeing and hearing things invisible and inaudible to less favored mortals. Quite unconsciously to herself she became the lion of the season, when the next season opened. She had been so difficult to know, that as soon as she was willing to be known invitations poured in upon her, and her house was invaded by a throng of visitors, many of them more or less distantly related to her.

To Hilda this new life was one of unexpected and exquisite delight. Phebe, also, with her genuine interest in her fellow-creatures, and her warm sympathy in all human joys and sorrows, enjoyed the change, though it perplexed her, and caused her to watch Felicita with anxiety. Felix saw less of it than any one, for he was down in Essex, leading the tranquil and not very laborious life of a country curate, chafing a little now and then at his inactivity, yet blissful beyond words in the close daily intercourse with Alice. There was no talk of their marriage, but they were young and together. Their happiness was untroubled.

CHAPTER XVI

THE VOICE OF THE DEAD

In his lonely garret in the East End, Jean Merle was living in an isolation more complete even than that of Engelberg. There he had known at least the names of those about him, and their faces had grown familiar to him. More than once he had been asked to help when help was sorely needed, and he had felt, though not quite consciously, that there was still a link or two binding him to his fellow-men. But here, an unit among millions, who hustled him at every step, breathed the same air, and shared the common light with him, he was utterly alone. "Isolation is the sum total of wretchedness to man," and no man could be more completely isolated than he.

Strangely enough, his Swiss proclivities seemed to have fallen from him like a worn-out garment. The narrow, humble existence of his peasant forefathers, to which he had so readily adapted himself, was no longer tolerable in his eyes. He felt all the force and energy of the life of the great city which surrounded him. His birthright as an Englishman presented itself to his imagination with a splendor and importance that it had never possessed before, even in those palmy days when it was no unthought-of honor that he might some day take his place in the House of Commons. He called himself Jean Merle, for no other name belonged to him; but he felt himself to be an Englishman again, to whom the life of a Swiss peasant would be a purgatory.

Other natural instincts were asserting themselves. He had been a man of genial, social habits, glad to gather round him smiling faces and friendly voices; and this bias of his was stirring into life and shaking off its long stupor. He longed, with intense longing, for some mortal ear into which he could pour the story of his sins and sufferings, and for some human tongue to utter friendly words of counsel to him. It was not enough to pour out his confessions before God in agonizing prayer; that he had done, and was doing daily. But it was not all. The natural yearning for man's forgiveness, spoken in living human speech, grew stronger within him. There was no longer a chance for him to make even a partial reparation of the wrong he had committed; he felt himself without courage to begin the long conflict again. What his soul hungered for now was to see his life through another man's eyes.

But his money, economize it as he might, was slowly melting away. Unless he could get work—and all his efforts to find it failed—it would not do to remain in England. At Engelberg had secured a position as a wood carver, and his livelihood was assured. There, too, he possessed a scanty knowledge of the neighbors, and they of him. It would be his wisest course to return there, to forget what he had been, and to draw nearer to him the simple and ignorant people, who might yet be won over to regard him with good-will. This must be done before he found himself penniless as well as friendless. He set aside a certain sum, when that was spent he must once more be an exile.

Until then, it was his life to pace to and fro along the streets of London. Somewhere in this vast labyrinth there was a home to which he had a right; a hearth where he could plant himself and claim it for his own. He was master of it, and of a wife, and children; he, the lonely, almost penniless man. It would be a small thing to him to pay the penalty the law could demand of him. A few years more or less in Dartmoor Prison would be nothing to him, if at the end of them he saw a home waiting for him to return to it. But he never sought to look at the exterior even of that spot to which he had a right. He made no effort to see Felicita.

He stayed till he touched his last shilling. It was already winter, and the short, dark days, with their thick fogs, made the wintry months little better than one long night. To-morrow he must leave England, never to return to it. He strayed aimlessly about the gloomy streets, letting his feet bear him whither they would, until he found himself looking down through the iron railings upon the deserted yard in front of the Houses of Parliament. The dark mass of the building loomed heavily through the yellow fog, but beyond it came the sound of bells ringing in the invisible Abbey. It was the hour for morning prayer, and Jean Merle sauntered listlessly onwards until he reached the northern entrance and turned into the transept. The dim daylight scarcely lit up the lofty arches in the roof or the farther end of the long aisles, but he gave no heed to either. He sank down on a chair and bent his gray head on the back of the chair before him; the sweet solemn chanting of the white-robed choristers echoed under the roof, and the sacred and soothing tones of prayer floated pest him. But he did not move or lift his head. He sat there absorbed in his own thoughts, and the hours seemed only as floating minutes to him. Visitors came and went, chatting close beside him, and the vergers, with their quiet footsteps, came one by one to look at this motionless, poverty-stricken form, whose face no man could see, but nobody disturbed him. He had a right to be there, as still, and as solitary, and as silent as he pleased.

But when Canon Pascal came up the long aisle to evening prayers and saw again the same gray head bowed down in the same despondent attitude as he had left it in the morning, he could scarcely refrain himself from pausing then and there, before the evening service proceeded, to speak to this man. He had caught a momentary glimpse of his face, and it had haunted him in his study in the interval, until he had half reproached himself for not answering to that silent appeal its wretchedness had made. But he had had no expectation of seeing it again.

It was dark by the time the evening service was over, and Canon Pascal hastily divested himself of his surplice, that he might not seem to approach the stranger as a clergyman, but rather as an equal. The Abbey was being cleared of its visitors, and the lights were being put out one by one, when he sat down on the seat next to Jean Merle's, and laid his hand with a gentle pressure on his arm. Jean Merle started and lifted up his head. It was too dark for them to see each other well; but Canon Pascal's voice was full of friendly urgency.

"They are going to close the Abbey," he said; "and you've been here all day, without food, my friend. Is there any special reason why you should pass a long, dark winter's day in such a manner? I would be glad to serve you if I can. Perhaps you are a stranger in London?"

"I have been seeking the guidance of God," answered Jean Merle, in a bewildered yet unutterably sorrowful voice.

"That is good," replied Canon Pascal; "that is the best. But it is good also at times to seek man's guidance. It is God, doubtless, who has sent me to you. As His servant, I earnestly desire to serve you."

"If you would listen to me under a solemn seal of secrecy!" cried Jean Merle.

"Are you a Catholic?" asked Canon Pascal. "Is it a confessor you want?"

"I am not a Catholic," he answered; "but there is a strong desire in my soul to confess. My burden would be lighter if any man would share it, so far as to keep my secret."

"Does it touch the life of any fellow-creature?" inquired Canon Pascal; "is there any great crime in it?"

"No; not what you are thinking," he said; "there is sin in it; ay, and crime; but not a crime like that."

"Then I will listen to it under a solemn promise of secrecy, whatever it may be," replied Canon Pascal. "But the vergers are waiting to close the Abbey. Come with me; my home is close by, within the precincts."

Jean Merle had risen obediently as he spoke, but, exhausted and weary, he staggered as he stood upon his feet. Canon Pascal drew his arm within his own. This simple action was to him full of a friendliness to which he had been long a stranger. To clasp another man's hand, to walk arm-in-arm with him, he felt keenly how much of implied brotherhood was in them. He was ready to go anywhere with Canon Pascal, almost as a child guided and cared for by an older and wiser brother.

They passed out of the Abbey into the cloisters, dimly lighted by the lamps, which had been lit in good time this dark November evening. The low, black-browed arches, which had echoed to the footsteps of sorrow-stricken men for more than eight hundred years, resounded to their tread as they walked beneath them in silence. Jean Merle suffered himself to be led without a question, like one in a dream. There seemed some faint reminiscence from the past of this man, with his harsh features, and kindly, genial expression, the deep-set eyes, beaming with a benign light from under the rugged eyebrows, and the firm yet friendly pressure of his guiding arm; and his mind was groping about the dark labyrinth of memory to seize his former knowledge of him, if there had ever been any. There was a vague apprehension about him lest he should discover that this friend was no stranger, and his tongue must be tied, even though what he was about to say would be under the inviolable seal of secrecy.

They had not far to go, for Canon Pascal turned aside into a little square, open to the black November sky, and stopping at a door in the gray, old walls, opened it with a latch-key. They entered a narrow passage, and Canon Pascal turned at once to his study, which was close by. As he pushed open the door, he said, "Go in, my friend; I will be with you in a moment."

Jean Merle saw before him an old-fashioned room with a low ceiling. There was no light besides the warm, red glow of a fire, which was no longer burning with yellow flame, but which lit up sufficiently the figure of a woman seated on a low stool on the hearth, with her head resting on the hand that shaded her eyes. It was a figure familiar to him in his old life—that life which lay on the other side of Roland Sefton's grave. He had seen the same well-shaped head, with its soft brown hair, and the round outline of the averted cheek and chin, a thousand times in old Marlowe's cottage on the uplands, sitting in the red firelight as she was sitting now. All the intervening years were swept away in an instant—his bitter anguish and unavailing repentance—the long solitude and gnawing remorse—all was swept clean away from his mind. He felt the strength and freshness of his boyhood come back to him, as if the breeze of the uplands was blowing softly yet keenly across his throbbing and fevered temples. Even his voice caught back for the moment the ring of his early youth as he stood on the threshold, forgetting all else but the sight that filled his eyes. "Phebe!" he cried; "little Phebe Marlowe!"

The cry startled Phebe, but she did not move. It was the voice of one long since dead that rang in her ears—dead, and faithfully mourned over; and every nerve tingled, and her heart seemed to stay its beating. Roland Sefton's voice! She did not doubt it or mistake it. The call had been too real. She had answered to it too many times to be mistaken now. In those days of utter silence, when dumb signs only had passed between her and her father, Roland's pleasant voice had sounded too gladly in her ears ever to be forgotten or confounded with another. But how could she hear it now? The voice of the dead! how could it reach her? A strange pang of mingled joy and terror paralyzed her. She sat motionless and bewildered, with a thrill of passionate expectation quivering through her. Let Roland speak again; she could not answer his first call!

"Phebe!" She heard the cry again; but this time the voice was low, and lamentable, and despairing. For in the few seconds he had been standing, arrested on the threshold, the whole past had flitted through his brain in dismal procession. She lifted herself up slowly and mechanically from her low seat, and turned her face reluctantly towards the spot from which the startling call had come. In the dusky, red light stood the form of the one friend to whom she had been faithful with the utter faithfulness of her nature. Whence he came she knew not—she was afraid of knowing. But he was there, himself, and not another like him. There was a change, she could see that dimly; but not such a change as could disguise him from her. Of late, whilst she had been painting his portrait from memory, every recollection of him had been revived with keener vividness. Yet the terror of beholding him again on this side of death struck her dumb. She stretched out her hands towards him, but she could not speak.

"I must speak to Phebe Marlowe alone," said Jean Merle to Canon Pascal, and speaking in a tone of irresistible earnestness. "I have that to say to her which no one else can hear. She is God's messenger to me."

"Shall I leave you with this stranger, Phebe?" asked Canon Pascal.

She made a gesture simply; her lips were too parched to open.

"My dear girl, I will stay, if you please," he said again.

"No," she breathed, in a voice scarcely audible.

"There is a bell close at your hand," he went on, "and I shall be within hearing of it. I will come myself if you ring it however faintly. You know this man?"

"Yes," she answered.

She saw him look across at her with an encouraging smile; and then the door was shut, and she was alone with her mysterious visitor.

CHAPTER XVII

NO PLACE FOR REPENTANCE

They stood silent for a few moments;—moments which seemed hours to Phebe. The stranger—for who could be so great a stranger as one who had been many years dead?—had advanced only a step or two from the threshold, and paused as if some invisible barrier was set up between them. She had shrunk back, and stood leaning against the wall for the support her trembling limbs needed. It was with a vehement effort that at last she spoke.

"Roland Sefton!" she faltered.

"Yes!" he answered, "I am that most miserable man."

"But you died," she said with quivering lips, "fourteen years ago."

"No, Phebe, no," he replied; "would to God I had died then."

Once more an agony of mingled fear and joy overwhelmed her. This dear voice, so lamentable and hopeless, so well remembered in all its tones, told her that he was still living, whom she had mourned over so many years. But what could this mystery mean? What had he passed through? What was about to happen now? A tumult of thoughts thronged to her brain. But clearest of all came the assurance that he was alive, standing there, desolate, changed, and friendless. She ran to him and clasped his hands in hers; stooping down and kissing them, those hard worn hands, which he left unresistingly in her grasp. These loving, and deferential caresses belonged to the time when she was a humble country girl, and he the friend very far above her.

"Come closer to the fire, your hands are cold, Mr. Roland," she said, speaking in the old long-disused accent of her early days, as she might have spoken to him while she was yet a child. She threw a few logs on the fire, and drew up Canon Pascal's chair to the hearth for him. She felt spell-bound; and as if she had been suddenly thrust back upon those old times.

"I am no longer Roland Sefton," he said, sinking down into the chair; "he died, as you say, many a long year ago. Do not light the lamp, Phebe; let us talk by the firelight."

The flicker of the flames creeping round the dry wood played upon his face, and her eyes were fastened on it. Could this man really be Roland Sefton, or was she being tricked by her fancy? Here was a scarred and wrinkled face, blistered and burnt by the summer's sun, and cut and frost-bitten by the winter's cold; the hair was gray and ragged, and the eyes far sunk in the head met her gaze with a despairing and uneasy glance, as if he shrank from her close scrutiny. His bowed shoulders and hands roughened by toil, and worn-out mechanic's dress, were such a change, that perhaps, she acknowledged it reluctantly to herself, if he had not spoken as he did she might have passed him by undiscovered.

"I am Jean Merle," he said, "not Roland Sefton."

"Jean Merle?" she repeated in a low, bewildered tone, "not Roland Sefton, but Jean Merle?"

But she could not be bewildered or in doubt much longer. This was Roland indeed, the hero of her life, come back to her a broken-down, desolate, and hopeless man. She knelt down on the hearth beside him, and laid her hand compassionately on his.

"But you are Roland himself to me!" she cried. "Oh! be quick, and tell me all about it. Why did we ever think you were dead?"

"It was best for them all," he answered. "God knows I believed it was best. But it was a second sin, worse than the first, Phebe. I did the man who died no wrong, for he told me as he lay dying that he had no friends to grieve for him, and no property to leave. All he wanted was a decent grave; and he has it, and my name with it. The grave at Engelberg contains a stranger. And I, Jean Merle, have taken charge of it."

"Oh!" cried Phebe, with a pang of dread, "how will Felicita bear it?"

"Felicita has known it; she consented to it," said Jean Merle. "If she had uttered one word against my desperate plan, I should have recoiled from it. To be dead whilst you are yet in the body; to have eyes to see and ears to hear with, and a thinking brain and a hungry heart, whilst there is no sign, or sound, or memory, or love from your former life; you cannot conceive what that is, Phebe. I was dead, yet I was too keenly alive in Jean Merle, the poor wood-carver and miser. They thought I was imbecile; and I was almost a madman. I could not tear myself away from the grave where Roland Sefton was buried; but oh! what I have suffered!"

He ended with a long shuddering sigh, which pierced Phebe to the heart. The joy of seeing him again was vanishing in the sight of his suffering; but the thought uppermost in her mind was of Felicita.

"And she has known all along that you were not dead?" she said, in a tone of awe.

"Yes, Felicita knew," he answered.

"And has she never seen you, never written to you?" she asked.

"She knows nothing of me," he replied. "I was to be dead to her, and to every one else. We parted forever in Engelberg fourteen years ago this very month. Perhaps she believes me to be dead in reality. But I could live no longer without knowing something of you all, of Felix and Hilda; and I came over to England in August. I have seen all of you, except Felicita."

"Oh! it was wicked! it was cruel!" sobbed Phebe, shivering. "Your mother died, believing she was going to rejoin you; and I, oh! how I have mourned for you!"

"Have you, Phebe?" he said sorrowfully; "but Felicita has been saved from shame, and has been successful. She is too famous now for me to retrace my steps, and get back into truthfulness. I can find no place for repentance, let me seek it ever so carefully and with tears."

"But you have repented?" she whispered.

"Before God? yes!" he answered, "and I believe He has forgiven me. But there is no way by which I can retrieve the past. I have forfeited everything, and I am now shut out even from the duties of life. What ought I to have done, Phebe? There was this way to save my mother, and my children, and Felicita; and I took it. It has prospered for all of them; they hold a different position in the world this day than they could have done if I had lived."

"In this world, yes!" answered Phebe, with a touch of scorn in her voice; "but cannot you see what you have done for Felicita? Oh! it would have been better for her to have endured the shame of your first sin, than bear such a burden of guilt. And you might have outlived the disgrace. There are Christian people in the world who can forgive sin, even as Christ forgives it. Even my poor father forgave it; and Mr. Clifford, he is repenting now that he did not forgive you; it weighs him down in his old age. It would have been better for you and Felicita if you had borne the penalty of your crime."

"And our children, Phebe?" he said.

"Could not God have made it up to them?" she asked. "Did He make it necessary for you to sin again on their account? Oh! if you had only trusted Him! If you had only waited to see how Christ could turn even the sins of the father into blessings for his children! They have missed you; it may be, I cannot see clearly, they must miss you now all their lives. It would break their hearts to learn all this. Whether they must know it, I cannot tell."

"To what end should they know it?" he said. "Don't you see, Phebe, that the distinction Felicita has won binds us to keep this secret? It cannot be disclosed either to her or to them. I came to tell it to the man who brought me here under a seal of secrecy."

"To Canon Pascal?" she exclaimed.

"Pascal?" he repeated, "ay? I remember him now. It would have been terrible to have told it to him."

"Let me think about it," said Phebe, "it has come too suddenly upon me. There must be something we ought to do, but I cannot see it yet. I must have time to recollect it all. And yet I am afraid to let you go, lest you should disappear again, and all this should seem like a dreadful dream."

"You care for me still, Phebe?" he answered mournfully. "No, I shall not disappear from you; I shall hold fast by you, now you have seen me again. If that poor wretch in hell who lifted up his eyes, being in torments, had caught sight of some pitying angel, who would now and then dip the tip of her finger in water and cool his tongue, would he have disappeared from her vision? Wouldn't he rather have had a horrible dread lest she should disappear? But you will not forsake me, Phebe?"

"Never!" replied Phebe, with an intense and mournful earnestness.

"Then I will go," he said, rising reluctantly to his feet. The deep tones of the Abbey clock were striking for the second time since he had entered Canon Pascal's study, and they had been left in uninterrupted conversation. It was time for him to go; yet it seemed to him as if he had still so much to pour into Phebe's ear, that many hours would not give him time enough. Unconstrained speech had proved a source of ineffable solace and strength to him. He had been dying of thirst, and he had found a spring of living waters. To Phebe, and to her alone, he was still a living man, unless sometimes Felicita thought of him.

"If you are still my friend, knowing all," he said, "I shall no longer despair. When will you see me again?"

"I will come to morning service in the Abbey to-morrow," she answered.

CHAPTER XVIII

WITHIN AND WITHOUT

After speaking to Canon Pascal for a few minutes, with an agitation and a reserve which he could not but observe, Phebe left the house to go home. In one of the darkest corners of the cloisters she caught sight of the figure of Jean Merle, watching for her to come out. For an instant Phebe paused, as if to speak to him once more; but her heart was over-fraught with conflicting emotions, whilst bewildering thoughts oppressed her brain. She longed for a solitary walk homewards, along the two or three miles of a crowded thoroughfare, where she could how feel as much alone as she had ever done on the solitary uplands about her birth-place. She had always delighted to ramble about the streets alone after nightfall, catching brief glimpses of the great out-door population, who were content if they could get a shelter for their heads during the few, short hours they could give to sleep, without indulging in the luxury of a home. When talking to them she could return to the rustic and homely dialect of her childhood; and from her own early experience she could understand their wants, and look at them from their stand-point, whilst feeling for them a sympathy and pity intensified by the education which had lifted her above them.

But to-night she passed along the busy streets both deaf and dumb, mechanically choosing the right way between the Abbey and her home, nearly three miles away. There was only one circumstance of which she was conscious—that Jean Merle was following her. Possibly he was afraid in the depths of his heart that she would fail him when she came to deliberately consider all he had told her. He wronged her, she said to herself indignantly. Still, whenever she turned her head she caught sight of his tall, bent figure and gray head, stealing after her at some distance, but never losing her. So mournful was it to Phebe, to see her oldest and her dearest friend thus dogging her footsteps, that once or twice she paused at a street corner to give him time to overtake her; but he kept aloof. He wished only to see where she lived, for there also lived Felicita and Hilda.

She turned at last into the square where their house was. It was brilliantly lighted up, for Felicita was having one of her rare receptions that evening, and in another hour or two the rooms would be filled with guests. It was too early yet, and Hilda was playing on her piano in the drawing-room, the merry notes ringing out into the quiet night. There was a side door to Phebe's studio, by which she could go in and out at pleasure, and she stood at it trying to fit her latch-key into the lock with her trembling hands. Looking back she saw Jean Merle some little distance away, leaning against the railings that enclosed the Square garden.

"Oh! I must run back to him! I must speak to him again!" she cried to her own heart. In another instant she was at his side, with her hands clasping his.

"Oh!" she sobbed, "what can I do for you? This is too miserable for you; and for me as well. Tell me what I can do."

"Nothing," he answered. "Why, you make me feel as if I had sinned again in telling you all this. I ought not to have troubled your happy heart with my sorrow."

"It was not you," she said, "you did not even come to tell me; God brought you. I can bear it. But oh! to see you shut out, and inside, yonder, Hilda is playing, and Felix, perhaps, is there. They will be singing by-and-by, and never know who is standing outside, in the foggy night, listening to them."

Her voice broke into sobs, but Jean Merle did not notice them.

"And Felicita?" he said.

Phebe could not answer him for weeping. Just yet she could hardly bring herself to think distinctly of Felicita; though in fact her thoughts were full of her. She ran back to her private door, and this time opened it readily. There was a low light in the studio from a shaded lamp standing on the chimney-piece, which made the hearth bright, but left all the rest of the room in shadow. Phebe threw off her bonnet and cloak with a very heavy and troubled sigh.

"What can make you sigh, Phebe?" asked a low-toned and plaintive voice. In the chair by the fire-place, pushed out of the circle of the light, she saw Felicita leaning back, and looking up at her. The beauty of her face had never struck harshly upon Phebe until now; at this moment it was absolutely painful to her. The rich folds of her velvet dress, and the soft and costly lace of her head-dress, distinct from though resembling a widow's cap, set off both her face and figure to the utmost advantage. Phebe's eyes seemed to behold her more distinctly and vividly than they had done for some years past; for she was looking through them with a dark background for what she saw in her own brain. She was a strikingly beautiful woman; but the thought of what anguish and dread had been concealed under her reserved and stately air, so cold yet so gentle, filled Phebe's soul with a sudden terror. What an awful life of self-approved, stoical falsehood she had been living! She could see the man, from whom she had just parted, standing without, homeless and friendless, on the verge of pennilessness; a dead man in a living world, cut off from all the ties and duties of the home and the society he loved. But to Phebe he did not appear so wretched as Felicita was.

She sank down on a seat near Felicita, with such a feeling of heart-sickness and heart-faintness as she had never experienced before. The dreariness and perplexity of the present stretched before her into the coming years. For almost the first time in her life she felt worn-out; physically weary and exhausted, as if her strength had been overtaxed. Her childhood on the fresh, breezy uplands, and her happy, tranquil temperament had hitherto kept her in perfect health. But now she felt as if the sins of those whom she had loved so tenderly and loyally touched the very springs of her life. She could have shared any other burden with them, and borne it with an unbroken spirit and an uncrushed heart. But such a sin as this, so full of woe and bewilderment to them all, entangled her soul also in its poisonous web.

"Why did you sigh so bitterly?" asked Felicita again.

"The world is so full of misery," she answered, in a tremulous and troubled voice; "its happiness is such a mockery!"

"Have you found that out at last, dear Phebe?" said Felicita. "I have been telling you so for years. The Son of Man fainting under the Cross—that is the true emblem of human life. Even He had not strength enough to bear His cross to the place called Golgotha. Whenever I think of what most truly represents our life here, I see Jesus, faltering along the rough road, with Simon behind Him, whom they compelled to bear His cross."

"He fainted under the sins of the world," murmured Phebe. "It is possible to bear the sorrows of others; but oh! it is hard to carry their sins."

"We all find that out," said Felicita, her face growing wan and white even to the lips. "Can one man do evil without the whole world suffering for it? Does the effect of a sin ever die out? What is done cannot be undone through all eternity. There is the wretchedness of it, Phebe."

"I never felt it as I do now," she answered.

"Because you have kept yourself free from earthly ties," said Felicita mournfully; "you have neither husband nor child to increase your power of suffering a hundred-fold. I am entering upon another term of tribulation in Felix and Hilda. If I had only been like you, dear Phebe, I could have passed through life as happily as you do; but my life has never belonged to myself; it has been forced to run in channels made by others."

Somewhere in the house behind them a door was left open accidentally, and the sound of Hilda's piano and of voices singing broke in upon the quiet studio. Phebe listened to them, and thought of the desolate, broken-hearted man without, who was listening too. The clear young voices of their children fell upon his ears as upon Felicita's; so near they were to one another, yet so far apart. She shivered and drew nearer to the fire.

"I feel as cold as if I was a poor outcast in the streets," she said.

"And I, too," responded Felicita; "but oh! Phebe, do not you lose heart and courage, like me. You have always seemed in the sunshine, and I have looked up to you and felt cheered. Don't come down into the darkness to me."

Phebe could not answer, for the darkness was closing round her. Until now there had happened no perplexity in her life which made it difficult to decide upon the right or the wrong. But here was come a coil. The long years had reconciled her to Roland's death, and made the memory of him sacred and sorrowfully sweet, to be brooded over in solitary hours in the silent depths of her loyal heart. But he was alive again, with no right to be alive, having no explanation to give which could reinstate him in his old position. And Felicita? Oh! what a cruel, unwomanly wrong Felicita had been guilty of! She could not command her voice to speak again.

"I must go," said Felicita, at last. "I wish I had not invited visitors for to-night."

"I cannot come in this evening," Phebe answered; "but Felix is there, and Canon Pascal is coming. You will do very well without me."

She breathed more freely when Felicita was gone. The dimly-lighted studio, with the canvases she was at work upon, and the pictures she had painted hanging on the walls, and her easels standing as she had left them three or four hours ago, when the early dusk came on, soothed her agitated spirit now she was alone. She moved slowly about, putting everything into its place, and feeling as if her thoughts grew more orderly as she did so. When all was done she opened the outer door stealthily, and peeped out. Yes; he was there, leaning against the railings, and looking up at the brilliantly-lighted windows. Carriages were driving up and setting down Felicita's guests. Phebe's heart cried out against the contrast between the lives of these two. She longed to run out and stand beside him in the darkness and dampness of the November night. But what good could she do? she asked bitterly. She did not dare even to ask him in to sit beside her studio fire. The same roof could not cover him and Felicita, without unspeakable pain to him.

It was late before the house was quiet, and long after midnight when the last light was put out. That was in Phebe's bedroom, and once again she looked out, and saw the motionless figure, looking black amidst the general darkness, as if it had never stirred since she had seen it first. But whilst she was gazing, with quivering mouth and tear-dimmed eyes, a policeman came up and spoke to Jean Merle, giving him an authoritative shake, which seemed to arouse him. He moved gently away, closely followed by the policeman till he passed out of her sight.

There was no sleep for Phebe; she did not want to sleep. All night long her brain was awake and busy; but it found no way out of the coil. Who can make a crooked thing straight? or undo that which has been done?

CHAPTER XIX

IN HIS FATHER'S HOUSE

When Phebe entered Westminster Abbey the next day the morning service was already begun. Upon the bench nearest the door sat a working-man, in worn-out clothes, whose gray hair was long and ragged, and whose whole appearance was one of poverty and suffering. She was passing by, when a gleam of recognition in the dark and sunken eyes of this poor man arrested her. Could he possibly be Roland Sefton? The night before she had seen him only in a friendly obscurity, which concealed the ravages time, and sorrow, and labor had effected; but now the daylight, in revealing them, cast a chill shadow of doubt into her heart. It was his voice she had known and acknowledged the night before; but now he was silent, and, revealed by the daylight, she felt troubled and distrustful. Such a man she might have met a thousand times without once recalling to her memory the handsome, manly presence and prosperous bearing of Roland Sefton.

Yet she sat down beside him in answer to that appealing gleam in his eyes, and as his well-known voice joined hers in the responses to the prayers, she acknowledged him again in her heart of hearts. And now all thought of the sacred place, and of the worship she was engaged in, fled from her mind. She was a girl at home again, dwelling in the silent society of her dumb father, with this voice of Roland Sefton's coming to break the stillness from time to time, and to fill it with that sweetest music, the sound of human speech. If he had lost every vestige of resemblance to his former self, his voice only, calling "Phebe" as he had done the evening before, must have betrayed him to her. Not an accent of it had been forgotten.

To Jean Merle Phebe Marlowe was little altered, save that she had grown from a simple rustic maiden into a cultivated and refined woman. The sweet and gentle face beside him, with the deep peaceful blue of her eyes, and the sensitive mouth so ready to break into a smile, was the same he had seen when, on that terrible evening so many years ago, he had craved her help to escape from his dreaded punishment. "I will help you, even to dying for you and yours," she had said. He remembered vividly how mournfully the girlish fervor of her manner had impressed him. Even now he had no one else to help him; this woman's little hand alone could reach him in the gulf where he lay; only the simple, pitiful wisdom of her faithful heart could find a way for him out of this misery of his into some place of safety and peace. He was willing to follow wherever she might guide him.

"I can see only one duty before us," she said, when the service was over, and they stood together before one of the monuments in the Abbey; "I think Mr. Clifford ought to know."

"What will he do, Phebe?" asked Jean Merle. "God knows if I had only myself to think of I would go into a convict-prison as thankfully as if it was the gate of heaven. It would be as the gate of heaven to me if I could pay the penalty of my crime. But there are Felicita and my children; and the greater shock and shame to them of my conviction now."

"Yet if Mr. Clifford demanded the penalty it must even now be paid," answered Phebe; "but he will not. One reason why he ought to know is that he mourns over you still, day and night, as if he had been the chief cause of your death. He reproaches himself with his implacability both towards you and his son. But even if the old resentment should awaken, it is right you should run the risk. Why need it be known to any one but us two that Felicita knew you were still alive?"

"If we could save her and the children I should be satisfied," said Jean Merle.

"It would kill her to know you were here," answered Phebe, looking round her with a terrified glance, as if she expected to see Felicita; "she is not strong, and a sudden agitation and distress might cause her death instantly. No, she must never know. And I am not afraid of Mr. Clifford; he will forgive you with all his heart; and he will be made glad in his old age. I will go down with you this evening. There is a train at four o'clock, and we shall reach Riversborough at eight. Be at the station to meet me."

"You know," said Jean Merle, "that the lapse of years does not free one from trial and conviction? Mr. Clifford can give me into the hands of the police at once; and to-night may see me lodged in Riversborough jail, as if I had been arrested fourteen years ago. You know this, Phebe?"

"Yes, I know it, but I am not afraid of it," she answered.

She had not the slightest fear of old Mr. Clifford's vindictiveness. As she travelled down to Riversborough, with Jean Merle in a third-class carriage of the same train, her mind was very busy with troubled thoughts. There was an unquiet joy stirring in the secret depths of her heart, but she was too full of anxiety and bewilderment to be altogether aware of it. Though it was not more than twenty-four hours since she had known otherwise, it seemed to her as if she had never believed that Roland Sefton was dead, and it appeared incredible that the report of his death should have received such full acceptance as it had everywhere done. Yet though he had come back, there could be no welcome for him. To her and to old Mr. Clifford only could this return from the grave contain any gladness. And was she glad? she asked herself, after a long deliberation over the difficulties surrounding this strange reappearance. She had sorrowed for him and comforted his mother in her mourning, and talked of him as one talks fondly of the dead to his children; and all the sacred healing of time had softened the grief she once felt into a tranquil and grateful memory of him, as of the friend she had loved most, and whose care for her had most widely influenced her life. But she could not own yet that she was glad.

Old Mr. Clifford was sitting in the wainscoted dining-room, his favorite room, when Phebe opened the door silently, and looked in with a pale and anxious face. His sight was dim, and a blaze of light fell upon the dark, old panels, and the old-fashioned silver tankards and bright brass salvers on the carved sideboard. Two or three of Phebe's sunniest pictures hung against the oaken panels. There was a blazing fire on the hearth, and the old man, with his elbows resting on the arms of his chair, and his hands clasped lightly, was watching the play and dance of the flames as they shot up the chimney. Some new books lay on a table beside him, but he was not reading. He was sitting there in utter loneliness, with no companionship except that of his own fading memories. Phebe's tenderness for the old man was very great; and she paused on the threshold gazing at him pitifully; whilst Jean Merle, standing in the hall behind her, caught a glimpse of the hearth so crowded with memories for him, but occupied now by one desolate old man, before the door was closed, and he was left without.

"Why, it's little Phebe Marlowe!" cried Mr. Clifford gladly, looking round at the light sound of a footstep, very different from Mrs. Nixey's heavy tread; "my dear child, you can't tell what a pleasure this is to me."

He had risen up, and stood holding both her hands and looking fondly into her face.

"This moment I was thinking of you, my dear," he said; "I was inditing a long letter to you in my head, which these lazy old fingers of mine would have refused to write. Sandon, the bookseller, has been in here, bringing these books; and he told me a queer story enough. He says that in August last a relation of Madame Sefton's was here, in Riversborough; and told him who he was, in his shop, where he bought one of Felicita's books. Why didn't Sandon come here at once and tell us then, so that you could have found him out, Phebe? You and Felix and Hilda were here. He was a poor man, and seemed badly off; and I guess he came to inquire after Madame. Sandon says he reminded him of Roland—poor Roland! Why, I'd have given the poor fellow a welcome for the sake of that resemblance; and I was just thinking how Phebe's tender heart would have been touched by even so faint a likeness."

"Yes," she murmured.

"And we could have lifted him up a little; quite a poor man, Sandon says," continued Mr. Clifford; "but sit down, my dear. There is no one in the wide world would be so welcome to me as little Phebe Marlowe, who refused to be my adopted daughter."

He had drawn a chair close beside his own, for he would not loose her hand, but kept it closely grasped by his thin and crooked fingers.

"You have altogether forgiven Roland?" she said tremulously.

"Altogether, my dear," he answered.

"As Christ forgives us, bearing away our sins Himself?" she said.

"As Christ forgave us," he replied, bowing his head solemnly.

"And if it was possible—think it possible," she went on, "that he could come back again, that the grave in Engelberg could give up its dead, he would be welcome to you?"

"If my old friend Sefton's son, could come back again," he said, "he would be more welcome to me than you are, Phebe. How often do I fancy him sitting yonder in Sefton's chair, watching me with his dear eyes!"

"But suppose he had deceived us all," she continued, "if he had escaped from your anger by another fraud; a worse fraud! If he had managed so as to bury some one else in his name, and go on living under a false one! Could you forgive that?"

"If Roland could come back a repentant man, I would forgive him every sin," answered Mr. Clifford, "and rejoice that I had not driven him to seek death. But what do you mean, Phebe? why do you ask?"

"Because," she answered, speaking almost in a whisper, with her face close to his, "Roland did not die. That man, who was here in August, and called himself Jean Merle, is Roland himself. He saw you, and all of us, and did not dare to make himself known. I can tell you all about it. But, oh! he has bitterly repented; and there is no place of repentance for him in this world. He cannot come back amongst us, and be Roland Sefton again."

"Where is he?" asked the old man, trembling.

"He is here; he came with me. I will go and fetch him," she answered.

Mr. Clifford leaned back in his arm-chair, and gazed towards the half-open door. His memory had gone back twenty years, to the last time he had seen Roland Sefton, in the prime of his youth, handsome, erect, and happy, who had made his heart ache as he thought of his own abandoned son, lying buried in a common grave in Paris. The man whom he saw entering slowly and reluctantly into the room behind Phebe, was gray-headed, bent, and abject. This man paused just within the doorway, looking not at him but round the room, with a glance full of grief and remembrance. The eager, questioning eyes of old Mr. Clifford did not arrest his attention, or divert it from the aspect of the old familiar place.

"No, no, Phebe!" exclaimed Mr. Clifford, "he's an impostor, my dear. That's not my old friend's son Roland."

"Would to God I were not!" cried Jean Merle bitterly, "would to God I stood in this room as a stranger! Phebe Marlowe, this is very hard; my punishment is greater than I can bear. All my life comes back to me here. This place, of all other places in the world, brings my sin and folly to remembrance."

He sank down on a chair, and buried his face in his hands, to shut out the hateful sight of the old home. He was inside his Paradise again; and behold, it was a place of torment. There was no room in his thoughts for Mr. Clifford, it was nothing to him that he should be called an impostor. He came to claim nothing, not even his own name. But the avenging memories of the past claimed him and held him fast bound. Even last night, when in the chill darkness of the November night he had watched the house which held Felicita and their children, his pain had been less poignant than now, within these walls, where all his happy life had been passed. He was unconscious of everything but his pain. He could not hear Phebe's voice speaking for him to Mr. Clifford. He saw and felt nothing, until a gentle and trembling hand pressing on his shoulder feebly and as tenderly as his mother's made him look up into the gray and agitated face of Mr. Clifford bending over him.

"Roland! Roland!" he said, in a voice broken by sobs, "my old friend's son, forgive me as I forgive you. God be thanked, you have come back again in time for me to see you and bid you welcome. I bless God with all my heart. It is your own home, Roland, your own home."

With his feeble but eager old hands he drew him to the hearth, and placed him in the chair close beside his own, where Phebe had been sitting, and kept his hand upon his arm, lest he should vanish out of his sight.

"You shall tell me nothing more to-night," he said; "I am old, and this is enough for me. It is enough that to-night you and I have pardoned one another from 'the low depths of our hearts.' Tell me nothing else to-night."

Phebe had slipped away from them to help Mrs. Nixey to prepare a room for Jean Merle. It was the one that had been Roland Sefton's nursery, and the nursery of his children, and it was still occupied by Felix, when he visited his old home. The homely hospitable occupation was a relief to her; but in the room that she had left the two men sat side by side in unbroken silence.

CHAPTER XX

AS A HIRED SERVANT

From a profound and dreamless sleep Jean Merle awoke early the next morning, with the blessed feeling of being at home again in his father's house. The heavy cross-beams of black oak dividing the ceiling into panels; the low broad lattice window with a few upper panes of old stained glass; the faded familiar pictures on the wall; these all awoke in him memories of his earliest years. In the corner of the room, hardly to be distinguished from the wainscot, was the high narrow door communicating with his mother's chamber, through which he had often, how often! seen her come in softly, on tiptoe, to take a look at him. His own children, too, had slept there; and it was here that he had last seen his little son and daughter before fleeing from his home a self-accused criminal. All the happy, prosperous life of Roland Sefton had been encompassed round by these walls.

But the dead past must bury the dead. If there had ever been a deep, buried, hidden hope, that a possible return to something of the old life lay in the unknown future, it was now utterly uprooted. Such a return was only possible over the ruined lives and broken hearts of Felicita and his children. If he made himself known, though he was secure against prosecution, the story of his former crime would revive, and spread wider, joined with the fair name of Felicita, than it would have done when he was merely a fraudulent banker in a country town. However true it might be what Phebe maintained, that he might have suffered the penalty of his sin, and afterwards retrieved the past, whilst his children were too young to feel the full bitterness of the shame, it was too late to do it now. The name he had dishonored was forever forfeited. His return to his former life was hedged up on every hand.

But a new courage was awaking in him, which helped him to grapple with his despair. He would bury the dead past, and go on into the future making the best of his life, maimed and marred as it was by his own folly. He was still in the prime of his age, thirty years younger than Mr. Clifford, whose intellect was as keen and clear as ever; there was a long span of time stretching before him, to be used or misused.

"Come unto Me all ye that be weary, and heavy laden, and I will give you rest." He seemed to see the words in the quaint upright characters in which old Marlowe had carved them under the crucifix. He had fancied he knew what coming to Christ meant in those old days of his, when he was reputed a religious man, and was first and foremost in all religious and philanthropic schemes, making his trespass more terrible and pernicious than if it had been the transgression of a worldly man. But it was not so when he came to Christ this morning. He was a broken-hearted man, who had cut himself off from all human ties and affections, and who was longing to feel that he was not forsaken of the universal Brother and Saviour. His cry was, "My soul thirsteth for thee; my flesh longeth for thee, in a dry and weary land, where no water is." It was his own fault that he was in the dry and weary wilderness; but oh! if Christ would not forsake him then, would dwell with him, even in this desert made desolate by himself, then at last he might find peace to his soul.

There was a deep inner consciousness, the forgotten but not obliterated faith of his boyhood and youth, before the world with its pomps and ambitions had laid its iron hand upon him, that Christ was with him, leading him day by day, if he would but follow nearer to God. Was it impossible to follow His guidance now? Could he not, even yet, take up his cross, and be willing to fill any place which he could yet fill worthily and humbly; expiating his sins against his fellow-men by truer devotion to their service, as Jean Merle, the working-man; not as Roland Sefton, the prosperous and fraudulent banker?

This return to his father's house, and all its associations, solemn and sacred with a peculiar sacredness and solemnity, seemed to him a pledge that he could once more be admitted into the great brotherhood and home of Christ's disciples. Every object on which his eye rested smote him, but it was with the stroke of a friend. A clear and sweet light from the past shed its penetrating rays into the darkest corners of his soul. Forgiven! God had forgiven him; and man had forgiven him. Before him lay an obscure and humble path; but the heaviest part of his burden was gone. He must go heavy-laden to the end of his days, treading in rough paths; but despair had fled, and with it the sense of being separated from God and man.

He heard the feeble yet deep old voice of Mr. Clifford outside his door inquiring from Mrs. Nixey if Mr. Merle was gone down-stairs yet. He made haste to go down, treading the old staircase with something of the alacrity of former days. Phebe was in the dining-room, and the servants came in to prayer as they had been used to do forty years ago when he was a child. An old-world tranquillity and peacefulness was in the familiar scene which breathed a deep calm over his tempest-tossed spirit.

"Phebe has been telling me all," said Mr. Clifford, when breakfast was over; "tell me what can be done to save Felicita and the children."

"I am Jean Merle," he answered with a melancholy smile, "Jean Merle, and no one else. I come back with no claims, and they must never know me. Why should I cross their path and blight it? I cannot atone for the past in any way, except by keeping away forever from them. I shall injure no one by continuing to be Jean Merle."

"No," said Phebe, "it is too late now, and it would kill Felicita."

"This morning a thought struck me," he continued, "a project for my future life, which you can help me to put into execution, Phebe. I have an intolerable dread of losing sight of you all again; let me be at least somewhere in England, when you can now and then give me tidings of my children and Felicita."

"I will do anything in the world to help you," cried Phebe eagerly.

"Then let me go to your little farm," he answered, "and take up your father's life, at least for a time, until I can see how to make myself of greater use to my fellow-men. I will till the fields as he did, and finish the carvings he has left undone, and live his simple, silent life. It will be good for me, and I shall not be banished from my own country. I shall be a happier man then than I have any right to be."

"Have you no fear of being recognized?" she asked.

"None," he replied. "Look at me, Phebe. Should you have known me again if I had not betrayed myself to you?"

"I should have known you again anywhere," she exclaimed. But it was her heart that cried out that no change could have concealed him from her; there was a dread lying deep down in her conscience that she might have passed him by with no suspicion. He shook his head in answer to her assertion.

"I will go out into the town," he continued, "and speak to half-a-dozen men who knew me best, and there will be no gleam of recognition in their eyes. Recollect Roland Sefton is dead, and has been dead so long that there will be no clear memory left of him as he was then to compare with me. And any dim resemblance to him will be fully accounted for by my relationship to Madame Sefton. No, I am not afraid of the keenest eyes."

He went out as he had said, and met his old townsmen, many of whom were themselves so changed that he could barely recognize them. The memory of Roland Sefton was blotted out, he was utterly forgotten as a dead man out of mind.

As Jean Merle strayed through the streets crowded with market-people come in from the country, his new scheme grew stronger and brighter to him. It would keep him in England, within reach of all he had loved and had lost. The little place was dear to him, and the laborious, secluded peasant life had a charm for him who had so long lived as a Swiss peasant. By-and-by, he thought, the chance resemblance in the names would merge that of Merle into the more familiar name of Marlowe; and the identity of his pursuits with those of the deaf and dumb old man would hasten such a change. So the years to come would pass by in labor and obscurity; and an obscure grave in the little churchyard, where all the Marlowes lay, would shelter him at last. A quiet haven after many storms; but oh! what a shipwreck had he made of his life!

All the morning Mr. Clifford sat in his arm-chair lost in thought, only looking up sometimes to ply Phebe with questions. When Jean Merle returned, his gray, meditative face grew bright, with a faint smile shining through his dim eyes.

"You are no phantom then!" he said. "I've been so used to your company as a ghost that when you are out of sight I fancy myself dreaming. I could not let Phebe go away lest I should feel that all this is not real. Did any one know you again?"

"Not a soul," he answered; "how could they? Mrs. Nixey herself has no remembrance of me. There is no fear of my being known."

"Then I want you to stay with me," said old Mr. Clifford eagerly; "I'm a lonely man, seventy-seven years old, with neither kith nor kin, and it seems a long and dreary road to the grave. I want one to sit beside me in these long evenings, and to take care of me as a son takes care of his old father. Could you do it, Jean Merle? I beseech you, if it is possible, give me your services in my old age."

"It will be hard for you," pleaded Phebe in a low voice, "harder than going out alone to my little home. But you would do more good here; you could save us from anxiety, for we are often very anxious and sorrowful about Mr. Clifford. I can take care that you should always know before Felix and Hilda come down. Felicita never comes."

How much harder it would be for him even Phebe could not guess. To dwell within reach of his old home was altogether different from living in it, with its countless memories, and the unremitting stings of conscience. To have about him all that he had lost and made desolate; the empty home, from which all the familiar faces and beloved voices had vanished; this lot surely was harder than the humble, laborious life of old Marlowe on the hills. Yet if any one living had a claim upon him for such self-sacrifice, it was this feeble, tottering old man, who was gazing up into his face with urgent and imploring eyes.

"I will stay here and be your servant," he answered, "if there appears no reason against it when we have given it more thought."

CHAPTER XXI

PHEBE'S SECRET

For the first time in her life those who were about Phebe Marlowe felt that she was under a cloud. The sweet sunny atmosphere, as of a clear and peaceful day, which seemed to surround her, had fled. She was absent and depressed, and avoided society, even that of Hilda, who had been like her own child to her. Towards Felicita there was a subtle change in Phebe's manner, which could not fail to impress deeply her sensitive temperament. She felt that Phebe shrank from her, and that she was no longer welcome to the studio, which of all places in the world had been to her a place of repose, and of brief cessation of troubled thought. Phebe's direct and simple nature, free from all guile and worldliness, had made her a perfect sympathizer with any true feeling. And Felicita's feeling with regard to her past most sorrowful life had been absolutely real; if only Phebe had known all the circumstances of it as she had always supposed she did.

Phebe was, moreover, fearful of some accident betraying to Felicita the circumstance of Jean Merle living at Riversborough. There had never been any direct correspondence between Felicita and Mr. Clifford, except on purely business matters; and Felix was too much engrossed with his own affairs to find time to run down to Riversborough, or to keep up an animated interchange of letters with his old friend there. The intercourse between them had been chiefly carried on through Phebe herself, who was the old man's prime favorite. Neither was he a man likely to let out anything he might wish to conceal. But still she was nervous and afraid. How far from improbable it was that through some unthought-of channel Felicita might hear that a stranger, related to Madame Sefton, had entered the household of Mr. Clifford as his confidential attendant, and that this stranger's name was Jean Merle. What would happen then?

She was burdened with a secret, and her nature abhorred a secret. There was gladness, almost utterly pure, to her in the belief that there was One being who could read the inmost recesses of her heart, and see, with the loving-kindness of an All-wise Father, its secret faults, the errors which she did not herself understand. That she had nothing to tell to God, which He did not know of her already, was one of the deepest foundations of her spiritual life. And in some measure, in all possible measure, she would have had it so with those whom she loved. She did not shrink from showing to them her thoughts, and motives, and emotions. It was the limit of expression, so quickly reached, so impassable, that chafed her; and she was always searching for fresh modes of conveying her own feeling to other souls. Possibly the enforced speechlessness in which she had passed her early years had aided in creating this passionate desire to impart herself to those about her in unfettered communion, and she ardently delighted in the same unreserved confidence in those who conversed with her. But now she was doomed to bear the burden of a secret fraught with strange and painful consequences to those whom she loved, if time should ever divulge it.

The winter months passed away cheerlessly, though she worked with more persistent energy than ever before, partly to drive away the thoughts that troubled her. She heard from Mr. Clifford, but not more frequently than usual, and Jean Merle did not venture upon sending her a line of his hand-writing. Mr. Clifford spoke in guarded terms of the comfort he found in the companionship of his attendant, in spite of his being a sad and moody man. Now and then he told Phebe that this attendant of his had gone for a day or two to her solitary little house on the uplands, of which Mr. Clifford kept the key, and that he stayed there a day or two, finishing the half-carved blocks of oak her father had left incomplete. It would have been a happier existence, she knew, for himself, if Jean Merle had gone to dwell there altogether; but it was along this path of self-sacrifice and devotion alone lay the road back to a Christian life.

One point troubled Phebe's conscience more than any other. Ought she not at least to tell Canon Pascal what she knew? She could not help feeling that this second fraud would seem worse in his estimation than the first one. And Felicita, the very soul of truth and honor, had connived at it! It seemed immeasurably more terrible in Phebe's own eyes. To her money had so small a value, it lay on so low a level in the scale of life, that a crime in connection with it had far less guilt than one against the affections. And how unutterable a sin against all who loved him had Roland and Felicita fallen into! She recalled his mother's mourning for him through many long years, and her belief in death that she was going soon to rejoin the beloved son whom she had lost. Her own grief she put aside, but there was the deep, boyish sorrow of Felix, and even little Hilda's fatherlessness, as the children had grown up through the various stages of childhood. It might have been bad for them to bear the stigma of their father's shame, but still Phebe believed it would have been better for every one of them to have gone bravely forward to bear the just consequences of sin.

She went down into Essex to spend a day or two at Christmas, carrying with her the fitful spirit so foreign to her. The perfect health that had been hers hitherto was broken; and Mrs. Pascal, a confirmed invalid, to whom Phebe's physical vigor and evenness of temper had been a constant source of delight and invigoration, felt the change in her keenly.

"She has something on her mind," she said to her husband; "you must try and find it out, or she will be ill."

"I know she has a secret," he answered, "but it is not her own. Phebe Marlowe is as open as the day; she will never have a secret of her own."

But he made no effort to find out her secret. His searching, kindly eyes met hers with the trustfulness of a frank and open nature that recognized a nature akin to its own, and Phebe never shrank from his gaze, though her lips remained closed. If it was right for her to tell him anything of the stranger who had been about to make him his confessor, she would do it. Canon Pascal would not ask any questions.

"Felix and Alice are growing more and more deeply in love with each other," he said to her; "there is something beautiful and pleasant in being a spectator of these palmy days of theirs. Felicita even felt something of their happiness when she was here last, and she will not withhold her full approbation much longer."

"And you," answered Phebe, with an eager flush on her face, "you do not repent of giving Alice to the son of a man who might have been a convict?"

"I believe Alice would marry Felix if his father had been a murderer," replied Canon Pascal; "it is too late to alter it now. Besides, I know Felix through and through, he is himself; he is no longer the son of any person, but a true man, one of the sons of God."

The strong and emphatic tone of Canon Pascal's words brought great consolation to Phebe's troubled mind. She might keep silence with a good conscience, for the duty of disclosing all to Canon Pascal arose simply from the possibility that his conduct would be altered by this further knowledge of Roland and Felicita.

"But this easy country life is not good for Felix," she said in a more cheerful tone; "he needs a difficult parish to develop his energies. It is not among your people he will become a second Felix Merle."

"Patience! Phebe," he answered, "there is a probability in the future, a bare probability, and dimly distant, which may change all that. He may have as much to do as Felix Merle by and by."

Phebe returned to her work in London with a somewhat lighter heart. Yet the work was painful to her; work which a few months before would have been a delight. For Felicita, yielding to the urgent entreaties of Felix and Hilda, had consented to sit for her portrait. She was engaged in no writing, and had ample leisure. Until now she had resisted all importunity, and no likeness of her existed. She disliked photographs, and had only had one taken for Roland alone when they were married, and she could never bring herself to sit for an artist comparatively a stranger to her. It was opposed to her reserved and somewhat haughty temperament that any eye should scan too freely and too curiously the lineaments of her beautiful face, with its singularly expressive individuality. But now that Phebe's skill had been so highly cultivated, and commanded an increasing reputation, she could no longer oppose her children's reiterated entreaties.

Felicita was groping blindly for the reason of the change in Phebe's feeling towards her, for she was conscious of some vague, mysterious barrier that had arisen between her and the tender, simple soul which had been always full of lowly sympathy for her. But Phebe silently shrank from her in a terror mingled with profound, unutterable pity. For here was a secret misery of a solitary human spirit, ice-bound in a self-chosen isolation, which was an utter mystery to her. All the old love and reverence, amounting almost to adoration, which she had, offered up as incense to some being far above her had died away; gone also was the child-like simplicity with which she could always talk to Felicita. She could read the pride and sadness of the lovely face before her with a clear understanding now, but the lines which reproduced it on her canvas were harder and sterner than they would have been if she had known less of Felicita's heart. The painting grew into a likeness, but it was a painful one, full of hidden sadness, bitterness, and infelicity. Felix and Hilda gazed at it in silence, almost as solemn and mournful as if they were looking on the face of their dead mother. She herself turned from it with a feeling of dread.

"How much do you know of me?" she cried; "how deep can you look into my heart, Phebe?" Phebe glanced from her to the finished portrait, and only answered by tears.

CHAPTER XXII

NEAR THE END

Felicita had followed the urgent advice of her physicians in giving up writing for a season. There was no longer any necessity for her work, as some time since the money which Roland Sefton had fraudulently appropriated, had been paid back with full interest, and she began to feel justified in accepting the income from her marriage settlement. During the winter and spring she spent her days much as other women of her class and station, in a monotonous round of shopping, driving in the parks, visiting, and being visited, partly for Hilda's sake, and partly driven to it for want of occupation; but short as the time was which she gave to this life, she grew inexpressibly weary of it. Early, in May she turned into Phebe's studio, which she had seldom entered since her portrait was finished. This portrait was in the Academy Exhibition, and she was constantly receiving empty compliments about it.

"Dear Phebe!" she exclaimed, "I have tried fashionable life to see how much it is worth, and oh! it is altogether hollow and inane. I did not expect much from it, but it is utter weariness to me."

"And you will go back to your writing?" said Phebe.

Felicita hesitated for a moment. There was a worn and harassed expression on her pale face, as if she had not slept or rested well for a long time, which touched Phebe's heart.

"Not yet," she answered; "I am going on a journey. I shall start for Switzerland to-night."

"To Switzerland! To-night!" echoed Phebe. "Oh, no! you must not, you cannot. And alone? How can you think of going alone?"

"I went alone once," she answered, smiling with her lips, though her dark eyes grew no brighter, "and I can go again. I shall manage very well. I fancied you would not care to go with me," she added, sighing.

"But I must go with you!" cried Phebe; "did I not promise long ago? Only don't go to-night, stay a day or two."

"No, no," she said with feverish impatience, "I have made all my arrangements. Nobody must know, and Hilda is gone down into Essex for a week, and my cousins fancy I am going to the sea-side for a few days' rest. I must start to-night, in less than four hours, Phebe. You cannot be ready in time?"

But she spoke wistfully, as if it would be pleasant to hear Phebe say she would go with her. For a few minutes Phebe was lost in bewildered thought. Felicita had told her some months ago that she must go to Engelberg before she could give her consent to Felix marrying Alice, but it had escaped her memory, pushed out by more immediate and more present cares. And now she could not tell what Jean Merle would have her do. To discover suddenly that he was alive, and in England, nay, at Riversborough itself, under their old roof, would be too great a shock for Felicita. Phebe dared not tell her. Yet, to let her start off alone on this fruitless errand, to find only an empty hut at Engelberg, with no trace of its occupant left behind, was heartless, and might prove equally injurious to Felicita. There was no time to communicate with Riversborough, she must come to a decision for herself, and at once. The white, worn face, with its air of sad determination, filled her with deep and eager pity.

"Oh! I will go with you," she cried. "I could never bear you to go alone. But is there nothing you can tell me? Only trust me. What trouble carries you there? Why must you go to Engelberg before Felix marries?"

She had caught Felicita's small cold hand between her own and looked up beseechingly into her face. Oh! if she would but now, at last, throw off the burden which had so long bowed her down, and tell her secret, she could let her know that this painful pilgrimage was utterly needless. But the sweet, sad, proud lips were closed, and the dark eyes looking down steadily into Phebe's, betrayed no wavering of her determined reticence.

"You shall come with me as far as Lucerne, dear Phebe," she answered, stooping down to kiss her uplifted face, "but I must go alone to Engelberg."

There was barely time enough for Phebe to make any arrangements, there was not a moment for deliberation. She wrote a few hurried words to Jean Merle, imploring him to follow them at once, and promising to detain Felicita on their way, if possible. Felicita's own preparations were complete, and her route marked out, with the time of steamers and trains set down. Through Paris, Mulhausen, and Basle she hastened on to Lucerne. Now she had set out on this dreary and dolorous path there could be no rest for her until she reached the end. Phebe recognized this as soon as they had started. It would be impossible to detain Felicita on the way.

But Jean Merle could not be far behind them, a few hours would bring him to them after they had reached Lucerne. Felicita was very silent as they travelled on by the swiftest trains, and Phebe was glad of it. For what could she say to her? She was herself lost in a whirl of bewilderment, and of mingled hope and fear. Could it possibly be that Felicita would learn that Jean Merle was still living, and the mode and manner of his life through this long separation, and yet stand aloof from him, afar off, as one on whom he had no claim, claim for pity and love? But if she could relent towards him, how must it be in the future? It could never be that she would own the wrong she had committed openly in the face of the world. What was to happen now? Phebe was hardly less feverishly agitated than Felicita herself.

It was evening when they arrived at Lucerne, and Felicita was forced to rest until the morning. They sat together in a small balcony opening out of her chamber, which overlooked the Lake, where the moonbeams were playing in glistening curves over the quiet ripples of the water. All the mountains round it looked black in the dim light, and the rugged summit of Pilatus, still slightly sprinkled with snow, frowned down upon them; but southward, behind the dark range of lower hills, there stood out against the almost black-blue of the sky a broken line of pale, mysterious peaks, which might have been merely pallid clouds lying along the horizon but for their stedfast, unaltering immobility. They were the Engelberg Alps, with the snowy Titlis gleaming highest among them; and Felicita's face, wan and pallid as themselves, was set towards them.

"You will let me come with you to-morrow?" said Phebe, in a tone of painful entreaty.

"No, no," she answered. "I could not bear to have even you at Engelberg with me. I must visit that grave alone. And yet I know you love me, dear Phebe."

"Dearly!" she sobbed.

"Yes, you love me dearly," she repeated sorrowfully, "but not as you once did; even your heart is changed towards me. If you went with me to-morrow I might lose all the love that is left. I cannot afford to lose that, my dear."

"You could never lose it!" answered Phebe. "I love you differently? Yes, but not less. I love you now as Christ loves us all, more for God's sake than our own; and that is the deepest, most faithful love. That can never be worn out or repulsed. As Christ has loved me, so I love you, my Felicita."

Her voice had fallen into an almost inaudible whisper, as she knelt down beside her, pressing her lips upon the thin, cold hands lying listlessly on Felicita's lap. It had been as an impulsive girl, worshipping her from a lowly inferiority, that Phebe had been used long ago to kiss Felicita's hand. But this was the humility of a great love, willing to help, and seeking to save her. Felicita felt it through every fibre of her sensitive nature. For an instant she thought it might be possible that Phebe had caught some glimmer of the truth. With her weary and dim eyes lifted up to the pale crests of the mountains, beneath which lay the miserable secret of her life, she hesitated as to whether she could tell Phebe all. But the effort to admit any human soul into the inner recesses of her own was too great for her.

"Christ loves me, you say," she murmured, "I don't know; I never felt it. But I have felt sure of your love; and next to Felix and Hilda you have stood nearest to me. Love me always, and in spite of all, my dear."

She lifted up her bowed head and kissed her lips with a long and lingering kiss. Then Phebe knew that she was bent upon going alone and immediately to Engelberg.

The icy air of the morning, blowing down from the mountains where the winter's snow was but partially melted, made Felicita shiver, though her mind was too busy to notice why. Phebe had seen that she was warmly clad, and had come down to the boat with her to start her on this last day's journey; but Felicita had scarcely opened her pale lips to say good-by. She stood on the quay, watching the boat as long as the white steam from the funnel was in sight, and then she turned away, blind to all the scenery about her, in the heaviness of heart she felt for the sorrowful soul going out on so sad and vain a quest. There had been no time for Jean Merle to overtake them, and now Felicita was gone when a few words from her would have stopped her. But Phebe had not dared to utter them.

Felicita too had not seen either the sunlit hills lying about her, or Phebe watching her departure. She had no thought for anything but what there might be lying before her, in that lonely mountain village, to which, after fourteen years, her reluctant feet were turned. Possibly she might find no trace of the man who had been so long dead to her and to all the world, and thus be baffled and defeated, yet relieved, at the first stage of her search. For she did not desire to find him. Her heart would be lightened of its miserable load, if she should discover that Jean Merle was dead, and buried in the same quiet cemetery where the granite cross marked the grave of Roland Sefton. That was a thing to be hoped for. If Jean Merle was living still, and living there, what should she say to him? Wild hopes and desires would be awakened within him if he found her seeking after him? Nay, it might possibly be that he would insist upon making their mutual sin known to the world, by claiming to return to her and her children. It seemed a desperate thing to have done; and for the first time since she left London she repented of having done it. Was she not sowing the wind to reap the whirlwind? There was still time for her to retrace her steps and go back home, the home she owed altogether to herself; yet one which this man, whom she had not seen for so long a time, had a right to enter as the master of it. What fatal impulse had driven her to leave it on so wild and fruitless an errand?

Yet she felt she could no longer live without knowing the fate of Jean Merle. Her heart had been gnawing itself ever since they parted with vague remorses and self-accusations, slumbering often, but now aroused into an activity that could not be laid to rest. This morning, for the first time, beneath all her perplexity and fear and hope to find him dead, there came to her a strange, undefined, scarcely conscious tenderness towards the miserable man, whom she had last seen standing in her presence, an uncouth, ragged, weather-beaten peasant. The man had been her husband, the father of her children, and a deep, keen pain was stirring in her soul, partly of the old love, for she had once loved him, and partly of the pity she felt for him, as she began to realize the difference there had existed between her lot and his.

She scarcely felt how worn out she was, how dangerously fatigued with this rapid travelling and the resistless current of agitation which had possessed her. As she journeyed onwards she was altogether unconscious of the roads she traversed, only arousing herself when any change of conveyance made it necessary. Her brain was busy over the opinion, more than once expressed by Phebe, that every man could live down the evil consequences of his sin, if he had courage and faith enough. "If God forgives us, man will forgive us," said Phebe. But Felicita pondered over the possibility of Roland having paid the penalty of his crime, and going back again to take up his life, walking more humbly in it evermore, with no claim to preeminence save that of most diligently serving his fellow-men. She endeavored to picture herself receiving him back again from the convict prison, with all its shameful memories branded on him, and looking upon him again as her husband and the father of her children; and she found herself crying out to her own heart that it would have been impossible to her. Phebe might have done it, but she—never!

The journey, though not more than fourteen miles from Stans to Engelberg, occupied several hours, so broken up the narrow road was by the winter's rains and the melting snow. The steep ascent between Grafenort and Engelberg was dangerous, the more so as a heavy thunderstorm broke over it; but Felicita remained insensible to any peril. At length the long, narrow valley lay before her, stretching upwards to the feet of the rocky hills. The thunderstorm that had met them on the road had been raging fiercely in this mountain caldron, and was but just passing away in long, low mutterings, echoed and prolonged amid the precipitous walls of rock. Tall, trailing, spectre-like clouds slowly followed each other in solemn and stately procession up the valley, as though amid their light yet impenetrable folds of vapor they bore the invisible form of some mysterious being; whether in triumph or in sorrow it was impossible to tell. The sun caught their gray crests and tinged them with rainbow colors; and as they floated unhastingly along, the valley behind them seemed to spring into a new life of sunshine and mirth.

CHAPTER XXIII

THE MOST MISERABLE

It was past noon when Felicita was driven up to the hotel in the village, where, when she had last been at Engelberg, she had gone to look upon the dead face of the stranger, who was to carry away the sin of Roland Sefton, with the shame it would bring upon her, and bury it forever in his grave. It seemed but a few days ago, and she felt reluctant to enter the house again. In two or three hours when the horses were rested, she said to the driver, she would be ready to return to Stans. Then she wandered out into the village street, thinking she might come across some peasant at work alone, or some woman standing idly at her door, with whom she could fall into a casual conversation, and learn what she had come to ascertain. But she met with no solitary villager; and she strayed onward, almost unwittingly in the direction of the cemetery. In passing by the church, she pushed open one of the heavy, swinging doors, and cast a glance around; there was no one in sight, but the gabble of boys' voices in some vestry close by reached her ear, and a laugh rang after it, which echoed noisily in the quiet aisles. The high altar was lit up by a light from a side-window and her eye was arrested by it. Still, whether she saw and heard, or was deaf and blind, she scarcely knew. Her feet were drawn by some irresistible attraction towards the grave where her husband was not buried.

She did not know in what corner of the graveyard it was to be found; and when she entered the small enclosure, with its wooden cross at the head of every narrow mound, she stood still for a minute or two, hesitatingly, and looking before her with a bewildered and reluctant air, as if engaged in an enterprise she recoiled from. A young priest, the curé of the nearest mountain parish, who visiting the grave of one of his parishioners lately buried at Engelberg, was passing to and fro among the grassy mounds with his breviary in his hands, and his lips moving as if in prayer; but at the unexpected sight of a traveller thus early in the season, his curiosity was aroused, and he bent his steps towards her. When he was sufficiently near to catch her wandering eye, he spoke in a quiet and courteous manner—

"Is madame seeking for any special spot?" he inquired.

"Yes," answered Felicita, fastening upon him her large; sad eyes, which had dark rings below them, intensifying the mournfulness of their expression, "I am looking for a grave. The grave of a stranger; Roland Sefton. I have come from England to find it."

Her voice was constrained and low; and the words came in brief, panting syllables, which sounded almost like sobs. The black-robed priest looked closely and scrutinizingly into the pallid face turned towards him, which was as rigid as marble, except for the gleam of the dark eyes.

"Madame is suffering; she is ill!" he said.

"No, not ill," answered Felicita, in an absent manner, as if she was speaking in a dream, "but of all women the most miserable."

It seemed to the young curé that the English lady was not aware of what words she uttered. He felt embarrassed and perplexed: all the English were heretics, and how heretics could be comforted or counselled he did not know. But the dreamy sadness of her face appealed to his compassion. The only thing he could do for her was to guide her to the grave she was seeking.

For the last nine months no hand had cleared away the weeds from around it, or the moss from gathering upon it. The little pathway trodden by Jean Merle's feet was overgrown, though still perceptible, and the priest walked along it, with Felicita following him. Little threads of grass were filling up the deep clear-cut lettering on the cross; and the gray and yellow lichens were creeping over the granite. Since the snow had melted and the sun had shone hotly into the high-lying valley there had been a rapid growth of vegetation here, as everywhere else, and the weeds and grass had flourished luxuriantly; but amongst them Alice's slip of ivy had thrown out new buds and tendrils. The priest paused before the grave, with Felicita standing beside him silent and spell-bound. She did not weep or cry, or fling herself upon the ground beside it, as he had expected. When he looked askance at her marble face there was no trace of emotion upon it, excepting that her lips moved very slightly, as if they formed the words inscribed upon the cross.

"It is not in good order just at present," he said, breaking the oppressive silence; "the peasant who took charge of it, Jean Merle, disappeared from Engelberg last summer, and has never since been seen or heard of. They say he was paid to take care of this grave; and truly when he was here there was no weed, no soil, no little speck of moss upon it. There was no other grave kept like this. Was Roland Sefton a relation of Madame?"

"Yes," she whispered, or he thought she whispered it from the motion of her lips.

"Madame is not a Catholic?" he asked.

Felicita shook her head.

"What a pity! what a pity!" he continued, in a tone of mild regret, "or I could console her. Yet I will pray for her this night to the good God, and the Mother of Sorrows, to give her comfort. If she only knew the solace of opening her heart; even to a fellow-mortal!"

"Does no one know where Jean Merle is?" she asked, in a low but clear penetrating voice, which startled him, he said afterwards, almost as much as if the image of the blessed Virgin had spoken to him. With the effort to speak, a slight color flushed across the pale wan face, and her eyes fastened eagerly upon him.

"No one, Madame," he replied; "the poor man was a misanthrope, and lived quite alone, in misery. He came neither to confession nor to mass; but whether he was a heretic or an atheist no man knew. Where he came from or where he went to was known only to himself. But they think that he must have perished on the mountains, for he disappeared suddenly last August. His little hut is falling into ruins; it was too poor a place for anybody but him."

"I must go there; where is it?" she inquired, turning abruptly away from the grave, without a tear or a prayer, he observed. The spell that had bound her seemed broken; and she looked agitated and hurried. There was more vigor and decision in her face and manner than he could have believed possible a few moments before. She was no longer a marble image of despair.

"If Madame will go quite through the village," he answered, "it is the last house on the way to Stans. But it cannot be called a house; it is a ruin. It stands apart from all the rest, like an accursed spot; for no person will go near it. If Madame goes, she will find no one there."

With a quick yet stately gesture of farewell, Felicita turned away, and walked swiftly down the little path, not running, but moving so rapidly that she was soon out of sight. By and by, when he had had time to think over the interview and to recover from his surprise, he followed her, but he saw nothing of her; only the miserable hovel where poor Jean Merle had lived, into which she had probably found an entrance.

Felicita had learned something of what she had come to discover. Jean Merle had been living in Engelberg until the last summer, though now he had disappeared. Perished on the mountains! oh! could that be true? It was likely to be true. He had always been a daring mountaineer when there was every motive to make him careful of his life; and now what could make it precious to him? There was no other reason for suddenly breaking off the thread of his life here in Engelberg; for Felicita had never imagined it possible that he would return to England. If he had disappeared he must have perished on the mountains.

Yet there was no relief to her in the thought. If she had heard in England that he was dead there would have been a sense of deliverance, and a secret consciousness of real freedom, which would have made her future course lie before her in brighter and more tranquil light. She would at least be what she seemed to be. But here, amid the scenes of his past life, there was a deep compunction in her heart, and a profound pity for the miserable man, whose neighbors knew nothing about him but that he had disappeared out of their sight. That she should come to seek him, and find not even his grave, oppressed her with anguish as she passed along the village street, till she saw the deserted hut standing apart like an accursed place, the fit dwelling of an outcast.

The short ladder that led to it was half broken, but she could climb it easily; and the upper part of the door was partly open, and swinging lazily to and fro in the light breeze that was astir after the storm. There was no difficulty in unfastening the bolt which held the lower half; and Felicita stepped into the low room. She stood for awhile, how long she did not know, gazing forward with wide open motionless eyes, the brain scarcely conscious of seeing through them, though the sight before her was reflected on their dark and glistening surface. A corner of the roof had fallen in during the winter, and a stream of bright light shone through it, irradiating the dim and desolate interior. The abject poverty of her husband's dwelling-place was set in broad daylight. The windowless walls, the bare black rafters overhead, the rude bed of juniper branches and ferns, the log-seat, rough as it had come out of the forest—she saw them all as if she saw them not, so busy was her brain that it could take no notice of them just now.

So busy was it that all her life seemed to be hurrying and crowding and whirling through it, with swift pictures starting into momentary distinctness and dying suddenly to give place to others. It was a terrifying and enthralling phantasmagoria which held her spell-bound on the threshold of this ruined hovel, her husband's last shelter.

At last she roused herself, and stepped forward hesitatingly. Her eyes had fallen upon a book or two at the end of a shelf as black as the walls; and books had always called to her with a voice that could not be resisted. She crept slowly and feebly across the mouldering planks of the floor, through which she could see the grass springing on the turf below the hut. But when she lifted up the mildewed and dust-covered volume lying uppermost and opened it, her eyes fell first upon her own portrait, stained, faded, nearly blotted out; yet herself as she was when she became Roland Sefton's wife.

She sank down, faint and trembling, on the rough block of wood, and leaned back against the mouldy walls, with the photograph in her hand, and her eyes fastened upon it. His mother's portrait, and his children's, he had given up as evidence of his death; but he had never parted with hers. Oh! how he had loved her! Would to God she had loved him as dearly! But she had forsaken him, had separated him from her as one who was accursed, and whose very name was a malediction. She had exacted the uttermost farthing from him; his mother, his children, his home, his very life, to save her name from dishonor. It seemed as if this tarnished, discolored picture of herself, cherished through all his misery and desolation, spoke more deeply and poignantly to her than anything else could do. She fancied she could see him, the way-worn, haggard, weather-beaten peasant, as she had seen him last, sitting here, with the black walls shutting him out from all the world, but holding this portrait in his hands, and looking at it as she did now. And he had perished on the mountains!

Suddenly all the whirl of her brain grew quiet; the swift thoughts ceased to rush across it. She felt dull and benumbed as if she could no longer exert herself to remember or to know anything. Her eyes were weary of seeing, and the lids drooped over them. The light had become dim as if the sun had already set. Her ears were growing heavy as though no sound could ever disturb her again; when a bitter and piercing cry, such as is seldom drawn from the heart of man, penetrated through all the lethargy creeping over her. Looking up, with eyes that opened slowly and painfully, she saw her husband's face bending over her. A smile of exceeding sweetness and tenderness flitted across her face, and she tried to stretch out both her hands towards him. But the effort was the last faint token of life. They had found one another too late.

CHAPTER XXIV

FOR ONE MOMENT

She had not uttered a word to him; but her smile and the tender gesture of her dying hands had spoken more than words. He stood motionless, gazing down upon her, and upon Phebe, who had thrown herself beside her, encircling her with her arms, as if she would snatch her away from the relentless grasp of death. A single cry of anguish had escaped him; but he was dumb now, and no sound was heard in the silent hut, except those that entered it from without. Phebe did not know what had happened, but he knew. Quite clearly, without any hope or self-deception, he knew that Felicita was dead.

The dread of it had haunted him from the moment that he had heard of her hurried departure in quest of him. When he read Phebe's words, imploring him to follow them, the recollection had flashed across him of how the thread of Lord Riversdale's life had snapped under the strain of unusual anxiety and fatigue. Felicita's own delicate health had been failing for some months past. As swiftly as he could follow he had pursued them; but her impatient and feverish haste had prevented him from overtaking them in time. What might have been the result if he had reached her sooner he could not tell. That there could ever have been any knitting together again of the tie that had ever united them seemed impossible. Death alone, either hers or his, could have touched her heart to the tenderness of her farewell smile and gesture.

In after life Jean Merle never spoke of that hour of agony. But there was nothing in the past which dwelt so deeply or lived again so often in his memory. He had suffered before; but it seemed as nothing to the intensity of the anguish that had befallen him now. The image of Felicita's white and dying face lying against the darkened walls of the hovel where she had gone to seek him, was indelibly printed on his brain. He would see it till the hour of his own death.

He lifted her up, holding her once more in his arms, and clasping her to his heart, as he carried her through the village street to the hotel. Phebe walked beside him, as yet only thinking that Felicita had fainted. His old neighbors crowded out of their houses, scarcely recognizing Jean Merle in this Monsieur in his good English dress, but with redoubled curiosity when they saw who it was thus bearing the strange English lady in his arms. When he had carried her to the hotel, and up-stairs to the room where he had watched beside the stranger who had borne his name, he broke through the gathering crowd of onlookers, and fled to his familiar solitudes among the mountains.

He had always told himself that Felicita was dead to him. There had not been in his heart the faintest hope that she could ever again be anything more to him than a memory and a dream. When he was in England, though he had not been content until he had seen his children and his old home, he had never sought to get a glimpse of her, so far beyond him and above him. But now that she was indeed dead, those beloved eyes closed forever more from the light of the sun, and the familiar earth never again to be trodden by her feet, the awful chasm set between them made him feel as if he was for the first time separated from her. Only an hour ago and his voice could have reached her in words of entreaty and of passionate repentance and humble self-renunciation. They could have spoken face to face, and he might have had a brief interval for pouring out his heart to her. But there had been no word uttered between them. There had been only that one moment in which her soul looked back upon him with a glance of tenderness, before she was gone from him beyond recall. He came to himself, out of the confused agony of his grief, as the sun was setting. He found himself in a wild and barren wilderness of savage rocks, with a small black tarn lying at his feet, which just caught the glimmer of the setting sun on its lurid surface. The silence about him was intense. Gray clouds stretched across the mountains, out of which a few sad peaks of rock rose against the gray sky. The snowy dome of the Titlis towering above the rest looked down on him out of the shadow of the clouded heavens with a ghostly paleness. All the world about him was cold and wan, and solemn as the face of the dead. There was death up here and in the valley yonder; but down in the valley it bore too dear and too sorrowful a form.

As the twilight deepened, the recollection of Phebe's loneliness and her distress at his absence at last roused him. He could no longer leave her, bewildered by this new trouble, and with slow and reluctant steps he retraced his path through the deep gloom of the forests to the village. There was much to be turned over in his mind and to be decided upon before he reached the bustling hotel and the gaping throng of spectators, marvelling at Jean Merle's reappearance under circumstances so unaccountable. He had met with Phebe as she returned from starting Felicita in the first boat, and they had waited for the next. At Grafenort they had dismissed their carriage, thinking they could enter the valleys with less observation on foot; and perhaps meet with Felicita in such a manner as to avoid making his return known in Engelberg. He had turned aside to take shelter in his old hut, whilst Phebe went on to find Felicita, when his bitter cry of pain had called her back to him. The villagers would probably take him for a courier in attendance upon these ladies, if he acted as one when he reached the hotel. But how was he to act?

Two courses were open to him. There was no longer any reason to dread a public trial and conviction for the crime he had committed so many years ago. It was quite practicable to return to England, account plausibly for his disappearance and the mistake as to identity which had caused a stranger to be buried in his name, and take up his life again as Roland Sefton. It was improbable that any searching investigation should be made into his statements. Who would be interested in doing it? But the old memories and suspicions would be awakened and strengthened a hundred-fold by the mystery surrounding his return. No one could compel him to reveal his secret, he had simply to keep his lips closed in impenetrable silence. True he would be a suspected man, with a disgraceful secrecy hanging like a cloud about him. He could not live so at Riversborough, among his old towns-people, of whom he had once been a leader. He must find some new sphere and dwell in it, always dreading the tongue of rumor.

And his son and daughter? How would they regard him if he maintained an obstinate and ambiguous silence towards them? They were no longer little children, scarcely separate from their father, seeing through his eyes, and touching life only through him. They were separate individuals, living souls, with a personality of their own, the more free from his influence because of his long absence and supposed death. It was a young man he must meet in Felix, a critic and a judge like other men; but with a known interest in the criticism and the judgment he had to pass upon his father, and less apt to pass it lightly. His son would ponder deeply over any account he might give of himself. Hilda, too, was at a sensitive and delicate point of girlhood, when she would inevitably shrink from any contact with the suspicion and doubt that would surround this strange return after so many years of disappearance.

Yet how could he let them know the terrible fraud he had committed for their mother's sake and with her connivance? Felix knew of his other defalcations; but Hilda was still ignorant of them. If he returned to them with the truth in his lips, they would lose the happy memory of their mother and their pride in her fame. He understood only too well how dominant must have been her influence over them, not merely by the tender common ties of motherhood, but by the fascinating charm of her whole nature, reserved and stately as it had been. He must betray her and lessen her memory in their sorrowful esteem. To them, if not to the world, he must disclose all, or resolve to remain a stranger to them forever. During the last six months it had seemed to him that a humble path lay before him, following which he might again live a life of lowly discipleship. He had repented with a bitter repentance, and out of the depths into which he had fallen he had cried unto God and been delivered. He believed that he had received God's forgiveness, as he knew that he had received men's forgiveness. Out of the wreck of his former life he had constructed a little raft and trusted to it bearing him safely through what remained of the storm of life. If Felicita had lived he would have remained in the service of his father's old friend, proving himself of use in numberless ways; not merely as an attendant, but in assisting him with the affairs of the bank, with which he was more conversant, from his early acquaintanceship with the families transacting business with it, than the stranger who was acting manager could be. He had not been long enough in Riversborough to gain any influence in the town as a poor foreigner, but there had been a hope dawning within that he might again do some good in his native place, the dearer to him because of his long and dreary banishment. In time he might perform some work worthy of his forefathers, though under another name. If he could so live as to leave behind him the memory of a sincere and simple Christian, who had denied himself daily to live a righteous, sober, and godly life, and had cheerfully taken up his cross to follow Christ, he would in some measure atone for the disgrace Roland Sefton's defalcations had brought upon the name of Christ.

This humble, ambitious career was still before him if he could forego the joy of making himself known to his children—a doubtful joy. For had he not cut himself from them by his reckless and despairing abandonment of them in their childhood? He could bring them nothing now but sorrow and shame. The sacrifice would be on their side, not his. It needs all the links of all the years to bind parents and children in an indestructible chain; and if he attempted to unite the broken links it could only be by a knowledge of their mother's error as well as his. Let him sacrifice himself for the last and final time to Felicita and the fair name she had made for herself.

He was stumbling along in the dense darkness of the forest with no gleam of light to guide him on his way, and his feet were constantly snared in the knotted roots of the trees intersecting the path. So must he stumble along a dark and rugged track through the rest of his years. There was no cheering gleam beckoning him to a happy future. But though it was thorny and obscure it was not an ignoble path, and it might end at last even for him in the welcome words, "Well done, good and faithful servant; enter thou into the joy of thy Lord."

His mind was made up before he reached the valley. He could not unravel the warp and woof of his life. The gossamer threads of the webs he had begun to weave about himself so lightly in the heyday of his youth and prosperity and happiness had thickened into cables and petrified; it was impossible to break through the coil of them or find a way out of it. Roland Sefton had died many years ago. Let him remain dead.

CHAPTER XXV

THE FINAL RESOLVE

It was dark, with the pitchy darkness of a village street, where the greater part of the population were gone to bed, when he passed through Engelberg towards the hotel, where Phebe must be awaiting his return anxiously. In carrying out his project it would be well for him to have as little as possible to do with the inmates of the hotel, and he approached it cautiously. All the ground-floor was dark, except for a glimmer of light in a little room at the end of a long passage; but the windows of the salon on the floor above were lit up, and Jean Merle stepped quietly up the staircase unheard and unseen.

Phebe was sitting by a table, her head buried in her arms, which rested upon it—a forlorn and despondent attitude. She lifted up her face as he entered and gazed pitifully into his; but for a minute or two neither of them spoke. He stood just within the door, looking towards her as he had done on the fateful night when Felicita had told him that she chose his death rather than her share of the disgrace attaching to his crime. This day just drawn to a close had been the bitterest fruit of the seed then sown. Jean Merle's face, on which there was stamped an expression of intense but patient suffering, steadfastly met Phebe's aching eyes.

"She is dead!" she murmured.

"I knew it," he answered.

"I did not know what to do," she went on after a slight pause, and speaking in a pitiful and deprecating tone.

"Poor Phebe!" he said; "but I am come to tell you what I have resolved to do—what seems best for us all to do. We must act as if I was only what I seem to be, a stranger to you, a passing guide, who has no more to do with these things than any other stranger. We will do what I believe she would have desired; her name shall be as dear to us as it was to her; no disgrace shall stain it now."

"But can you never throw off your disguise?" she asked, weeping. "Must you always be what you seem to be now?"

"I must always be Jean Merle," he replied. "Roland Sefton cannot return to life; it is impossible. Let us leave her children at least the tender memory of their mother; I can bear being unknown to them for what remains to me of life. And we do no one any harm, you and I, by keeping this secret."

"No, we wrong no one," she answered. "I have been thinking of it ever since I was sure she was dead, and I counted upon you doing this. It will save Felix and Hilda from bitter sorrow, and it would keep her memory fair and true for them. But you—there will be so much to give up. They will never know that you are their father; for if we do not tell them now, we must never, never betray it. Can you do it?"

"I gave them up long ago," he said; "and if there be any sacrifice I can make for them, what should withhold me, Phebe? God only knows what an unutterable relief it would be to me if I could lay bare my whole life to the eyes of my fellow-men and henceforth walk in their sight in simple honesty and truthfulness. But that is impossible. Not even you can see my whole life as it has been. I must go softly all my days, bearing my burden of secrecy."

"I too shall have to bear it," she murmured almost inaudibly.

"I shall start at once for Stans," he went on, "and go to Lucerne by the first boat in the morning. You shall give me a telegram to send from there to Canon Pascal, and Felix will be here in less than three days. I must return direct to Riversborough. I must not perform the last duties to the dead; even that is denied to me."

"But Felicita must not be buried here," exclaimed Phebe, her voice faltering, with an accent of horror at the thought of it. A shudder of repugnance ran through him also. Roland Sefton's grave was here, and what would be more natural than to bury Felicita beside it?

"No, no," he cried, "you must save me from that, Phebe. She must be brought home and buried among her own people. Promise to save her and me from that."

"Oh, I promise it," she said; "it shall never be. You shall not have that grief."

"If I stayed here myself," he continued, "it would make it more difficult to take up my life in Riversborough unquestioned and unsuspected. It can only be by a complete separation now that I can effect my purpose. But I can hardly bear to go away, Phebe."

The profound pitifulness of Phebe's heart was stirred to its inmost depths by the sound of his voice and the expression of his hopeless face. She left her seat and drew near to him.

"Come and see her once more," she whispered.

Silently he made a gesture of assent, and she led the way to the adjoining room. He knew it better than she did; for it was here that he had watched all the night long the death of the stranger who was buried in Roland Sefton's grave. There was little change in it to his eyes. The bare walls and the scanty homely furniture were the same now as then. There was the glimmer of a little lamp falling on the tranquil figure on the bed. The occupant of this chamber only was different, but oh! the difference to him!

"Do not leave me, Phebe!" he cried, stretching out his hand towards her, as if blind and groping to be led. She stepped noiselessly across the uncarpeted floor and looked down on the face lying on the pillow. The smile that had been upon it in the last moment yet lingered about the mouth, and added an inexpressible gentleness and tenderness to its beauty. The long dark eyelashes shadowed the cheeks, which were suffused with a faint flush. Felicita looked young again, with something of the sweet shy grace of the girl whom he had first seen in this distant mountain village so many years ago. He sank down on his knees, and shut out the sight of her from his despairing eyes. The silent minutes crept slowly away unheeded; he did not stir, or sob, or lift up his bowed face. This kneeling figure at her feet was as rigid and as death-like as the lifeless form lying on the bed; and Phebe grew frightened, yet dared not break in upon his grief. At last a footstep came somewhat noisily up the staircase, and she laid her hand softly on the gray head beneath her.

"Jean Merle," she said, "it is time for us to go."

The sound of this name in Phebe's familiar voice aroused him. She had never called him by it before; and its utterance was marked as a thing irrevocably settled that his life henceforth was to be altogether divorced from that of Roland Sefton. He had come to the last point which connected him with it. When he turned away from this rigid form, in all the awful loveliness of death, he would have cut himself off forever from the past. He laid his hand upon the chilly forehead; but he dared not stoop down to touch the sweet sad face with his lips. With no word of farewell to Phebe, he rushed out into the dense darkness of the night and made his way down the valley, and through the steep forest roads he had traversed only a few hours ago with something like hope dawning in his heart. For in the morning he had known that he should see Felicita again, and there was expectation and a gleam of gladness in that; but to-night his eyes had looked upon her for the last time.

CHAPTER XXVI

IN LUCERNE

Phebe found herself alone, with the burden of Jean Merle's secret resting on her unshared. It depended upon her sagacity and tact whether he should escape being connected in a mysterious manner with the sad event that had just transpired in Engelberg. The footstep she had heard on the stairs was that of the landlady, who had gone into the salon and had thus missed seeing Jean Merle as he left the house. Phebe met her in the doorway.

"I have sent a message by the guide who brought me here," she said in slowly pronounced French; "he is gone to Lucerne, and he will telegraph to England for me."

"Is he gone—Jean Merle?" asked the landlady.

"Certainly, yes," answered Phebe; "he is gone to Lucerne."

"Will he return, then?" inquired the landlady.

"No, I suppose not," she replied; "he has done all he had to do for me. He will telegraph to England, and our friends will come to us immediately. Good-night, Madame."

"Good-night, Mademoiselle," was the response. "May you sleep well!"

But sleep was far away from Phebe's agitated brain that night. She felt herself alone in a strange land, with a great grief and a terrible secret oppressing her. As the night wore on a feverish dread took possession of her that she should be unable to prevent Felicita's burial beside Roland Sefton's grave. Even Felix would decide that it ought to be so. As soon as the dawn came she rose and went out into the icy freshness of the morning air, blowing down from the snow-fields and the glaciers around her.

The village was beginning to arouse itself. The Abbey bells were ringing, and at the sound of them, calling the laborers to a new day's toil, here and there a shutter was thrown back or a door was opened, and light volumes of gray wood-smoke stole upwards into the still air. There was a breath of serenity and peace in this early hour which soothed Phebe's fevered brain, as she slowly sauntered on with the purpose of finding the cemetery, where the granite cross stood over the grave that had occupied so much of her thoughts since she had heard of Roland Sefton's death. She reached it at last and stood motionless before it, looking back through all the years in which she had mourned with Roland's mother his untimely death. He whom she had mourned for was not lying here; but did not his life hold deeper cause for grief than his death ever had? Standing there, so far from home, in the quiet morning, with this grave at her feet, she answered to herself a question which had been troubling her for many months. Yes, it was a right thing to do, on the whole, to keep this secret—Felicita's secret as well as Roland's—forever locked in her own heart. There was concealment in it closely verging, as it must always do, on deception. Phebe's whole nature revolted against concealment. She loved to live her life out in the eye of day. But the story of Roland Sefton's crime, and the penance done for it, in its completeness could never be given to the world; it must always result in some measure in misleading the judgment of those most interested in it. There was little to be gained and much to be sacrificed by its disclosure. Felicita's death seemed to give a new weight to every reason for keeping the secret; and it was safe in her keeping and Mr. Clifford's: when a few years were gone it would be hers alone. The cross most heavy for her to bear she must carry, hidden from every eye; but she could bear it faithfully, even unto death.

As her lips whispered the last three words, giving to her resolution a definite form and utterance, a shadow beside her own fell upon the cross. She turned quickly and met the kindly inquisitive gaze of the mountain curé who had led Felicita to this spot yesterday. He had been among the first who followed Jean Merle as he carried her lifeless form through the village street; and he had run to the monastery to seek what medical aid could be had there. The incident was one of great interest to him. Phebe's frank yet sorrowful face, turned to him with its expression of ready sympathy with any fellow-creature, won from the young priest the cordial friendliness that everywhere greeted her. He stood bareheaded before her, as he had done before Felicita, but he spoke to her in a tone of more familiar intercourse.

"Madame, pardon," he said, "but you are in grief, and I would offer you my condolence. Behold! to me the lady who died yesterday spoke her last words—here, on this spot. She said not a word afterwards to any human creature. I come to communicate them to you. There is but little to tell."

It was so little that Phebe felt greatly disappointed; though her eyes grew blind with tears as she thought of Felicita standing here before this deceptive cross and calling herself of all women the most miserable. The cross itself had had no message of peace to her troubled heart. "Most miserable," repeated Phebe to herself, looking back upon yesterday with a vain yearning that she had been there to tell Felicita that she shared her misery, and could help her to bear it.

"And now," continued the curé, "can I be of any service to Madame? You are alone; and there are a few formalities to observe. It will be some days before your friends can arrive. Command me, then, if I can be of any service."

"Can you help me to get away," she asked, in a tone of eager anxiety, "down to Lucerne as quickly as possible? I have telegraphed to Madame's son, and he will come immediately. Of course, I know in England when a sudden death occurs there are inquiries made; and it is right and necessary. But you see Madame died of a heart disease."

"Without doubt," he interrupted; "she was ill here, and I followed her down the village, and saw her enter Jean Merle's hut. I was about to enter, for she had been there a long time, when you appeared with your guide and went in. In a minute there was a cry, and I saw Jean Merle bearing the poor lady out into the daylight and you following them. Without doubt she died from natural causes."

"There are formalities to observe," said Phebe earnestly, "and they take much time. But I must leave Engelberg to-morrow, or the next day at the latest, taking her with me. Can you help me to do this?"

"But you will bury Madame here?" answered the curé, who felt deeply what interest would attach to another English grave in the village burial-ground; "she told me yesterday Roland Sefton was her relative, and there will be many difficulties and great expenditure in taking her away from this place."

"Yes," answered Phebe, "but Madame belongs to a great family in England; she was the daughter of Baron Riversborough, and she must be buried among her own people. You shall telegraph to the consul at Geneva, and he will say she must be buried among her own people, not here. It does not signify about the expenditure."

"Ah! that makes it more easy," replied the curé, "and if Madame is of an illustrious family—I was about to return to my parish this morning; but I will stay and arrange matters for you. This is my native place, and I know all the people. If I cannot do everything, the abbot and the brethren will. Be tranquil; you shall leave Engelberg as early as possible."

It was impossible for Phebe to telegraph to England her intention of returning immediately to Lucerne; for Felix must have set off already, and would be on his way to the far-off valley among the Swiss mountains, where he believed his father's grave lay, and where his mother had met her death. Phebe's heart was wrung for him, as she thought of the overwhelming and instantaneous shock it would be to him and Hilda, who did not even know that their mother had left home; but her dread lest he should judge it right to lay his mother beside this grave, which had possessed so large a share in his thoughts hitherto, compelled her to hasten her departure before he could arrive, even at the risk of missing him on the way. The few formalities to be observed seemed complicated and tedious; but at last they were ended. The friendly priest accompanied her on her sorrowful return down the rough mountain-roads, preceded by the litter bearing Felicita's coffin; and at every hamlet they passed through he left minute instructions that a young English gentleman travelling up to Engelberg was to be informed of the little funeral cavalcade that was gone down to Lucerne.

Down the green valley, and through the solemn forests, Phebe followed the rustic litter on foot with the priest beside her, now and then reciting a prayer in a low tone. When they reached Grafenort carriages were in waiting to convey them as far as the Lake. It was only a week since she and Felicita had started on their secret and disastrous journey, and now her face was set homewards, with no companion save this coffin, which she followed with so heavy a spirit. She had come up the valley as Jean Merle had done, with vague, dim hopes, stretching vainly forward to some impossible good that might come to him when he and Felicita stood face to face once again. But now all was over.

A boat was ready at Stans, and here the friendly curé bade her farewell, leaving her to go on her way alone. And now it seemed to Phebe, more than ever before, that she had been living and acting for a long while in a painful dream. Her usually clear and tranquil soul was troubled and bewildered as she sat in the boat at the head of Felicita's coffin, with her dear face so near to her, yet hidden from her eyes. All around her lay the Lake, with a fine rapid ripple on the silvery blue of its waters, as the rowers, with measured and rhythmical strokes of their oars, carried the boat's sad freight on towards Lucerne. The evening sun was shining aslant down the wooded slopes of the lower hills, and dark blue shadows gathered where its rays no longer penetrated. That half-consciousness, common to all of us, that she had gone through this passage in her life before, and that this sorrow had already had its counterpart in some other state of existence, took possession of her; and with it came a feeling of resigning herself to fate. She was worn out with anxiety and grief. What would come might come. She could exert herself no longer.

As they drew near to Lucerne, the clangor of military music and the merry pealing of bells rang across the water, jarring upon her faint and sorrowful heart. Some fête was going on, and all the populace was active. Banners floated from all the windows, and a gay procession was parading along the quay, marching under the echoing roof of the long wooden bridge which crossed the green torrent of the river. Numberless little boats were darting to and fro on the smooth surface of the Lake, and through them all her own, bearing Felicita's coffin, sped swiftly on its way to the landing-stage, on which, as if standing there amid the hubbub to receive it, her sad eyes saw Canon Pascal and Felix.

They had but just reached Lucerne, and were waiting for the next steamer starting to Stans, when Felix had caught sight of the boat afar off, with its long, narrow burden, covered by a black pall; and as it drew nearer he had distinguished Phebe sitting beside it alone. Until this moment it had seemed absolutely incredible that his mother could be dead, though the telegram to Canon Pascal had said so distinctly. There must be some mistake, he had constantly reiterated as they hurried through France to Lucerne; Phebe had been frightened, and in her terror had misled herself and them. No wonder his mother should be ill—dangerously so, after the fatigue and agitation of a journey to Engelberg; but she could not be dead. Phebe had had no opportunity of telegraphing again; for they had set off at once, and from Basle they had brought on with them an eminent physician. So confident was Felix in his asseverations that Canon Pascal himself had begun to hope that he was right, and but that the steamer was about to start in a few minutes, they would have hired a boat to carry them on to Stans, in order to lose no time in taking medical aid to Felicita.

But as Felix stood there, only dimly conscious of the scene about them, the sight of the boat bringing Phebe to the shore with the covered coffin beside her, extinguished in his heart the last glimmering of the hope which had been little more than a natural recoil from despair. He was not taken by surprise, or hurried into any vehemence of grief. A cold stupor, which made him almost insensible to his loss, crept over him. Sorrow would assert itself by and by; but now he felt dull and torpid. When the coffin was lifted out of the boat, by bearers who were waiting at the landing-stage for the purpose, he took up his post immediately behind it, as if it were already the funeral procession carrying his mother to the grave; and with all the din and tumult of the streets sounding in his ears, he followed unquestioningly wherever it might go. Why it was there, or why his mother's coffin was there, he did not ask; he only knew that she was there.

"My poor Phebe," said Canon Pascal, as they followed closely behind him, "why did you start homewards? Would it not have been best to bury her at Engelberg, beside her husband? Did not Felicita forgive him, even in her death?"

"No, no, it was not that," answered Phebe; "she forgave him, but I could not bear to leave her there. I was with her just as she died; but she had gone up to Engelberg alone, and I followed her, only too late. She never spoke to me or looked at me. I could not leave Felicita in Engelberg," she added excitedly; "it has been a fatal place to her."

"Is there anything we must not know?" he inquired.

"Yes," she said, turning to him her pale and quivering face, "I have a secret to keep all my life long. But the evil of it is spent now. It seems to me as if it is a sin no longer; all the selfishness is gone out of it, and Felix and Hilda were as clear of it as Alice herself; if I could tell you all, you would say so too."

"You need tell me no more, dear Phebe," he replied; "God bless you in the keeping of their secret!"

CHAPTER XXVII

HIS OWN CHILDREN

The tidings of Felicita's death spread rapidly in England, and the circumstances attending it, its suddenness, and the fact that it had occurred at the same place that her husband had perished by accident many years before, gave it more than ordinary interest and excited more than ordinary publicity. It was a good deal talked of in literary circles, and in the fashionable clique to which she belonged through her relationship with the Riversford family. There were the usual kindly notices of her life and works in the daily papers; and her publisher seized the occasion to advertise her books more largely. But it was in Riversborough that the deepest impression was made, and the keenest curiosity aroused by the story of her death, obscure in some of its details, but full of romantic interest to her old towns-people, who were thus recalled to the circumstances attending Roland Sefton's disappearance and subsequent death. The funeral also was to be in the immediate neighborhood, in the church where all the Riversfords had been buried time out of mind, long before a title had been conferred on the head of the house. It appeared quite right that Felicita should be buried beside her own people; and every one who could get away from business went down to the little country churchyard to be present at the funeral.

But Phebe was not there: when she reached London she was so worn out with fatigue and agitation that she was compelled to remain at home, brooding over what she had come through. And Jean Merle had not trusted himself to look into the open grave, about to close over all that remained of the woman he had so passionately loved. The tolling of the minute-bell, which began early in the day and struck its deep knell through the tardy hours till late in the evening, smote upon his ear and heart every time the solemn tone sounded through the quiet hours. He was left alone in his old home, for Mr. Clifford was gone as one of the mourners to follow Felicita to the grave; and all the servants had asked to be present at the funeral. There was nothing to demand his attention or to distract his thoughts. The house was as silent as if it had been the house of death and he himself but a phantom in it.

Though he had been six months in the house, he had never yet been in Felicita's study—that quiet room shut out from the noise both of the street and the household, which he had set apart and prepared for her when she was coming, stepping down a little from her own level to be his wife. It was dismantled, he knew; her books were gone, and all the costly decorative fittings he had chosen with so much joyous anxiety. But the panelled doors which he had worked at with his own hands were there, and the window, with its delicately tinted lattice-frames, through which the sun had shone in daintily upon her at her desk. He went slowly up the long staircase, pausing now and then lost in thought; and standing, at last before the door, which he had never opened without asking permission to enter in, he hesitated for many minutes before he went in.

An empty room, swept clean of everything which made it a living habitation. The sunshine fell in pencils of colored light upon the bare walls and uncarpeted floor. It bore no trace of any occupant; yet to him it seemed but yesterday that he had been in here, listening to the low tones of Felicita's sweet voice, and gazing with silent pride on her beautiful face. There had been unmeasured passion and ambition in his love for her, which had fatally changed his whole life. But he knew now that he had failed in winning her love and in making her happy; and the secret dissatisfaction she had felt in her ill-considered marriage had been fatal both to her and to him. The restless eagerness it had developed in him to gain a position that could content her, had been a seed of worldliness, which had borne deadly fruit. He opened the casement, and looked out on the familiar landscape, on which her eyes had so often rested—eyes that were closed forever. The past, so keenly present to him this moment, was in reality altogether dead and buried. She had ceased to be his wife years ago, when she had accepted the sacrifice he proposed to her of his very existence. That old life was blotted out; and he had no right to mourn openly for the dead, who was being laid in the grave of her fathers at this hour. His children were counting themselves orphans, and it was not in his power to comfort them. He knelt down at the open window, and rested his bowed head on the window-sill. The empty room behind him was but a symbol of his own empty lot, swept clean of all its affections and aspirations. Two thirds of his term of years were already spent; and he found himself bereft and dispossessed of all that makes life worth having—all except the power of service. Even at this late hour a voice within him called to him, "Go work to-day in my vineyard." It was not too late to serve God who had forgiven him and mankind whom he had wronged. There was time to make some atonement; to work out some redemption for his fellow-men. To Roland Sefton had arisen a vision of a public and honorable career, cheered on by applause of men and crowned with popularity and renown for all he might achieve. But Jean Merle must toil in silence and difficulty, amid rebuffs and discouragements, and do humble service which would remain unrecognized and unthanked. Yet there was work to do, if it were no more than cheering the last days of an old man, or teaching a class of the most ignorant of his townsfolk in a night school. He rose from his knees after a while, and left the room, closing the door as softly as he had been used to do when afraid of any noise grating on his wife's sensitive brain. It seemed to him like the closing up of the vault where she was buried. She was gone from him forever, and there was nothing left but to forget the past if that were possible.

As he went lingeringly down the staircase, which would henceforth be trodden seldom if ever by him, he heard the ringing of the house-bell, which announced the return of Mr. Clifford and of Felix and Hilda, who were coming to stay the night in their old home, before returning to London on the morrow. He hastened down to open the door and help them to alight from their carriage. It was the first time he had been thus brought into close contact with them; but this must happen often in the future, and he must learn to meet them as strangers, and to be looked upon by them as little more than a hired servant.

But the sight of Hilda's sad young face, so pale and tear-stained, and the expression of deep grief that Felix wore, tried him sorely. What would he not have given to be able to take this girl into his arms and soothe her, and to comfort his son with comfort none but a father can give? He stood outside the sphere of their sorrows, looking on them with the eyes of a stranger; and the pain of seeing them so near yet so far away from him was unutterable. The time might come when Jean Merle could see them, and talk with them calmly as a friend, ready to serve them to the utmost of his power; when there might be something of pleasure in gaining their friendship and confidence. But so long as they were mourning bitterly for their mother and could not conceal the sharpness of their grief, the sight of them was a torture to him. It was a relief to him and to Mr. Clifford when they left Riversborough the next morning.

CHAPTER XXVIII

AN EMIGRATION SCHEME

Several months passed away, bringing no visitor to Riversborough, except Phebe, who came down two or three times to see Mr. Clifford, whose favorite she was. But Phebe never spoke of the past to Jean Merle. Since they had determined what to do, it seemed wiser to her not to look back so as to embitter the present. Jean Merle was gradually gaining a footing in the town as Mr. Clifford's representative, and was in many ways filling a post very few could fill. Now and then, some of the elder townsmen, who had been contemporary with Roland Sefton, remarked upon the resemblance between Jean Merle and their old comrade; but this was satisfactorily accounted for by his relationship to Madame Sefton: for Roland, they said, had always had a good deal of the foreigner about him, much more than this quiet, melancholy, self-effacing man, who never pushed himself forward, or courted attention, yet was always ready with a good sound shrewd opinion if he was asked for it. It had been a lucky thing for old Clifford that such a man had been found to take care of him and his affairs in his extreme old age.

Felix had gone back to his curacy, under Canon Pascal, in the parish where he had spent his boyhood and where he was safe against any attack upon his father's memory. But in spite of being able to see Alice every day, and of enjoying Canon Pascal's constant companionship, he was ill at ease, and Phebe was dissatisfied. This was exactly the life Felicita had dreaded for him, an easy, half-occupied life in a small parish, where there was little active employment for either mind or body. The thought of it troubled and haunted Phebe. The magnificent physical strength and active energy of Felix, and the strong bent to heroic effort and Christian devotion given to him in his earliest years, were thrown away in this tranquil English village, where there was clearly no scope for heroism. How was it that Canon Pascal could not see it? His curacy was a post to be occupied by some feebler man than Felix; a man whose powers were only equal to the quiet work of carrying on the labors begun by his rector. Besides, Felix would have recovered from the shock of his mother's sudden death if his time and faculties had been more fully occupied. She must give words to her discontent, and urge Canon Pascal to banish him from a spot where he was leading too dull a life.

Canon Pascal had been in residence at Westminster for some weeks, and was about to return to his rectory, when Phebe went down to the Abbey one day, bent upon putting her decision into action. The bitterness of the early spring had come again; and strong easterly gales were blowing steadily day after day, bringing disease and death to those who were feeble and ailing, yet not more surely than the fogs of the city had done. It had been a long and gloomy winter, and in this second month of the year the death rates were high. As Phebe passed through the Abbey on her way to his home in the cloisters, she saw Canon Pascal standing still, with his head thrown back and his eyes uplifted to the noble arches supporting the roof. He did not notice her till her clear, pleasant voice addressed him.

"Ah, Phebe!" he exclaimed, a swift smile transforming his grave, marked face, "my dear, I was just asking myself how I could bear to say farewell to all this."

He glanced round him with an expression of unutterable love and pride and of keen regret. The Abbey had grown dearer to him than any spot on earth; and as he paced down the long aisle he lingered as if every step he took was full of pain.

"Bid farewell to it!" repeated Phebe; "but why?"

"For a series of whys," he answered; "first and foremost, because the doctors tell me, and I believe it, that my dear wife's days are numbered if she stays another year in this climate. All our days are numbered by God, I know; but man can number them also, if he pleases, and make them longer or shorter by his obedience or disobedience. Secondly, Phebe, our sons have gone on before us as pioneers, and they send us piteous accounts of the spiritual needs of the colonists and the native populations out yonder. I preach often on the evils of over-population and its danger to our country, and I prescribe emigration to most of the young people I come across. Why should not I, even I, take up the standard and cry 'Follow me'? We should leave England with sad hearts, it is true, but for her good and for the good of unborn generations, who shall create a second England under other skies. And last, but not altogether least, the colonial bishopric is vacant, and has been offered to me. If I accept it I shall save the life most precious to me, and find another home in the midst of my children and grand-children."

"And Felix?" cried Phebe.

"What could be better for Felix than to come with us?" he asked; "there he will meet with the work he was born for, the work he is fretting his soul for. He will be at last a gallant soldier of the Cross, unhampered by any dread of his father's sin rising up against him. And we could never part with Alice—her mother and I. You would be the last to say No to that, Phebe?"

"Oh, yes!" she answered, with tears standing in her eyes, "Felix must go with you."

"And Hilda, too," he went on; "for what would become of Hilda alone here, with her only brother settled at the antipodes? And here we shall want Phebe Marlowe's influence with old Mr. Clifford, who might prevent his ward from quitting England. I am counting also on Phebe herself, as my pearl of deaconesses, with no vow to bind her, if the happiness and fuller life of marriage opened before her. Still, to secure all these benefits I must give up all this."

He paused for a minute or two, looking back up the narrow side aisle, and then, as if he could not tear himself away, he retraced his steps slowly and lingeringly; and Phebe caught the glistening of tears in his eyes.

"Never to see it again," he murmured, "or if I see it, not to belong to it! To have no more right here than any other stranger! It feels like a home to me, dear Phebe. I have had solemn glimpses of God here, as if it were indeed the gate of heaven. To the last hour of my life, wherever I go, my soul will cleave to these walls. But I shall give it up."

"Yes," she said, sighing, "but there is no bitterness of repentance to you in giving it up."

"How sadly you spoke that," he went on, "as if a woman like you could know the bitterness of repentance! You have only looked at it through other men's eyes. Yes, we shall go. Felix and Hilda and you are free to leave Mr. Clifford, now he is so admirably cared for by this Jean Merle. I like all that I hear of him, though I never saw him; surely it was a blessing from God that Madame Sefton's poor kinsman was brought to the old man. Could we not leave him safely in Merle's charge?"

"Quite safely," she answered.

"I have a scheme for a new settlement in my head," he continued, "a settlement of our own, and we will invite emigrants to it. I can reckon on a few who will joyfully follow our lead, and it will not seem a strange land if we carry those whom we love with us. This hour even I have made up my mind to accept this bishopric. Go on, dear Phebe, and tell my wife. I must stay here alone a little longer."

But Phebe did not hasten with these tidings through the cloisters. She walked to and fro, pondering them and finding in them a solution of many difficulties. For Felix it would be well, and it was not to be expected that Alice would leave her invalid mother to remain behind in England as a curate's wife. Hilda, too, what could be better or happier for her than to go with those who looked upon her as a daughter, who would take Alice's place as soon as she was gone into a home of her own? There was little to keep them in England. She could not refuse to let them go.

But herself? The strong strain of faithfulness in Phebe's nature knitted her as closely with the past as with the present; and with some touch of pathetic clinging to the past which the present cannot possess. She could not separate herself from it. The little home where she was born, and the sterile fields surrounding it, with the wide moors encircling them, were as dear to her as the Abbey was to Canon Pascal. In no other place did she feel herself so truly at home. If she cut herself adrift from it and all the subtly woven web of memories belonging to it, she fancied she might pine away of home-sickness in a foreign land. There was Mr. Clifford too, who depended so utterly upon her promise to be near him when he was dying, and to hold his hand in hers as he went down into the deep chill waters of death. And Jean Merle, whose terrible secret she shared, and would be the only one to share it when Mr. Clifford was gone. How was it possible for her to separate herself from these two? She loved Felix and Hilda with all the might of her unselfish heart; but Felix had Alice, and by and by Hilda would give herself to some one who would claim most of her affection. She was not necessary to either of them. But if she went away she must leave a blank, too dreary to be thought of, in the clouded lives of Mr. Clifford and poor Merle. For their sakes she must refuse to leave England.

CHAPTER XXIX

FAREWELL

But it was more difficult than Phebe anticipated to resist the urgent entreaties of Felix and Hilda not to sever the bond that had existed between them so long. Her devotion to them in the past had made them feel secure of its continuance, and to quit England, leaving her behind, seemed impossible. But Mr. Clifford's reiterated supplications that she would not forsake him in his old age drew her as powerfully the other way. Scarcely a day passed without a few lines, written by his own feeble and shaking hand, reaching her, beseeching and demanding of her a solemn promise to stay in England as long as he lived. Jean Merle said nothing, even when she went down to visit them, urged by Canon Pascal to set before Mr. Clifford the strong reasons there were for her to accompany the party of emigrants; but Phebe knew that Jean Merle's life, with its unshared memories and secrets, would be still more dreary if she went away. After she had seen these two she wavered no more.

It was a larger party of emigrants than any one had foreseen; for it was no sooner known that Canon Pascal was leaving England as a colonial Bishop, than many men and women came forward anxious to go out and found new homes under his auspices. He was a well-known advocate of emigration, and it was rightly deemed a singular advantage to have him as a leader as well as their spiritual chief. Canon Pascal threw himself into the movement with ardor, and the five months elapsing before he set sail were filled with incessant claims upon his time and thought, while all about him were drawn into the strong current of his work. Phebe was occupied from early morning till late at night, and a few hours of deep sleep, which gave her no time for thinking of her own future, was all the rest she could command. Even Felix, who had scarcely shaken off the depression caused by his mother's sudden death, found a fresh fountain-head of energy and gladness in sharing Canon Pascal's new career, and in the immediate prospect of marrying Alice.

For in addition to all the other constant calls upon her, Phebe was plunged into the preparations needed for this marriage, which was to take place before they left England. There was no longer any reason to defer it for lack of means, as Felix had inherited his share of his mother's settlement. But Phebe drew largely on her own resources to send out for them the complete furnishing of a home as full of comfort, and as far as possible, as full of real beauty, as their Essex rectory had been. She almost stripped her studio of the sketches and the finished pictures which Felix and Hilda had admired, sighing sometimes, and smiling sometimes, as they vanished from her sight into the packing cases, for the times that were gone by, and for the pleasant surprise that would greet them, in that far-off land, when their eyes fell upon the old favorites from home.

Felix and Hilda spent a few days at Riversborough with Mr. Clifford, but Phebe would not go with them, in spite of their earnest desire; and Jean Merle, their kinsman, was absent, only coming home the night before they bade their last farewell to their birth-place. He appeared to them a very silent and melancholy man, keeping himself quite in the background, and unwilling to talk much about his own country and his relationship with their grandmother's family. But they had not time to pay much attention to him; the engrossing interest of spending the few last hours amid these familiar places, so often and so fondly to be remembered in the coming years, made them less regardful of this stranger, who was watching them with undivided and despairing interest. No word or look escaped him, as he accompanied them from room to room, and about the garden walks, unable to keep himself away from this unspeakable torture. Mr. Clifford wept, as old men weep, when they bade him good-by; but Felix was astonished by the fixed and mournful expression of inward anguish in Jean Merle's eyes, as he held his hand in a grasp that would not let him go.

"I may never see you again," he said, "but I shall hear of you."

"Yes," answered Felix, "we shall write frequently to Mr. Clifford, and you will answer our letters for him."

"God bless you!" said Jean Merle. "God grant that you may be a truer and a happier man than your father was."

Felix started. This man, then, knew of his father's crime; probably knew more of it than he did. But there was no time to question him now; and what good would it do to hear more than he knew already? Hilda was standing near to him waiting to say good-by, and Jean Merle, turning to her, took her into his arms, and pressed her closely to his heart. A sudden impulse prompted her to put her arm round his neck as she had done round old Mr. Clifford's, and to lift up her face for his kiss. He held her in his embrace for a few moments, and then, without another word spoken to them, he left them and they saw him no more. The marriage was celebrated a few days after this visit, and not long before the time fixed for the Bishop and his large band of emigrants to sail. Under these circumstances the ceremony was a quiet one. The old rectory was in disorder, littered with packing cases, and upset from cellar to garret. Even when the wedding was over both Phebe and Hilda were too busy for sentimental indulgence. The few remaining days were flying swiftly past them all, and keeping them in constant fear that there would not be time enough for all that had to be done.

But the last morning came, when Phebe found herself standing amid those who were so dear to her on the landing-stage, with but a few minutes more before they parted from her for years, if not forever. Bishop Pascal was already gone on board the steamer standing out in the river, where the greater number of emigrants had assembled. But Felix and Alice and Hilda lingered about Phebe till the last moment. Yet they said but little to one another; what could they say which would tell half the love or half the sorrow they felt? Phebe's heart was full. How gladly would she have gone out with these dear children, even if she left behind her her little birth-place on the hills, if it had not been for Mr. Clifford and Jean Merle!

"But they need me most," she said again and again to herself. "I stay, and must stay, for their sakes." As at length they said farewell to one another, Hilda clinging to her as a child clings to the mother it is about to leave, Phebe saw at a little distance Jean Merle himself, looking on. She could not be mistaken, though his sudden appearance there startled her; and he did not approach them, nor even address her when they were gone. For when her eyes, blinded with tears, lost sight of the outward-bound vessel amid the number of other craft passing up and down the river, and she turned to the spot where she had seen his gray head and sorrowful face he was no longer there. Alone and sad at heart, she made her way through the tumult of the landing-stage and drove back to the desolate home she had shared so long with those who were now altogether parted from her.

CHAPTER XXX

QUITE ALONE

It was early in June, and the days were at the longest. Never before had Phebe found the daylight too long, but now it shone upon dismantled and disordered rooms, which reminded her too sharply of the separation and departure they indicated. The place was no longer a home: everything was gone which was made beautiful by association; and all that was left was simply the bare framework of a living habitation, articles that could be sold and scattered without regret. Her own studio was a scene of litter and confusion, amid which it would be impossible to work; and it was useless to set it in order, for at midsummer she would leave the house, now far too large and costly for her occupation.

What was she to do with herself? Quite close at hand was the day when she would be absolutely homeless; but in the absorbing interest with which she had thrown herself into the affairs of those who were gone she had formed no plans for her own future. There was her profession, of course: that would give her employment, and bring in a larger income then she needed with her simple wants. But how was she to do without a home—she who most needed to fill a home with all the sweet charities of life?

She had never felt before what it was to be altogether without ties of kinship to any fellow-being. This incompleteness in her lot had been perfectly filled up by her relationship with the whole family of the Seftons. She had found in them all that was required for the full development and exercise of her natural affections. But she had lost them. Death and the chance changes of life had taken them from her, and there was not one human creature in the world on whom she possessed the claim of being of the same blood.

Phebe could not dwell amid the crowds of London with such a thought oppressing her. This heart-sickness and loneliness made the busy streets utterly distasteful to her. To be here, with millions around her, all strangers to her, was intolerable. There was her own little homestead, surrounded by familiar scenes, where she would seek rest and quiet before laying any plans for herself. She put her affairs into the hands of a house-agent, and set out alone upon her yearly visit to her farm, which until now Felix and Hilda had always shared.

She stayed on her way to spend a night at Riversborough—her usual custom, that she might reach the unprepared home on the moors early in the day. But she would not prolong her stay; there was a fatigue and depression about her which she said could only be dispelled by the sweet fresh air of her native moorlands.

"Felix and Hilda have been more to me than any words could tell," she said to Mr. Clifford and Jean Merle, "and now I have lost them I feel as if more than half my life was gone. I must get away by myself into my old home, where I began my life, and readjust it as well as I can. I shall do it best there with no one to distract me. You need not fear my wishing to be too long alone."

"We ought to have let you go," answered Mr. Clifford. "Jean Merle said we ought to have let you go with them. But how could we part with you, Phebe?"

"I should not have been happy," she said, sighing, "as long as you need me most—you two. And I owe all I am to Jean Merle himself."

The little homely cottage with its thatched roof and small lattice windows was more welcome to her than any other dwelling could have been. Now her world had suffered such a change, it was pleasant to come here, where nothing had been altered since her childhood. Both within and without the old home was as unchanged as the beautiful outline of the hills surrounding it and the vast hollow of the sky above. Here she might live over again the past—the whole past. She was a woman, with a woman's sad experience of life; but there was much of the girl, even of the child, left in Phebe Marlowe still; and no spot on earth could have brought back her youth to her as this inheritance of hers. There was an unspoiled simplicity about her which neither time nor change could destroy—the childlikeness of one who had entered into the kingdom of heaven.

It was a year since she had been here last, with Hilda in her first grief for her mother's death; and everywhere she found traces of Jean Merle's handiwork. The half-shaped blocks of wood, left unfinished for years in her father's workshop, were completed. The hawk hovering over its prey, which the dumb old wood-carver had begun as a symbol of the feeling of vengeance he could not give utterance to when brooding over Roland Sefton's crime, had been brought to a marvellous perfection by Jean Merle's practised hand, and it had been placed by him under the crucifix which old Marlowe had fastened in the window-frame, where the last rays of daylight fell upon the bowed head hidden by the crown of thorns. The first night that Phebe sat alone, on the old hearth, her eyes rested upon these until the daylight faded away, and the darkness shut them out from her sight. Had Jean Merle known what he did when he laid this emblem of vengeance beneath this symbol of perfect love and sacrifice?

But after a few days, when she had visited every place of yearly pilgrimage, knitting up the slackened threads of memory, Phebe began to realize the terrible solitude of this isolated home of hers. To live again where no step passed by and no voice spoke to her, where not even the smoke of a household hearth floated up into the sky, was intolerable to her genial nature, which was only satisfied in helpful and pleasant human intercourse. The utter silence became irksome to her, as it had been in her girlhood; but even then she had possessed the companionship of her dumb father: now there was not only silence, but utter loneliness.

The necessity of forming some definite plan for her future life became every day a more pressing obligation, whilst every day the needful exertion grew more painful to her. Until now she had met with no difficulty in deciding what she ought to do: her path of duty had been clearly traced for her. But there was neither call of duty now nor any strong inclination to lead her to choose one thing more than another. All whom she loved had gone from London, and this small solitary home had grown all too narrow in its occupations to satisfy her nature. Mr. Clifford himself did not need her constant companionship as he would have done if Jean Merle had not been living with him. She was perfectly free to do what she pleased and go where she pleased, but to no human being could such freedom be more oppressive than to Phebe Marlowe. She had sauntered out one evening, ankle-deep among the heather, aimless in her wanderings, and a little dejected in spirits. For the long summer day had been hot even up here on the hills, and a dull film had hidden the landscape from her eyes, shutting her in upon herself and her disquieting thoughts. "We are always happy when we can see far enough," says

Emerson; but Phebe's horizon was all dim and overcast. She could see no distant and clear sky-line. The sight of Jean Merle's figure coming towards her through the dull haziness brought a quick throb to her pulse, and she ran down the rough wagon track to meet him.

"A letter from Felix," he called out before she reached him. "I came out with it because you could not have it before post-time to-morrow, and I am longing to have news of him and of Hilda."

They walked slowly back to the cottage, side by side, reading the letter together; for Felix could have nothing to say to Phebe which his father might not see. There was nothing of importance in it; only a brief journal dispatched by a homeward-bound vessel which had crossed the path of their steamer, but every word was read with deep and silent interest, neither of them speaking till they had read the last line.

"And now you will have tea with me," said Phebe joyfully.

He entered the little kitchen, so dark and cool to him after his sultry walk up the steep, long lanes, and sat watching her absently, yet with a pleasant consciousness of her presence, as she kindled her fire of dry furze and wood, and hung a little kettle to it by a chain hooked to a staple in the chimney, and arranged her curious old china, picked up long years ago by her father at village sales, upon the quaintly carved table set in the coolest spot of the dusky room. There was an air of simple busy gladness in her face and in every quick yet graceful movement that was inexpressibly charming to him. Maybe both of them glanced back at the dark past when Roland Sefton had been watching her with despairing eyes, yet neither of them spoke of it. That life was dead and buried. The present was altogether different.

Yet the meal was a silent one, and as soon as it was finished they went out again on to the hazy moorland.

"Are you quite rested yet, Phebe?" asked Jean Merle.

"Quite," she answered, with unconscious emphasis.

"And you have settled upon some plan for the future?" he said.

"No," she replied; "I am altogether at a loss. There is no one in all the world who has a claim upon me, or whom I have a claim upon; no one to say to me 'Go' or 'Come.' When the world is all before you and it is an empty world, it is difficult to choose which way you will take in it."

She had paused as she spoke; but now they walked on again in silence, Jean Merle looking down on her sweet yet somewhat sad face with attentive eyes. How little changed she was from the simple, faithful-hearted girl he had known long ago! There was the same candid and thoughtful expression on her face, and the same serene light in her blue eyes, as when she stood beside him, a little girl, patiently yet earnestly mastering the first difficulties of reading. There was no one in the wide world whom he knew as perfectly as he knew her; no one in the wide world who knew him as perfectly as she did.

"Tell me, Phebe," he said gravely, "is it possible that you have lived so long and that no man has found out what a priceless treasure you might be to him?"

"No one," she answered, with a little tremor in her voice; "only Simon Nixey," she added, laughing, as she thought of his perseverance from year to year. Jean Merle stopped and laid his hand on Phebe's arm.

"Will you be my wife?" he asked.

The brief question escaped him before he was aware of it. It was as utterly new to him as it was to her; yet the moment it was uttered he felt how much the happiness of his life depended upon it. Without her all the future would be dreary and lonely for him. With her—Jean Merle did not dare to think of the gladness that might yet be his.

"No, no," cried Phebe, looking up into his face furrowed with deep lines; "it is impossible! You ought not to ask me."

"Why?" he said.

She did not move or take away her eyes from his face. A rush of sad memories and associations was sweeping across her troubled heart. She saw him as he had been long ago, so far above her that it had seemed an honor to her to do him the meanest service. She thought of Felicita in her unapproachable loveliness and stateliness; and of their home, so full to her of exquisite refinement and luxury. In the true humility of her nature she had looked up to them as far above her, dwelling on a height to which she made no claim. And this dethroned king of her early days was a king yet, though he stood before her as Jean Merle, still fast bound in the chains his sins had riveted about him.

"I am utterly unworthy of you," he said; "but let me justify myself if I can. I had no thought of asking you such a question when I came up here. But you spoke mournfully of your loneliness; and I, too, am lonely, with no human being on whom I have any claim. It is so by my own sin. But you, at least, have friends; and in a year or two, when my last friend, Mr. Clifford, dies, you will go out to them, to my children, whom I have forfeited and lost forever. There is no tie to bind me closely to my kind. I am older than you—poorer; a dishonor to my father's house! Yet for an instant I fancied you might learn to love me, and no one but you can ever know me for what I am; only your faithful heart possesses my secret. Forgive me, Phebe, and forget it if you can."

"I never can forget it," she answered, with a low sob.

"Then I have done you a wrong," he went on; "for we were friends, were we not? And you will never again be at home with me as you have hitherto been. I was no more worthy of your friendship than of your love, and I have lost both."

"No, no," she cried, in a broken voice. "I never thought—it seems impossible. But, oh! I love you. I have never loved any one like you. Only it seems impossible that you should wish me to be your wife."

"Cannot you see what you will be to me," he said passionately. "It will be like reaching home after a weary exile; like finding a fountain of living waters after crossing a burning wilderness. I ought not to ask it of you, Phebe. But what man could doom himself to endless thirst and exile! If you love me so much that you do not see how unworthy I am of you, I cannot give you up again. You are all the world to me."

"But I am only Phebe Marlowe," she said, still doubtfully.

"And I am only Jean Merle," he replied.

Phebe walked down the old familiar lanes with Jean Merle, and returned to the moorlands alone whilst the sun was still above the horizon. But a soft west wind had risen, and the hazy heat was gone. She could see the sun sinking low behind Riversborough, and its tall spires glistened in the level rays, while the fine cloud of smoke hanging over it this summer evening was tinged with gold. Her future home lay there, under the shadow of those spires, and beneath the soft, floating veil ascending from a thousand hearths. The home Roland Sefton had forfeited and Felicita had forsaken had become hers. There was deep sadness mingled with the strange, unanticipated happiness of the present hour; and Phebe did not seek to put it away from her heart.

CHAPTER XXXI

LAST WORDS

Nothing could have delighted Mr. Clifford so much as a marriage between Jean Merle and Phebe Marlowe. The thought of it had more than once crossed his mind, but he had not dared to cherish it as a hope. When Jean Merle told him that night how Phebe had consented to become his wife, the old man's gladness knew no bounds.

"She is as dear to me as my own daughter," he said, in tremulous accents; "and now at last I shall have her under the same roof with me. I shall never be awake in the night again, fearing lest I should miss her on my death-bed. I should like Phebe to hold my hand in hers as long as I am conscious of anything in this world. All the remaining years of my life I shall have you and her with me as my children. God is very good to me."

But to Felix and Hilda it was a vexation and a surprise to hear that their Phebe Marlowe, so exclusively their own, was no longer to belong only to them. They could not tell, as none of us can tell with regard to our friends' marriages, what she could see in that man to make her willing to give herself to him. They never cordially forgave Jean Merle, though in the course of the following years he lavished upon them magnificent gifts. For once more he became a wealthy man, and stood high in the estimation of his fellow-townsmen. Upon his marriage with Phebe, at Mr. Clifford's request, he exchanged his foreign surname for the old English name of Marlowe, and was made the manager of the Old Bank. Some years later, when Mr. Clifford died, all his property, including his interest in the banking business, was left to John Marlowe.

No parents could have been more watchful over the interests of absent children than he and Phebe were in the welfare of Felix and Hilda. But they could never quite reconcile themselves to this marriage. They had quitted England with no intention of dwelling here again, but they felt that Phebe's shortcoming in her attachment to them made their old country less attractive to them. She had severed the last link that bound them to it. Possibly, in the course of years, they might visit their old home; but it would never seem the same to them. Canon Pascal alone rejoiced cordially in the marriage, though feeling that there was some secret and mystery in it, which was to be kept from him as from all the world.

Jean Merle, after his long and bitter exile, was at home again; after crossing a thirsty and burning wilderness, he had found a spring of living water. Yet whilst he thanked God and felt his love for Phebe growing and strengthening daily, there were times when in brief intervals of utter loneliness of spirit the long-buried past arose again and cried to him with sorrowful voice amid the tranquil happiness of the present. The children who called Phebe mother looked up into his face with eyes like those of the little son and daughter whom he had once forsaken, and their voices at play in the garden sounded like the echo of those beloved voices that had first stirred his heart to its depths. The quiet room where Felicita had been wont to shut herself in with her books and her writings remained empty and desolate amid the joyous occupancy of the old house, where little feet pattered everywhere except across that sacred threshold. It was never crossed but by Phebe and himself. Sometimes they entered it together, but oftener he went there alone, when his heart was heavy and his trust in God darkened. For there were times when Jean Merle had to pass through deep waters; when the sense of forgiveness forsook him and the light of God's countenance was withdrawn. He had sinned greatly and suffered greatly. He loved as he might never otherwise have loved the Lord, whose disciple he professed to be; yet still there were seasons of bitter remembrance for him, and of vain regrets over the irrevocable past.

It was no part of Phebe's nature to inquire jealously if her husband loved her as much as she loved him. She knew that in this as in all other things "it is more blessed to give than to receive." She felt for him a perfectly unselfish and faithful tenderness, satisfied that she made him happier than he could have been in any other way. No one else in the world knew him as she knew him; Felicita herself could never have been to him what she was. When she saw his grave face sadder than usual she had but to sit beside him with her hand in his, bringing to him the solace of her silent and tranquil sympathy; and by and by the sadness fled. This true heart of hers, that knew all and loved him in spite of all, was to him a sure token of the love of God.

SARAH SMITH (writing as Hesba Stretton) – A CONCISE BIBLIOGRAPHY

Short Stories & Periodicals
The Lucky Leg (19th March 1859)
The Ghost in the Clock Room (Christmas, 1859)
The Postmaster's Daughter (All the Year Round, 5th November 1859)
A Provincial Post Office (All the Year Round, 28 February 1863)
Jessica's First Prayer (Sunday at Home, July 1866)
The Travelling Post-Office (All the Year Round, Mugby Junction, December 1866)
Jessica's Mother (1867)

Books
Fern's Hollow (1864)
Enoch Roden's Training (1865)
The Children of Cloverley (1865)
Jessica's First Prayer (Sunday at Home, July 1866)
The Fishers of Derby Haven (1866)
Jessica's Mother (Periodical 1867, book 1904)
Pilgrim Street (1867)
Little Meg's Children (1868)

Alone in London (1869)
Nellie's Dark Days (1870)
The Doctor's Dilemma (1872)
The King's Servants (1873)
Lost Gip (1873
Cassy (1874)
Brought Home (1875)
In Prison and Out (1878)
Two Secrets (1882)
The Lord's Purse-Bearers (1883)
Sam Franklin's Savings Bank (1888)
Little Meg's Children (1905)
The Christmas Child (1909 in US)

Other Works
Brought Home
Cobwebs And Cables